P9-CMR-829

EASY INNOCENCE

EASY INNOCENCE

BY

LIBBY FISCHER HELLMANN

BLEAK HOUSE BOOKS

MADISON | WISCONSIN

Published by Bleak House Books
a division of Big Earth Publishing
923 Williamson St.
Madison, WI 53703
www.bleakhousebooks.com

This is a work of fiction. Any similarities to people or places, living or dead, is purely coincidental.

ISBN 13: 978-1-932557-66-4 (Trade Cloth)
ISBN 13: 978-1-932557-69-5 (Evidence Collection)

Library of Congress Cataloging-in-Publication Data has been applied for.

Printed in the United States of America

11 10 09 08   2 3 4 5 6 7 8 9 10

Set in Perpetua

Interior by Von Bliss Design
www.vonbliss.com

For Robin
whose song brings
joy and sunshine to my life

ACKNOWLEDGMENTS

I AM continually amazed by the generosity and patience of so many people, without whose help this book would not have been written. Thanks (again) to Mike Green, Deputy Chief of Police in Northbrook, Illinois; Detective Mike O'Malley of Northbrook; Cook County Prosecutor Robert Egan; P.I. Joel Ostrander (who put up with endless questions); Sue Trowbridge; Attorney Dan Franks; and therapist Rick Tivers. Also thanks to Illinois EPA official Bob Carson; Judy Bobalik (is there anything she hasn't read?), Kent Krueger, Roberta Isleib, Deborah Donnelly, and Ruth Jordan. And, of course, the Red Herrings.

The transcript of an Oprah show on high school and teen prostitution was also useful.

Finally, sincere thanks to Jacky Sach, who helped conceive the story; Nora Cavin, whose editorial expertise shaped it; Ann Rittenberg, whose insight strengthened it; and Alison Janssen, whose sharp eye polished it.

CHAPTER ONE

LONG AFTER she moved on, she would remember the smells. Her eyes, she kept closed—she'd never been a watcher, and most of the time there wasn't anything worth looking at. But the smells were always there. Sometimes she made a game out of it. She could usually tag them by their aftershave. Brut. Old Spice. The man who reeked of Opium. Those were easy. It was when they didn't bother to clean up, when their greasy hair or body odor or foul breath made her gag, that it got hard. Then she stopped playing the game and took shallow breaths through her mouth.

There was also the dusty smell of the blankets. The starchy scent of the sheets. The faint residue of smoke in the rug and curtains. In nicer hotels, she might catch a lingering trace of disinfectant.

But the smell of sex—that was always the same. It didn't matter whether the man was white or black or Asian. It didn't matter the state of his personal hygiene. Sex gave off that slightly chemical, briny odor.

Sometimes yeasty. Sometimes flavored with sweat. It wasn't offensive. Just different.

As she rolled off his body, his aftershave cut through the smell of sex. Spicy but sweet. She didn't recognize it, but she knew it was expensive. She sat up. The room was large and elegantly furnished. Late afternoon sun spilled through wooden window slats. He always brought her to nice hotels. And he paid well. They never haggled.

She grabbed the small towel she'd left at the end of the bed and gently rubbed his cock. He moaned and stretched out his arms. He claimed he liked to clean up right away, but she knew he just wanted some extra attention.

She kept rubbing. "How we doing?"

He kept his eyes shut, but a smile tickled his lips, and he angled his pelvis up toward the towel. "Mmmm."

Men were so predictable. But this was what made it worthwhile. Besides the money. She loved the moment when they reached the edge of passion and couldn't hold on any longer. When they shot into her, relinquishing everything. The feeling of power at that moment was incredible. And addictive.

She massaged him for another minute, then stopped. Always leave them wanting, she'd learned. Sometimes it meant another round. And more money. This time, though, he didn't move. He lay so still she wondered if he had fallen asleep. She hoped not. She had another appointment.

She bunched up the towel and lobbed it across the room. It landed on her black leather mini-skirt. Damn. She'd paid nearly two hundred dollars for it, another two for the jacket. No way she'd let it get ruined by a sex-stained towel. She got out of bed, picked up the clothes and the Coach bag lying nearby. She remembered when she bought the bag. How she handed over the three hundred dollar bills with a blasé expression, trying not to show how proud she was to have that kind of cash. How the sales clerk at Old Orchard Mall squinted, trying to hide her envy. Yes, it was worth it.

She headed into the bathroom, making sure to leave the door open. He liked to watch her get dressed. She tried to remember if he'd always been that way. She thought not. Of course, things were different then. She smiled to herself. If he only knew. She cleaned herself up and put on the skirt, then the filmy see-through blouse. She checked herself out in the mirror, pirouetting left then right. She'd lost a few pounds over the summer, and she liked her new lean look. She'd be shopping for winter clothes soon. That would be fun.

She was reapplying her makeup, thinking about Prada boots and Versace sweaters when his cell chirped. She heard him curse, then fumble around for his jacket. She heard the metallic click as he flipped the phone open.

"Yeah?"

She studied her hair in the mirror. It had come down, and her blond waves framed her face. But she had another job, so she rolled it back up into a twist. With her hair, her makeup and clothes, no one recognized her. Including "Charlie." She almost giggled. Charlie. What kind of name was that for a john? He should have been more creative. Sometimes she said her name was Stella. The object of desire. Better than that stupid streetcar.

"I'm in a meeting," he said into the cell.

She couldn't hear who he was talking to, but the long exhalation that followed told her he wasn't going to be hanging up.

"That's what we're meeting about." A pause. "The funeral's at Christ Church up here. She refuses to go back to the old neighborhood." Another pause. "Memorial Park."

She stopped fiddling with her hair.

"I told you. I don't want to talk about this. I told you I would handle Fred. But you couldn't wait. Now we're both up shit creek."

Fred? She dropped her arms and slowly turned around. He sat on the edge of the bed, his profile to her. His cell was glued to his ear, and he was trying to pull up his pants with his free hand. She leaned against the bathroom door.

"Of course, she's upset." He snapped the button of his trousers. "He's the only one in the family she talked to. For him to die—alone—in a fire—she's devastated. Everyone is. I told you not to jump the gun. We were practically there."

She bit her lip, trying to piece it together. When she thought she had it, she sucked in a breath.

He twisted around and stared at her. The anger that ran hard across his face disappeared, and his expression grew puzzled. Then his eyes narrowed. "I'll call you back." He released the cell from his ear and snapped it closed.

She looked down. But not fast enough.

CHAPTER TWO

A PRINCESS. That's what she looked like to him. A fairy princess.

Shh. Quiet. Don't make a sound. Have to watch the silky, golden-haired girl. See her twist and twirl in the clearing.

He slipped behind a tree. As quiet as a mouse. *A furry mouse. Mousekeeters. Karen and Cubby.* But the girls with her in the clearing were not quiet. They shouted and laughed. And made the princess spin around in a circle. She stumbled from one to another while they clapped and cheered. They should stop, he thought. Fairy princesses are not meant to fall. Fairy princesses are meant to smile, to soar, to glide. Their wands flickered as they touched the anointed, and the anointed rose up strong and powerful.

No. Must not touch myself. It is bad. Everyone says so.

The branch he'd been holding fell back, but the girls, absorbed in their chanting, didn't notice. He waited a moment, then lifted the branch again.

The girls had gone. The princess was alone. But she did not flutter from spot to spot, bestowing magic with her wand. She stomped around the clearing, her arms out in front. Long, bare arms, her summer tan not quite faded. He imagined the shapely, tanned legs beneath her jeans. He felt himself stiffen.

She couldn't see. A white metal bucket covered her head. A foul smell came from the bucket. Fish. Dead fish. How did that happen? She pulled at the bucket, tugging, yanking, trying to take it off. But it would not come off. Her ring made a tinny sound against the metal. A quiet clang. *Knock knock. Who's there? Who's coming?*

"Is anybody there?" He could barely hear her muffled cries. "Please. Help. It's getting hard to breathe!"

He let the branch fall again. Her ladies-in-waiting had abandoned her. He, the gallant prince, would rescue her. But first he had to attend to the urge. It was strong, his urge. Sometimes it consumed him. It was what he did when he saw beauty. It was the only thing that soothed him. And the fairy princess was very beautiful. He hid behind a tree and dropped his pants. *Quiet. Very quiet. Can't let anyone see.*

"Hey. Come on! I need help!"

His heart began to pound. She was calling. I am here, your highness, he wanted to say. I will be there. But first, I need to do this. It will only be a minute. *Minute rice. Minute men. Minute. Minute. Minute.*

A moment later, he sagged and clung to the tree. He had finished. He peered around. The princess was standing strangely still. Had she heard him? No. How could she? He was always quiet. And she had that bucket on her head.

Bushes rustled on the other side of the clearing. Who was creeping out of the woods toward the princess? Was that a baseball bat in their hands? Or was it his imagination? The doctors kept saying he saw things that weren't there. Did things he shouldn't do.

His father had bought him a Louisville Slugger when he was young. Told him about Ted Williams and Harmon Killebrew. Taught him how to swing from his hips. He remembered that day. It was a good one.

Wait. What was happening? The bucket wasn't a ball. *Stop striking the bucket. The princess will get hurt!* Already she was swaying from side to side. But the bat kept pounding the metal. *Swing and a miss. Strike one.* The princess fell to her knees, still clutching the bucket. *Ashes, ashes, they all fall down.* The princess was down for the count. *Ten, nine, eight.* One more swing connected with the bucket with a loud clannngggg. The princess dropped to the ground.

Home run. The home team won! Where are the bells? The whistles? The scoreboard lit up like the Fourth of July? A trickle of red seeped under the rim of the bucket onto the ground.

Suddenly it was quiet. Even the crickets stifled their song. He stared at the princess. She wasn't moving. *Oh God, it was good.* He was good. His pants were stained. He was wet. Sticky. So was the princess. *Have to mop up. Clean us both. Little Miss Muffet sat on her tuffet. Cleaning her curds and whey.*

Her sweet, milky neck. The soft, golden hair. Streaked with red now. Did he do this? He was going to be her salvation. The leaves on the trees shivered. He did too.

The Louisville Slugger. It lay close to the princess. He had wanted to play Little League. Shortstop, he thought. *Stop short.* But he didn't make the team. His father was angry. He remembered that day, too. It hurt. He stood up and raised the bat to his shoulders. *Swing and a miss. Strike two.*

Screams pierced the silence of the woods. The ladies in waiting were back. Their hands flew to their mouths. Their eyes grew wide with horror. *You are too late*, he wanted to call out. *You could not save your Princess.*

He dropped the bat and knelt down next to her body. He touched the bloody rim of the bucket. He wiped his hands on his shirt. The silence of the woods pressed in. He would have cried, if only he knew how.

CHAPTER THREE

THAT TWO-TIMING bitch," he spat. "She's going to pay. Big time."

Georgia Davis tried to ignore the man's venom, but the more he talked, the more vicious he grew. A potential client, he'd met her at Starbucks and immediately started to rant about his wife. Georgia listened, hoping she could remain dispassionate. "When did you first suspect she was seeing someone?"

"About six months ago."

"You waited a long time to act on it."

"I thought maybe she was telling the truth about the Goddammed class. Then I called the school, and they had no fucking record of her registration." His face grew so crimson, his body so rigid she was afraid he might explode. "She's a whore. A Goddamned cheating whore. After all

I've done for her. She was nothing before she married me." He bunched his hands into fists. "A fucking nobody!"

Georgia sipped her coffee. The guy had come in as a referral from a PI she hardly knew. The dick worked in the western suburbs, but the client lived on the North Shore, and he thought Georgia would be better suited to the case. She'd gratefully snapped it up, but now she wasn't so sure. Did the PI know what an asshole this guy was? Maybe she should have grilled him more before she jumped.

Except the guy was paying good money. He hadn't blinked when she gave him her per diem, payable up front, and he agreed to a bonus if she came up with the goods.

"Let me look into it, Mr. Colley." She put down her coffee. "If it's true, you'll have your proof."

"What, pictures? Videotape? Or other crap?"

"Something like that."

"It's gonna have to hold up in court."

"It will."

He eyed her skeptically. "Lamont says you're new to this game."

Georgia looked him in the eye. "I was a cop for ten years."

"Where?"

"Up here. On the North Shore."

"You spent your days tracking down lost bicycles and cats?"

And covered a lot of domestics, she thought. "Among other things."

"This job—well—it's not like handing out speeding tickets on Happ Road. How do I know you can handle it?"

She leveled another look at him. "You don't." She paused. "But if you have any doubts, you're free to find someone else." She lifted her bag off the back of the chair, and hiked it up on her shoulder. "Thanks for the coffee." She stood up and turned around.

"Hold on." Colley raised his hand. "I'll write out a check."

***

Something was off, Georgia realized the next night.

The woman threw her arms around her boyfriend, her face so full of joy and abandon it lit up the motel parking lot. As she pressed against him, he tipped up her chin and kissed her eyes, her nose, her throat. Then he tenderly brushed the side of her cheek. She winced. He wrapped his arms around her, and the two of them clung together, as if they might melt into each other through sheer will. The man fished a key out of his pocket and opened the door to the room. The woman followed him in.

Georgia frowned and stopped her digital camera. They didn't look like a couple in the throes of a tawdry, furtive affair. They looked like a couple in love, the kind of love that makes old people smile indulgently and causes the envious to avert their eyes. The kind of love that refuses to hide, even when it should. She'd been less than fifty yards away from the motel, filming their every move, and they never bothered to check if anyone was watching.

She curled her fingers around the camera and played back the tape through the view finder. When she got to the part where the man brushed his fingers along his lover's cheek, Georgia zoomed in. She saw a discolored spot on the woman's skin. A bruise.

Georgia weighed her options. She *could* delete the tape. Blame it on a screwed-up camera. Being married to that asshole was punishment enough. Then again, this was her living. She couldn't afford the luxury of scruples. The domestics, the skip traces, the occasional insurance fraud— they all added up. She panned from the motel to the rear of the woman's white Mercedes and zoomed in on a shot of her license plate. Then she panned into the rear windshield. One of those dogs with drooping folds at its neck bobbed in the window. Brown and white markings and floppy ears. A Beagle.

Finished, she headed back to her car and put the camera back in its case. She was about to start the engine for the drive back to Evanston when she changed her mind. Sliding out of the car, she made her way to the motel room and tapped lightly on the door.

At least they'd have a day's head start.

***

Georgia watched the steam swirl around her bathroom as she toweled off the next morning. With all the humidity, she ought to buy a fern for the window ledge. But she knew she'd never do it. She had a knack for killing things.

The phone rang in the living room. She scrambled to get it. "Davis here."

"Georgia Davis?" It was a woman's voice. Soft. Tentative.

"That's right."

The woman cleared her throat. "Hello My name is Ruth Jordan and I'm—uh—I'm calling at the suggestion of Sergeant Dan O'Malley."

"O'Malley. How is the old—er—coot?"

The woman didn't reply.

"Sorry, he's a—well, sometimes, I get, well ..." Georgia stopped, feeling embarrassed. "How can I help you?"

"I—I don't quite know how to explain. I think I'm still in shock. But the Sergeant thought you might be able to help."

O'Malley referring someone to her? That was a first. "Just start at the beginning and go slowly."

The woman let out a breath. "Yes. Of course. Like I said, my name is Ruth Jordan. I live in Northbrook. I'm calling about my brother, Cameron. Cam, we call him."

Wrapping the towel around her, Georgia went to her desk and grabbed a pad of paper and a pen. "Go on."

"Cam's always been—well, how shall I say it—he's not right in the head. Hasn't been since—since he was a little boy." She hesitated. "Not that he's violent or anything. He's just—well, they never knew quite how to diagnose him. Autistic, we're pretty sure. But other things, too. We tried everything, of course. Sometimes he seems better for a while. It's hard to tell. And now that our parents are gone, well, it's just the two of us, and I—it's hard, you know?"

Georgia tapped the pen against the pad of paper. "What's the problem, Ms. Jordan?"

"Cam—well, Cam is in a lot of trouble." She cleared her throat again. "He was arrested a few weeks ago, and he's in jail. They say he killed a teenage girl."

CHAPTER FOUR

SHINY LINOLEUM floors, naugahyde booths, and lots of mirrors tagged the Villager restaurant as a newly renovated diner, but a diner nonetheless. Tucked away on a side street not far from the police station, it had been serving good food at reasonable prices for twenty years. A few years ago the place had been bought by two Greek brothers and their sister, and while the menu now reflected an ethnic flavor, it was still a popular hangout for cops. O'Malley was nursing a bowl of soup. It was mid-afternoon, and the place was practically empty. O'Malley would never have met her here at rush hour, Georgia knew. It wasn't wise for a cop and a PI to be seen together, even if the PI had once been on the force. So why had he suggested the Villager? Maybe he didn't care. She slid into the booth across from him.

"Hey, Danny. I appreciate this."

"Gotta make it quick." O'Malley picked up his spoon. His red hair, marginally flecked with gray, made him look younger than his forty-five years, but there was no trace of the eager police officer he'd been when Georgia first met him. His face now held a world-weary cast, and his expression was naturally suspicious, even in repose. They'd come onto the force around the same time, but O'Malley was promoted after a couple of years. In fact, he'd been her supervisor when she left. He was a good one, too. Never got tied up in knots over political correctness or idiotic regulations, some of which were designed to keep her a few rungs behind the men. O'Malley told her when she did good and when she screwed up.

She pretended not to notice his thickening gut and chalky complexion. Was he okay? Should she ask? They'd always been straight with each other. Still, she wasn't on the force any more. She glanced at his soup, a steaming, thick, buttery mass with a few pieces of bacon thrown in.

She motioned to the bowl. "That your idea of healthy eating?"

"Careful, there," he said, spooning soup into his mouth. He took his time swallowing. "I already have a food cop in my life."

If anything was wrong with him, his wife Joyce, a strong plain-speaking woman with so much energy she could power the lights at Wrigley Field by herself, would be all over him with a list of remedies she'd discovered on the Internet.

Georgia righted her coffee cup, which had been upside down. As a waitress came over to fill it, she caught a glimpse of herself in a mirrored panel on the wall. Some said she had hard features, especially when she wasn't wearing makeup. Today, with her blond hair pulled into a butterfly clip, she looked all nose, blue eyes, and pale skin. She started to tug at her fisherman's sweater, then stopped. She was what she was. She ran her hands down her thighs. The denim of her jeans was comforting.

"So to what do I owe the honor of this referral?"

"Don't call it that, okay? I told her I wasn't sure there was anything you—or anyone—could do. But she was—well—persistent." He put his spoon down and studied her. "Hey. You doing all right?"

Georgia sipped her coffee. "I'm doing fine. There is life after the force."

"Good." He shook his head. "The way all that went down, it—it wasn't right. Olson shouldn't have … well … Shit."

"It's okay, Dan. I'm moving on. You should too. Gotta live for the present, you know what I mean?"

"That's for sure." He started to nod then caught himself. "You sound— different." His eyes narrowed. "You doing some kind of religious stuff? Or yoga?"

Georgia laughed. "Church of life, Dan. Church of Life."

He snorted and spooned up more soup. It left a trace of white on his mustache.

"So." Georgia ran a finger over her lips. "Tell me about Sara Long and what she was doing in the Forest Preserve on September 17th."

He looked up. "You did your homework."

"It's not hard when it's all over the papers. Seventeen years old. A junior at Newfield High School in Winnetka. Clubbed to death with a baseball bat in the Forest Preserve. Her friends find the offender kneeling over her body, holding the bat. The girls run away and call the police on their cells. Police pick him up wandering near the crime scene a few minutes later. Turns out to be one Cameron Jordan, a registered sex offender, and crazy as a loon."

"That's just about it."

"So?"

"So what?"

"So, it sounds pretty cut and dry. Why'd you have his sister give me a call?"

O'Malley pushed his soup bowl away from him, folded his hands on the table, and stared at Georgia. "I don't like it." He paused. "And there's nothing I can do about it."

Georgia hunched forward, leaning her elbows on the table. She kept her mouth shut. It was a trick she'd picked up from—she forced his image out of her mind. It didn't matter. The technique worked.

"This one flew up to the State's Attorney so fast you'd need wings to track it," O'Malley said. "I never saw anything like it. Wasn't even half an hour after they picked up the boy that we got the call. Felony Review was here like a shot. We did a show-up, and they approved murder charges right away."

"Without a CI?"

"They claimed they didn't need a continuing investigation. Said they had everything they needed. Two days later, they sent the package to 26th and Cal, and the grand jury indicted him for first degree murder. He was arraigned in Skokie two weeks after that."

Holy—"That is fast. Who does her family know?"

O'Malley shrugged. "Good question. Word is the State's Attorney's Office wants it taken care of yesterday."

"Who's handling the case?"

"Jeff Ramsey."

"Don't know him."

"He's First Assistant. From New York. Went to Northwestern Law. Joined the State's Attorney's Office four years ago. They say he's interested in higher office."

"Aren't they all?"

O'Malley shrugged. "What's interesting is that he lives on the North Shore."

"Is that right?"

"Winnetka," O'Malley nodded. "Has a daughter at Newfield."

"Oh."

Newfield was considered one of the most prestigious public schools in the country, but it was a place that mirrored both the best and the worst of teenage life. People talked about the famous actors, cabinet secretaries, and CEOs who graduated from the school, but with over four thousand students, how any one of them got enough personal attention so they could rise to the top was a mystery to Georgia. She'd gone to St. Michael's parish school on the West Side of Chicago, where there were forty kids in the entire grade.

"Tell me about the suspect."

"Cam Jordan is thirty-five. In and out of institutions his entire life. Yes, he's a sex offender. But he never attacked anyone and he's never shown any signs of violent behavior. He's basically just a peeping tom who whacks off in parks and other public places."

"And scares the shit out of high school girls."

"There is that," O'Malley admitted. "But you know the law. You don't have to be much more than a wand waver to get registered these days. But that's only one of his problems." He went on. "We have his prints on the bat, and her blood on his shirt."

"Sounds like a lock," Georgia said. "How come you think it's fucked up?"

O'Malley didn't answer.

She leaned forward. "Who's Jordan's lawyer?"

"A public defender at first. But I heard the sister just got a private defense lawyer."

"You don't know who?"

He shook his head. "She told me, but I didn't know the name. Kelly, I think."

"Who's lead detective on your end?"

O'Malley hesitated. "Robby Parker."

Robby Parker had been Georgia's partner for two years. She'd endured him. Barely. "Parker's a dick now?"

"Just."

Georgia rolled her eyes. "Christ, man, what are you doing to me?"

"That's not the best part."

Their waitress appeared with a pot of coffee. Although she'd only had a sip, Georgia let her warm it up. When the waitress left, Georgia leaned back. "So, what is—the best part?"

"What the girls were doing in the Forest Preserve."

Georgia thought about it. Two years ago, when she was still on the force, a group of high school senior girls had attacked some juniors in the Forest Preserve during what was supposed to be an all-girls powder puff football game. Several of the girls were hurt badly enough to go to the ER. Unfortunately, someone brought a video camera, and when shots of the fracas appeared on TV, a scandal broke nationwide.

She'd been the youth officer on the force at the time, and she remembered questioning some of the kids. It turned out the incident was part of a hazing tradition that had been going on for years. It also turned out that some of the students, including boys, who'd witnessed the hazing, had been drinking beer. And the beer, as well as baseball bats, buckets, and other materials used during the hazing, were supplied by the kids' parents. Some of the victims filed suits against the school and each other, and nearly thirty students were suspended. Strict anti-hazing rules were enacted, but no one believed the practice had disappeared. It had just gone underground.

"Hazing," Georgia said softly.

"There's no video this time, but that's the operative theory."

"Was there booze?"

"Looks that way."

Georgia nodded. "The reports say the girls found her body in a secluded part of the woods."

"Part of the ritual. They blindfolded her, dumped a bucket of fish guts on her head, then ditched her. She was supposed to find her way back to the picnic area."

"What about clubbing her with a baseball bat? Was that part of the ritual?"

O'Malley shot her a look. "Just the fish guts. They claim they never used the bat."

"Right." She laced her fingers together. "So tell me, Dan. Why do you think the case is moving so fast?"

O'Malley shrugged.

Georgia didn't say anything. Then, "It hasn't been reported by the press. The hazing part."

"It will be. They've been sniffing around."

"But it's been a few weeks since her murder."

O'Malley just looked at her.

"Maybe they needed time to get the girls all lawyered up," she said.

O'Malley spread his hands. "Hey, this is the North Shore."

CHAPTER FIVE

GEORGIA HEADED home on Ridge, turning west and then south on Asbury. She started looking for a place to park on a side street, but a large orange U-Haul in the middle of the road blocked her. She cursed, squeezed by the truck, and drove further down the block. Five minutes later, she found a spot, parked the car, and jogged back to her building. As she approached, two men were hefting a large bureau toward her front door.

She cut across the grass past the men and climbed up three steps. The door opened into a vestibule just big enough for six brass mailboxes and a small table. Normally junk mail, coupons, and flyers were fanned across the table, but today they were strewn on the floor. She scooped up a couple of pizza delivery coupons. She hoped whoever was moving in was almost done. It was nearly dusk, and despite what the Chamber of Commerce proclaimed, Evanston wasn't the kind of place to keep your front door open after dark.

She started up the stairs to the second floor. A loud thump made her stop.

"Hey, man. Can't you be more careful? This belonged to my grandmother."

"You want a professional mover, hire one," the other man grumbled.

Georgia peeked over her shoulder. The men looked about her age. One was husky and big like a defensive tackle. The other was tall and thin with sandy hair, long on top, but razor short on the sides. A pair of glasses slipped down his nose. He was wearing jeans and a t-shirt with the sleeves cut off. The strain of the load made his biceps stand out nicely.

She watched them brace the bureau against the railing as they hoisted it up the steps. It would be a sharp ninety degree turn to get it inside. As the man with the glasses gripped the table and maneuvered it sideways through the door, the light glinted off a thin gold band on his left hand. Georgia turned around and continued up the steps.

She let herself into her apartment, kicked off her boots, and grabbed a pop from the fridge. She took it back into the living room, which doubled as her office. The apartment was spare, even severe. A plain brown couch, beige curtains, two easy chairs, a desk with several shelves above. Once upon a time, she'd collected things: candles, a clock, a bronze rooster, a cloisonné bowl. They were packed away now. Better not to have too many possessions. Who said that? Some French writer, she thought.

She had two jobs lined up: a skip trace, which, if the Internet Gods were favorable, might only take a few hours, and a possible insurance fraud scam. There was no reason she couldn't handle another job. As a cop, she'd multi-tasked for years.

The problem—as it always was—was money. There probably wouldn't be much if she took Cam Jordan's case. Then again, this was the kind of work she'd been yearning for. Something that required more than taping an adulterous affair. She hadn't confirmed it with Ruth Jordan or the public defender, but she assumed her task would be to establish reasonable doubt that Cam Jordan had killed Sara Long. At least enough to convince a jury.

She'd have to insert herself in the middle of other people's lives. Which presented a problem. People on the North Shore didn't take kindly to interference by outsiders. And up here people considered anyone they didn't already know an outsider. There was also the pressure of a heater case, one that the State's Attorney apparently wanted to wrap up fast. And she'd be facing her former partner on the other side. That didn't bother her; she could run rings around Robby Parker. And she did have some knowledge of teenagers on the North Shore from her stint as youth officer. She even knew one or two who might talk to her.

Peeling off her jeans, she went into the bathroom in her underwear. As she splashed cold water on her face, she heard banging and a curse coming from the hall. Groans and scuffles as the furniture was hauled up to the third floor. The new tenants must be moving into the apartment one floor up and across from hers. At least they wouldn't be thumping on her ceiling.

She rolled the can of soda across her forehead and sat down, tapping a finger against the can. Then she got up and grabbed the cordless phone on her desk. She punched in a number.

***

Lauren Walcher's hand shook so much she was afraid she might stab herself in the eye. She lowered the mascara brush and stared at herself in the mirror. Thick black hair framed an oval face with blue eyes, thick lashes, and pale skin. With or without the mascara, she knew she was attractive. Even her mother, during those rare moments of intimacy, still called her Snow White. She remembered as a little girl trying to find the magic mirror on the wall. She was sure it was hidden underneath the wallpaper in her bedroom. All she needed were the right words, and the mirror would magically swim to the surface and tell her who was the fairest one of all.

Now, her face illuminated by the theater lights, Lauren knew better. The mirror would never appear. People carried their mirrors on the inside. They should. Most people were ugly. She raised the brush again and leaned toward the glass. She'd bought the mascara at Sephora last week for twenty-five dollars. It was good stuff. Everyone used it. She tried again to apply it, taking care there were no clumps or goop, but the tremor in her hand wouldn't stop.

She took a breath to steady herself. She couldn't fall apart. Everything depended on her. Where was he? She'd called him an hour ago. He always called back. A chirp from the computer sounded, alerting her to an incoming e-mail. He did have a Treo. Maybe he was e-mailing.

She went into her bedroom, a lavender and white kingdom with a huge four poster bed. The dainty print canopy matched the quilt which blended with the curtains and the carpet. A collection of teddy bears and other stuffed animals were piled in a corner. Her mother kept telling her to get rid of them, to give them to needy children. But Lauren couldn't bear to part with them. She'd named them all.

Next to the menagerie was an arrangement of shelves, drawers, and desk, holding her CD-DVD player, TV, and computer. She clicked on the e-mail. It wasn't him. She read the message, made some notes, and typed a message back. Then she rummaged in her bag for her cell and made a call.

When she finished, she popped in a CD and lay down on her bed. John Mayer's mellow voice welled out of Bose speakers. She closed her eyes. What was the last thing Sara heard before she died?

***

It was the beginning of junior year. The toughest year, everyone said. Term papers, ACTs, grades that counted. The powder puff football game in the Forest Preserve was the last frivolous activity before they knuckled down. Even so, Sara hadn't wanted to go. Neither did Lauren, but she thought it was important to make an appearance. Sara wasn't convinced until the night before when she called Lauren to say she'd come after all.

"How come you changed your mind?" Lauren asked.

"I need to talk to you about something," Sara said.

"Is something wrong?"

"No. I—I just want to talk."

Lauren and Sara had drifted apart recently. After being best friends for years, she wasn't sure why. Maybe it was just the way it had to be. Now Sara seemed to be opening the door again. At least a crack.

"Okay," Lauren replied. "We don't have to stay long. We don't even have to play."

The morning of the game was one of those late summer days that breaks your heart with its perfection. A warm sun, a soft, cloudless blue sky, the trees and bushes still plump and green. Lauren waited for Sara at the field. They'd be in and out in a flash, then head over to Starbucks.

She hadn't counted on the seniors. She didn't know they were planning to haze them that day. When Heather and Claire ran up, breathlessly whispering what they'd overheard, Lauren scowled. How could her friends be so excited? They seemed almost hungry for the chance to be humiliated. Lauren wanted to leave right then. She should have.

Two seniors sauntered over, both holding cans of beer. Lauren knew them; uninspiring girls whose interests were limited to boys, clothes, and cars. One of them twirled a lock of hair. They wanted Sara, they said.

"Sara?" Lauren replied. "What for?"

The girls exchanged glances. "She needs some attitude readjustment," one said.

Lauren crossed her arms.

"She thinks she's hot shit," the other chimed in. "It's time to teach her a lesson."

"Sara? Are you kidding? What the fuck are you talking about?"

"You know." The first girl threw her a meaningful look.

An icicle of fear slid down Lauren's spine. "No. I don't." Sara was beautiful. Every boy in school probably had wet dreams about her. But Sara didn't flirt. Or lead them on. Lauren had seen her back off when some guy mustered up the courage to approach her. Still, that didn't stop people from being jealous.

"You ever heard about invasion of privacy?" The second girl took a swig of beer.

So that was it. Lauren broke eye contact with her.

"She's got to stop messing around in everybody's business. Trying to know it all," the first girl said. "She's not Diane Sawyer. Time for her to realize that."

Lauren shrugged, as if it couldn't mean less to her. Except it did. Sara had been getting a reputation for asking personal questions. Trying to find out who was doing what with whom. She read other people's notes, and someone even accused her of stealing their diary, although why anyone was dumb enough to bring a diary to school was another thing. Lauren thought she knew why Sara was doing it and warned her to tone it down. Sara countered that she wasn't the only one. Heather, for example, was worse. But Heather wasn't beautiful like Sara.

Now Lauren steeled herself. "What are you going to do?"

"Actually, you're going to do it. You and her other little friends."

When they told her what they wanted her to do, Lauren didn't like it. Still, if she didn't go along, the seniors would make her life miserable. Sara's too. That was something they didn't need. So when Sara arrived, Lauren told her to be cool and just go with the program. Let them take her into the clearing and put the bucket on her head. Sara hesitated but finally agreed once Lauren promised it would be over in a few minutes and everyone would tell her what a good sport she'd been. Sara always wanted everyone to like her.

Lauren was sure Sara would find her way back to the field. But then she heard the clang of the bat against the bucket. And what sounded like screams. Not just screams of surprise or annoyance. Lauren knew they were screams of pain. Unbearable, excruciating pain.

***

Lauren turned the music up. Shake it off, she ordered herself. She went to her closet, threw open the door, and pulled out a pair of jeans and her Prada jacket. She glanced at the clock-radio on her nightstand. Almost seven. Her parents had strict rules about being home on school nights, even if she didn't have any homework. Which was usually the case. Unless there was a paper, Lauren could get most of her work done during classes or study hall. Whoever said high school was hard must have been stupid. She slipped on her clothes, then shut down the computer.

As she crept down the stairs, she stayed close to the banister. The stairs didn't creak on that side. The wicked witch was talking on the phone in the kitchen. Lauren pictured her mother perched on a stool near the wall where the granite counter met the Mexican wall tiles. She'd have downed two glasses of wine by now, but her makeup and hair would still be perfect. So too, the body she spent hours sculpting at the gym, just so she could replicate what Lauren took for granted. Lauren couldn't resist a smirk.

The hard part was getting out the door. Usually she went out through the garage, but that meant walking through the kitchen. If she was quiet, she could probably duck out the front. The red alarm signal would blink, but with her mother on the phone, chances were she wouldn't notice.

She slunk past the Chagall in the hall. Her parents never tired of telling everyone it was an original, and if anyone had the gall to ask how much it cost—which was exactly what they wanted—they'd paste on a bland look and say, "Oh, that's something we never discuss."

She got to the door and stopped. No warm, mouth-watering aromas drifted out from the kitchen. Only the antiseptic smell of cleaner and furniture polish. Homey smells were for company only. Her mother had taken to bringing things home from FoodStuffs. There was no reason to cook, her mother claimed. Lauren's father rarely made it home for dinner, and he didn't like to eat things that had been sitting out. The first part was true. Her father never came home before ten. But the "sitting out" part was bullshit. The meals her mother brought home from FoodStuffs had been "sitting out" in the store for hours, sometimes days.

Lauren listened to her mother's conversation. It was about Uncle Fred; how he died in the fire a couple of weeks ago. Just when he was struggling to come back from the stroke. Lauren had loved Uncle Fred, and she cried when she heard the news. When she was younger and her parents were out of town, he'd take her out for dinner. Sometimes a movie. But then there was the stroke, and he wasn't the same. Her mother thought that's how the fire started. He probably turned on the stove to cook something and forgot all about it.

Then Sara was killed by that creep a few days later, and Lauren cried again. Why did death take the people she loved? If this was what life had in store for her, she didn't want any part of it.

Now she pulled the door open, slipped out, and quietly closed it. She skipped down the three concrete pads over the goldfish pond. Her mother always corrected her. They were koi, not goldfish. How many other people had fishponds in their front yard? Then again, how many other people lived in a house like this?

She opened the door to her Land Rover and got in. Keying the engine would give her away. Even her half-drunk mother couldn't help but notice. She started the car anyway.

CHAPTER SIX

GEORGIA'S HEART pounded, her palms were sweaty, and it was only with a huge effort that she was able to put one foot in front of other. She had been inside Cook County jail before, but each time she went in, her chest tightened and she hyperventilated. The air seemed so much thinner inside. She couldn't wait to get out. Thank God she could. She thought about the tenuous line that separated cops and criminals and shivered.

This time, though, she'd *asked* to come down. She wanted to interview Cam Jordan. She arranged to meet his sister, Ruth, at the visitor's entrance after she checked out the crime scene.

She hadn't seen much. The clearing in the Forest Preserve where Sara Long was killed was fifty yards from the field where the powder puff football game took place. The only hint it had been disturbed were bits of yellow crime scene tape twisted among the fallen leaves. They'd released it fast, O'Malley said. Then again, there wasn't any reason not to. They had their man. The had their evidence.

She trod carefully, dodging shafts of sunlight that penetrated the still dense, leafy ceiling. In heater cases, the village cops usually brought in techs from Nortaf or the Crime Lab rather than process the scene themselves. It was safer.

The ground was matted with leaves, but underneath it was bone dry. No chance of footprints. Even if there were, they probably belonged to the girls who brought Sara here. The techs would have looked for hair, fibers, even skull fragments, anything that didn't belong. She wished she knew what they'd bagged, apart from the baseball bat and Cam Jordan's shirt. She sighed, missing the access and information that came with being a cop.

An hour later, she met Ruth Jordan at 26th and California. They introduced themselves while the guards ran their ID's and made them fill out three forms each.

Cam's sister was a small, slender woman with what Georgia called worry-hair: frizzy, mostly gray strands that looked like they had been scratched and pulled and chewed in frustration. An equally worried expression lined her face.

"Cam's fifteen years younger than me," Ruth said as they sat on a bench. Her voice was quiet and sad, and Georgia had to lean forward to catch everything. "My parents waited a long time between kids. It must have been like having a grandson, so many years had passed." She looked at Georgia. "You have kids?"

"No." It came out fast. Georgia avoided looking at the woman.

"Me neither. I guess with Cam—well ..." She ran her fingers across her forehead, wiping away nonexistent sweat.

A burly guard called Ruth's name, and they both stood up. After searching their bags, he gave them a sticker for their jackets and motioned them to follow him. As he led them outside and around to another building, Ruth added, "I'm not sure you'll get much. He won't talk. I can hardly get him to talk to me."

The guard took them inside a gloomy building, up a flight of stairs, and down a long hallway. Beneath Georgia's shoes the floor felt sticky. The smell was part dumpster and part gym locker, overlaid with the stench of urine and stale smoke. She breathed through her mouth.

She heard a few catcalls and whistles as she passed. Most of Cook County jail was divided into wards consisting of large, well-lit day rooms ringed by cells. Tables and benches were bolted to the floor, and a TV was mounted high on the wall. Prisoners spent most of their time lounging at the tables. A wire cage the size of a parking lot booth occupied the front of the room—it was there that guards kept watch on their prisoners. Georgia caught a glimpse of the bathrooms as she passed. Just a row of toilets. No stalls, no seats, no privacy.

The guard stopped at a closed door off the central passageway. Georgia peered through a small window in the door. They'd moved Cam Jordan from his cell, and he sat hunched over a table, his legs shackled. She was surprised they'd brought him to an interview room; she'd been prepared for the dingy glass partitions of the visitors' area. The ceiling of the room was full of exposed pipes covered with chipped beige paint. Everything in Cook County was beige, she thought. The walls, the floor, the uniforms, sometimes even the people.

The guard opened the door. Cam started to rock back and forth. His brown hair was lank and greasy, and his beige jumpsuit hung on his frame. He might have been handsome, given the proper grooming and clothes, if not for his eyes. They were dark and glittering, fixed on some inner vision.

Ruth walked over and gently squeezed his shoulder. Cam stared straight ahead. Ruth sat across from him. Georgia sat next to her. Ruth pressed her hands and feet together. She was holding herself together with effort.

"How are you, Cammy?" She said.

He stopped rocking and issued a series of raspy, phlegmy coughs.

"He's sick!" Ruth said sharply. She turned to the guard. "Please, can you do something for him?"

"We got nursing personnel 24 hours a day. They're aware of his—his condition," the guard replied.

Ruth shot Georgia a helpless look. The guard was referring to the medical staff in Division VIII, the ward where the mentals were housed. But the docs there were looking for things like schizophrenia, homicidal tendencies, and other psychotic compulsions. They'd probably just laugh at a cough.

"Are you eating all your food, Cammy?" Ruth tried again.

No answer.

She bit her lip. "Isn't there any way we can get him out of here?"

"What was his bail?" Georgia asked.

Ruth looked down at her hands as if she'd just noticed she'd folded them. "The judge set it at three million dollars."

Three million meant business. Big business. "Your lawyer could ask him to lower it."

"He said he'll try, but not to expect much."

Georgia nodded. No one wanted the man who might have murdered a North Shore teenager walking around.

Ruth turned to her brother. "Cammy, this lady is going to try and help you. Her name is Georgia. Just like the state. You remember the states, don't you?"

"Florida, Georgia, South Carolina, North Carolina, Virginia, Maryland ..."

"That's good, sweetie. Very good."

Cam's expression didn't change, but his rocking slowed.

Ruth looked at Georgia. "Sometimes when he's relaxed—and in his own environment, he'll answer questions. And, once in a while, I catch him smiling. But here ..." Her voice trailed off.

"He lives with you?"

She nodded. "In the basement. It's finished, of course. Nice carpet, paneling on the walls. Soft lights. Quiet. He likes it there. It's a big room, and he has his own bathroom. With a shower." She emphasized the last fact like she was proud of it.

"What does he do all day?"

"When he's home, he plays games. Board games for kids. You know, like *Candyland, Chutes and Ladders. Connect Four.* He loves them."

"By himself?"

"Sometimes I play. He watches TV, too. And he's trying to learn how to ride a bike. But most of the time, he takes walks."

"Alone?"

"Sometimes. He has a route he usually follows."

"Through the Forest Preserve?"

She hesitated. "Yes."

"What about your parents?"

"They're both gone. My father died about eight years ago. Mother went a year later."

"Run, hide." Cam piped up. "Papa has the belt."

Georgia and Ruth exchanged looks. "My father refused to—well, he never really accepted Cam. He thought he could work it out of him—make him better."

"He beat him."

"And the beat goes on," Cam chanted softly off-key. His voice was thin, sing-song, as high-pitched as a girl's.

"He uses songs to communicate sometimes," Ruth explained.

Georgia wondered if there was some way to use that.

"Our father was—a strict disciplinarian. He was a born-again Christian." Ruth looked at her hands, but Georgia heard the disdain. "I'm Catholic."

No wonder the kid was crazy. A religious nut for a father who tried to beat Cam's mental illness out of him. Too bad it wasn't the kind of thing that would sway a jury. Aloud she said, "I know Cam is a registered sex offender. How did that happen?"

Cam's rocking sped up again.

Ruth shrank into her chair. "It was about six years ago. He was … I already told you. He liked to take walks in the Forest Preserve. I went with him sometimes, you know? And he was fine. We'd just walk along the path, pick up rocks, things like that. But one day—I wasn't with him—we got a call from the police. He'd been well, masturbating behind a tree, and this couple saw him. A man and a woman. They were jogging. When they told him to fuck off, he didn't do anything. Or go anywhere. Just finished what he was doing. The woman thought that was 'aggressive.'"

"Because he didn't stop or run away."

"It's my fault." A tortured look came over Ruth. "See, the thing is I knew about his … habit. I've known for years. But I never did anything about it. Even if I wanted to, what could I do? Despite everything, Cam is a man, with a man's hormones … and proclivities. If he wasn't hurting anyone, what was the harm? I doubt he understands what he's doing. Or why. And I'm sure he doesn't know it's wrong."

Any more than the monkey in the zoo, Georgia thought.

"But I know—I just know—he'd never hurt anyone. He's just not capable of it. This business with the baseball bat …" Ruth's eyes sparked anger. "Look at him. He hasn't swung a bat since he was six. I'm sure he doesn't know how."

Georgia looked over at the waifish man, rocking back and forth, lost in his own world. He looked incapable of withstanding the slightest blow. But how did his sister know he didn't have another side? A dark, murderous side? What if he'd been in some kind of fugue state, driven by an unknown urge or rage? Could he have summoned up enough strength to wield a bat? Things like that had happened before, especially with the mentally ill. Ruth had told her that Cam was autistic, but there was something else, too. *What was it*, she wondered.

"Does he have a doctor, a social worker, someone I could see about his—his condition?"

Ruth nodded. "He sees a social worker at North Shore Mental Health Center. I'll put you in touch with her. And our new lawyer. My parish priest talked him into taking the case."

"That's a good sign," Georgia said. "Ruth ... can I talk to Cam?"

"You can try," she motioned. "But don't expect much."

Georgia moved and sat directly across from Cam. His rocking sped up. "Hello. I'm a friend of your sister's. I'm here to help you. Do you think you can tell me your name?"

Cam looked down. He kept rocking but his movements slowed.

"My name is Georgia. Like the state. I heard you naming the states before. That was very good."

No response. Cam seemed alternately terrified and mollified by the chaos inside his mind.

"I'd like to get to know you better."

Nothing.

Georgia sighed. "Okay. Maybe another time. I'd like to come back and visit. Would that be okay?"

Cam blinked.

Georgia looked over at Ruth.

"By the way," Ruth said, "in case you're wondering, I have some money from a trust fund that my grandparents set up for Cam. I'm going to use it to pay the lawyer. And you. There won't be much left afterwards, but I—well ..."

"You're a good sister."

"That's not it," Ruth persisted. "I just can't stand the thought that he might be locked up for the rest of his life for something that—well—I know he didn't do. Where would he have gotten the bat, anyway? He doesn't own one. Hasn't for years."

Cam rocked back and forth, singing off-key. "Do do do do do do do do. Batman."

***

"Cermak evaluated him but didn't move him into Division VIII," Paul Kelly said later that afternoon. A small man in a shabby navy jacket, khaki pants, and a blue shirt, he leaned back in his chair and folded his hands behind his neck. Fluorescent light bounced off his shiny, bald head.

The sign above Kelly's door said "Paul Kelly: Lawyer & Insurance Agent." Was that a sign of the health of the law business or Paul Kelly's competence? His office consisted of two good-sized but sparsely furnished rooms in Rogers Park, a neighborhood on the northern edge of Chicago.

"Why didn't they admit him?" Georgia sat down across his battered desk. "He's clearly out of it."

"Overcrowding," Kelly said. "Only room for the real sickos. So they do some bullshit tests and then fold 'em back into the general population."

Georgia crossed her legs. "You're officially his lawyer now?"

"As of two days ago." He smirked. "You should have seen the PD. Kid was so grateful he almost kissed me on the mouth."

"Can't you insist he be admitted?"

"I can insist till I'm blue in the face, but it won't make any difference." His voice was thin and reedy, but he spoke with a careful, almost melodic inflection, as if compensating for his timbre. "Ms.——er Davis. You've heard of a tsunami, right?"

She nodded.

"Well, that's what this case is shaping up to be. I've never seen anything like it. The guy was indicted in three days and arraigned two weeks later.

But—get this—the State's Attorney's Office has already complied with discovery."

Georgia jerked her head up. "That's unheard of!"

"Don't I know it." He motioned to a pile of documents on one side of his desk. "That's what this is. Someone wants this case to go away fast."

"Why?"

"Who knows?" He shrugged. "The State's Attorney ran a tough-as-nails campaign last year. He's probably trying to make good on it."

"But why this case?"

"Because it's a slam dunk."

"Nothing else?"

"Why? What are you getting at?"

"I was told that Ramsey, the First Assistant State's Attorney and the prosecutor handling the case, lives in Winnetka. His daughter goes to the same school as the victim."

"Interesting."

"You think he might be under some kind of pressure?"

"Someone's always under pressure in Chicago. Why do you think they say you can indict a ham sandwich in Cook County?" He paused. "But if you're talking about *undue* pressure …" His voice rose on the word "undue."

"The murder happened in one of the most affluent—and white—areas of Chicagoland. And yes, if the girl went to school with Ramsey's daughter, there could be pressure. From the school. The neighbors. The village honchos. No one wants this hanging over the community. At the same time, Ramsey's got to be pretty damn sure he's gonna win. I mean, they got the guy's prints on the bat and her blood on his shirt."

"I'm guessing that doesn't give me much time," Georgia said.

"You got it." Kelly eyed her. "Look. I know why Ruth Jordan hired you. I know she's convinced he didn't do it. But I can't, in good faith, tell either of you that it's gonna make a difference. I think our best shot is to plead it out. Let the boy go into the system. They'll get him a shrink. Who knows? Might even do him some good."

Georgia uncrossed her legs. If Kelly didn't want to mount a defense, working with him would be a nightmare. She considered her options. She could tell him what O'Malley said, but she didn't want to get O'Malley in trouble. Still, she had to give him something, if only to keep him from pleading it out right away. "Actually, the idea of getting me involved came from a cop on the North Shore."

Kelly arched his eyebrows.

"Ruth didn't mention that?"

"No." He leaned forward. For the first time he looked interested in the conversation. "If the cops get their man, they usually don't go looking for evidence to exonerate them. What's the deal?"

"A hazing incident was going on at the time of the crime."

"Hazing?" He frowned.

"The public defender didn't brief you?"

Kelly shook his head. "I was lucky the PD knew his client's name."

"I figured it would be in the police reports. The hazing, I mean."

"Haven't read them yet."

Georgia pinched the bridge of her nose. "Okay. Let me fill you in."

As she explained about the hazing incident two years ago, Kelly started to nod. "I remember that." He shifted. "Hold on. Are you saying another kid clubbed her to death?"

"It's a possibility."

Kelly shook his head. "But how could—"

"What if things—just spun out of control? They were drinking, don't forget. What if someone had a few too many and tackled a girl by accident?"

"By accident?"

"It was supposed to be a touch football game."

"Oh."

"And, say, a few minutes later, another girl tackles her back. Then someone else picks up a baseball bat, and it escalates. And if one of them had a grudge against the other ..." She leaned forward, mirroring his movements. "You know how high school girls are."

"No. How are they?"

Somehow Georgia wasn't surprised. "Like quicksilver. They operate mostly on hormones. Which means they can turn on their friends in a heartbeat. Especially if the 'group', whoever that group is at the moment, says to. The need for acceptance makes kids do wacko things."

"A girl would have had to be pretty damn strong to do the kind of damage that was done to the victim."

"A six-year-old could do plenty of damage with a baseball bat." She shrugged. "And what if it wasn't a girl? What if it was a guy? There were boys in the Forest Preserve, too."

For a moment Kelly looked curious, even engaged, and Georgia dared to hope. Then his expression turned grim. "So there's a few kids in the woods. And they're running around half drunk whooping it up. That doesn't mitigate the evidence against my client. He's a registered sex offender. You can't get around that."

"Mr. Kelly, we don't know what your—our—client was really doing in the woods. The girls saw him kneeling over the body, but the police found him a quarter mile from the crime scene. Despite his prints on the bat, as far as I know, no one actually saw him kill the girl. And he can't tell us, one way or the other." Georgia looked at her hands. "There are a lot of questions that haven't been answered. Where the bat came from, for instance. His sister insists it wasn't his."

"I don't know," Kelly said doubtfully. "I still think pleading him out is our best shot."

Georgia bit her lip. She was close, she could feel it. She couldn't let it slip through her fingers. She dealt her last card. "Look. I used to be on the force up there, and, like I said, someone I respect—who's still on the force—thinks we should take a closer look."

"You were a cop?"

She nodded. "But apparently, no one is—looking into it, I mean. At least not seriously. Which begs the question, why not? Is it possible this Ramsey's daughter was involved in the hazing? Or another VIP's kid? Or is it something entirely different that we don't know yet? We need to find out, but I need time. You're his lawyer. Can you get me some?"

Kelly drummed his fingers on the desk. The smell of exhaust from a passing bus drifted through the window. Georgia looked out. The bus disgorged a bunch of school kids, who jostled each other and laughed. She turned back to Kelly. She wondered what Ruth Jordan's parish priest had said to strong-arm Kelly into taking the case.

As if he had read her mind, he sighed. "Father Carroll and I grew up together on the West Side. He begged me to take the case. Told me Ruth Jordan was a decent soul who was carrying a hideous burden. It was the Christian thing to do, he told me." Kelly laughed. "If I had a dollar for all the Christian things I've done, I could buy my ticket to heaven." He folded his hands on his desk. "I'll be honest. I'm not optimistic. Like I said, I've never seen a case fly through the courts this fast. Not even Gacy. These people mean business. You need to be prepared for that."

"But what if he didn't do it?"

"Wouldn't be the first time."

Georgia just looked at him.

He scratched his head. "But since you're determined to play Joan of Arc ... I have to examine the forensic evidence. That will take time." He dropped his hand. His scratching had left two whitish streaks on his shiny head.

"How much?"

"Maybe a week or so."

"That's not enough."

"And then there's the BCX." He sounded aggrieved that she'd interrupted him.

"BCX? That's some kind of shrink report, isn't it?"

"Behavioral Clinical Exam. A psychological exam that's supposed to determine whether the defendant understands the charges against him, if he's able to cooperate in his defense, and if he was sane at the time of the crime."

"You already know he's not. Why do you need a test?"

"It'll buy us more time."

Us, Georgia thought. He said *us*. "How much?"

Again he tipped his head to the side. "If somebody decides to railroad it, which we can't discount, given what's already gone down, maybe a couple of weeks. Then again, you're dealing with bureaucrats and shrinks who couldn't turn on a dime if their lives depended on it. It could take a month. Maybe longer."

That's better, Georgia thought.

"And …"The hint of a smile appeared on his face. "Depending on what the report says, I might have to ask for a second opinion. From a private shrink. Which could give us another month."

This time she returned the smile. "So when can you request this BCX?"

A twinkle came into his eyes. "I already did. At the arraignment."

Georgia's mouth opened.

Kelly gave her a lopsided but genuine grin.

"Smooth, counselor." She'd underestimated the man. She made some calculations. Today was the eighth of October. "So it's possible we might have to go back into court till December?"

"It's up to the judge. Remember, the prosecution is in the catbird seat. They might even have the judge in their pocket."

"But you're trying."

"Apparently."

Georgia stood up. "So why did you come on so—hard-assed—in the first place?"

He shrugged.

"You were checking me out."

He stood up too. "Maybe." He paused. "Or maybe it was what I told you."

"What's that?"

He smiled. "I'm buying my way into heaven."

She almost believed him.

After copying the discovery documents at a nearby Kinko's, Georgia returned them to Kelly. She was surprised when he handed her a check from Ruth Jordan.

"A down payment," he said.

She slipped it into her pocket and headed back to Evanston, grateful she'd passed muster.

CHAPTER SEVEN

THE WHITE Volvo careened around the corner so fast the driver had to slam on the brakes. Georgia knew the woman behind the wheel. Ellie Foreman was involved in a case Georgia worked on when she was still on the force. In fact, it was the case that had triggered her suspension. Despite that, Georgia ended up liking Foreman. Except for moments like this when the woman displayed a sense of entitlement that made Georgia bristle. Why did some people assume they could break the rules? To be fair, though, Foreman wasn't alone. Especially on the North Shore.

"Comes with the territory," O'Malley used to say. "They're all lawyers and doctors and VIPs who tell you how connected they are. Some are. Some aren't. Still, always address them as Miss or Mr. And treat 'em with kid gloves, even more so when you catch them red-handed."

As the Volvo lurched to a stop on the driveway, Georgia decided to keep her mouth shut. She wasn't a cop anymore. What did she care if someone broke the rules? A moment later, the driver opened the door and climbed out, pulling off the baseball cap she wore and releasing a mop of blond curls.

Not Ellie. Rachel, her daughter.

Georgia watched as the girl, oblivious to Georgia, retrieved her back pack and a white plastic bag. She stuffed the bag into her backpack and hoisted it up on her shoulder. When had she turned sixteen? Georgia used to resent it when her grandmother got her age wrong, which happened all the time. She'd vowed never to do that to a young person; it was insulting. She tugged on her corduroy jacket.

"Rachel!"

The girl spun around. "Georgia!" A string of emotions paged across her face: surprise, joy, finally guilt. "Oh, God. I didn't see you."

"No kidding," Georgia said dryly. "You always race around the corner that fast? How long have you had your license?"

The girl's cheeks reddened. "Please don't tell my mom. I won't do it again. It was just—" She cut herself off. "Hey, you're not in uniform. You have the day off?"

"Nice try. But changing the subject won't do it. What if one of the little kids you used to babysit was running up the street?"

Rachel nervously unrolled the cuff of her sweater, although it already reached to her wrist. "I won't do it again. Really."

Georgia nodded. She didn't want to be too hard on the kid. Rachel was the reason she'd come over.

Rachel seemed to realize the all-clear had been given and relaxed. "Hey, why are you here? Is something wrong?"

"No."

Rachel started to shrug the backpack off her shoulder.

"But I do want to ask you a few questions."

She squinted and furrowed her brow. "About what?"

"How 'bout we go inside?"

As they walked up to the house, Georgia guessed Rachel had grown at least two inches; she was almost as tall as Georgia. Her blond curls, as distinctive as her mother's dark ones, were cut short and held in place with a wide headband. Her blue eyes were clear and bright, and the hint of a smile touched her lips, as if she was just waiting for the right punch line to burst out laughing. Rachel was turning out to be quite a young woman.

"What's up?" Rachel went around to the back door and twisted the knob. It was open.

Georgia stepped into the kitchen. It looked the same as it did the last time she was here: butcher block table, white appliances, dark wood cabinets. "I want to ask you about Sara Long."

"I thought so." Rachel rolled her eyes. "That's all anyone is talking about."

"It was a ..." Georgia chose her words carefully. "... significant event."

"No sh—kidding."

"Hey, Rach." A voice from upstairs called down. "Did you get what you needed?"

"Yeah, Mom." Rachel slipped her backpack off her shoulder and took out the plastic bag. "Shampoo. It's new. Cleans, conditions, and highlights all in one step." She peered at Georgia's hair. "You should try it."

Georgia was about to reply when the voice cut in again. "Who's with you, Rachel? I thought we agreed. Homework first."

Rachel grinned conspiratorially. "Why don't you come down and see?"

Georgia heard the scuffle of feet scrambling down the steps. A moment later an attractive, dark-haired woman in sweats and a t-shirt bounded into the kitchen.

"Georgia!" Ellie Foreman's face lit up, and she threw her arms around her in a hug. "What a surprise!"

Georgia tried not to let her awkwardness show. "I was in the neighborhood ..."

Ellie stepped back, a shrewd look in her eyes. "Sure you were."

Georgia pretended not to notice. "Actually, I wanted to talk to Rachel about Sara Long."

Ellie looked at Rachel, then back at Georgia.

Georgia went on. "She was just starting to tell me what it's been like at school."

"Oh. Well. Don't let me bother you." Ellie turned around, opened the refrigerator, and rummaged inside. Georgia pulled out a chair and sat down.

"Like I was saying," Rachel said self-importantly, "we've had advisories and meetings up the wazoo. Social workers and counselors are all over the place, and there's some new resource every day we're supposed to know about. Like we don't have enough help already."

Georgia stifled a smile. She sounded like her mother.

"They even had the police talk to us." She paused. "But then, you already know that."

Ellie turned around, leaving the refrigerator door open. She and Georgia exchanged glances. Apparently, Ellie hadn't told her daughter about Georgia's suspension. Not that there was any reason to. Or not to. Georgia answered, keeping her eyes on Ellie. "No, I didn't."

"Aren't you working on the case?"

Georgia had rehearsed her answer, but she hadn't expected to say it with Ellie in the room. "I am. I'm doing some—research."

"Why?" Rachel said. "I thought they already got the guy."

"There are still some ... loose ends to tie up." She and Ellie exchanged another glance. If Ellie was going to blow Georgia's cover, it would be now. Ellie looked like she wanted to say something, then turned back to the refrigerator. "Who wants a pop?"

"Me," Rachel answered.

"How about you, Georgia?"

"I'm fine."

Ellie pulled out two cans of soda and handed one to Rachel. "Well, I guess I'll go back upstairs. Give a call sometime," she said to Georgia.

Georgia nodded.

Ellie gave her one more look before leaving the room. She was okay, Georgia concluded. For a civilian. "So there's been a lot of attention on the incident at school?" Georgia asked Rachel.

Rachel nodded. "They want to make sure everyone who needs it has help."

"Her friends?"

"Some. But there are plenty of wannabes. You know. Kids who weren't really her friends but want the attention." She popped the top off her can.

"Did you know her?"

"Sara? Not well."

"You weren't friends?"

"No. I'm not in that crowd."

"What crowd is that?"

"They don't really have a name, at least a name anyone would use in public."

"What do you mean?"

"Well, the girls are kind of Barbie dolls, you know? Pretty but dumb, cool clothes and stuff. They spend all their time buying makeup and texting each other."

"Sara was part of that group?"

Rachel nodded. "Yeah. She was gorgeous. She was a year older than me." She took a swig of her soda. "How come you're asking all these questions?"

"I told you. I'm just trying to tie up some loose ends."

"What loose ends?"

Georgia didn't answer.

Rachel cocked her head. "You don't think he did it?"

"It isn't my job to think one way or the other. That's up to a judge and jury."

Rachel stared hard at Georgia. "My mother does that."

"What?"

"Gives me those non-answer answers when she doesn't want to tell me what's really going on."

Georgia bypassed the comment. "Who are Sara's friends? Can you give me some names?"

Rachel took another sip of her pop. "You're not gonna tell me, are you?" When Georgia kept quiet, she sighed. "Okay. I know she was friends with Heather Blakely. She's the anchor for the school news in the morning."

"The school news?"

"Every morning during advisory, they make us watch the school news on these monitors."

"You have TVs in the classroom?"

She nodded. "The PTA bought them a few years ago. I don't know why. We don't need them. I think making us watch the news is just an excuse to get some use out of them. Anyway, Heather's the main anchor person. She thinks she's Katie Couric."

Georgia pulled out a memo pad and pen. "Anyone else?"

"Well, there's Claire Tennenbaum. She's probably one of the dumbest girls you'll ever meet. But in a cute, puppy-dog kind of way. You know they're stupid, but you can't help liking them. Oh. How could I forget? Lauren Walcher. She lives in this incredible house in Glencoe with a pool and a separate guest house, and this goldfish pond that's supposed to be amazing."

"You've been there?"

Rachel took a swig of her soda and shook her head. "No. Only the cool kids get invited over to Lauren's. I'm not in with that crowd."

"For which we should all say a prayer of thanks," Georgia muttered. She looked up from her notes to find Rachel regarding her, her eyes challenging. Georgia smiled. "You don't need to hang out with the cool crowd. You're already one of the coolest kids I know."

Rachel couldn't quite suppress a grin.

Georgia hoped she believed it. "What about a boyfriend?"

A blush crept up Rachel's neck. "Craig? I—I'm not really—"

"Not you," Georgia cut in.

"Oh." She smiled sheepishly. "I don't know. Guys are—were—always drooling over Sara. And her friends. At least in the hall and things. But I don't know if she was going with anyone."

"What boys?"

She shrugged. "I don't know."

"Okay. Do any of the girls you mentioned have cars?"

"I think Claire does. Oh, and Lauren too. She has a black Land Rover. She used to give people rides." Rachel frowned. "Come to think of it, I haven't seen her much recently."

"Got it." Georgia finished writing, closed her memo pad, and dumped it in her jacket pocket. "Tell me something. Isn't there someone named Ramsey at your school?"

Rachel nodded. "Monica Ramsey. She's a senior."

"Was she a friend of Sara's?"

Rachel shrugged. "I don't know. Why?"

Georgia shrugged back. "Just curious."

"Her father's a big wheel, isn't he?"

"A very big wheel." Georgia agreed. "Hey. Do you happen to have a yearbook I could borrow?"

Rachel nodded.

"Maybe you could point out some of the people you just named?"

"Sure. I'll get it."

Georgia smiled her thanks. "Including Craig."

***

Back in her apartment that night, Georgia waded through the police reports, grand jury transcripts, and witness statements. She found interview summaries from all the girls Rachel had mentioned. All three were at the Forest Preserve for the junior/senior powder puff football game.

Georgia pressed her lips together. The hazing incident two years ago had started the same way. Why hadn't anyone stopped it this time? Surely some adults, teachers, or other school officials must have suspected it could happen again. Memories weren't that short. She got up from the couch and went into the kitchen. Adults make a decree, the kids ignore it, then the adults do nothing to enforce it. And they wonder why kids have trouble with authority figures.

She got a glass of water and drank all of it down. She was trying to keep herself hydrated. They said it helped. But eight glasses a day? That was overkill. Not to mention all the trips to the john. She finished the water anyway.

The transcripts confirmed what she already knew. The girls came back to the clearing where they saw Cam Jordan kneeling over Sara Long's body, the bat on the ground beside him. They ran to call the police, and he apparently fled. The police found him wandering around a quarter mile from the crime scene.

Next she reviewed the police reports. They, too, were in line with what she already knew; nevertheless, she went through them carefully. The word "hazing" wasn't mentioned, and no one confessed to bringing the bucket, the blindfold, or the bat. *So how did they get there*, Georgia wondered. Did they materialize out of thin air?

Georgia finished reading, then stacked the files in a neat pile on the floor. She knew about powder puff football, and she knew girls sometimes changed the rules to suit themselves. But she couldn't imagine any rule that would involve Sara Long off by herself with a bucket on top of her head. More significantly, none of the police officers, apparently, had thought to ask. Or if they did, the answer wasn't reported.

She went into her kitchen and stared out the window. The sun had set hours ago and the blackness outside lay in sharp contrast to her white curtains. The simplicity of the polar opposites was appealing. Black and white could never be confused, misread, or manipulated. She leaned her forehead against the glass. Somehow she doubted Sara Long's case would have the same clarity.

CHAPTER EIGHT

THE BELL rang, signaling the end of the period. Lauren was startled—she'd been deep into a worksheet analyzing the characters of Willy Stark and Jack Burden. She gathered her books, hoisted her Prada bag over her shoulder, and headed out of the classroom. A throng of students pushed and crowded and shoved their way down the hall. Lauren skirted the edges, staying close to the rows of lockers. As she reached the end of the corridor, she spotted Claire and Heather waiting for her around the corner.

"What's up?" She was irritated by their presence. She had things to do. But they all had a free period at the same time—they'd planned it that way last spring. With Sara.

"You want to go outside?" Heather Blakely, petite and waiflike, prided herself on wearing a size two. Lauren thought she was borderline anorexic—she never ate a thing, at least in front of them. Today she was wearing a denim Citizen skirt with a flounce at the bottom and a pale green t-shirt that looked like it was Express. Feminine. Neat. Very Heather.

Lauren dug out her cell to check the time. "I only have a couple of minutes. Got to do some stuff. And I'm hungry. Let's go to the cafeteria."

Claire Tennenbaum, who was tall and slim and towered over Heather, shook her head. Her long brown hair was streaked with blond, and it shimmered, even in the fluorescent school light. "I gotta talk to you guys."

Lauren frowned. "What about?"

Claire's denim jacket covered her torso, just barely, and her Sevens jeans were low riders. She looked around and gestured toward the stairwell.

"Why do we have to go up?" Heather's voice was suspicious. Shit. The girl couldn't take yes for an answer. She had to know everything, right away. At least Sara had been more subtle.

"Just come upstairs." Claire usually had a dull, vacant look, as though the neurons in her brain were slow to fire. But today, she looked anxious. Almost scared.

Lauren headed toward the stairwell which led up to a little-used corner on the third floor. Sometimes they camped out up there during free period. Few teachers came up there, if they could avoid it—too many steps to climb.

As they entered the stairwell, a wave of kids flowed around them. There were only five minutes between classes, and teachers enforced it by doling out detention whenever a student was late. Once on the third floor, they pushed through a set of double glass doors. Heather thumped down the hall. In Michael Kors clogs, Lauren noted.

Claire flopped down on the floor at the end of the hall. Heather arranged herself more carefully.

Lauren leaned against the wall, planning to cut out after she heard whatever Claire had to say. "So what is it, Claire?"

Claire's jaws pumped up and down. She was chewing gum. She leaned forward. "I was coming into school this morning. It was early, 'cause I was supposed to meet my math teacher to go over some stuff for a test. Anyway, I parked across the street in the lot, and—"

Heather rolled her eyes. "Get to the point, Claire."

Claire glared at Heather. "I am." She angled herself away from Heather toward Lauren. "Well, this woman stopped me near my car. Said she wanted to talk about Sara."

Lauren straightened. Heather, Lauren noticed, took her cue and became interested too.

"What woman?" Lauren said.

"Georgia Davis."

Lauren frowned. "Was she a cop?"

Claire clacked her gum. "I—I think so."

"You didn't ask?"

"She had a bunch of papers, and she kept going through them. I—I figured she was."

"Was she wearing a uniform?" Heather asked.

Claire shook her head.

Heather stole a glance at Lauren, then pronounced, "Cop or no cop, you know we're not supposed to talk about anything without our parents there."

"That's what I told her." Claire nodded energetically.

"And?" Lauren said.

"She said we could call them, if it made me feel more comfortable, or we could go home and talk."

Heather threw an exasperated what-are-you-gonna-do look at Lauren.

Lauren ignored it. "What happened next?"

Claire slowly folded her legs Indian-style and popped a gum bubble. *She was thrilled to be the center of attention*, Lauren thought. "Well, first, she looked inside the Jeep."

"What for?" Heather cut in.

"I don't know. Drugs, maybe?"

"You don't have any drugs." Heather scoffed.

"Of course not."

"Claire ..." Lauren cut in. "What did she want to know?"

"Well, she asked me about the powder puff game."

"What about it?"

"She wanted to know how many girls were there ... what the score was ... stuff like that."

"I don't get it," Heather piped up. "Why would she ask that? The police already know. It doesn't make—"

"Shut up, Heather." Lauren waved a hand at Claire. "Go on."

Heather shrank against the wall.

"I asked her why I had to go over it all again," Claire said. "Like, did I say something wrong the first time?"

"And?"

"She said they go over the same thing again and again. That sometimes people remember stuff they didn't the first time. You know, details and things."

Two geeky looking boys appeared at the other end of hall, talking boisterously. Both had the gang-wannabe look: oversized pants that hung below their waists, long t-shirts, and baseball hats on backwards. They trudged toward the girls, waving their cell phones, comparing features and games. Having a cell phone on during school was a breach of rules, but you could get away with it on the third floor.

Claire smiled at them.

Lauren shot Claire a stern look, then glared at the boys. All at once they quieted, scurried past, and disappeared through the door. Lauren caught a powerful whiff of aftershave. One of them probably dumped an entire bottle on his face. She turned back to Claire, who was snapping her gum. "How many times do I need to tell you not to waste your time on these guys, Claire? They're—immature."

Claire's jaws stopped moving. She looked like she'd been slapped.

"So what else did this—Davis woman ask?" Lauren said.

Claire picked at her jacket, although there was no lint in sight. "She wanted to know who took Sara away."

"What did you tell her?"

"The truth." When Lauren winced, she added, "I had to. The cops already know anyway."

"Of course. You're right. What else?"

Claire shrugged.

Heather gave a theatrical sigh. "Claire, I'm sure you can be more specific. Think."

"Well …" Claire looked from Heather to Lauren, drawing out the moment. "I told her about Sara sticking her nose into everyone's business."

Heather winced.

"You know, all the stuff we talked about. Like how Sara had to know what everyone was doing."

Lauren didn't react.

"What's wrong?" Claire asked, her tone defensive. "The police know that too."

"Did you tell her about the blindfold?" Heather asked.

Claire nodded. "And the bucket. How grody it was, and how bad it smelled."

"What else?" Lauren asked.

"I said the seniors may have wanted to teach her a lesson, but nobody wanted her to get hurt. I told her the crazy guy definitely did it." She looked back at Lauren as if for approval.

"Did she ask who the seniors were?" Lauren asked.

Claire nodded.

"What names did you give her?"

"Annie Chernow, Judy Bobalik, Monica Ramsey …" Claire recited.

"You told her Monica Ramsey was there?"

Claire nodded.

"Anything else?" Heather asked.

"That was it. The first bell rang, and I had to go."

"Nothing else?"

"No. Why are *you* asking so many questions, Heather?" Claire shot Heather an angry glance. "You can't broadcast this on the school news."

Lauren stifled a smile.

"I sit next to Monica Ramsey in Spanish," Heather said in her self-important voice. A totally irrelevant piece of information, Lauren thought. But you couldn't blame them. They were both clueless.

"And, like, I know Sara was our friend," Heather went on. "And that boys were hot for her. But she wasn't perfect. I mean, there were things she did—well, you know what I mean."

"No." Lauren frowned. "I don't. What things?"

"The thing with Cash, for instance."

Lauren waved a dismissive hand. "Ancient history."

"Well, I haven't forgotten."

"Better not tell the cops that. Or the investigator," Lauren said. "They might think you had something to do with her murder."

"Ewww ..." Heather whined, stretching the sound into three syllables. "That's disgusting."

"And to top it all off, the woman made me late for my math teacher." Claire clacked her gum again. "I'm gonna fail this quarter for sure."

Lauren yanked her thumb toward Heather. "She's smart. She'll tutor you, won't you, Heather?"

Heather pursed her lips.

CHAPTER NINE

SO FAR the job had been routine. So mundane, in fact, that he wondered why his employer needed protection. Maybe he was the type who thought his footsteps made an indelible imprint, who was sure nothing could be accomplished without his intervention. Sitting at the right hand of God.

One thing was clear, he thought as he wiped down the Jag. The man *was* a micromanager. Down to his instructions on how to wash the car. What cloths to use. How much wax. How long to buff. Still, he was grateful to be working at all. It had been a while. He'd provided references. Impressed them with his resume. And they'd scooped him up. Good thing, too. Any longer and his skills might have deteriorated. He practiced, tried to make sure he was still sharp. But until you were actually on the street, you never knew.

He was the back door guy, the outsider. He didn't even have chauffeur status. It would stay that way until he earned their trust. But he'd expected that, and he was prepared to take it slow. It was important to be a team player.

He finished buffing the car and went around to the back. A huge turquoise swimming pool bordered by marble statues lay behind a wide veranda. Beyond that was a sweep of broad, sloping lawn with thick green grass. His employer emerged from the water, sun-sparkled droplets beading the gray hair on his chest. A silver mezuzah around his neck flashed in the morning light. Wrapping himself in a soft white towel, he gazed around his estate with a satisfied expression.

A cell phone trilled. The man grabbed it, listened, barked a response. Then he tossed the phone down on the table. He spotted him at the edge of the cabana. His bushy eyebrows rose.

"Lawyers!" His boss spat out. "They don't do what you want, and they fuck you while they're not doing it."

CHAPTER TEN

THE PUNGENT smell of pizza from someone's apartment wafted through the air vents, making Georgia realize she hadn't eaten since breakfast. She finished her notes, went into the kitchen, and opened the refrigerator. Nothing but mayo, wilted lettuce, eggs, and a hunk of muenster cheese. She got out her one good Cutco knife, sliced a piece off the cheese, and wolfed it down.

Her first full day on the case, but it wasn't very productive. First she'd played telephone tag with Cam Jordan's social worker. It was just a courtesy—she figured the social worker would echo what Ruth Jordan said. Still, the call had to be made. Paul Kelly might be able to use the information in his defense, particularly if it turned out Cam had never been known to be violent. But the woman was either in a meeting or out of the office, and when she called back, Georgia was at the gym. She dutifully left her number on the woman's voice mail again.

She did manage to question Claire Tennenbaum, one of Sara Long's friends, before school. She hadn't found out much that wasn't in the police reports—just that Sara had been taken away from the game "to teach her a lesson," the girl said. When Georgia asked why, she admitted Sara was a busybody. "Sara had to know what everyone was doing. She'd read people's notes. Diaries, too."

"Why?"

"I don't know. She wasn't always that way."

"So this—behavior just started recently?"

Claire looked uncomfortable, as if she'd said too much. "I guess. Maybe."

The most interesting piece of information she'd picked up was the name of one of the seniors who'd been at the Forest Preserve. Monica Ramsey.

Now, she went back into the living room and turned on the news. She was startled to see a photo of Sara Long behind the shoulder of the anchor woman. She turned up the volume.

"... a high school hazing was taking place during the powder puff football game at which Sara Long was killed last month," the newscaster said. "According to sources, the victim was taken to another part of the forest where she was subjected to taunting and a series of practical jokes. As you recall, hazing is not a new activity on the North Shore ..."

File footage from someone's video camera two years ago flashed across the screen, including shots of girls on the ground covered in what Georgia knew were feces, urine, paint, pig intestines, and fish guts. More video showed girls being punched, kicked, and pummeled with buckets.

The story cut to Police Chief Eric Olson, Georgia's former boss, who said while the hazing was regrettable, it would not change the course of justice. In a statement that sounded scripted, Olson maintained they had apprehended the offender and had solid evidence to back up their case. They would, however, continue to conduct a thorough investigation into every aspect of this heinous crime. Robby Parker, tall, blond, and smug, stood at Olson's side, hands clasped behind his back.

So much for keeping the hazing under wraps. Now that it was out, the question of why it had been kept quiet in the first place would undoubtedly surface. Who would take the heat, Georgia wondered? Would school officials claim something about an internal investigation and wanting to be sure before they went public? Would parents admit pressuring the authorities to keep it quiet? Or would the cops and the State's Attorney's Office offer some half-assed explanation?

She turned off the TV. The good news was that the fact of a cover-up, however short-term or benign, could help raise reasonable doubt about Cam Jordan. She and Kelly ought to brainstorm some strategies. Maybe talk to a friendly reporter. She'd call Kelly tomorrow.

She looked around the apartment, aware she'd been alone most of the day. Too much isolation wasn't good. She grabbed her jacket, locked her door, and went down the stairs.

The night air had a snap to it, and a breeze carried the tang of burning leaves. She zipped up her jacket. Another month and she'd be wearing her down jacket. She jogged the six blocks to Mickey's on the east side of Ridge and pushed through the door.

"Hey, Davis." Owen Dougherty, Mickey's owner, grinned. A big man, he wore a flowing white shirt and a bartender's apron over his pants. He looked a lot like Jackie Gleason in the reruns of *The Honeymooners* she'd caught on cable. Even the same mustache.

"How's it goin' Owen?" she asked, enjoying the rhyme for about the thousandth time.

"Can't complain." Over the past few years Evanston had become fashionable, its new condos, upscale eateries, and shops a haven for empty-nesters and singles who didn't want to live downtown. With its dim light, scarred wood, and good burgers at decent prices, Mickey's was one of the last of the old neighborhood places. "What about you, Davis?" He wiped down the bar with a damp cloth.

Everyone went by last names at Mickey's except Owen, and, presumably, the Mickey who owned it before him. She didn't mind. It made her feel she belonged.

"Surviving."

Dougherty had bought the place eight years ago. "Didn't have to change a thing," he'd said proudly. Gazing at the old neon signs, shabby tables, and scuffed floor, Georgia wasn't sure that was a good thing. While its grunginess was comfortable, almost endearing, Mickey's *was* becoming a dinosaur. Which made it ripe for a buyout. Of course, that could have been Dougherty's plan all along, which would make him a lot cagier than she thought. She slid onto a stool at the end of the bar.

"So what'll it be, tonight? The usual?"

She nodded. Dougherty filled a tall glass with ice, reached under the bar for a nozzle and spritzed cola into the glass. He reached under the bar again and came up a slice of lemon which he anchored on the rim. "One Coke, plenty of ice and lemon."

"Thanks." She took a pull, wondering why Coke always tasted better here than at home. Swiveling around, she checked out the crowd. The bar was half-filled; most of the faces were familiar. Of the five booths, three were taken, two by couples, and one by a family with two kids. A jukebox stood in the corner, but no music was playing. Instead, a TV above the bar tuned to ESPN was replaying clips from Sunday's games. At least it wasn't the news. Georgia took her drink to one of the empty booths. "This okay?" she called out.

He nodded. "Gemma's not here tonight. You want food, order through me."

"Make it a burger and fries. Rare, this time."

He appraised her. "Raw meat, huh? You got something going I should know about?"

"Nope. I'm saving myself for you."

He ducked into the kitchen. Georgia settled herself in the booth, and thought about the hazing announcement. Two days after she talked to O'Malley, the hazing surfaced. Had he leaked it? It was possible; he clearly wasn't happy with the way the case was going. But O'Malley was a team player. No matter how unhappy he was, he wouldn't cause trouble. Or stick his neck out. Leaking the hazing took guts.

She stared up at the TV. A pretty boy with a blow-dry haircut breathlessly proclaimed that last week's offensive play by Number 49 was a masterpiece. She hardly listened, preoccupied with another issue—this one of her own making. When she interviewed Claire Tennenbaum that morning, she'd had the stack of discovery documents with her, and she pored through them at strategic points during the conversation. She'd let the girl think she was a cop—at least, she hadn't said anything to contradict it.

The problem was she wasn't a cop any more. And it was against the law to impersonate one. Ironically, when she was a cop, she'd learned it was okay to lie in certain situations. She'd watched O'Malley extort information from suspects by playing them off against each other, insisting—falsely—that one was framing the other. The tactic usually worked. But Claire Tennenbaum was a kid. Lying to a kid—even misleading her—didn't feel right.

There was another problem too. Georgia no longer had the insulation that being a cop provided. What if Claire Tennenbaum told her parents she'd been questioned by a cop, and her parents called to verify it? When they found out she'd been posing as one, she could be in trouble. She stared up at the TV, willing her stomach to stop churning.

Ten minutes later Owen arrived with her food. "Burger and fries. Rare." He set the plate down. "You could do the breast stroke in the blood."

She took a bite. "Perfect."

He went back behind the bar, but she knew he was pleased. She remembered the first time she'd come to Mickey's. Matt had brought her here one rainy spring night three years ago. He'd said it was a comfort zone, the kind of place where people knew you on the surface and didn't need to dig any deeper. He'd been right. To this day she wasn't sure Owen knew she—or Matt—had ever been a cop.

She watched Owen flip a white towel over his shoulder. They'd come here so often that she knew the rhythms of the place. How many times an hour Owen wiped down the bar—about twelve. How many TV stations Owen would let customers watch—only two. How many brands of bourbon he carried—seven. She recalled one night, giggling, a few brews to the high side, when she tried to swipe Owen's towel, just to see what he'd do. She figured he'd freak out and frisk everyone in the place 'till he found it. She sneaked up behind Owen, ready to snatch it off his shoulder when he whipped around to face her, and the chance was lost. Matt laughed so hard he knocked over his beer. They used Owen's cloth to wipe it up.

Now, she dipped a fry in ketchup and crammed it in her mouth. When would she stop using Matt to mark time? They'd split up two years ago, but he still haunted her dreams, his face appearing unbidden when she was cuffing an offender, writing tickets, doing laundry. She saw his crooked grin, the way he pushed his hair off his face. Once he'd let it get so long that Olson threatened to buck Matt back to patrol if he didn't get a haircut. That afternoon Matt came back from lunch with a shaved head. She remembered how he walked up and down the hall past Olson's office—it had to be twenty times—before the Chief finally noticed. And never said a word.

She wiped her mouth with her napkin. Those were the heady days. When the touch of his finger sent shivers down her spine. When just being alone made them tear their clothes off, drunk with the smell, taste, and feel of each other. She thought it would never end. She took another bite of her burger. It was starting to taste like cardboard.

CHAPTER ELEVEN

THE SOCIAL worker rooted around in a pile of olive green folders, extracted one, and scanned the first page. "Oh, here we go."

Georgia sat across from Carol Moore, a young woman with ash blond hair and enormous glasses. She was wearing jeans and a ribbed sweater, and she looked like she'd just graduated from high school. She and Georgia sat on either side of a metal desk in the North Shore Mental Health Clinic. The clinic operated out of an Evanston building near Oakton and Ridge that had once been a parochial school. A quick glance around revealed the same peeling paint, green walls, and chipped tiles Georgia remembered from St. Michael's. A grimy, institutional odor seeped out of the walls. Georgia remembered that too.

"Cam Jordan has been my client for over a year," Moore said.

"That doesn't sound like a long time." Georgia breathed through her mouth.

"Let's see. I took over from …" Moore paged through the file. "… Margie Hanson. She got married and had a baby. And before that, Shauna Alexander was his caseworker."

Georgia fidgeted. Passed from hand to hand, Cam was just another file to these people. A case number to justify their budget.

"You *have* met with him?"

"Of course." Moore looked offended. "And now that he's in the news, we've gotten more calls. We can't comment, of course."

"As I told you, I'm a private investigator working on his case. Anything you can tell me about his mental state would be helpful."

Moore nodded. "I talked to the director before you came, and—" She looked up. "Hey, am I going to be called to testify?"

"I don't know if there will be a trial."

"But is it a possibility."

"Yes."

"I just wondered, you know." Moore flipped up a lock of hair. Then she went back to the file. "The last time he came in was almost five months ago. In June."

"How often did you see him?"

"Every six months. Unless there was a crisis."

"Only twice a year?"

"Do you know how many clients I have, Ms. Davis? Some are victims of abuse. Child abuse. Sexual abuse. One of my clients was put in a cage by her father for two years. Another has been in thirty foster homes. Between home visits, clinical practice, and writing reports, it's a miracle I see him that much."

Not something we'd want brought out in a trial, Georgia thought. She could just imagine Ramsey: "With forty-two clients and only two visits a year, in reality, you have no idea whether he was violent or not, do you, Ms. Moore?"

Aloud she said, "What can you tell me about those visits?"

"His sister brings him in. I talk mostly to her. It looks like she takes good care of him. He's always been calm. Not agitated. At least the times I've seen him."

"Is he on any medications?"

She frowned, pulled her glasses down her nose, and sifted through the file. "There's a note from Margie that he was on Seroquel for a year. And Remeron. But it doesn't say if they helped. I don't know if he's still on the meds."

"What do those drugs do?"

"One's an antidepressant. The other is specifically for bipolar disorder and schizophrenia." She looked at Georgia. "Psychopharmacological agents can improve quality of life for the mentally ill. But the best catalyst for change is still a positive and trusting relationship with a therapist."

"But you weren't that therapist."

"I told you. We only see patients during physical or mental health crises. And check-ups. There's nothing here about any other therapist." She closed the file. "I'm guessing there wasn't enough money for it."

Georgia motioned toward the file. "May I look through that? Make some copies?"

"The director said you need to put any request in writing. Then it has to go before our internal committee for approval. And then to the state."

"Well then, may I look through it so I know which reports to request?"

"I'm sorry." Moore leaned back with an expression that said she was really doing Georgia a favor. "But I can tell you what they say."

Georgia bit back a reply. It infuriated her when people doled out information a bit at a time. They were usually sadists. Assholes who liked to watch people beg. They'd have to subpoena the records if they needed them. "Go ahead," she said tersely.

Moore took her time reopening the file and looking through it. "It doesn't appear that there was any instance of real communication—at least while he was here. When he did talk it was mostly the repetition of certain words, or phrases from nursery rhymes."

"Are there any notes about his sexual offense?"

"Let's see ..." She pushed her glasses back onto the bridge of her nose. "Everyone agrees he masturbated in public. But apparently, there was some question about physical contact. His sister contends he never touched the woman in the Forest Preserve. The couple said otherwise, of course." She read on. "Apparently, he had a history of being abused. His father beat him."

"Yes, I know."

She tipped her head. "That could be a contributing factor."

"What do you mean?"

She looked up. "You know. If an individual was abused them-selves, they're more likely to—Oh." She stopped. A frown creased her forehead.

"What?" Georgia said.

"Well, it says here the couple dropped the case a few months later."

"Dropped it? How come?"

"Apparently, they separated and got a divorce." She snorted. "Guess they found other lawyers to give their money to."

If the couple dropped the case, without a conviction, how had Cam been labeled a sex offender? Georgia made a note to follow up. "Is there *anything* in his file about him being violent, threatening violence, or doing harm to anyone?"

Moore looked through the file one more time. She shook her head.

"Do you think it's possible that someone like him, given his record, could suddenly snap and murder a complete stranger?"

Moore gazed at her. "Anything is possible with mentally impaired in-dividuals. But, based on his file and my experience with him, I would be surprised."

Georgia felt an unexpected sense of relief. "We'll probably have to subpoena the entire file."

Moore waved a noncommittal hand. "Whatever."

Before heading home, Georgia stopped to buy copies of the newspapers. Word about the hazing was splashed above the fold in the *Trib* and on the front page of the *Sun Times*. While experts rued the growing violence among teenagers, Chief of Police Eric Olson denied it would affect the outcome of the case. There was no comment from the State's Attorney's Office.

CHAPTER TWELVE

"*SARA HATED* to get up in the morning," A sad smile flickered across Melinda Long's face. "I still wake up thinking it's time to get her out of bed."

"I'm so sorry," Georgia said, aware how useless the words were even as they came out of her mouth.

A tall, lanky blonde, Sara Long's mother retrieved some hangers and garments from the dressing room at New Ideas, an upscale but casual women's dress store in Northfield. After reading where she worked in the police reports, Georgia decided to take a chance. She wasn't sure Sara's mother would be back at work, but she figured it would be less painful to talk outside her home. If she talked at all.

When Georgia walked into the store, she was surprised at its cozy, comfortable feel. A cheerful jumble of brightly patterned sweaters, pants, and even jewelry, New Ideas had a mix of the countrified, horsy fashions worn by North Shore matrons as well as the trendier workout styles favored by the young. Drawn to a rack of sweatshirts and pants, she let her fingers slide down the soft, fleecy garments. She even imagined herself in one of them—the blue one—until she saw the $240 price tag.

"People are shocked I'm back at work," Melinda said a few minutes later. She nodded toward a woman behind the cash register who was chatting with a customer. "I know Janelle was. But what am I supposed to do? I took a week off, but I just couldn't bear staring at four walls." She shivered. "Sara's brother, Jamie, went back to school. And Jerry's at work." She frowned. "I'm sorry. What did you say your name was?"

"Georgia Davis." It hadn't been hard to talk to Sara's mother. She'd recognized her right away. Melinda had the same blonde hair and slim build as her daughter. When she asked if Georgia needed help, Georgia nodded. The conversation had turned to Sara almost immediately. In fact, her eagerness to talk—especially to a stranger—puzzled Georgia, until she recalled that people dealt with grief in all sorts of ways.

"You're an investigator?"

"That's right."

A strange look came over the woman's face. "Forgive me, did you say you're with the police?"

Georgia tensed. She didn't want to mislead the woman, as she'd done with Claire Tennenbaum, but telling the truth might mean the end to their conversation. Still. "Actually, I'm working for some people who want to make sure the right person is held accountable for your daughter's murder."

Melinda clutched the hangars and clothes to her stomach. "You're working for that—that creature, aren't you?"

"Yes," she said quietly. "But I'm just trying to find out the truth. I have no bias."

Georgia figured she had about five seconds before the woman kicked her out of the store. But Melinda's expression was unreadable, and after a moment she headed to a nearby rack and started to hang the garments.

"You know, if you had come in here a week ago, I would have thrown your butt out of here."

Georgia nodded. The woman could see inside her soul.

"I wanted to nail Cam Jordan. I wanted to tear him from limb to limb. Make sure his sorry ass never saw the light of day. It was all so—senseless." Melinda sighed. "But then, I don't know. Things started moving so fast it made my head spin. Everything all tied up in three or four days. With a big, shiny ribbon on top. Closure, they say."

"You had a problem with that?"

"While I was at home, I started to think about it. And now—well—I guess it doesn't really matter."

"Oh, but it does," Georgia blurted out. "If you have any reason to feel Cam Jordan might not be responsible for Sara's death, you have to speak out."

"I don't *have* to do a damn thing." Melinda turned around, her eyes flashing.

Georgia's stomach flipped. Great move, she scolded herself. Her first break in the case, and she'd patronized the victim's grief-stricken mother. She started to apologize but was cut off by a woman loaded down with jewelry who called over to Melinda in a high-pitched voice. "Do you have this in a six?" She picked up a striped black and white outfit that looked like a zebra costume.

Melinda stiffened just for an instant. "Let me check." Her voice was tight.

"I'm sorry," Georgia said. "I was out of line."

Melinda gave her a curt nod.

"Please. Let me buy you a cup of coffee."

Melinda looked at her watch. "I'm off in twenty minutes, but I have to go home and start dinner."

"I can meet you at your house."

"I—I don't know. I don't think it's such a good—"

"Fifteen minutes. That's all."

Melinda started over to Zebra lady. Then, "Fifteen minutes. No more."

***

Georgia pulled up to a small house in western Wilmette, an area some considered the "wannabe" section of the North Shore. Just inside the boundaries of Newfield High School, the neighborhood consisted of mostly split-level homes on tiny lots, although realtors inexplicably called them colonials.

The bricks on the house needed tuck-pointing, and the white shutters could use a coat of paint. There was an older model blue Camaro in the driveway. Still, it looked like the kind of house Georgia's parents aspired to, once upon a time. Georgia remembered her mother chattering on about how they'd move to the suburbs, live in a house with a garage. Georgia would take the bus to school every morning, and her mother would meet her every afternoon when she came home. They'd make cookies together in winter, play in the back yard in summer. She was little, maybe five or six. Even then, had she believed any of it would happen?

Melinda led her into a living room so choked with furniture that Georgia pulled on the neck of her sweater.

"I'll make a pot of coffee," Melinda said. "Make yourself comfortable."

Georgia squeezed past an oversized sofa patterned in red and blue and sat gingerly in a large red-brocade chair. The fabric on the arms was frayed. Framed family photographs sat on an end table. A foursome, then the two kids by themselves. The pictures of Sara looked recent.

"Thank you for letting me come," Georgia called.

"Actually, I was wondering how long it would take for someone to get around to it," Melinda answered from the kitchen. "Now that the hazing's out."

"What do you mean?" Georgia noticed some brownish stains on the white carpet. She hadn't seen a dog.

"When you live in an area like this, you learn to size it up pretty fast." Melinda came into the living room carrying only one coffee mug. She sat down on the sofa and took a sip. "We knew moving out here was a risk."

"In what way?"

"We knew the kids would be exposed to—to different values. That they'd be around people with a lot of money. But Newfield is a good school. We wanted them to have a chance."

"Where were you living?"

"In the Austin neighborhood. Jerry and I grew up there. No, that's not true. I grew up on the East side near Cal Park but moved to Austin when we got married. The schools down there ... well, we knew we could do better. So we scraped together what we could, and moved up here ..." She looked around as if seeing the room for the first time. "We're hanging on, but barely."

Georgia nodded, unsure where Melinda was going. "You said you were wondering how long it would take ..."

Melinda took another sip of coffee. "I wait on women who come into New Ideas and drop a grand on clothes as casually as you and I—well me, at least—drop a couple of bucks for a latte. Then they come back a week later and do it all over again." She hesitated. "When people throw money around like that, I wonder what else they're throwing around."

"What do you mean?"

Melinda gazed at her. "I mean there are people around here who, because of their wealth or their position, expect certain things ... to be taken care of. Fast."

"Do you mean covering up the hazing or coming up with a suspect in your daughter's murder?"

"What's the difference?" Melinda set her mug on a dark wood coffee table with a thud. When the coffee sloshed over the rim, Georgia realized where the carpet stains had come from. "Sara was a little girl when we moved up here. Her brother was even younger. They didn't know why certain kids never invited them to birthday parties. Or sleepovers. Jamie didn't care so much, but I remember Sara crying when she discovered a party she hadn't been invited to. That happened less as she got older. But there were always some girls who excluded her. And then, when she got so pretty, those same girls—well—they resented her. They were jealous."

Georgia glanced at the family photographs. With her long blond hair, blue eyes, and clear, rosy skin, Sara *was* beautiful. "What girls?"

Melinda shook her head.

"Mrs. Long, I can't do anything unless you can be more specific." When she still didn't answer, Georgia leaned forward. "Do you have any reason to believe Cam Jordan didn't kill your daughter?"

Melinda fixed Georgia with a grim look. "Look. I knew what they were planning to do in the Forest Preserve. And I wasn't the only one."

Georgia arched her eyebrows.

"The rumors were flying for weeks. Ever since school started."

"Did Sara tell you?"

"No. Actually, I heard it in the store. Customers—some of the mothers—were talking. It had been two years since the last hazing incident. The girls had learned their lesson. They were going to resurrect the game. After all, it was a school tradition. But it would be harmless this time. Well, maybe a little teasing. But nothing major. Nothing violent."

"Did you know Sara would be one of the targets?"

"Of course not." Anger hardened her face. "Sara might not have been part of the 'in' crowd, but she had friends. Enough, or so I thought, to keep her from being picked on." Melinda went on. "She wasn't like them, anyway. She had a job. She worked after school and on weekends."

"Where?"

Melinda picked up her mug. "At the café in Old Orchard. Inside the book store. She paid for all her clothes. And cell phone. Got discounts on books, too. She knew the value of a dollar."

"So you weren't aware of any problems."

"What are you getting at?"

"One of Sara's friends said Sara was too involved in everyone else's business. Reading diaries. Stealing notes. There was some talk about teaching her a lesson."

"Sara? That's just—ridiculous. Sara spent her time, except when she was working, trying to look like them and sound like them ... it's got to be gossip. High school girls being bitchy." But Georgia saw the hurt spilling out of her eyes.

"Who were her friends?" Georgia asked gently.

Melinda struggled to regain her composure. "Heather and Claire, of course. She's known them since grade school. And Lauren Walcher."

"Do you like them?"

Melinda shrugged. "I—I accepted them. Maybe I shouldn't have." A faraway look came into her eyes. "You know, now that I'm thinking about it, that was why she went there in the first place."

"Went where?"

"To the Forest Preserve. She said she wanted to talk to Lauren."

"She said that?"

Melinda nodded. "I was surprised. She'd said the night before she wasn't planning to go."

"Did she say why she wanted to talk to Lauren?"

"No."

"You didn't ask?"

"I didn't want to pry."

"Do you know the Walchers?"

"Andrea, Lauren's mother, comes into the store sometimes." She looked down. "She pretends she doesn't know who I am."

"So you haven't talked to any of Sara's friends since ..."

"Even if I wanted to I couldn't. Their parents have locked them down tight. That's my point."

Georgia cocked her head.

"The hazing. It was a such a brutal ... savage act. Throwing a bucket of fish guts on her head? Threatening her with a baseball bat? Can you imagine the hatred they must have had toward my daughter? And then, when you realize the same thing happened two years ago, and several girls went to the ER, well, I just don't understand. Why didn't anyone anticipate it could happen again? Why didn't the school prevent it?"

"They did forbid it."

Melinda shook her head violently. "No. They issued an edict. Then they buried their heads in the sand, and prayed like hell it wouldn't happen again. Can you imagine the stupidity? Where were the counselors? The social workers? No one, not the school, not the parents, ever tried to get to the bottom of it. No one took the responsibility to make sure a child would never be hurt from this—this ..." Her voice cracked, and she didn't finish her sentence. "My daughter paid the price for their—incompetence."

"Are you saying you think one of the girls killed Sara?"

"I don't know who killed Sara. Maybe it was that ... excuse for a man they found in the woods. Maybe it wasn't. The problem is I don't think we're ever going to find out. Everything's 'solved'. Done. That's what's driving me crazy. I need to know the truth. And I don't think I'm gonna get it." Tears rimmed her eyes.

Georgia waited until she pulled herself together. "Mrs. Long, would you mind if I looked at Sara's room?"

She looked at her watch. "I don't know. It's almost five—"

"I'll be fast."

"The police were here, you know. They took her laptop and her cell phone. It was one of those camera phones. She just bought it." After everything she'd endured, Melinda's voice still held touch of pride. "You won't take anything ..."

"Of course not."

Melinda hesitated, then stood and led Georgia down a hall. Sara's room was the second on the right. It felt as oppressive as the rest of the house. Wallpaper teeming with tiny flowers. A double bed. A bureau with several drawers open, a closet with a bi-fold door.

"I haven't been able to go through her things," Melinda said, her voice raw.

When Georgia opened the closet door, she was greeted by a pile of clothes on the floor. She rummaged through shorts, tank tops, halters, and high-heeled sandals. She checked the shoes. Manolo. Then she moved to the bureau. Two pairs of Guess jeans. More tops, some of them glittery and revealing. A price tag was still attached to one: Fifty-nine ninety five. Opening the bottom drawer, she found a large mint green purse. The label said Marc Jacobs. Next to it was a digital camera and an iPod. She closed the drawers. Sara must have made a lot of lattes.

"Do you remember if Sara took her cell phone to the Forest Preserve?"

"No. It was here on her bureau when the police came."

Georgia wondered if the police had checked the call log on the cell. If so, it would have been in the discovery documents, but she hadn't seen anything. Which either meant they hadn't checked it or they hadn't gotten the log back yet. Knowing Robby Parker, she'd bet on the former.

Georgia turned around. "Okay, Mrs. Long, I think that about wraps it up. Thank you. I know this wasn't easy."

Melinda stepped heavily back down the hall. Georgia followed her back to the living room.

"How was Sara doing in school?"

"She had a B average. Mostly level three classes. Which was good considering how much she worked. Truth was, between her work schedule and ours, we didn't see that much of her."

"She always did her homework?"

"She had a couple of free periods at school. She did her homework there."

"Who was her advisor?" Georgia recalled that Newfield girls shared the same advisor during all four years of high school. Advisors were teachers who met with small groups of students before class every morning. With over three thousand students at Newfield, daily advisories were like homeroom, designed to give students a sense of belonging to *something*.

"Ms. Beaumont. Jill. Teaches social studies. Nice woman. She's called a couple of times." Melinda faced Georgia. "Tell me. What are you looking for? You obviously think the guy they arrested didn't do it."

Georgia weighed her response. "I do know that Cam Jordan is not considered a violent man. And while he is a registered sex offender, his offenses never involved direct physical contact with anyone. I also know his sister is convinced he didn't do it. And that Jeff Ramsey seems to be rushing this through the courts."

"Ramsey," Melinda said. "He's the prosecutor, isn't he?"

Georgia nodded.

Melinda tugged on a lock of hair. "If it turns out this man didn't kill Sara, if it turns out that the girls—that this idiotic *hazing* was responsible—you're going to hear about it. I know a few parents sued the school two years ago when it first happened, but believe me, that's nothing compared to what I'll do if that—that caused my baby's death. This has got to be stopped. Once and for all. No parent should ever have to go through— to suffer like us. It's—"

A key rattled the front door. The door opened, and a male voice called out, "Mel, whose car is in the driveway?"

Melinda went to her husband, a stocky, tired-looking man somewhere in his forties. As she explained who Georgia was, the lines on his forehead deepened. He brushed by his wife and planted himself in front of Georgia. "I don't know if this is a good idea. I don't think we should be talking to you."

"Jerry," Melinda pleaded. "We talked about this possibility. It's not so far-fetched. Please listen."

Jerry shook his head. "If you're working for Cam Jordan, we have nothing to say to you. Our daughter is dead. Someone has got to pay."

"But what if they have the wrong person?" Georgia asked.

"No. We're not going there." He placed his hand on her arm and guided her toward the door. "It's time for you to leave."

CHAPTER THIRTEEN

LAUREN COULD always tell when her parents argued. There were no screams or shouts; her parents didn't yell. Instead a frigid hostility would permeate the air, like some unseen but deadly toxin. Her mother, the ice queen, had perfected the technique. She could rip your insides out with a few wintry words, then turn around and talk to a stranger on the phone, all warm and honey charm.

Her father was either too gutless or indifferent to stand up to her. Lauren had only heard him raise his voice once in sixteen years, and it had been at her, when she rode her bike into the side of his new Porsche and scratched the paint. Even then, she suspected the only reason he got so pissed was because her mother was.

She closed the door to her room, a little surprised her parents were home together at the same time. That didn't happen often. She went to her iPod and turned it on. Sarah McLachlan poured her heart out from the speakers. Her father said the singer reminded him of Linda Ronstadt and Bonnie Raitt. Lauren tried not to focus on McLachlan's first name.

***

A Sunday night in February. Lauren was twelve, and her parents were in Acapulco—they went to Mexico every winter for ten days. The Walchers' live-in housekeeper took care of Lauren while they were gone: cooking, cleaning, making sure she got to school. It was usually a quiet week, boring even, except when Uncle Fred took her to dinner.

That evening the doorbell rang promptly at six. Lauren skipped down the stairs and opened the door. Uncle Fred, a burly, bearish man with gray hair curling at the temples, gave her a cheerful hug. Tonight they were going to a Chinese restaurant in Wilmette, and Sara was coming with them. Lauren directed him to Sara's house, feeling very adult when Uncle Fred complimented her for knowing the way.

Sara was waiting in front of her house. She climbed into the back seat of the Pontiac and leaned her arms on the back of the front seat. They chattered about last week's episode of "Friends," the new movie with Brad Pitt, the basketball game their middle school team won against their archenemy. Then Sara handed Lauren a sweater she'd borrowed.

"Oh, just keep it," Lauren said. "I have plenty of others."

Sara shook her head. "My mom says I have to give it back."

Lauren shrugged and took the sweater.

At the restaurant, they sat at a table with a white tablecloth. Uncle Fred let them order whatever they wanted, and they splurged on egg roll, sweet and sour pork, chicken chow mein, and ice cream for dessert. They tried to put on their best manners and act mature, but when the main course came, Sara started giggling at something Lauren said and couldn't stop. That made Lauren giggle, too, and for the rest of the meal both girls erupted into periodic gales of laughter.

Uncle Fred, who was unmarried and had no children of his own, smiled but looked slightly puzzled, as if he wasn't sure what sort of species twelve-year-old girls were. Still, he gave them both his arm on the way out, and told them he'd never dined with such pleasant company. That prompted more peals of laughter.

Sara told her afterwards Lauren was lucky. She wished she had an Uncle Fred.

***

Lauren roused herself with a start. She must have dozed off. She pushed away the wispy memories and checked the time. Shit. She needed to catch up with Derek. They had to talk.

She got up and shuffled into the bathroom. Staring at her reflection in the mirror, she dug some dark lip gloss out of her cosmetics drawer and applied it carefully, resisting the urge to smack her lips. Next she pulled on her black Armani sweatshirt she'd worn last night. It still smelled of Black Cashmere. She loved the musky, cinnamon tang. Then she wriggled into a new pair of Joe's Jeans, the ones with the embroidery up and down the legs. Her long, dark hair lay straight today. Her zits were under control, too. All in all, not bad.

She checked the time again. Thursday night at the mall was tricky. You couldn't be sure about the crowds. People were gearing up for the weekend, buying a last minute pair of shoes or pants or just hanging out at the Food Court. Derek would be there; it was one of their regular haunts. Plus, she was hungry. She couldn't have cared less about the lobster bisque and chicken salad her mother brought home. She needed real food. Corner Bakery, maybe. Or Johnny Rocket's.

Before leaving, she checked her e-mail. She'd checked an hour ago, but you had to keep on top of things. It had been easy to set up. Everyone, especially girls, thought you had to be a geek to do it. Not true. She clicked on her email program. Nothing new.

She was just shutting down when she heard the crunch of tires on the gravel. She went to her window and looked out onto the driveway. A car was rolling up to the house. In the fading light, she didn't recognize it. For a split second, she panicked. Derek wouldn't come here. She'd forbidden it. Then she remembered he didn't drive a Toyota, and now that the car had stopped, she could see that's what it was.

It seemed to take forever, but finally the driver climbed out. A woman. Blond hair pulled back. Wearing jeans and a blazer. The woman came around to the front of her car and looked uncertainly in both directions. The kitchen door was only a few feet away, but she trudged to the front door.

CHAPTER FOURTEEN

THE WALCHER home—or was it a mansion—
stood at the top of a rise that overlooked Lake Michigan. At the moment
the water was calm, Georgia noted, almost glassy, but the lake was as
fickle as a teenager and could change quickly.

The house had three stories, but the front, a sandy shade of granite,
was a monolithic façade like one of those modern museums. A thick grove
of trees just now starting to turn provided a natural barrier between the
home and the street. She pulled into a driveway shaped like a lower case
"h" and parked at the top. The front door occupied the rounded part of the
"h." She walked around.

Three circular concrete slabs, each one higher than the other, bridged
a small fishpond at the front entrance. Glimpses of orange and silver
flashed in the water. She moved to the side of an enormous wooden door
and rang the bell.

A series of musical notes echoed in ever quieter pools of sound. Georgia shuffled her feet. In the past her badge, her weapon, and her uniform had given her instant credibility. Now she had nothing, except her wits.

The tall, thin woman who opened the door was dressed in black crepe pants and a beige shirt. Her dark hair was cut short above her ears, which sported gold hoops. Her angular face and pronounced cheekbones were softened by age and a flawless makeup job. She wasn't a beauty, but with her dark gypsy looks she was exotic, and she carried herself like she knew it.

Georgia fastened one of the buttons on her blazer. "Good evening, Mrs. Walcher. My name is Georgia Davis." She peered into a pair of dark, suspicious eyes.

"I thought they said seven-thirty."

"Pardon me?"

"Seven thirty. You're from the school, aren't you?" The eyebrows above the dark eyes rose into perfectly formed arches.

Someone from the school was coming here? Georgia flashed back to her conversation with Rachel. Counselors and social workers were making home visits to help students cope with Sara's death. She took in Mrs. Walcher's hauteur, the icy expression. This might be her only chance to interview the girl about Sara Long. She She sucked in a breath and made a split decision.

"Um, is this a bad time? I was only a few blocks away ..."

The woman's arched eyebrows were replaced by an irritated look down her nose. "I suppose we might as well get it over with." She turned around and called down a long hall with a cold-looking marble floor. "Tom, Lauren's social worker is here. I know it's early, but we're both here, and so is Lauren."

Georgia felt her stomach knot. What was she doing? She'd never get away with it.

"Certainly," a voice boomed. "Andrea, let the poor woman in."

As Andrea Walcher opened the door, a man with a broad but curiously flat face that looked too large for his body joined her. His blond hair was parted on the side. Ruddy cheeks framed small eyes and a weak chin. But he was tall and well built, and he wore jeans and a soft-looking green shirt which made him appear younger and less formal than his wife. "I'm Tom Walcher." He smiled. "You're from Newfield?"

Georgia remembered Cam Jordan's social worker. The weary self-importance. The officious manner. She drew herself up. "Georgia Davis." She sighed and faked another smile.

Walcher smiled back, but it failed to reach his eyes. "Come in."

Andrea Walcher gazed coolly at her husband.

Georgia stepped inside. Walcher led her into the living room, a huge space with a sunken floor, a thick white carpet over which lay oriental rugs, and a giant picture window. Through the window Georgia saw woods that ended precipitously at a rocky bluff. Rachel had told her there was a pool and a guest house, but they must have been on the other side of the property, because the only thing in front of the window was a bricked patio with a built-in barbecue pit and grill. A pair of tongs and oven mitts lay next to the grill.

A sudden memory of ribs, smoking in an open pit on a hot summer day came over Georgia. Picnic tables loaded with bowls of slaw and cornbread. Peaches too. Bushels of fresh peaches. "We named you for them, darling," a musical voice was saying. "But you're sweeter and pinker and softer."

"Can I get you something to drink?" Tom Walcher walked around the room, turning on lamps. As the reflection of the lights popped up in the picture window, the view outside dimmed. Georgia forced herself back. The contrast between the Walcher home and Sara Long's was dramatic. None of the trinkets, sentimental objects, and framed photos she'd seen at the Longs'. The Walcher home felt sterile.

She cleared her throat. "Please, don't go to any trouble. I—I just wanted to check up on Lauren."

Andrea Walcher stayed at the entrance to the sunken living room, her arms crossed. Yet her husband seemed to be extending himself to be gracious. Were they playing her? Or just astonishingly dysfunctional?

"Andrea?" Walcher held out his hand to his wife. She took two steps down, but remained at the edge of the oriental rug, her foot poised on the fringe.

"Please, sit down," Walcher motioned. "You must be as tired as we are. You're sure you don't want something?"

"No thank you." Georgia sat stiffly on a nubby beige sofa with thick cushions. "How has Lauren been? Since the—Sara died?"

Walcher's face turned solemn, and he clasped his hands together, almost prayer-like. "Well, it's been—"

"Actually, she's been fine," Andrea cut in.

Walcher gave a little sigh and continued. "We all like to put a good face on things, especially Andrea." He glanced over. "But that's not altogether true. Sara and Lauren were close friends. This has been a very difficult time for her. Especially on top of her uncle's death."

"I'm sorry," Georgia said. "I didn't know ..."

Walcher nodded. "We're all—well, we're all under a good deal of stress." He looked over at Andrea. Was he apologizing for his wife's behavior? She glared at him. "But Lauren's strong. She'll make it. We're planning to take her to a therapist."

Georgia heard an intake of breath from Andrea.

"And, thankfully, the legal wrangling seems to be moving along." Walcher went on. "I'm a lawyer myself, and I know what legal sparring in the midst of grief is like."

"Are you involved in the case?"

"No." He unclasped his hands and leaned his elbows on the back of one of the wingback chairs. "I'm—well, let's just say I know the players involved." A trace of self-importance curled his lip.

Did that mean Jeff Ramsey? Were they "buddies?" Georgia wanted to follow up, but she was supposed to be a social worker from the school. Social workers didn't ask about murder investigations. She leaned back against the couch. Tom Walcher was continuing to play the genial host, but there was something disingenuous about him. And his wife was an arctic wind. What would they do if they realized she wasn't the person they thought? She should never have come. Too late now. She dug her thumb nail into her index finger and squeezed. "May I talk to Lauren?"

Walcher gestured. "Of course." He turned to Andrea. "Would you get her, dear?"

Andrea didn't move. Walcher shot her a questioning look. When Andrea still didn't move, he moved past her toward the stairs and called out. "Lauren, sweetie. Could you come down for a minute?"

There was no response.

Walcher flashed Georgia an embarrassed smile. "Her door must be closed. I'll get her." He started up the stairs.

The few moments she was alone with Andrea Walcher seemed interminable. The woman leveled her with a suspicious look and made no attempt at chitchat. The message was clear: "You don't belong here, I don't like you, and I won't do anything to make it easier." Georgia's pulse throbbed against her temple.

At length a noise at the top of the steps distracted her, and a girl's voice shouted defiantly, "No. I don't have time."

A two-way mumble followed, and while Georgia couldn't catch the words, the girl's defiance became a whine, and eventually an exasperated, "Oh, all right." Feet shuffled down the stairs, and Lauren Walcher spilled into the room.

The girl was a younger version of her mother, but with sharper features. Tall for her age, and slim, she had hair the same dark shade as Andrea's, but longer and thicker. Like her mother, she dressed in clothes that flattered her body. And looked expensive. Lauren's expression was just as suspicious as her mother's, and when she saw Georgia, her eyes narrowed.

"Who are you? Where's Beaumont?"

"What are you talking about, Lauren?" Andrea said. "She's your counselor from school."

"I've never seen her before. She doesn't work at Newfield."

Before Andrea could react, Georgia jumped in. "That's true. I've been brought in as a private counselor. I work in Evanston." It wasn't a complete lie.

"Why would they do that?" Lauren's tone was belligerent. "You didn't know Sara."

"Right again," Georgia said. "But sometimes that can work to your advantage. I'm not bringing any baggage. And I do know how to work with people in crisis." She gave Lauren the hint of a smile. "It's my job." That wasn't so far from the truth either.

Lauren looked at her watch. "I only have a few minutes. I'm going out."

"Where?" Her mother asked.

"Just out." She turned a chilly voice to her mother. "You said to be home by seven thirty. It's not even five."

Andrea shrugged in Georgia's direction. "That was before *she* showed up."

If only she could get the girl alone. Georgia turned to Walcher, who had followed his daughter back downstairs. "Would it be okay if Lauren and I talked privately?"

A glance passed between the adults, then Walcher answered. "Normally, I wouldn't hesitate. But in this case . . ." he threw his hand over his daughter's shoulder. ". . . there's been so much pressure. I don't want Lauren to be burdened any more than she already is. I'm sure you understand."

Georgia struggled to maintain a calm facade. "I do." She prayed the words that came out of her mouth next sounded convincing. "But it's hard for me to do my job if Lauren doesn't feel comfortable and safe. She needs to know she's not being measured or judged. Which is my goal. As a lawyer, sir, I'm sure you understand."

Walcher got up and turned on another lamp, which threw a yellow pool of light into the room. It wasn't totally dark outside, but the reflections of the four of them in the picture window obscured the view. "I do." He smiled. "But my decision stands."

Skirmish over. Walcher wins.

Georgia faked another smile. Andrea turned around and left the room. Lauren slouched in one of the wingback chairs. Throwing a jeaned leg over the arm, she swung it back and forth, as if she couldn't be less interested in the conversation.

Georgia bypassed the preliminaries. "I know there were—difficulties—with Sara and some of her friends. Which might have played a role in what happened in the Forest Preserve." She cleared her throat.

Lauren glanced at her father. "I don't think I should be talking about that. With you."

"Actually, I have no interest in that part of it. My concerns right now are just you girls. You. Heather. And Claire."

Lauren didn't say anything. Her leg continued to swing back and forth.

"There can often be a lot of embedded guilt after an experience like this. I want to make sure you know you did nothing to cause it."

Lauren eyed her.

"Guilt can be the most destructive part of grief. If you are feeling it, I want you to feel free to own it, with me, your therapist, or anyone of your choosing."

"I don't feel guilty." Lauren's chin lifted. "And my parents are getting me a therapist."

"I'm glad." Georgia paused. "So the information I have isn't true?"

"What information?"

Tom Walcher perched on the end of the sofa. He reminded Georgia of a tiger preparing to attack by feigning disinterest in its prey.

"That Sara came to the Forest Preserve specifically to talk to you."

Lauren's leg stopped swinging. A stunned look came over her.

Just then Georgia heard a voice from the kitchen. "Thank you. No, we'll take care of it." The phone was put down. Footsteps clacked, and Andrea Walcher came into the living room. All the way in, this time. Planting herself in front of the picture window, she glared at Georgia. "I just called Newfield. They haven't hired any free-lance social workers, and they've never heard of anyone named Georgia Davis. Which means you're impersonating someone you're not."

Georgia gulped air.

"So, who the hell are you and what do you want?"

CHAPTER FIFTEEN

ON THE way home, Georgia felt like counting her fingers and toes to make sure they were still there. When Andrea Walcher confronted her, she confessed she was a private investigator working for Cam Jordan. Tom Walcher's face turned crimson, and he told her to get the hell out of their house. He also vowed to make Goddamned sure she never worked anywhere in the state if he ever found her within a hundred yards of their daughter. He would get a restraining order if he had to. Or take her to court.

She made a speedy exit.

Heading south on Sheridan Road, she slammed her fist on the steering wheel. She'd known it was risky. Why the hell did she do it? Now she had two enemies, and if Walcher followed through on his threats, she might be in deep shit. Particularly since Walcher implied he and Ramsey were pals. What would happen if word got back to the State's

Attorney about her "visit"? What would that do to Kelly? Or Cam? She'd screwed up. Big time.

She cut across to Green Bay Road and parked at the Jewel. Inside she pushed her grocery cart through the aisles. Although food was the last thing on her mind, she grabbed milk, lettuce, bread, and eggs. Then she browsed the pre-cooked foods and threw a pizza in her cart. She didn't want to go out, and she certainly didn't have the energy to go to Mickey's. She paid for her groceries, headed back to her car, and threw the bags in the back seat.

The liquor store was only a block away. This had been one shitty day. Maybe she should stop in.

She was steering the cart into the cart corral when she felt a presence at her back. Her senses went on alert. It was practically dark, and the shadows in and around the parking lot were deep enough to shelter someone. *Great. Getting mugged would be a fitting end to this day.* Then instinct kicked in. Pretending not to notice anything, she tightened her grip on the cart's handlebar. With any luck, the attacker would hold off long enough for her to swing the cart out of the corral and launch it toward his groin. Then she would run like hell. Slowly, she started to back the cart out of the corral.

"Hey!" A voice said.

Georgia whipped the cart around, her hands curled into fists, prepared to let the cart fly.

"Wait! No. Don't!" A girl's voice.

Georgia froze.

Lauren Walcher emerged from the shadows, waving her arms.

Georgia took a deep breath. Her stomach slowly descended to its proper place. "What—what the hell are you doing here?"

"I followed you."

"All the way from Glencoe? Why?"

"I want to talk."

She steered the car back into the corral. "Do your parents know you're here?"

"Of course not."

Georgia loosened her grip on the cart. The adrenaline flowing through her began to ebb. "You realize they'd probably lock you up if they found out."

"No, they wouldn't." She shrugged. "I'd just tell them that you waited for me outside the house and forced me go with you."

Georgia gazed at Lauren. This girl had balls.

Lauren shot Georgia a condescending smile, trotted over to her Land Rover, and levered herself up on the hood. "Here's the thing. Sara was my friend. If that psycho didn't do it, I want to know who did."

Georgia had gotten nothing from Lauren at her house. Her presence here was a gift. Matt used to say never look a gift horse in the mouth—just be careful it's not a Trojan. She followed Lauren to the Land Rover. "What makes you think he didn't do it?"

"You tell me." Lauren crossed one leg over the other.

A sodium vapor light high above them crackled and buzzed. "Why don't you tell me about Sara's problems with her friends?"

"What problems?"

"No more games," Georgia said. "What did Sara want to talk to you about in the Forest Preserve?"

"What are you talking about?" Lauren asked uneasily.

"Come on, Lauren. Her mother told me she was coming to the Forest Preserve to see you. Why?"

The girl shrugged but didn't say anything.

Georgia forced herself to stay patient. "She didn't leave a message on your cell? Or text message?"

Lauren jiggled her foot. "No."

Georgia couldn't tell if she was lying. "So you have no idea what she wanted?"

"Nope." Lauren's foot continued to jiggle.

"You sure it had nothing to do with her ... activities?"

She looked up. Her foot stopped jiggling. "What activities?"

"Claire Tennenbaum told me that Sara had a tendency to—well, let's say she was very curious about other people's business."

"Oh, that." Lauren's shoulders relaxed. "Claire couldn't keep anything straight if her life depended on it."

"Excuse me?"

"Claire is sweet, but she's as dumb as a plate."

"So what she said isn't true?"

"I never saw Sara do anything like that." But she wouldn't meet Georgia's eyes.

"Lauren, when I was your age, I remember thinking that a real friend was someone who kept my secrets. Who would never tell anyone what I said or did. But I realize now that isn't always true. Sometimes you're a more responsible friend if you do tell someone those secrets. Especially if it helps us discover why she was killed." She paused. "Are you sure there's nothing you want to tell me?"

Lauren hesitated for just a fraction of a second. It was enough.

"Lauren?"

The girl fingered a leather band around her neck. A silver charm attached to it flashed in the orange glow of the sodium vapor light.

Georgia prodded gently. "Did Sara have any secrets she didn't want people to know?"

Lauren ran a tongue around her lips.

"Something that involved other people?"

The girl stared at her. Then she dropped her hand from the necklace and swung herself down from the hood of her car. She cleared her throat. "Sara was going out with somebody's boyfriend. Last summer. There were bad feelings about that."

"What boy? Whose boyfriend?"

"It didn't last, but that wasn't Sara's fault." Lauren started talking faster. "I mean, she was hot. Guys liked her. You can't do much about that."

"Who was the boy?" Georgia crossed her arms. Lauren cut her eyes to the ground.

"Okay. Who was the girl?" Georgia asked.

"Look, I've got to go. Maybe you're right. I shouldn't have followed you here." She dug out her keys from her pocket and unlocked the Land Rover.

"Lauren ..."

She opened the door and climbed up into the front seat. "Monica Ramsey," she said softly.

"The daughter of the State's Attorney?" Georgia's arms dropped to her sides.

She nodded.

"And Monica Ramsey was in the Forest Preserve the day Sara was killed."

"Yes," she said, as if the thought had just come to her. "She was there."

***

Georgia was lugging the groceries up to her apartment thinking about families and friendship and secrets when she heard the fight.

"I don't care what you said. It doesn't mean shit." A woman's voice. Georgia stopped and looked up, as if she expected see angry words stabbing the air.

"What do you want from me, Sheila?" A man's voice. Controlled. But tense.

"I want you to come home."

"Not after what happened. It's not going to work. It's over."

"Why can't you forgive me?" Her voice again. "I made a mistake, okay? A bad mistake."

"For two years?" His voice spiked. Georgia cringed. She could hear the rawness and pain.

"You're a sanctimonious prick, you know that?"

"Get out, Sheila. Now."

Footsteps pounded on the floor. Georgia fumbled her key into the lock. She let herself in just as the door upstairs opened.

"You'll regret this."

"Goodbye, Sheila."

The door slammed, and footsteps clomped down the steps. Georgia quietly closed her door.

***

Lauren checked the rear view mirror as she drove to the Mall. Ever since Sara was killed, Lauren had started to look over her shoulder, worrying that someone was watching her. Even the arrest of the freak in the woods hadn't stopped the feeling. She kept remembering *The Ring*, the movie that came out a few years ago. Once you watched a certain video, you died seven days later. Okay, it was just a trashy movie. But the thought that someone might—just might—be setting her up the way they did in *The Ring* was creepy.

No. She was just on edge. Stressed out. No one was after her. Sara was killed by a psycho. That's what the police said. So did everyone else. The guy was a registered sex offender, for Christ's sake. So why was this private investigator asking so many questions? Lauren had given her Monica Ramsey. Sent her off on a wild goose chase. Maybe she would leave *her* alone. The less anyone knew, the better.

Lauren gripped the wheel. She was tired. Weary. Why was she doing everything herself? Wasn't this supposed to be the time of her life? The bloom of the young rose and all that other crap her father handed down?

"You're young, white, rich, and gorgeous. Spread your wings."

Sure, Dad. Like you'd know how to do that. Although compared to the ice queen, he might have a trick or two up his sleeve. Still, nothing ever stopped the ache in her heart each time she thought about her family. She felt like they'd lost something important. Which was weird. How could you lose something you never had?

She parked the Land Rover and hurried into the mall. She spotted Derek as soon as she reached the main promenade. He was lounging on a bench outside Bath and Body Works, thumbing through the pages of one of those graphic novels. Nothing but a stupid comic book, except it cost as much as a CD. Still, she knew why he was carrying it, and it wasn't a bad prop. She crept up behind him. He looked like he was deep into the book, but she knew he sensed her presence. That was part of the come-on. Don't act too interested.

"Hey, dude." She walked around to the front of the bench.

Derek Janowitz looked up. His nose was sharp, and his lips were thin, giving him a haughty expression. He wasn't that big, but he was a wrestler, and his body was wiry and strong. His best features were his eyes, deep pools of blue that seemed to burrow straight into your soul. It was only skin deep, of course. What did he know about compassion or wisdom? But more times than not, it worked—he got plenty of second glances.

"Whassup?" He put the book down and fiddled with the leather band around his neck. It was similar to the necklace Lauren wore.

"We gotta talk."

"I'm busy, in case you didn't notice. Can't it wait?"

A spit of annoyance shot through Lauren. "No. It can't."

He slouched on the bench. "So talk."

She snuck a look around. A large woman and a teenage boy sat on a bench across from them. The boy looked as if he'd rather be anywhere else in the world than with his mother. But the woman kept her eyes pinned on Derek. *Holy shit!* She had to be at least forty, and she was ogling him.

"Not here." Lauren scowled. "Follow me."

She walked back to the escalator and headed up to the food court,
checking over her shoulder to make sure he was following. When she
got to Auntie Anne's, she scooped up a couple of samples on the counter
and popped them in her mouth. Asiago cheese. She stopped at a dimly lit
table in the back of the food stalls and sat down. A combination of greasy
Chinese food smells, pizza and fresh baked cookies drifted over.

Derek joined her a few seconds later. "So, what's the deal?"

Lauren clasped her hands together. "We have a problem."

"What now?" He sighed, but she picked up the irritation in his voice.

"No. This is serious."

"That's what you said last week, when—"

"That was different. I dealt with it. Not that you were much help."

"Right," he scoffed. "You wouldn't have even known about it without me."

He was right, but she glared at him anyway. He was starting to tick her
off. Claiming she couldn't get along without him. That she needed him
more than he needed her. Were all men like that, or was it just Derek?
Her father had his faults, but he didn't put people down all the time. At
least not around her.

Derek raised his palm in a so-what gesture.

"A private eye is working Sara's case."

A startled look came over him. "How do you know?"

"She came to the house today. Tried to impersonate a shrink."

Derek's eyebrows shot up. "She?"

"Name's Georgia Davis. Said she was a social worker. Turned out she
wasn't."

"No shit."

"You know her?"

"Naw. But a chick. That's pretty tight."

Lauren shrugged. "It did take balls. But it's not good. I had a little talk
with her afterwards."

Derek focused on something behind Lauren, as if intent on some inner thought. She'd been through a range of possibilities on the way over but didn't have any answers. She certainly didn't expect Derek to have any. He'd dropped out of high school last year. She wasn't with him because of his smarts.

She twisted around to see what he was staring at. A tall, thin blonde was passing behind her. She was hot but had on too much makeup. The girl favored Derek with a smile. Derek smiled back.

Lauren snapped. "Not now, asshole!"

Derek flicked his eyes back. He was pissed. Good. At least the smugness was gone.

Derek leaned forward. "How much does this Davis know?"

"She knows Sara came to the Forest Preserve to talk to me."

"She did?" Derek looked interested. "What did she want?"

"I don't know. I never got a chance to find out."

Derek's eyes narrowed into slits. "I thought you knew everything."

"Well, compared to some people ..."

His eyes turned nasty. She should back off. She continued. "Listen. I wouldn't be here if I didn't need your help. I tried to sidetrack her, and I think I did. But we need to make sure. Think, okay? Has there been anything—well, strange—on your end?"

"Like what?"

"I don't know. People asking too many questions? Saying weird things?"

His gaze turned calculating. "You mean besides Sara?"

Lauren ignored the crack. "You know what I mean."

He slouched in his chair, his brow furrowed. After a long moment, he shook his head. "I don't like it."

"Me neither." Lauren said. A throng of noisy teenagers suddenly appeared and commandeered the table beside them. She had to raise her voice to be heard. "What should we do?"

"Lemme think about it." He sat up, throwing a withering look toward the boys at the table. One of the boys threw an equally withering look back. Keeping his eye on the boy, Derek added, "But I'll tell you one thing not to do."

She glanced at the boy Derek had confronted. He looked younger, maybe about fourteen, but he glared at Derek like he was spoiling for a fight. Why did men always have to stake out their turf? All that testosterone with nowhere to go. "What?"

"Stop looking so freaked."

"You think I'm scared?" When he didn't answer, she shook her head. "You really do have delusions of grandeur."

Derek's eyes narrowed. "Delusions of what?"

She gestured to the comic book. "You'd know if you ever picked up a real book."

"I don't need books for the kind of work I do."

"Fuck it, Derek. You work in a gas station."

"I know what people want and how far they're willing to go to get it."

Lauren almost rose to the bait, but something inside told her this wasn't the right time. She took a deep breath. "Just be careful, okay?"

"Always am." He scooted the chair back. "Time to get back."

She nodded. She'd have to be satisfied with that. "Anything new?"

"Maybe. If you hadn't screwed it up."

She looked at her watch. "I have time. I could stick around."

"No way. I'm cool. Go home and jump into that fancy hot tub of yours. Let the water chill you out."

Pity he didn't know what a mixed metaphor was. It was a hundred and four degrees in her Jacuzzi.

CHAPTER SIXTEEN

CRISP MORNING sunlight angled through the car window, highlighting the steam rising from Georgia's coffee. She watched it dissipate into tendrils of fog. She was parked a few houses away from Jeff Ramsey's home in Winnetka. A rehabbed Victorian on a quiet street off Willow, the house was large but not showy, and it blended well with the other homes on the block. She was surprised—she'd expected him to live on one of the private roads in Winnetka that were little more than drive-ways. She was grateful he didn't. It would have been tough to stake out.

She checked her watch. Barely seven. She didn't have to be here, but she felt more in control of a case when she could ID the people involved. Not that she ascribed motives to people based on their looks—people were consummate actors—but she liked to watch how they carried themselves, whether they looked you in the eye, how they interacted with others. And since she had no reason to contact the Ramseys directly and probably wouldn't get through if she tried, this was the best she could do.

She riffled through the pages she'd printed out last night. Thanks to Google and Kroll, a security company with a huge electronic database that she could access for a fee, she now had solid background on Jeff Ramsey. Raised in the New Jersey suburbs; graduated fourth in his high school class. Had a scholarship to Penn—the Wharton School—but majored in political science. Ended up at Columbia Law, where he met his wife, Janet. Worked his way through law school—at least partially—playing the piano at private parties and corporate events. Clerked for a federal judge in New York, then got hired by the DA's office where he emerged as a star trial lawyer with an impressive won-lost record. Came to Chicago four years ago in one of Daley's sweeps to find fresh talent.

His wife Janet was a lawyer, too, although she didn't practice. She was the Executive Director of the North Shore seniors organization. She was also active in local politics, and there were rumors she planned to run for the Village Caucus. Monica was their only child.

Two ambitious overachievers in one house. That could put stress on a marriage. Not to mention a teenage daughter.

The front door to the house swung open, and a man with wavy brown hair falling over his forehead came out. Georgia glanced down at the photo she'd printed out. Ramsey. He was followed by a young girl in jeans and a pink sweat shirt.

Monica was about five-four. Her dark hair was pulled back in a ponytail. She hoisted a backpack on her shoulder and started down a bricked path to the street. She stopped when Ramsey called out to her. Georgia rolled down her window hoping to catch his words. She was still too far away, but Monica nodded, threw him a kiss, and proceeded to a red Honda Civic in front of the house. Wide-eyed, with a pug nose and bow-shaped lips, she was pretty in a fresh, wholesome way. She looked sweet, too. Not like someone who might club another girl over the head with a baseball bat. Then again, Ted Bundy had been a handsome charmer who walked with a cane.

Monica slid into the Honda, and Ramsey cut across the grass to the garage. He was average height and wore a blue pinstripe suit and a red tie, and he walked with an easy, charged grace. Georgia's throat suddenly went dry. He walked the way Matt did. It had made her smile, Matt's walk—until the day she watched him walk away from her.

Ramsey watched his daughter drive off, then raised the garage door and climbed into a silver Beamer. He backed out of the driveway and disappeared around the corner. Georgia considered hanging around to check out Janet Ramsey but decided it could wait. She finished her coffee, pitched the cup on the floor, and started her car. As she doubled back to Hibbard, she punched in Kelly's number on her cell. It was still early, and she reached his voice mail. Rather than leave a message, she hung up and headed for the gym.

She reached him after her workout.

"Kelly." His morning voice was thin and gravelly.

"Hi, Paul. This is Georgia Davis."

"I didn't know if I'd hear from you again."

"Hey. Does that mean you missed me?"

He groaned.

"I'll take that as a 'yes.' I've been checking things out."

He paused. "And?"

She told him about her interviews with Claire Tennenbaum and Melinda Long.

"How'd you get the Long woman to talk to you?" He sounded impressed.

She told him how she'd dropped into New Ideas and ended up at the woman's house.

"Yeah?"

"Yeah." She told him about Melinda's feelings about the speed of Cam's indictment and the hazing.

Kelly muttered something under his breath.

"Excuse me?" she asked.

"Nothing." He cleared his throat again.

Georgia let it go. "Her husband wasn't as … open-minded." She described how he'd come home from work and promptly asked her to leave.

"That's more like it," Kelly said. "Still, we might have some leverage. You think the mother'd testify for us?"

"I'd say it's a long shot. She's getting pressure from her husband to steer clear of us. I guess it depends on what else we find." She told him about the expensive clothes in Sara's closet. "I'm gonna talk to her boss at the bookstore just to confirm things. But that's not the best part."

"You got more?"

"Do I." She told him about her visit to the Walcher home. "They weren't cooperative."

"Walcher? Who the hell are they?"

She explained the relationship between Lauren and Sara. "Of course, it might have been my fault."

"Why?"

There was no sense keeping it from him—he'd find out eventually. She told him how she'd impersonated a social worker and had been caught.

"Why in hell did you do that?"

"It was kind of—well, it just happened. I didn't plan it."

"Sure you didn't."

"It's true." She wondered why she was defending herself. She didn't have anything to prove to Paul Kelly. "I wanted to try to get something before they shut down."

"Yeah, but showing up at their house under false pretenses? He could make trouble."

"It wasn't … that deliberate an action. It was more like taking advantage of an opportunity, but you're right. It won't happen again."

Silence.

"I think we can work around it," she added.

"We?"

Georgia kept her mouth shut.

"What do you want from me?" He sounded pained.

"Tom Walcher—the girl's father—is a lawyer. He claims he's not involved in the case. But I'd feel better knowing for sure. Could you check him out?"

More silence. Then, "Maybe."

"Thanks."

"Anything else?" He groused.

"As a matter of fact, there is." She told him what she'd learned about Monica Ramsey. That Sara had apparently stolen someone's boyfriend, possibly Monica Ramsey's. That the Ramsey girl might have been in the Forest Preserve at the hazing. That she'd staked out the house.

"Hold on," Kelly cut her off. "Are you saying the Ramsey girl might be involved in the Long girl's murder?"

"I'm saying we ought to find out more about their relationship."

"Whoa. Stop. Right now. What proof do you have that she was even in the Forest Preserve?"

"Two of the girls said so."

"There was no mention of Monica Ramsey in the discovery documents."

"That's true, but—"

"So you're going to take the word of a couple of teenagers?"

"I can get corroboration."

"Jesus Christ. You can't do this. I knew this was a bad idea. I should never have let Father Carroll talk me into—"

"You were ready to plead him out." She reminded him. "Without any investigation."

"I'm a lawyer. That's what I do."

"Send innocent people to prison?"

"Cut the drama, okay? We both knew this was a long shot from the get-go. Davis, you can't go after Ramsey's daughter. What are you gonna tell me next? That he covered up news of the hazing? That he's railroading Jordan to protect his daughter?"

Georgia forced herself to stay calm. "I'm not *going after* anyone. I'm just following the evidence."

"What evidence? Where?" Kelly's voice was as sharp as a razor blade. "From where I sit, you've got nothing but gossip. Can't even call it hearsay. It's—you're …" He sputtered. "Do you know what the State's Attorney could—could do to me? And you?"

"I understand. But—"

"No. I don't think you do. I could lose my license. You could never work again."

"If that happens you'll have the insurance business to fall back on."

"Is that a joke?"

"Well, you don't seem to be working the legal angles too hard."

A cold silence followed. Then, "Back off the Ramsey girl, Davis. Even if she was in the Forest Preserve, there had to be twenty other girls there, too."

"Paul, if there's a chance any one of those twenty is implicated in the death of Sara Long, I need to follow it."

She heard an exasperated sigh.

***

It was still early, and the aroma of roasting coffee coated the air inside the bookstore. Georgia sniffed her way to the café and bought a latte, hoping the milk would neutralize the acid eating away her stomach. She sipped her drink and looked around, trying not to feel intimidated. She'd never spent much time in bookstores. Her high school English teacher, a shriveled old nun who used to quote Shakespeare at the beginning of every class, tried her best to introduce Georgia to the world of literature. Sister Marion had waxed eloquent about the worlds that would open up to her through reading—except it never happened. Georgia had struggled just to make sense of the words. She found out later she'd been dyslexic: her brain didn't want to read letters in the right order.

Now, she wandered over to the counter where a twenty-something guy with lots of earrings punched through his eyebrows was working the register. There was only one customer in line, a woman pushing a stroller. Georgia waited until the woman left. "Hi."

The guy looked up from the register.

"Is the manager here?"

He pointed to the back of the store. "Back there."

Georgia turned around. The store was as big as a football field. "Where?"

"That door marked 'employees.'"

She nodded her thanks and made her way to the back, winding through stacks of books, mostly paperbacks. The dry, flat scent of paper replaced the smell of coffee. Had she missed something by not reading? Kids staffed stores like this. Did they know something she didn't? Had they entered the secret world of literature? Or were they just here because it was cushier than McDonald's?

She reached the employees' door and knocked. Nothing. She knocked again. This time she heard a rustle, and the door opened. Another youngish man in a denim shirt and jeans stuck out his head.

"Are you the manager?"

"That's right." He looked harried.

"My name's Georgia Davis. I'd like to ask you about one of your employees. Well, former employee."

He frowned. "Yeah?"

"Sara Long. She worked at the café."

He frowned for a moment. Then recognition lit his face. "The girl who got killed in the Forest Preserve."

"That's right." Why did it take him so long to remember? Didn't everyone at the store know about Sara's murder?

He scrutinized Georgia more carefully. "Who are you?"

"Georgia Davis. I'm an investigator working the case. What's your name?"

"Brian Pucinski."

She noted it down. "Brian, her mother says she worked here pretty much every day after school and on weekends."

A frown creased his brow. "She did?"

"Yes." Georgia looked up.

"That's weird."

"Why?"

"I don't think—well, let me check her file."

"Good idea."

He held the door open, and Georgia stepped into a cramped room filled with metal shelves from floor to ceiling. Each shelf was crammed with books or cardboard boxes full with books. Some lay flat, some were stacked vertically. More books were piled on the floor, and even more spilled onto counters and cabinets. If they were arranged in some order, Georgia didn't catch it—except one that would give a non-book person claustrophobia. She took a breath.

Pucinski bent over a metal file cabinet and pulled out a manila folder. He paged through it slowly, then stopped. After scanning a sheet of paper, he lifted it out of the folder and nodded. "That's what I thought."

"What?"

"Sara hasn't worked here in a while."

"What's a while?"

"She quit a long time ago." He held up a sheet of paper. "It's here on her sheet."

"When?"

"Middle of April." He passed her the sheet. "Last spring."

CHAPTER SEVENTEEN

SOMETHING WAS up. Something he wasn't privy to. It could have happened before he signed on. Or maybe it just happened, and they were keeping him in the dark. He'd witnessed a flurry of private conversations between Lenny, the security chief and the guy who'd hired him, and his employer. He'd overheard a fragment of one— his boss demanding to know when they would move. Whatever was going had to be serious; his superior was more short-tempered and impatient than usual.

He figured they weren't going to let him in on it, so he was surprised when Lenny came up to him while he was hosing down the Jag.

"Got a job for you."

"Sure."

"Surveillance."

He looked up, twisted off the flow of water.

"With your experience, it should be a slam dunk. Assuming all those references you gave us weren't bullshit."

"You checked 'em."

"Umm." Lenny hesitated, hands in his pockets, as if he was still deciding whether to give him the job. "I don't have to tell you how important this is. You come through, you're on your way up. You don't, well ..." The unsaid threat hung in the air.

He cleared his throat. "I won't let you down."

Lenny shot him a glance. "The target is a woman. A P.I. Used to be a cop. She's been nosing around things we're not ... comfortable with. We want you to find out who she's been talking to. Where she's been going. We need to know how much she knows."

"About what?"

Again Lenny hesitated. Then, "You been watching the news?"

"There's a lot of stories on the news."

"The girl who was killed in the Forest Preserve."

"I heard about it."

"The target is the PI working the case."

He started winding the hose, making big loops with his hands. "Why her?"

Lenny shook his head. "Sorry. Need to know basis only."

He shrugged. "She got a name?"

Lenny gave him an edgy look, almost as if he didn't want to say the name out loud. "Here." Lenny scrawled something on a scrap of paper and handed it over.

Matt set the hose on the ground and peered at the name. Then he stuffed the paper in his pocket. He picked up the hose and met Lenny's cool gaze with one of his own. "When do I start?"

CHAPTER EIGHTEEN

OUTSIDE, INDIAN summer was at its peak, the bright October sun igniting flames of reds, yellows, and oranges. Droves of people would abandon Chicago for Michigan and Wisconsin this weekend, all of them converging on the *Chicago Tribune's* "Best of Autumn" leaf-viewing sites. They'd trample through decomposing forests, click their digital cameras, and scold their kids who'd be whining about missing TV or the mall. Then they'd drive back on Sunday afternoon in bumper-to-bumper traffic, satisfied that they'd "done fall."

Relieved she didn't have to do things like that, or even pretend to like them, Georgia went back to her car. Sara was supposed to be working at the café in the bookstore. Except she wasn't. Why had she lied? Did she have another job? If not, how was she getting the money to pay for her cell phone, iPod, and those clothes in her closet?

Something had shifted. Georgia didn't know what, but the ground under her feet felt less firm. And the most disturbing part was that she might be the only one who knew it. Before leaving the bookstore, she'd casually remarked to the manager, "I guess the police are all over this, huh?"

Pucinski's brow furrowed. "They haven't been around."

Now she tried to recall if she'd read anything about Sara's job in the police reports. She didn't think so. She could see Robby Parker letting it slide. Especially when he could reap the fame that came with sewing the case up fast. But this was a homicide. Why didn't someone follow up? She would have. O'Malley would have, too. Unless his hands were tied.

Driving home, she decided it was time to question Jill Beaumont, Sara's advisor at Newfield. Advisors knew the child from a more or less long-term perspective. Some became a surrogate parent, some were pals, and some—the good ones—made themselves the adult ally kids needed as they ventured into the world. But she couldn't meet Beaumont at Newfield. The Walchers had reported her subterfuge to the school; no one would be rolling out the welcome wagon for her. They might even forbid her from going inside.

Back in her apartment, she checked the time. Noon. There was nothing more she could do now. She sighed, booted up her computer, and started the skip trace she'd promised another client.

Jeraldo Gutierrez, a mechanic from the West Side, had made off with twenty thousand of his employer's hard-earned dollars. His employer, Hector Montoya, was most interested in getting the money back but knew the police wouldn't be much help. He'd called his lawyer, a kid Georgia had grown up with from the old neighborhood. The lawyer referred the matter to her.

Luck was with her. After searching the Cook County Assessor's records online, she discovered a bungalow owned by Gutierrez's wife. Two hours after that, after culling through two more subscription websites, she called a number in Tucson, Arizona belonging to Maria Rodriguez, Gutierrez's wife's cousin. Georgia told the woman who answered the phone that she was calling from Mr. Gutierrez's bank in Chicago, and that a substantial sum of money had just been wired into his account. Was he by any chance there? The woman on the phone said he wasn't but was expected later that afternoon. Georgia said she'd call back, then called her client with the information.

As she logged off, she felt the ripple of satisfaction that comes with cracking a case. She loved feeling that—it's what had attracted her to becoming a cop in the first place. The notion that she—ordinary Georgia Davis from the West Side—could actually right a wrong, mete out justice. She and Matt used to talk about what had brought them into law enforcement. For her it was the need for that affirmation. Recognition. For him, it was the need for redemption. Or so he claimed. But when she asked what sins he'd committed, he'd press his lips together and go quiet.

Suddenly she felt a twinge of what—regret? Loneliness? Pain? Time had made these pangs almost second nature, but she still couldn't quite identify them. That must be part of the process, she guessed. You go on, one day at a time, and for a while the fog of misery thins, even lifts for a moment or two. Then, without warning, tiny knives reappear and slash their way through your psyche.

She and Matt had talked about leaving the force one day. Setting up shop as the "Nick and Nora Charles of the North Shore," Matt said. Georgia wasn't sure who Nick and Nora Charles were and had to sneak online to find out. They were different that way. Matt was well-educated. Georgia barely finished Oakton. Matt was Jewish; she was a lapsed Catholic. That didn't seem to bother him. She didn't see a problem either. Then.

***

It wasn't hard to find out where Jill Beaumont lived, so that night Georgia drove down to Andersonville, a neighborhood on the north side of Chicago. Andersonville used to be mostly Swedish, working class and quiet. Now ethnic restaurants and shops elbowed the blander, blonder haunts. As she cruised down Clark Street, she caught a glimpse of a second-story gym in a regentrified building with blue fluorescent lighting. Two guys were lifting barbells, sweat slicking their torsos.

She searched for a legal parking spot and found one two blocks away. Before she was a cop, she parked wherever she wanted, tickets be damned. If a summons showed up in her mailbox, she'd pay a visit to Max, her father's friend in the Corporation Counsel's office. She'd bring a copy of the Sun-Times, making sure two hundred dollar bills were nestled between Page Four and Five. Her tickets disappeared.

Then she became a cop and realized she couldn't be beholden to anyone. Nor did she want to line anyone's pockets. So she stopped. Max eventually ended up doing two to five in East Moline, and the city's new computer-generated ticket system was incorruptible. Still, on nights like these, when everyone in the world seemed to have snagged a spot except her, she missed the old days.

She hiked back to Farragut, a quiet block north and east of Foster and stopped in front of a three-story greystone that looked like it had been renovated. Scanning the mailboxes inside a tiny vestibule, she spotted the names Beaumont and Podromos on #3A. She pressed the buzzer.

A tinny female voice replied through the speaker. "Yes."

"Hello. My name is Georgia Davis, and I'd like to talk to Jill Beaumont."

"Who are you?"

Georgia squared her shoulders. "I'm a private investigator."

Nothing happened for a long moment. Georgia imagined Beaumont running through the possibilities, weighing whether to talk to her. It could be she was ordered not to. The Newfield administration might have insisted. They were under enormous pressure, not to mention liability, should Sara's parents or any of the others decide to sue. She'd met the superintendent during the first hazing investigation. He was a spineless, nerdy type who tried to come on strong but capitulated at the first sign of conflict. When the buzzer finally sounded, she let out a breath.

The woman who opened the door was small and round and wore a curious expression.

"Ms. Beaumont? Thank you for seeing me. I was hoping you—"

"I'm not Jill. I'm her roommate."

"Oh." Georgia gave her a flustered smile. "Is Jill here?"

The roommate shook her head. She kept her hand on the doorknob, letting the door stay open just a crack. Even so, the tantalizing smell of pot roast seeped into the hall. Georgia's mouth watered.

"Does she know you?" She asked.

Georgia tensed. "We—we haven't met."

"Does this have anything to do with Sara Long?"

This woman was the gatekeeper, Georgia realized. She needed to play it straight. "Yes."

"I thought so." The woman continued to hold the door slightly ajar as though she was using it as a shield. "Jill's been under a lot of pressure. She was hoping to get away from it for a while."

"I wouldn't have come if it wasn't important."

"I don't know if she'll talk to you."

Georgia nodded. The tension in her neck and shoulders mounted.

The roommate's gaze swept over her. "But I guess you can try." She sighed. "She's at A Woman's Place for a poetry reading."

CHAPTER NINETEEN

TWO BOOKSTORES in one day. *Was this some kind of sign,* Georgia wondered as she walked back to Clark Street. Sister Marion would have said "of course" and would have quoted something appropriate from *Hamlet* or *Macbeth* to prove it.

A Woman's Place was sandwiched between Ann Sathers and a Greek restaurant, but it had started out on Lincoln Park, a few miles south. Within two years, however, it outgrew its space and moved up to Andersonville. Inside was the same cramped, cheery chaos she remembered from Lincoln Park. Books crowded on shelves and counters; colored flyers were tacked on the walls, announcing everything from lost pets and want-ads to spiritual counseling and yoga for same-sex couples. The only concession to modern technology seemed to be the electronic cash register in the front which was operated by a woman who looked familiar—a little grayer, perhaps, but surely the same owner as in Lincoln Park.

Unlike the bookstore this morning, A Woman's Place was warm and welcoming, and Georgia felt the tension drain out of her as she browsed. She wound around shelves labeled by subject: cookbooks, women's issues, best-sellers, mysteries, and a gay/lesbian section. At the back was a raised platform with chairs in front. A cardboard sign in block letters said that Red Sladdick would recite poetry at seven thirty. A table with a jug of white wine, Diet Coke, and a plate of cheese squares sat nearby.

Georgia checked her watch. Seven-twenty. Six people had straggled in, five of them women. Which one was Jill Beaumont? Two women sat near the front, holding hands. Their cropped grey hair reminded Georgia of the Sisters at St. Michael's. Two rows behind was a man seated between two women. The fifth woman sat toward the back, alone, reading a paper-back. Slim with blond curly hair, she wore a denim jumper over a long-sleeved tee. When she glanced up, Georgia saw deep-set eyes, prominent cheekbones, and bushy eyebrows. Dark half-moons rimmed her eyes. She looked exhausted. Was that Beaumont?

A few minutes later, another woman hurried in, trailing an exotic scent. Tall and willowy, she was dressed in a tight black sweater, short black skirt, and over the knee black leather boots. Her brown hair was tied back, and her mouth was a bright red slash. She strode to the stage, carrying a book in one hand and a Starbucks cup in the other. The room suddenly seemed charged. Georgia poured herself some soda and sat in the back row.

The woman at the register came to the platform and introduced Red Sladdick. Holding a slim book, she invited the audience to purchase the author's first collection of poems, *Secrets*, after the reading. She dimmed the lights and took a seat.

Red straddled a stool on the dais, opened her book, and started to read. Her voice was low and lazy. Georgia scanned the room. The couple in the first row were eye-fucking each other, oblivious to everyone else. The man behind them seemed to be giving Red his full attention, but the two women with him were nattering behind his back. The woman

Georgia thought was Beaumont gazed at Red dully, as if forcing herself to stay awake.

After listening to Red for a few minutes, Georgia felt sluggish, too. Whether it was the droning rhythm of Red's voice, the poetry, or just fatigue, her eyelids drooped and a series of languid images drifted through her mind: Matt's eyes when he made love to her; a brightly lit Christmas tree topped with a silver angel. She slouched in her seat, her index finger slowly circling the rim of her cup. They should have candles on the stage, she thought lazily, to chase away the shadows.

"We are one with nature … Undulating in the womb of life … So wet, so moist. I put your hand on my breast … you kiss me. I am home."

Georgia jerked her head up. Did anyone take this seriously? When her eyes focused, she saw that Red was staring directly at her, an amused smile on her face. Georgia's nerves jangled. For a split second, she was confused. Had Red spoken to her? Was she supposed to say something back?

When she heard weak applause, she relaxed. Red had just finished a poem; that was all. Georgia clapped too. But Red's eyes lingered on Georgia as if they shared a secret. Georgia's cheeks grew hot. Beaming as though she'd hit the bulls-eye, Red averted her gaze and thumbed through her book.

Georgia stood up, rolled her shoulders, and went to the back of the room. She was here to do a job. Not to be hit on by another woman. By the time Red was finished, Georgia was back in control. The owner of the store stood up, thanked everyone for coming, and embraced Red. The blond woman in the denim jumper zipped up her jacket and gathered her bag. Georgia hurried over.

"Jill Beaumont?"

The woman turned around. "Yes?"

"Hello. I'd like to talk to you. My name is Georgia Davis."

Beaumont looked startled. She took a step back. "You're the one who showed up at the Walchers." Her eyes turned steely.

"I made a mistake."

"That's an understatement." Her face looked pinched.

"I hope you didn't catch any flak from it. The last thing I want is to make life tough for you."

Beaumont pressed her lips together. "Well, you did. Even though I wasn't involved in your little stunt, some people are questioning my loyalties. One or two actually think I put you up to it." ·

"For God's sake, why?"

"Because Lauren Walcher is in my advisory."

"Oh shit. I didn't know." Georgia blinked. "So they thought you told me about her, then I turn up at the Walchers."

She nodded again.

"I'm so sorry."

Beaumont tugged at the sides of her jacket. "Under the circumstances, I have nothing to say to you." She started to walk away.

"Please," Georgia threw out a hand to block her. "If there's anything I can do ... write a letter, make a statement, call someone, I will."

The woman shook off Georgia's hand. "You've done enough. Just leave me alone, okay?"

Georgia barreled on. "But I have a few questions. About Sara Long."

Beaumont glanced around fearfully, as if she thought she might be under surveillance. "Look. The fact that we had another hazing was bad enough. We could probably have handled it, even with all the media. But then when you add the murder of a student, well, we're in crisis mode. I have too much to deal with. "

"I get it, and I can't make you talk to me. But I wish you'd reconsider. I'm only trying to make sure the right person is held accountable for Sara's death."

Beaumont faced Georgia. "They said you used to be a cop. Is that true?"

Georgia nodded uncertainly. Where was she going with this?

"But you don't think the crazy guy did it?"

"It's not my job to think one way or the other."

Beaumont was quiet for a moment. "If he didn't do it, who did?"

"I don't know."

"Do—do you think it was another student?" She asked softly.

"Do you?"

Beaumont looked away.

Georgia homed in. "You're not sure, are you?"

Beaumont didn't react. Then she shook her head. "I can't believe any student would—No. Not at Newfield."

"But it's keeping you awake at night, all the same."

She shot Georgia a look.

"Do you know of any problems between Sara and any other students?"

She took a breath, and her body sagged. "No. She and Lauren Walcher were pretty close." Beaumont's mouth twitched. "Then again, I gather you already know that."

Georgia almost smiled back. "Someone I spoke to said Sara stole somebody's boyfriend. Do you know anything about that?"

"No. But you have to remember something."

"What?"

"Sara was turning into a beautiful young woman. That can cause all sorts of problems. Jealousy. Sucking up. Saying things behind each other's backs. Girls can be vicious. This is high school."

"Had you seen any behavior like that—where Sara was concerned?"

"I'm their advisor. They don't reveal that side of themselves to me." She hesitated. "But Sara was fairly level-headed. She and Lauren both. I got the sense they didn't pay much attention to gossip."

"Would you happen to know which boys?"

Beaumont looked puzzled.

"Which boys were attracted to her?"

"No clue. But I'm sure the line would have formed to the right, if she'd allowed it to."

"What kind of student was she?"

"She was—well, to be honest, she was treading water."

"How?"

"Sara used to be a lot more ... involved. As a sophomore, for instance, she joined three different clubs and was in Chorus. Her grades were pretty consistent, too. B plus. But this year," She shook her head. "She dropped her clubs, and her grades—well—it was too early to tell—but she didn't seem ... invested."

"Did you ask why?"

She nodded. "She said she had a job and needed to work. To save for college. At the same time, she knew her junior year was going to be tough academically, and she promised to make more of an effort." Beaumont shrugged.

"You didn't believe her?"

"It's not that. I—I got the feeling she was telling me what I wanted to hear."

"Did she do that often?"

"She was a sweet kid. I think she wanted to please." The owner of the store started coming toward them, eyeing her watch. "I think we're being asked to leave."

"One last thing. Did Sara tell you where she was working?"

"Let me think." She frowned. "Oh yes. At the cafe. In the bookstore at Old Orchard. I remember thinking at their wages she'd have to put in a lot of hours to pay for college."

"When did she tell you this?"

"Not long after school started. Why?"

"Nothing." Georgia changed the subject. "One of the girls I spoke to said Sara always needed to know everyone else's business. Did you pick up anything like that?"

She shook her head again. "I guess I'm not much of a help."

"Oh, but you are," Georgia said. "Listen. I know you still have—questions—about Sara's death." When Beaumont started to protest, Georgia raised her hand. "You don't have to say anything more. And I'll stay out of your hair." They headed to the front of the store. "But if something else comes to you, anything at all, will you let me know?"

Beaumont didn't answer for a moment. Then, "How come you're not on the force anymore?"

Georgia was taken aback. "I was suspended," she said after a pause.

"Why?"

"For not following procedure during an incident at a strip club."

Beaumont threw her a look. "It figures."

***

After handing Beaumont her card, Georgia exited the store. Her mood had lightened. She'd leveled with Beaumont, and in return Beaumont had leveled back. She might even have gained an ally. At least defused an enemy.

She was heading down Clark Street when all at once a hand clamped down on her arm. Adrenaline flooded through her. Without thinking, she whacked the attacker's arm with a karate chop and whirled around, ready to gouge out their eyes with her fingers.

"Hey! Chill, sweetheart!" A female voice yelled. "It's me!"

Georgia froze, her hand in mid-air. Red Sladdick, the poet from A Woman's Place. She dropped her hand and staggered back. "Jesus Christ!" She sucked down air. "Didn't anyone ever teach you not to grab people on the street? Especially at night?"

Red threw her hands up. "Sorry! I wasn't—I didn't think you'd mind."

"Think again." Georgia tried to get her breathing under control.

"Like I said, I'm sorry." Red hung her head. "I just wanted—I wanted to know what you thought."

"About what?"

"My poetry."

Equal amounts of relief and rage poured through Georgia. "Your what?"

"My—my poetry." Red turned an anxious face to Georgia. "Did you like it?"

Georgia felt the muscles on her face tighten. No way was she going to discuss poetry on Clark Street at night with a stranger. In the dim light, the woman's eyes glittered. Suddenly comprehension dawned. "Look. No offense, but I'm not into your scene, okay? I'm not gay."

Red didn't reply for a moment. "Just window shopping, huh?"

"I'm a private investigator."

"That's cool." Red grinned. "I'm a nurse. At Illinois Masonic."

"No. You don't understand. I was working tonight."

Red looked her up and down with an expression that made Georgia think Red had her own experience with liars. Even so, it was time to end this conversation. Georgia started to walk away.

"Hold on," Red called out. "Can I have one?"

Georgia stopped and turned around. "One what?"

Red pointed to Georgia's pocket. "A card. You gave one to the other woman you picked up."

Red had been watching her conversation with Beaumont. For some reason, that creeped her out. "I told you I was working."

"Well, you never know when I might need a PI."

"You'll find plenty in the Yellow Pages."

"Who knows? You might need a nurse."

Georgia didn't answer.

Red shrugged. "Suit yourself. But you ever need anything, sweet thing ... anything at all ... just come on down to the Silver Slipper on Diversey. I'm there every night by ten."

Red turned around and headed north. Georgia set off in the opposite direction, trying not to run.

CHAPTER TWENTY

THERE WAS *more denim at Newfield High than a Levi's factory*, Georgia thought the next day. As she waited in the parking lot across from the school, a steady stream of teenagers flowed past, all of them in configurations of blue: jeans, skirts, vests, jackets. Some of the kids wore smiles, but most had the sullen, rebellious expression that said they were destined for greater things than high school.

A couple of students lit up cigarettes as they exited. They tried to look nonchalant, even bored, but she knew better. They were flaunting the little power they had. *See? You can't do anything about it, even though you're an adult.* Georgia remembered how that felt. She still harbored a gnawing irritation when she had to navigate through the labyrinth of bureaucracy.

Rachel had said Heather Blakely thought she was Katie Couric. Strangely enough, when Georgia checked out her picture in the yearbook earlier, she did resemble the broadcaster: the same chin-length brown hair, big mouth, and petite, self-assured looks. Judging from the photo in which the girl was shoving a mic at Barack Obama during a school visit, she was following the same path, too.

The October morning had been balmy, but now a chill, blustery wind swept fallen leaves into tiny eddies before they tumbled to the ground. Georgia hung back at the edge of the parking lot, checking out the students.

Finding an individual among hundreds or even thousands of people was tricky. She remembered taking part in a NORTAF investigation as a rookie. She and Robby were stationed inside the Rosemont Horizon, waiting for a U2 concert to end. The task force was trying to crack a narcotics ring in Niles, and they'd been told the kingpin of the operation would be at the concert. After analyzing a seating chart, NORTAF posted cops in all the aisles and distributed blurry photos of the target. But when the concert ended, a sea of people streamed past, and she couldn't identify anyone. It was only when she saw a scuffle a few aisles away that she realized someone else had made him. She hated to admit her relief.

At last, a girl who looked like Heather sauntered across the street. She was with another girl, and a boy who didn't look old enough for high school. As they reached the parking lot, the second girl peeled off. Heather and the boy went to a silver RAV4.

Georgia hurried over. "Heather?"

The girl turned around. Under her jacket, which was open, she was wearing a white peasant-style blouse and jeans with a beaded design. Some of the beads looked like pearls. It all looked expensive.

"I'm Georgia Davis. I'm investigating the death of Sara Long, and I'd like to talk to you."

Heather hesitated. Then, "I know who you are. I'm not supposed to talk to you."

Georgia stepped forward as if she hadn't heard. "I know you were a good friend of Sara's, and I know you want to make sure justice is done."

"Look, I told you. I have no comment."

Georgia had been trained in media relations back at the Academy, and the trainer said never to use the words "no comment." It made you look like you were hiding something. Tell them you're not going to say anything, sure. Just don't use those words.

"Not the right answer, Heather," Georgia replied.

Meanwhile, the boy with Heather spoke up. "You're a real PI?"

"Jason, shut up." Heather threw him a dark look.

Georgia ran with it. "Yes, Jason I am."

"Like Magnum? They have these reruns on cable, and—"

"That's right."

"Cool. What kind of training do you need to be a PI?"

"I used to be a cop."

"Magnum worked in Naval Intelligence."

Georgia nodded, wanting to keep the kid talking, but Heather cut in. "Jason, cool it. Get in the car." She started to shoo him away.

"Hold on. I just have a couple of questions. I've already talked to Claire Tennenbaum and Lauren Walcher."

"I know," Heather said.

"Then you know there's a chance the guy who's in jail didn't kill Sara."

Heather shot her a scornful look.

Georgia shrugged. "Seems to me you, of all people, would want to get the story right."

"Come on. Everyone knows he did it."

"Are you sure? Remember when the husband and mother of that judge were killed, and everyone was sure the murderer was a white supremacist?" She paused. "And then it turned out to be this guy who was suing all those doctors? You're a journalist. You know better than to make assumptions."

"A broadcast journalist," Heather corrected.

Georgia nodded solemnly. "Even more so."

Heather didn't look quite as sure of herself. "Look, I'll be in serious trouble if I talk to you."

"How about if I ask you a couple of questions and you just nod or shake your head? To confirm information I already have. You know—the two source rule?"

A smug expression came over Heather.

"I know Sara stole someone's boyfriend," Georgia went on. "And that she was always poking her nose into other people's business. I also know some of the girls wanted to teach her a lesson. What I need to confirm is whose boyfriend she stole."

Heather looked at Georgia, then Jason. Georgia looked at Jason, too. Jason slung his hands in his pockets and started to slink away. "Okay, okay, I'm going."

Georgia nodded. "Thanks, pal."

Jason shuffled to the trees at the edge of the parking lot. Georgia turned back to Heather. "I need your help, Heather. You're one of the few people I can trust. We're after the same thing, you and I." Jesus, she was laying it on thick. She waited. "Was it Monica's boyfriend Sara stole?"

Heather bit her lip. Then she nodded. "I'm really sorry she's dead, but the fact is Sara could have had anyone she wanted. She was that hot. But she picked Cash."

"Cash?"

"Monica's boyfriend. Sara hooked up with him last summer while Monica wasn't around. That wasn't—well, that was just bitchy."

"Don't you think Cash might have had something to do with it?"

Heather shrugged.

Georgia waited.

"Well, maybe," she said grudgingly. "Of course, I don't mean to say anything bad about Sara. She was one of my best friends."

"Of course." Georgia let it sink in. "So was Monica with you when you dumped the fish guts on Sara?"

Heather shot her a surprised look. "How do you know it was me?"

Georgia shook her head. "It doesn't matter."

"Claire told you, didn't she?" An irritated look came over her.

"I can't reveal my sources. You understand."

"Claire couldn't get it right if she tried." Heather's tone grew bolder. "Monica was there. But—"

"But what?"

"She didn't do anything to Sara."

"She didn't?" Finally, Heather was talking without being prompted. That was good. "Then who did?"

Heather wouldn't meet her eyes.

"Heather?"

The girl's voice was a whisper. "We had to."

"Why?"

"The seniors made us."

"'But you and Lauren and Claire were Sara's best friends."

"We didn't have a choice. They pulled us aside before the game started and told us what we had to do if we wanted to make it through the year. They knew the only way Sara would leave the clearing was if we took her."

"So you did." Georgia remembered Matt talking about the concentration camps. His grandparents were German Jews who narrowly escaped the Nazis in '36. Many of their friends didn't. Afterwards the survivors told stories about how Jews—prisoners themselves—persecuted other Jews in the camps: taunting, stealing, turning in other inmates. You did what you had to in order to survive.

"Who brought the bucket and fish entrails?"

"Don't know. They were there when I got there."

"But Monica Ramsey wasn't one of the seniors who intimidated you ... or Sara?"

"She had no reason to. She and Cash had hooked up again. When school started."

"How do you know?"

"Monica and I sit next to each other in Spanish. I'm in Spanish IV."

"Cool." Georgia paused. "So Monica told you she and Cash were back together?"

"She tells me everything."

"Tell me about Cash."

"He's a senior. He plays bass guitar in a blues band." It came out almost reverently.

"Was Monica still around, once you left Sara in the clearing and came back to the game?"

"I—I don't remember."

"But you just said—"

"I said she was there when we left. I don't remember when we got back. It was kind of confusing. Too many kids. All over the place."

"Is it possible Monica might have been hiding behind a tree in the clearing?"

"I—I don't know." Heather bit her lip again, her expression guarded. "Look. That's enough. I have to go now. "

Georgia nodded. "One more question. Do you know where Sara was working after school and on weekends?"

She shrugged and gave a little frown. "At the café in the bookstore."

"You're sure?"

"Of course."

"What would you think if you found out she hadn't worked there since last spring? Would you have any idea where she was instead?"

"She wasn't at the bookstore?" Her eyes got a faraway look, and Georgia could tell she was trying to work something out.

"What is it, Heather? What are you thinking?"

Heather didn't answer.

"Heather?"

The girl glared at Georgia. "That's it. I'm done." She spun around. "Jason, let's go. Now!"

***

Bill's had to be the yuppiest Blues bar in Chicago. Tucked away on a quiet street in Evanston, the place had a clean floor, polished tables, and wonder of wonders, a spotless bathroom. Unlike the blues joints downtown, which were full of smoke and booze and late night angst, Bill's sported gaily colored prints of dark-skinned dancers on the walls, and a card on tables explained that the first show of the night was non-smoking. There was even a "family" show on Sundays.

Only on the North Shore.

Ignoring interested glances from several men at the bar, Georgia ordered a soda. The second half of Joe Moss's set thundered through the speakers, and the place was packed. As Joe cried about his baby leaving him, Georgia tapped her fingers on her leg, feeling the wailing guitars and pulsing beat. Another number and she'd be transported to a place where the pain of unrequited love, of being broke or drunk, was tempered by a bass guitar, funky keyboard, and raspy tenor.

When her drink came, she forked over a couple of dollars and swiveled around. A couple was already dancing in the aisle. Her friend Samantha used to say you could tell how a guy would be in bed from the way he danced. Georgia wasn't so sure. Matt couldn't dance at all. He'd throw himself around with more energy than skill, his body all limp and wiggly. But he knew all the right moves between the sheets. She felt a tingle work up her spine. She forced it back.

At the back of the bar four fresh-faced guys sat around a small table, their eyes locked on the stage. She'd called Tommy Cashian's home earlier tonight. No, Tommy wasn't home, a harried-sounding woman said. No, she wasn't sure where he was, but he'd probably end up at Bill's. He usually did on Fridays. When the woman asked who was calling, Georgia thanked her and disconnected.

Now she picked up her drink and strolled to the back of the bar. Her long blond hair was down, and she was wearing tight jeans and a turtleneck. A multi-colored pashmina, her only concession to fashion, was draped around her neck. As she approached their table, one of the boys glanced up, gave her the once-over, and smiled. Normally she would have ignored him, but tonight, she smiled back. "Are you Tommy Cashian?"

Disappointment flickered across his face. Then a cagey expression took its place. "Who wants to know?"

A thousand possibilities came to her, but in the end, she played it straight. "I'm Georgia Davis and I'm a private investigator." She had to shout to be heard. "Which one of you is Cash?"

Heaving a sigh, the boy pointed to a young man sitting across the table with long dark hair, a slim build, and piercing eyes. He wore a Hawaiian shirt over his jeans. A long-sleeved thermal shirt poked out underneath. A pair of shades perched over his crown. At the sound of his name, he tore his eyes from the stage. He, too, checked Georgia out. She saw a glimmer of appreciation.

She moved to him. "Cash. Mind if I talk to you? Alone?"

He frowned. "Who are you?"

She introduced herself.

He turned back to the band. For a moment, Georgia thought he was ignoring her. Then he scooted back his chair and stood up. The drummer was into a solo riff, with Joe Moss, the keyboard player, and the bass player nodding approvingly. Georgia motioned Cash to follow her outside.

After the pounding noise in Bill's, the quiet outside was a welcome reprieve. "So what do you play?" She asked, although she already knew.

"Bass guitar."

"Blues?"

"And rock." He wiped his hand across his mouth. "Hey, what's this about? You didn't bring me out here to talk about music." But he didn't sound hostile, and he lounged against the wall of the building, looking comfortable and composed. Georgia couldn't help comparing this self-possessed kid to the bundle of insecurities and raw nerves she'd been at that age.

"It's about you and Monica and Sara Long," she answered.

A serious look came over him. Was he going over his script? The lines he'd rehearsed in case someone asked? He pushed off from the wall. "What do you want to know?"

"I think you know."

"I have an idea," he admitted.

"So tell me."

"You want to know about me and Sara. Why I broke up with Monica. And why we went back together. And if there's any connection to Sara's murder."

Not only composed, but smart. She could see why Monica Ramsey—and Sara—were attracted to him.

"Actually," he went on, "I was kind of wondering when someone was going to come around."

"Are you saying no one's asked you about any of this?" When he shook his head, she added, "Not even the police?"

"Nope."

The sound of the band inside was muted, but a few twangs from the guitars and thumps from the bass rumbled through the walls.

"You're not with the police," he said.

"I'm working for Cam Jordan." At his frown, she explained. "He was arrested for Sara's murder."

"Right. The crazy guy."

"You know him?"

He shook his head again. She saw no guile in his manner. Curiosity, but that was it.

"So tell me about Sara."

He straightened up and took his hands out of his pockets. "I bumped into Sara over the summer. She was—well—Monica was back East with her family. Sara and I—we hit it off right away. She was—fun. "

"While the cat's away ..." Georgia said.

He shrugged.

"So what happened?"

"We hung out a few times. Blues Fest. Printers Row. I took her to Buddy Guy's. Even brought her here once. I liked her." He stopped.

When he didn't go on, she asked, "How much—did you like her?"

Even in the dim light, she saw his face redden. "I wanted—hell, I was ready to get involved."

"But?"

"Sara put me off. Wouldn't let me. It wasn't for want of trying. I tried not to be an asshole, but she was so sweet. And so sexy. And just—well ..."

"So you and Sara were seeing each other while Monica was out of town. What happened when she came back?"

"The day Monica came back—in August—I told Sara I was going to break up with her. Monica, that is. I called her and was on my way over to her house when Sara called me. She said we had to meet." A sad look unfolded on his face.

"What happened?"

"I met her at the bookstore where she ... proceeded to dump me."

"Sara dumped you?"

"She told me not to break up with Monica. That I belonged with Monica. Not her." His eyes met Georgia's. "She said—it was weird, it kind of came out of left field—she said I was too good for her."

"What did she mean by that?"

"I don't know," he said, shaking his head. "I kept asking her but she wouldn't say more. Just said we weren't right for each other." He looked at Georgia with a pleading expression. "She wouldn't explain. She just kept telling me not to ask. Eventually ..." He looked down again. "Eventually, I let it go. And I left."

Georgia knew how that felt. She let the silence swirl around them for a minute. Then she asked in a soft voice, "Does Monica know?"

"I never said anything, but it got back to her."

"Through Sara?"

"I don't know. It doesn't matter. But she—you've got to understand something. Monica's a really sweet girl."

"You said the same thing about Sara."

"They both were. That's why—you know, I read someplace that you get one person in your life who's your passion, and someone else who's your partner." He broke off. "That's the way I feel. They're both incredible. Were. One was my passion, and one was ..." His words trailed off, and for the first time, he looked uncertain.

Georgia waited until he pulled himself together, wondering how a kid could be so young and wise at the same time. "Did Monica ever ask you about Sara?"

"Just once. It was after Sara dumped me but before school started. I knew she'd heard about it by then. She asked me if there was anything I wanted to tell her."

"And?"

"I told her that I missed her. And I was glad she was back."

"She didn't ask you anything else? Just let it go?"

"She seemed—satisfied. We just went back to the way we'd been. No problemo."

Or was Monica storing up her anger, planning to take revenge on Sara?

As if reading her mind, Cash added, "Monica doesn't have a mean bone in her body. She'd never hurt anyone. Including Sara."

"How do you know?"

"Because I was at the Forest Preserve that day." He slouched against the wall. "And I took Monica home."

"When?"

"After the others led Sara away. Monica didn't like what was going on. She said it wasn't right. She wanted to leave. So I finished my beer, and we split."

"Who brought the beer, incidentally?"

"I don't know."

"One of the parents?"

He shrugged. "Don't know."

If a parent brought the stuff, did they know in advance what was being planned? If so, they might be tagged as accessories. Which would explain why they tried to keep the hazing quiet.

"Who led Sara away?"

"Her friends. Heather and Lauren and the other one."

That matched. "Cash, did Monica bring a baseball bat to the game?"

"Of course not."

"Do you know who did?"

"No. It was there when we arrived."

Georgia nodded. "One more thing. When you were seeing Sara, was she still working at the bookstore?"

He brightened, as if remembering happier times. "I used to drop her off in front. Pick her up sometimes too."

"Did you ever go inside to meet her?"

"Ummm ... let me think. I was going to once, but you know how nuts parking is at Old Orchard. It was easier to wait outside."

"So you have no way of knowing whether Sara was really working there or not."

Cash looked confused. "I—I guess not. Why?"

Georgia shook her head. "It's not important."

CHAPTER TWENTY-ONE

TOMMY CASHIAN was poised, smart, and seemed to have the kind of sensibility you'd expect from a budding musician. But why did that make him too good for Sara? A person says that when they're feeling shame. Or guilt. Or insecurity. And while teenagers are, by nature, insecure, Georgia didn't have that impression of Sara. In fact, she'd come away with idea that, with the exception of too much curiosity perhaps, the girl was pretty sensible.

What was she missing? Georgia mulled it over as she went back to her car. Did it have something to do with quitting her job at the bookstore? She didn't think so—kids don't care that much about a minimum wage job. They might care about what replaced that job, though, and Sara had been doing *something* when she told her parents she was still working.

As she passed an alley, she slowed. Two dark forms lurked in the shadows beside a dumpster. A burst of orange flame flared briefly, followed by the familiar scent of weed. She picked up her pace. During the hazing two

years ago, parents brought the beer to the Forest Preserve. They rational-
ized it, claiming kids would have brought it anyway, and at least it wasn't
cocaine. And they wondered why their kids had no respect for authority.

She got in the Toyota and headed back to her apartment. None of
this—the beer, Sara quitting her job, her abbreviated relationship with
Cash—had been in the police reports. She could write off one, even two
omissions to sloppy work—and Robby was sloppy. But all of it? Georgia
couldn't help wondering if the skimpy police reports might—just
might—have something to do with the fact that the daughter of the State's
Attorney prosecuting the case was in the Forest Preserve at the time of
the murder.

Protection was a natural response when your child faced unwanted
scrutiny. It was also important when you were a rising political star. The
fact that his daughter was present when a hazing—and a murder—went
down could be a major embarrassment for one of the top law enforcement
officers in Cook County. Cam Jordan had given Jeff Ramsey a golden opportunity to protect his daughter—and himself. But was it convenience
or cover-up? One was politics as usual; the other could blow the lid off
Cook County government.

As she searched for a place to park, Georgia decided that despite
Tommy Cashian's smooth defense, she couldn't ignore Monica Ramsey's
presence in the Forest Preserve. The girl might not have had anything to
do with Sara Long's murder, but the cop in her said not to make assumptions. Kids knew how to gin the system and manipulate others. What if
there was a vengeful side to Monica? What if she'd hidden her fury over
Cash's relationship with Sara? There was only Cash's word they left the
Forest Preserve together. What if Monica picked up a bat and went back
to the clearing alone, determined to teach Sara a lesson? Or encouraged
someone else to do it? What if Cash himself was involved more than he'd
let on?

Then again, the murder just might have been the result of a hazing
that spun out of control. Kids half-looped. seniors wanting to flex their

muscles. Beer and baseball bats at the scene. What if all of them: Monica, Cash, even Lauren, Claire, and Heather had a hand in Sara's death? Wasn't she supposed to have read some book in high school about boys on an island who turned into barbarians and killed a kid? *Lord of The Flies*, she thought.

Or maybe she was overreaching. Maybe Cam Jordan did kill Sara Long in some type of insane frenzy, and she was just too unwilling or stubborn to admit it. As she snagged a parking spot, feeling lucky to have found one on a Friday night, she realized she had more digging to do.

She locked the car and started down the block. A raw, biting chill hung in the air, and leaves tumbled around the cars, almost raining down. The changing of the seasons always touched her with melancholy. Something to do with passage of time, she supposed. She hurried up the walk to her building. She pulled opened the door to the vestibule, anticipating a rush of warmth. Instead, she was knocked back, gagging, by a stench so thick it was palpable.

CHAPTER TWENTY-TWO

THE STINK slammed into Georgia like an angry ocean wave. Nausea climbed up her throat, and her skin turned clammy. She automatically reached for her holster before realizing she wasn't carrying. She stumbled back outside and gulped down deep breaths. Seconds ago she'd fretted about the coming of winter. Now she needed to suck clean, cold air into her lungs.

A few more breaths steadied her. Wrapping her pashmina around her nose and mouth, she went to the front door and peered in. Nothing looked disturbed. The usual assortment of flyers lay on the table; the floor was clean. She opened the door. Again, the smell attacked her, but this time she was prepared. She tightened the scarf and pushed through.

At first she thought it was a dead body, but aside from the problem of how a corpse managed to get into her building, the smell wasn't right. She'd been around corpses before. Underneath their rancid odor was a sickly sweet smell. This was fresher. More rotten. Fishier.

The doors to the first floor apartments were closed, and everything was quiet. Too quiet. Where were her neighbors? The smell had to have seeped into their living rooms. Why didn't she hear exhaust fans, street noise from open windows, loud complaints? For that matter, why was there no sign in the lobby? Unless no one was home. She considered it. It was Friday night, and most of her neighbors were young. They could be out. It was possible she was the first tenant to discover it.

She gripped the banister and forced herself to climb the stairs. The smell grew stronger with each step, and the clammy feeling overspread her skin. But her initial shock was gone, replaced with a grim anger. Who had the balls to do this? How did they get inside?

She saw it before she reached the second floor landing. On the floor outside her apartment door was a pile of what could only be described as gray muck. Disembodied fish heads with glassy eyes stared vacantly into space, while fish tails, entrails, and skeletons were splattered in clumps across the carpet. Bloody carcasses and scales covered the rug, glimpses of silver and red threaded through the mess. She tried not to let disgust overpower her, but there was no way to avoid stepping through it, and she cringed as she reached for her key.

Bits of muck clung to her shoes and the bottom of her jeans as if they had jumped of their own accord. The smell snaked into her nose, her throat, her clothes. She shuddered, imagining crud leaching through her shoes and socks onto her skin. Is this how Sara Long had felt at the Forest Preserve with the bucket of fish guts on her head? She stabbed her lock with her key. She and Sara Long now had something in common.

***

An hour later, after scooping up piles with a spatula, stuffing them into double-bagged garbage bags, and throwing them in the alley dumpster, most of the gunk was cleaned up. She left her apartment door open and opened her windows. She set two fans on the landing, hoping to vent the worst of the smell through her apartment rather than her neighbors.' She found rug shampoo under her sink and worked it into the hall carpet. It was only a first step; she'd rent a steam cleaner tomorrow. But there was no way she could get through the night at home. She called her friend Samantha and left a message on her cell.

She was on her hands and knees rinsing the carpet for the third time, cursing the specks of silver scales that had embedded themselves in the fibers, when the door to the vestibule downstairs swung open.

"Jesus Christ!" The voice was loud. "What the hell happened?"

Georgia peered over the landing. It was the man from the third floor. With the wife named Sheila. He clamped a hand over his mouth and nose. She called down. "There's a—a problem."

"That's an understatement." He yelled through his hand. "What in Christ's name happened?"

Georgia explained.

"This is outrageous. Who did this?"

She struggled to maintain her composure. "Don't know. I wasn't here."

"Great. A building under siege by rotting fish guts." His eyes flashed.

If she hadn't spent the past hour trying to clean it up, she might have smiled. "I didn't ask for it." A lame reply.

He looked up but didn't say anything. Then, "What did you do with the—the crap?"

"Cleaned it up and threw it away."

He wiped the back of his hand across his chin and started up the stairs. "In the dumpster?"

"Yes, as a matter of fact. I wrapped it in a couple of plastic bags."

"No, no." He waved his hands in the air. "That was wrong."

She frowned. "Excuse me?"

"Not only will the stench just move out there, but you'll get maggots by the million. Not to mention the rats and cats who'll come around. They're probably already digging in."

"What would you suggest?"

"The best thing would be to compost it."

She planted her hands on her hips. "And just where am I going to find compost this time of night?"

"The Botanic Gardens, maybe."

"At midnight? Are you crazy?"

He shrugged.

"Yeah, well, tell me something. Until I get this magic material, what am I supposed to do with the stuff?"

"You could throw it in your freezer."

"There are two huge garbage bags of the shit."

He shrugged again.

"Tell you what. Why don't you put a bag in *your* freezer?" He just stared at her. "You're kind of limiting my options." It was her turn to shrug. "Maybe I should just haul it over to the lake and drop them in."

He shook his head. "Not a good idea. If you got caught, you'd be fined. Maybe even arrested. Screwing up the environment and all."

"You're just full of useful information." She snapped. "The thing is I've got a situation that needs to be dealt with tonight. Not tomorrow, or Monday, or whenever I manage to rustle up some compost or an industrial-sized freezer."

He started up the steps. "You have no idea where it came from?"

"I'm guessing Burhops. Or some other fish market. Hey, how do you know so much about this, anyway?"

"Common sense." He passed by her on the second floor landing, covering his nose with his hand, and mounted the stairs to the third floor. "At least hose it down." His voice was muffled. "The dumpster, that is. And treat it with bleach. Or Lysol." He sniffed again but instantly looked like he regretted it. "And don't forget to call the police."

"Sure thing." Georgia watched him disappear up the stairs.

***

The patrol officer left, conceding that because there were no injuries and nothing had been stolen, it wouldn't be a top priority. Georgia took a shower, then went online to check out fish markets and restaurants. There were plenty of fish and seafood wholesalers downtown, but she suspected the stuff came from someplace on the North Shore. She came away with half a dozen possibilities, all within easy driving distance of Evanston.

Then, just for the hell of it, she Googled "Fish guts." Sure enough, one of the recommended ways to dispose of them was to compost them. As she read on, she realized her neighbor wasn't bullshitting about the rest either. Apparently, it was possible to freeze fish bones—assuming they weren't rancid or rotten—for soup. As if she'd ever made soup in her life.

The key thing, she learned, was to keep the stuff clean. If she hosed down the dumpsters, threw in a cup of bleach or Lysol, the smell wouldn't get too bad. She logged off, wondering how her neighbor knew that. Was he an environmental geek? A Save-the-Whales-and-along-with-them-the-world kind of guy?

She turned off the fans, locked up, and hosed down the dumpsters with Lysol. Then she drove over to Sam's.

She'd met Samantha Mosele at Oakton before entering the Police Academy. Sam wanted to be a graphic designer and was taking computer design classes. Georgia was taking sociology in the classroom next door. They'd eyeballed each other for six weeks before acknowledging the other's presence. Georgia found it hard to make friends with women, and, apparently, Sam was the same way. It wasn't until they'd finished their finals the same night, and found themselves in the pub down the street that they started to talk. They'd been friends ever since.

Sam wrinkled her nose when she opened the door. "Yuck."

"I took a shower, but I guess it's still all over me."

"Hold on." She went back into her apartment, returning a moment later with a bottle of perfume. "Here." She started to spritz Georgia's t-shirt and jeans.

Georgia held up her hands. "No, it's okay. I'll just——"

"Stop complaining. It's Obsession." Sam kept spritzing.

Sighing, Georgia submitted to Sam's ministrations. Probably better to smell like an object obsessed than a rotten fish.

"Who did it?" Sam asked once they were settled in her living room with a cup of tea. An attractive brunette with shoulder length hair, she pushed a lock of it behind her ear.

"I have no idea."

"But you're working on something, right?" When Georgia nodded, she added, "You think it's related?"

"It would seem so." Georgia explained the case to her.

"How did they get inside?"

Georgia shrugged. "They probably waited till the last person went out earlier tonight and propped the door open."

"You think they're sending you a message, huh? A warning to back off?"

"If so, it was a clumsy attempt."

She sipped her tea. "But the girl in the Forest Preserve with fish guts all over her was killed. Now you have fish guts all over you. Ergo ..."

Georgia cut her off. "If someone really wanted to send me a warning, don't you think a note, or a phone call, would have been more efficient? Why go to all the trouble and expense of buying the shit, transporting it to my place, and then spreading it around in the hall—just to get me to back off? It's stupid."

But Sam was enjoying playing armchair detective. "Hold on. Didn't they do something like that in *The Godfather*? Didn't someone send some-one a dead fish as a warning?"

"This isn't the movies, Sam."

Sam played with her lock of hair. "Well, maybe whoever did this doesn't realize that."

Georgia thought about it. She had a point.

CHAPTER TWENTY-THREE

MATT WAS staked out in the shadows of the house across the street from Georgia's apartment. He'd been tailing her for a couple of days. To the bookstore in Andersonville last night. Tonight to Bill's Blues where she'd tracked down some kid in a Hawaiian shirt. On her way back to her car, she'd slowed to check out an alley. Once a cop …

He'd been across the street from her building when she discovered the crap in the hall. At first he didn't know what it was; he had to recon the dumpster to find out. Fish guts? What was that about? He called it in to Lenny, who seemed surprised. After grilling him on the details, Lenny ordered him to stay where he was.

If he moved far enough back and used the binoculars, he could just see into her window. She'd been going from the kitchen to the hall with a bucket, brush, and rags. Forty-five minutes later, the to and fro stopped.

Lenny wanted a report every two hours. More often if there was any action. He pulled out his cell, about to tell Lenny she was in for the night. Then the lights in her apartment snapped off, and a minute later she emerged from the building, hefting a backpack over her shoulder. Her blond hair was down, catching golden sparks from the glow of the streetlight.

Dumping the cell in his pocket, he hurried down the street to his car. He pulled out just in time to get behind the Toyota, making sure to keep a few lengths back. Where was she going? To shack up with someone? She turned west on Dempster. He squinted through the windshield and made the turn. He'd know soon enough.

CHAPTER TWENTY-FOUR

DEREK JANOWITZ only worked half a day on Saturdays, but it was the most profitable day of the week. Not because he was a mechanic.

He'd been at Horner's gas station almost a year. He'd spend a few hours a day tinkering with cars, mostly nice ones, this being the North Shore and all. He'd adjust brakes, replace batteries, change the oil. Sometimes Horner would ask his opinion on a tricky fuel injector or transmission problem. The old man got stumped a lot these days. Everything was digital, he'd grouse. Too complicated. What happened to the time when all you needed to know were carburetors, distributors, and spark plugs?

The lucrative part of Derek's job came from his other customers. He wasn't kidding when he told Lauren he knew what people wanted and how far they would go to get it. Derek was a provider. He gave people what they wanted when they wanted it. In fact, he thought of himself as a self-made dude. Like Donald Trump. Or the guy who started that airline.

His reputation was growing. Pretty soon he'd be able to ditch this job and tell Horner where to go. Maybe Lauren, too. The bitch never gave him any credit.

He wheeled a white Acura onto the lift. A note from Horner said it needed new pads and a wheel alignment. The car looked vaguely familiar. Probably belonged to some spoiled brat in Northbrook or Glencoe who didn't know shit about car maintenance, who just fed it gas and expected it to run. He shook his head. If it weren't for him, a lot of people would be up the creek.

He was raising the lift when a silver Lexus turned into the station. The driver didn't stop at the pump but pulled up to the little mart. Derek didn't pay much attention at first. It was probably some asshole needing directions, or a woman who wanted her fix of sugar. Funny how many of them, older and loose around the middle, would come over to the mart to buy a candy bar or Wing-Ding, then sneak it into their purse like it was an illegal drug.

But when the driver got out and started toward him, Derek saw it was Charlie, one of his regulars. Usually, the guy drove a Porsche 911 Turbo. He lowered the lift and wiped his hands on his pants.

"Mornin." He walked to the edge of the garage where Charlie was waiting.

Charlie nodded.

Something in his nod wasn't right. Charlie normally booked online. And it was Saturday. Derek's regulars didn't do business on weekends. Weekends were for tourists. First-timers. Happily, there were usually plenty of them. And they often turned into regulars. "What's happening, man?" Derek said.

Charlie walked past Derek into the garage. Derek noticed the guy's pressed khaki slacks and silk sweater. The rich ones couldn't dress down even when they tried. Even their jeans were ironed. He watched Charlie slip his hands in his pockets, then take them out and clasp them together.

"I wanted to—check up on a matter," Charlie said.

Charlie was usually pretty laid back. Not today. "What's that?"

"You remember the girl I was seeing?"

Derek tensed. He knew who Charlie meant. The guy had sampled all the stock but settled on her. Until a few weeks ago.

"I know you talk to your girls," Charlie said. "To make sure they're being treated right. That they're not being hit or hurt or taken advantage of by their—clients."

Of course he did. In his line of business he couldn't risk trouble. He did a pretty good job, if he said so himself. Where was Charlie going with this?

"That's what I need to know," Charlie went on. "Did—well—did anyone ..." Charlie paused, carefully avoiding any names, Derek noticed. "Did anyone make any comments about unusual activities during their—client meetings?"

"Man, what the fuck are you talking about?"

Charlie hunched his shoulders. His face took on a surly expression. "I'm sure they tell you where they go. And what happens after they get there. Guys like you—I expect they give you—well—a blow by blow?"

Derek ignored the double entendre. Was Charlie some kind of pervert? He wouldn't have thought so. With his Porsche and nice clothes, Derek had him figured for a guy who just wasn't getting any at home. Maybe he had figured wrong. Sometimes they couldn't get it up. Maybe he was embarrassed about it. Until he knew for sure, he should play it cool. "Hey, man, what you do is nobody's business but yours and your lady's, you know what I mean?"

An even darker look came over Charlie's face. Arching his back, slung his hands in his pockets. He looked like he was fighting to control his anger. "That's not what I meant."

Derek shifted. "So, what do you mean?"

"Do they ever report back about what happens before and after? Calls or other business related things. Not yours. Mine."

"You mean who gets the money and how? You know that happens up front."

Charlie slipped his hands out of his pockets and waved them in front of Derek. "Forget it. This isn't working." He shook his head irritably. "Just forget it."

A chill raced up Derek's spine.

"Hey ..." Suddenly Charlie forced a smile, as if they were old pals. "... What about next Tuesday afternoon?" He crossed his arms. "Say around four? Can you set me up?"

Derek wasn't buying it. He replied cautiously. "What are you looking for?"

"I don't know. Something new and different. You decide."

"That's cool."

"Have them come to the usual place, okay?"

"Sure, man."

Charlie smile's widened, baring teeth so white Derek knew they were bleached. He dropped his arms, turned, and headed back to his Lexus. Derek watched him start the car, release the brake, and give a little wave as he drove away.

Derek went back to the lift. This was probably the longest conversation he'd ever had with the dude, but that didn't mean it made sense. What was he getting at? Derek hated it when people talked in that roundabout way, hiding their real intentions, making him figure out what they meant. Lauren did that sometimes. Must be something they all learned in rich school, he thought. He raised the Acura six feet off the ground and shone his light along the frame. Horner had some Nissan brake pads he thought would work. Derek went back to the storeroom to get them.

Thirty minutes later he was working on the car, still puzzling over Charlie's behavior when he remembered. She *had* said something. It was one of the last times she'd been with Charlie—maybe the last. A Wednesday afternoon, he recalled. Near the end of summer. When she reported in to give Derek his take, she wasn't cheerful like she usually was. He remembered asking if someone had roughed her up. No, she said. Nothing like that. Now Derek stared at the underside of the Acura. What was it she said? Something about bad things happening to good people. And that she would take care of it. Yeah. That was it.

Shit. Now that he was thinking about it, she'd been starting to do the same thing as Lauren. And Charlie. What the hell did it mean? She says something. Then Charlie comes around asking questions. The whole thing was weird. Definitely not cool. Not in their line of work. Derek stopped working, dug out his cell, and text messaged his partner.

CHAPTER TWENTY-FIVE

AFTER SPENDING an uncomfortable night on Sam's couch, Georgia rented a steam carpet cleaner, went home, and spent the day scrubbing. She scoured the steps and the landing with carpet shampoo and an enzyme cleaner until most of the smell was gone. The only way you could pick up anything at all was to burrow your nose into the carpet fibers. She half expected to run into her neighbor, but he didn't appear.

It was a crisp fall day with an achingly blue sky, and late that afternoon she went for a run. She jogged east to the lake and then up to Northwestern, making a loop around Evanston. As she reached the campus, she passed a couple strolling by the lake, their bodies melded together in a two-step of total absorption. She remembered that absorption: the overpowering need that only one person could satisfy, the joy that came from satisfying it. That joy, the joy that framed the corners of most people's lives, made only a temporary foray into Georgia's life. A dull pain gathered at the center of her chest.

Back home she showered, dressed, then returned the carpet cleaner to the supermarket. She must have still had soup on the brain, because she picked up a container of tomato bisque along with her other groceries. She wasn't exactly sure what bisque was. It looked like cream of tomato but was more expensive. What was the difference, besides the fancy French name? She poured it into a pan and set it on the stove.

She'd never been a soup person until Matt. He loved it. Said it must be the peasant stock in him. Shit. She was doing it again—using Matt as a benchmark for the events in her life. When would she stop? She stared at the bisque, then took it off the stove and poured it down the drain.

She was lugging a load of clean laundry up from the basement when the phone rang inside her apartment. She sprinted up the last flight to get it.

"Hello?"

"Davis," a tinny voice responded. "It's Paul Kelly."

Saturday night. She hadn't figured the lawyer for a weekend worker. "Hey, Paul. What's up?"

He cleared his throat, and there was a moment of silence. Then, "I was just going over my notes on the Jordan case and wanted to check in."

"It's been an interesting couple of days." She told him about the fish guts. "I could have used your help."

Kelly mumbled something she couldn't make out.

"What?" She smiled. "You don't think cleaning up fish crud is in the line of duty?"

"It was the first thing I learned in law school."

"Along with due process?" She opened her door to gaze at the now clean carpet. "Well, given that this was the same thing that was dumped on Sara Long's head, I'd say someone was trying to send me a message."

"Brilliant deduction," Kelly said. "But fish guts? It's crude."

"That may be the only thing they could think up."

"What do you mean?"

"I'm wondering if the perpetrator was a kid. From the hazing."

"You have any leads?"

"You're not going to like this, but one name keeps surfacing."

"And who would that be?"

"Monica Ramsey."

She heard him suck in his breath.

"Just listen, Paul. Apparently Tommy Cashian—he's the Ramsey girl's boyfriend—had the hots for Sara Long. They hooked up over the summer. It didn't last, but according to her friends, Monica knew about it. When I talked to the kid, he admitted he was crazy about Sara. He would have broken up with Monica, except Sara told him not to. In fact, she dumped him."

More silence.

"There's more. Ramsey was at the Forest Preserve during the game. Several people have backed that up, including her boyfriend. But there's no mention of Monica Ramsey in the police reports. Not one word. The boyfriend claims he took her home when the hazing started, but maybe he's covering for her. I'm going to dig deeper, and if we find evidence that she's unstable, or has some—"

"Davis," Kelly cut in. "You know how when you want something to be true, you can stack the deck, slant things, so it seems like it can't possibly be anything except what you want it to be?"

"I'm not doing that."

"Are you sure?"

"It's a lead, Paul."

"Is it the only one?"

Georgia hesitated. "No," she said quietly.

"What else do you have?"

"Sara lied about working at the bookstore."

"Really?"

"The manager says she quit her job last spring. Hasn't worked there in five months."

"What was she doing?"

"I don't know yet."

"Well now, that's what I call a lead." She heard him rustling papers. "What's more, I don't see anything about *that* in the police reports."

"You won't. They didn't follow up."

"Now that makes things interesting."

"Can you blame them? They're convinced Cam Jordan killed her."

"Like you're convinced it was the Ramsey girl?"

"I'm not—" She cut herself off.

"Look. Instead of chasing after the State's Attorney's daughter, why don't you concentrate on this job thing?"

"I will. But what about the fish guts in my hall? Whoever sent them clearly doesn't like me nosing around."

"Who else have you pissed off?"

"The line forms to the right."

"I'm listening."

"There's Tom Walcher. He's the lawyer I asked you to check out."

"I did. Big real estate lawyer. Successful. Very much on the up and up. As far as I can tell." Kelly harrumphed. "Who else?"

"Sara Long's father wasn't too pleased with me. And the girls I interviewed didn't want to talk to me. I wonder if one of them could be behind the fish guts."

"You thinking of someone in particular?"

"Not sure yet." Georgia tapped her finger on the phone. "You know, there's still the matter of those sketchy police reports."

"I'm on them."

"What do you mean?"

"I'm working on it."

"I thought you weren't going after Ramsey."

"That's correct."

"Well then, who are—" She caught herself. "Are you going after the cops?"

"It wouldn't be the first time."

She shifted uncomfortably. "I wish you wouldn't."

"Why not?"

"I used to be a cop, remember?"

"But you aren't any more. You can't have it both ways, Davis."

She thought about O'Malley. He was her mentor and her friend. She didn't want to make trouble for him. And though she couldn't defend Parker's sloppy ways, she'd been his partner for nearly ten years. When you risk your life every day, and your partner's the only one watching your back, it creates a bond that can transcend the rules.

"Paul, I think it's more personal. I've been picking around the edges, and someone doesn't like it. Don't go after the cops yet. Let me follow up."

"Going after the cops—or, at least, pointing out what's *not* in their reports—would buy us more time. And deflect attention away from the Jordan boy."

He had a point. "Enough to get him out of jail?" Cam Jordan was wasting away in Cook County in what was, for him, barbaric conditions. If there was a chance of getting his bail reduced so he could be released, it would be cruel not to try.

"It's possible," Kelly said. "Especially now that the hazing is out. Public opinion is bound to start softening." He paused. "You have any idea who leaked the hazing, by the way?"

"No." It came out quickly.

"I see." Kelly cleared his throat. "Probably just some enterprising reporter?"

"Probably." It was possible that someone had decided to play hero. O'Malley, for example. Of course, if it *was* him, he'd never admit it. And she'd never ask. "Paul, I still think we should wait on the cop angle. Keep it in reserve until, or if, our backs are up against the wall. It just doesn't feel ... right."

"Since when did scruples mean anything to a PI who lies to get what she needs?"

She didn't answer. She wasn't sure herself. On the other hand, at least Kelly was involved in the process: brainstorming strategies, trying out leads. One minute he didn't want to go after anyone, the next he was ready to charge ahead on half-assed theories. Talk about being unencumbered by morals.

"Your wife must love watching you weasel your way out of trouble," she said.

"I'm not married," he said in his reedy voice.

Somehow she had the feeling he'd say that.

CHAPTER TWENTY-SIX

NORTH SHORE Fitness was a suburban version of the East Bank Club, a successful downtown facility for exercise, business meetings, and the amenities that fuel them both. Located near the Skokie courthouse, the yellow brick complex met those expectations, right down to a row of glassed-in conference rooms with a view of the racquetball courts and pool. Georgia pulled into the parking lot, having tailed Lauren Walcher from Newfield. She couldn't imagine what business would draw the teenager to the Club.

Earlier that morning Georgia had visited five different fish markets in the area: two Burhops, Don's, the Davis Street Fishmarket, and Mitchell's in the Glen. No one remembered any waste products being taken away, although one of the Burhops managers suggested she come back during the afternoon shift. In an ideal world, she would have gone back to question Sara's friends, but both Heather Blakely and Claire

Tennenbaum were under strict orders not to talk to her. She'd goosed them as far as she could.

Which left Lauren Walcher. Lauren might have an idea about the fish guts, but getting to her was problematic. Georgia wouldn't be welcome at the Walchers' home, and another confrontation in a parking lot wasn't a good idea. She'd decided to tail her and "accidentally" bump into her in a neutral location where the girl might be willing to answer a few questions. Not perfect, but worth a shot.

Georgia parked two rows from Lauren's Land Rover and kept a discreet distance behind as the girl walked to the entrance. Lauren wasn't carrying a gym bag, but she might keep her workout clothes in a locker. Georgia would have to talk her way into the locker room or wait until Lauren finished exercising.

The interior of the club looked like a hotel lobby with elaborate chandeliers, floor to ceiling mirrors, and splashy art on the walls. On the left a marble floor led to a cocktail lounge with couches and chairs. On the right was a juice bar and restaurant surrounded by screens and potted palms. Overhead signs that looked like the scrolling marquees inside movie theaters directed visitors to the locker rooms, pool, and courts. It was a far cry from the smelly gym and locker rooms of high school. In fact, Georgia detected a light fruity aroma in the air—peach-scented disinfectant, maybe?

Georgia expected Lauren to go to the locker rooms, so she was surprised when the teenager headed into the juice bar. She followed the girl and peered inside. Half the tables were occupied. Two waiters chatted idly to each other. Lauren went to a table in the back corner where two men and a woman were seated. Georgia didn't want to show herself, so before she got a good look at them, she slipped around to the back and positioned herself behind a row of palms. The table Lauren had approached was a few feet away. Palm fronds blocked her view, but she could hear clearly.

"Hi, sweetheart," a man said. His voice was familiar.

"Hi, Daddy."

Tom Walcher.

Georgia heard a chair scrape. He was getting up to embrace her.

"You have the key to Mom's locker?"

"Right here."

Georgia imagined him digging into his pocket. Smiling as he handed it over.

"Thanks, Dad. You're the best." Lauren sounded almost pleasant. Daddy's little girl.

"You'll bring it home when you're done?"

"Duh." A trace of belligerence crept into the girl's voice.

"Honey, let me introduce you to some people. Harry, this is Lauren, my daughter. This is Harry Perl, sweetheart. He's a real estate developer."

"Nice to meet you, Mr. Perl." Lauren's voice sounded mechanical.

"You too," a nasally voice replied.

"And this is another successful developer. You could do worse than to follow in her footsteps."

"Now, Tom," the woman protested. "Don't do that to the poor girl."

"Nonsense. You are what you are. Lauren, this is Ricki Feldman."

Oh my fucking God. For a second Georgia thought she'd said it aloud.

***

They'd made her see a counselor after the suspension. It was part of the process, they said. She dutifully showed up. They moved past the incident in question quickly. Six months earlier Georgia had failed to turn in an offender's gun, and she'd brought a civilian to a stake-out. Both of those were clear violations of procedure, and she'd been suspended from the force. Georgia understood, took full responsibility for her actions, and told the counselor under the circumstances, she'd probably do the same thing again. There wasn't much more to say.

The counselor nodded and started asking about her personal life. In retrospect, Georgia realized she must have been feeling chatty, because she actually told the woman about Matt. It was the oldest story in the world, she began. They were dating. She thought they made a perfect couple. They were both cops, they understood each other. Then he found another woman, and he dumped her.

When prodded, Georgia admitted she'd underestimated the pull of his heritage. She'd heard how Jewish men liked to date gentile women. *Shiksas*, they called them. Especially if they were blond. But when it was time to settle down, they usually married a Jewish woman. It was his family, she told the counselor. His grandparents had escaped the Holocaust, and his parents never let him forget it. She'd met them once. At a Friday night Shabbos dinner. They were polite, even kind. Still, she felt like an outsider. At the time she didn't think it mattered.

But it did. Never mind that the woman he dumped her for was as shrewd and ambitious as a hungry fox. Never mind that her father had a reputation as a shark. She was Jewish, and Matt had fallen for her.

"What do you mean, 'shark'?" the counselor had asked.

Georgia explained. Thirty-five years ago, Stuart Feldman, Ricki's father, had built a housing development near Joliet. Beautiful homes; affordable, too. The problem was he conveniently neglected to tell anyone they were built on the remains of a toxic waste dump. When abnormally high rates of cancer, mostly neuroblastomas, surfaced among the children living there, Feldman faced a huge class action suit. His business collapsed, and he suffered a stroke from which he never recovered. After his death Ricki took over the business and quickly settled the case.

"But none of that mattered to Matt," she added. "None of it."

The counselor listened sympathetically, then tried to explain the five stages of grief according to some woman named Elisabeth Kübler-Ross. Georgia told her it was bullshit. She went through each and every stage at the same time. Grief clung to her, continually reminding her of what she had lost.

Maybe she was stuck, the counselor said, in that nice, antiseptic way of telling someone they were crazy. She should consider ongoing professional help. Georgia told the counselor they were done and walked out.

***

Now the woman she'd been dumped for was sitting next to Lauren's father.

Georgia's throat felt thick, her stomach jumped, and she felt hot and cold at the same time. As slowly as she could, she lifted a frond of the palm tree she was lurking behind and peeked through. Ricki Feldman was sitting directly across from her.

The first thing you noticed about the woman was her hair. Straight. Silky. Dark brown. No split ends in sight. Then her eyes—luminous, with thick lashes and perfect eyebrow arches. She had a slender, almost petite build and dressed in what had to be expensive but tasteful clothes. Georgia saw how the men in the room: waiters, businessmen, or exercisers, snuck looks in her direction. Even Lauren's gaze was admiring.

Screw it. Ricki knew the effect she had on people. Even drinking a pink smoothie, she displayed a studied arrogance, aware she was the center of attention. Georgia watched an enigmatic smile spread across Ricki's lips after a comment by Walcher. Saw her wave a carefully manicured hand in the air. It was all stage-managed. Orchestrated with the knowledge that even her slightest action was riveting.

Georgia ran a hand through her blond ponytail. She felt like a tacky bland giant in comparison. In a way she couldn't blame Matt for having been swept away. But she could blame Ricki for stealing him.

She forced herself back. Lauren was still standing by the table, looking speculatively at her father, who was talking to the other man.

"We're well on our way, Harry. The variance sailed through the zoning committee."

Georgia focused on Harry Perl. He didn't seem that tall, but he was sitting down. He appeared to be fit, and he had a full head of curly gray hair worn fashionably long. He wore a plush warm-up suit—he'd probably just come off the racquetball court. He wasn't unattractive, but something kept him from being truly handsome. Maybe it was his eyes, which darted from person to person but never lit for more than a second. His face was a blank slate.

Perl cleared his throat and opened his mouth. Gold flashed in the right side of his mouth. "Excellent." He looked over at Ricki.

Lauren watched as Ricki nodded. "Yes. It is."

Walcher, also in a warm-up suit, folded his hands, the way he'd done at his house. "There are still challenges ahead. The full board still has to approve it. And they're in the middle of all the low-income housing regs. Anything could happen."

Perl leaned forward. "That's why we hired you. To make nice with the board."

"It will require some—delicacy." Tom shot Perl a meaningful glance.

Lauren cocked her head.

"But you have—leverage." Ricki interjected.

"Whatever you need." Perl added.

Walcher's nostrils flared. Georgia couldn't tell if Walcher admired Perl, hated him, or was afraid of him.

There was a brief pause. Then Ricki offered up a dazzling smile. "Lauren, sweetheart," she said, revealing straight white teeth. "You are such the image of your mother. She's a gorgeous woman, isn't she?" She turned to the other men who nodded in unison.

Lauren shot her an almost angry look, Georgia thought, then tried to cover it. "Well, I'll be going now. Nice meeting you all. Bye."

Georgia watched her go. She felt heavy and lethargic. Questioning Lauren Walcher would wait. She turned around and headed back outside. As she pushed through the revolving door, she spotted a man getting into a car on the other side of the parking lot. She couldn't see his face, but he had a slim build and curly, dark hair. Like Matt. No. It was just her imagination.

CHAPTER TWENTY-SEVEN

WHEN GEORGIA went back to Burhops in Glenview, the afternoon manager told her someone *did* come in last Friday, looking for a bag of fish entrails.

From the back of the shop came the sound of a radio turned up too high. Spanish rock. "Can you describe the person?" She tried to rein in her excitement.

"A man. A boy, really," the manager said.

"How young?"

"Maybe in high school. Small. Skinny. Sharp nose."

"Clothes?"

"Jeans. T-shirt. Work shoes. Oh," He smirked. "And lots of jewelry."

"If I showed you a yearbook, could you identify him?"

The manager laughed. "No way! There's gotta be—what—three thousand pictures in those things? I don't have time."

Georgia bit her lip. "Well, tell me this. Did you give him the fish waste?"

He shrugged. "Sure. Less crap for us to get rid of."

Georgia thanked the manager and left. Was this the kid who was responsible for the mess in her apartment? She thought about running his description past Rachel, Ellie Foreman's daughter. And if he turned out to be a friend of Monica Ramsey ... Then she reconsidered. Better not to get Rachel involved. Lauren Walcher was still her best bet.

That night it rained. A cold, stinging rain that stripped the leaves from trees, clogged gutters, and turned the satisfying crunch of shoes on dry leaves into a slippery ordeal. Georgia started to wander around the apartment. It felt empty and brooding. Too big. She grabbed her jacket and umbrella and headed to Mickey's.

The place smelled like a combination of wet wool and grease, but because of the rain, it wasn't crowded. She went to a booth in the back. Owen brought her food promptly. She was on the second bite of her burger when she felt someone's gaze on her. She looked up. One of the men at the bar was watching her. The light was dim, and she couldn't quite make him out, but he looked friendly. Indeed, he was smiling. She squinted. He had sandy hair, long on top but short on the sides. Rimless glasses partway down his nose. Jesus! Her upstairs neighbor. She looked down at her plate.

He didn't get the message, because he picked up his drink and started over. She wanted to tell him she wasn't interested, but something stopped her. Afterwards, she admitted she didn't know what it was. Not his clothes; ordinary khakis and a button-down shirt with sleeves rolled up. Maybe it was that he didn't seem to care that his clothes were fifty years out of date. He looked comfortable with himself. Or maybe it was his smile. Not the plastic grimace she saw on so many men, especially men on the make. His was warm, and that warmth was mirrored in his eyes. Or maybe it was just that it was a bad night, and she was tired of feeling lonely. Whatever it was, when he reached her table, beer in hand, she gave him a nod.

He sat down, the scent of Aramis drifting over to her. "Catch any big ones lately?"

She blinked.

He put the glass down. "Fish. The fish guts."

"Oh." She ran a hand through her hair. "You were right, you know."

"About what?"

"Compost. As a disposal method."

"How did you figure it out?"

"I went online."

"First time."

"What?"

He looked at her. "First time someone said I've been right in a while."

She cocked her head and took a bite of her hamburger. It was missing something. Ketchup? Relish?

"My name's Pete Dellinger."

She swallowed her food. "Georgia Davis."

"Like the state?"

"You got a problem with the South?" But she grinned when she said it. He grinned back. Yes, it was a good smile.

He motioned to his glass. "Can I buy you one?"

She looked longingly at his beer. It had been a tough day, coming up against her nemesis. A beer would take the edge off. A lot more than Diet Coke. Probably make the burger taste better, too. She wanted it. Deserved it. Just this once. Anyway, it was free. The word tumbled out, almost of its own accord. "Sure."

He got up, went to the bar, and gave Owen the order. Owen dipped his head at Georgia, but she wouldn't meet his eyes. Owen shrugged and poured the beer into a glass. Pete brought it back.

"The bartender seems to know you. Do you come here often?"

The oldest line in the world and the guy said it with a straight face. She bit back a reply. "Yes," she said simply.

"I like it." He gazed around with a satisfied expression.

"Glad we have your approval." She lifted the glass of beer, hesitated, then took a long pull. Just like she remembered it. Frosty and tart with a grainy aftertaste that danced on her tongue. How long had it been? A year? Eighteen months? Damn. There was nothing like a cold brew. She set the glass down and stole a glance at the bar. Owen was watching her, hands on his hips. She looked away.

"So how do you like our building?" She focused on Pete.

"It's fine."

"Except when somebody spreads fish guts in the hall."

"I'm guessing there's a good story there."

Georgia took another long swallow. Half gone already. "I'm a private investigator," she began. Ten minutes and another beer later, she'd told him about the case. Again, she surprised herself. When she was on the force, she rarely talked to civilians about her cases.

Pete listened attentively—she had to give him that. Even though she left out some information, he didn't interrupt, something Matt used to do all the time. He'd claim he just wanted to understand, but it often felt like he was interrogating her. Pete nodded at all the right times and kept his mouth shut. When she was done, he leaned his elbows on the table.

"So what's your next step?"

"I'm not sure. Like I said, I have a theory, but not enough evidence." She finished off her beer.

"Want another?" He pointed to her empty glass.

She hesitated. She'd already downed two. A third would be asking for trouble. But he had to be on his fourth or even fifth by now. If he could handle it, so could she. "Okay."

He returned with their drinks and settled in, a smile tugging the corners of his mouth. She wondered what was so amusing but felt too shy to ask. Instead she asked, "So what about you? Why did you move in?"

"My wife and I separated."

"Sheila," she murmured.

A flush crept up his neck.

"I heard you two arguing the other night," she added, remembering how quickly Sheila had exploded.

"Oh." The flush spread to his face. "Yeah. She came over."

"Sounds like she wants you back."

"She's ... well ..." He shook his head, flustered. "It's not gonna happen ..." He looked over. "Let's not go there."

Georgia shrugged and took another bite of her burger. Pete watched with a curious expression.

She caught his look and pushed the food toward him. She wasn't hungry any more. Alcohol did that.

He frowned at the plate.

"Something wrong?" She asked.

He shook his head again.

She looked at him, then at her plate. "You're a vegetarian."

He shot her an embarrassed smile. "Will you still talk to me?"

"Hey, it's your life."

A vegetarian. Probably a "my body is my temple" guy. She sighed. How come she always ended up with the weird ones? Truth was, until Matt, her relationships with men had been limited. She'd only had sex with three men. They'd all been sweet, but slightly off: a software geek in high school, an accountant for a chain of pet stores a few years later, then Matt, who, for a cop, was bookish. She must have been sending out subtle signals: all nerds welcome.

She tossed back the rest of her beer. Ricki Feldman wouldn't do that, she'd lay odds. She'd set her sights on the richest, most handsome man in the room. And get him too. Georgia set her glass down carefully. Too carefully. The room was starting to wobble.

Pete's eyebrows arched. "You downed that one pretty fast."

"It's been a bad day."

"Aren't they all?" He asked a little sadly.

He was right. Everyone suffered. She wasn't so special. Why did she think she was? Suddenly, she couldn't think. Three beers and practically no food. What happened to her tolerance? She used to be able to toss back four or five with no problem. Now, her head felt too big and too far away from her body. She needed to lie down. She balled up her napkin, tried to pitch it on the table. She missed, and the napkin bounced onto the floor. She stood up unsteadily. "It's time for me to go."

CHAPTER TWENTY-EIGHT

THE THING was to act like you weren't there for anything important. Like you couldn't care less. That was what she'd told them. After a while you could layer on a smile if you wanted. Make them feel special. Lauren checked her watch. Being prompt was important, too. Clients didn't have all day. Neither did she. And Derek was late.

She slouched on the bench, wondering whether to call him. Not that it would do much good. He'd have to stop whatever he was doing and call her back. And time was growing short. She looked around the mall. Monday was always slow. Things didn't heat up until mid-week; Thursday and Friday were busy. And Saturdays were crazy. She usually took off the first two days of the week. Worked out, did her homework, chilled. Her cell phone buzzed. She checked the caller ID. Heather. She ignored the call.

Tonight was meant to be a business meeting. She and Derek had to talk. Derek was recruiting girls who—well—just weren't good enough. He'd started cruising Golf Mill and Woodfield, but frankly, Mount Prospect and Schaumburg weren't the North Shore. The girls weren't as classy— though she'd be the last to admit the North Shore had cornered the market on class. She'd seen plenty of clients who picked their noses, chewed with their mouths open, or sported bellies that hung over their belts. Still, there was a cachet about North Shore girls. After she trained them, they were good. She was proud of her work.

Derek's point was they had to expand, maybe even start another branch. To stay where they were meant they were falling behind. But this wasn't fast food, and they weren't McDonald's. She liked the control of a small operation. They were pulling down great money. That was important. People respected women with money. Their own money. Like Ricki Feldman. They'd only met for a minute, but they were two of a kind, she and Ricki. She could see it in the woman's eyes. They understood each other. Lauren recalled her comment about how beautiful her mother was. That was code. Ricki didn't like her mother. Lauren understood.

She and Derek had to discuss Sara, too. The PI had talked to Claire and Heather. Neither of them knew shit, but it wouldn't be long until she came back to her. Georgia Davis. Lauren scoffed. Who had a name like Georgia? She hoped Georgia was focusing on Monica Ramsey. She'd planted the seed herself the night she followed her to the grocery store. To take the heat off her and the business. Still, there were problems. The PI had just discovered Sara wasn't working at the bookstore. And now suddenly Heather was calling all the time, asking tons of questions, like she was going to do some big investigation for the school news. Lauren knew Heather was just being nosy, in that high school kind of way. She should just grow up.

Lauren crossed one leg over the other, letting her foot jiggle the air. Sara had screwed up the bookstore thing. The manager had been a client. He'd lied for Sara, took messages when someone called her at the store, even filled out bogus time sheets for her in return for a blowjob or two. But he had been fired over the summer—they'd caught the jerk with his hands in the cash register—and the new manager didn't know about Sara's "employment." Lauren had told Sara to find another "job"—fast— but two months had gone by, and Sara hadn't come up with one. Then she was killed.

Lauren's foot dangled back and forth. They had the crazy guy. The cops were still sure he did it, despite the hazing. Why was a PI on the case? That was the other reason she needed to talk to Derek. He said he would take care of Georgia Davis. She hadn't seen anything yet. And then there was that text message he'd sent a while back about Charlie, one of their regulars. Whether Lauren had heard from him and to let Derek know if she did.

She uncrossed her legs and checked her watch. Now Derek was re- ally late. She dug out her cell and punched in his number. The call went straight to voice mail. "Hi, leave your name and number." Nothing cute or fancy. All business. She disconnected.

She got up, walked over to Bath and Body Works, and ducked inside. She bought some Vanilla Cream body lotion but kept one eye on the mall. No Derek. She came back out, her irritation mounting. Damn him. How dare he stand her up?

***

Derek's apartment in Deerfield was only twenty minutes from the mall, but driving on rain-slicked streets made it take longer. He had two roommates. She'd met them once; she didn't like either of them. They talked with heavy European accents, and they were a lot older than Derek. One of them wore thick gold chains around his neck, and the other had an ear that was pierced in five places. But when she asked Derek about them, he said they were cool.

How would he know, she wondered as she cut across Deerfield Road. Derek didn't talk much about his life. His family lived—or used to live— in a small ramshackle house in Wilmette. He had a brother who died two years ago; after that the family fell apart. His mother drank herself to death, and his father didn't care about anything. Derek had dropped out of school.

She'd first met him in a chat room and started emailing. When he told her he'd gone to Newfield, she met him for coffee. One thing led to another, and they decided to work together. From then on, the business took off. They were both pulling down serious money. So were the girls.

The streetlamps cast pale, watery shadows as she pulled into the rear of the apartment complex. It was only seven, but night came faster now. Daylight savings time would be over in a week. That was the final indignity. Once the sun went down before five o'clock, winter couldn't be avoided. She parked her Land Rover in the lot behind one of four identical red brick buildings. As she rounded the corner to the front, she fiddled with her umbrella and didn't immediately notice the flashing lights. When she did, she was almost on top of them. A police cruiser. And a crowd of about twenty people beside it. She froze.

The police car was empty, but one of the doors was open, and the lights on the roof revolved in twin bursts of red and blue. The crowd hovered near the car, craning their necks toward the building's entrance. Derek's building. The front door was open. Lauren couldn't barge inside without the crowd—and the police—seeing her. If they'd let her in at all. She didn't remember what apartment Derek lived in, anyway. She pulled out her cell and called him again. Again the call went to voice mail.

She was pocketing the cell when a siren cut through the air. She spun around. An ambulance raced into the complex and screeched to a stop outside the building. The crowd parted to let it through. Her breath caught in her throat. She tried to tell herself it was nothing. Someone fell. Cut themselves. Had a heart attack. That's all.

But when two more police cars and a black van with a blue flashing light swung into the lot, her stomach clenched. The cars sped over to Derek's building and stopped. Three cops and two other men in uniform climbed out and hurried inside, leaving the engine running. Lauren started to shake in the night chill. She pulled her jacket close. One of the cops came back out and picked up a bullhorn.

"Everybody go home now. Everything's under control." He shouted. His voice sounded tinny, mechanical.

Where was Derek? She felt like she was being sucked into a vortex. She stared at the revolving lights on top of the police cruisers. The lights were spinning in time to her racing pulse. She thought about those Japanese cartoons that were supposed to trigger seizures in kids. Was she losing it? Then her brain kicked in. She was fine, damn it. She just needed to know what was going on.

She willed herself to take a step forward. The knot of gapers had moved to the side, but no one seemed in a hurry to leave. Umbrellas sprouted. The sight of the crowd and their umbrellas comforted her. Maybe that's why people flocked to the scene of fires and accidents. To celebrate that they were okay, that the horror of whatever they were witnessing wasn't happening to them. She crept closer.

"The kid didn't have a chance. Shot point blank," Lauren heard one man say knowingly.

What kid? Panic lodged in her throat.

"Anyone know him?" A woman asked.

"Not me," the same man answered.

"I might. Doesn't he live with those Serbians?" Another woman asked.

Lauren tightened her fist around her umbrella. The pressure in her chest moved up to her Adam's apple. She wanted to escape. Run away. Instead she made herself tap the shoulder of the woman who said she might know him. "Excuse me, what happened?" Her voice was hardly above a whisper.

A dumpy woman turned around, her face alternately blue and pink from the lights.

"One of the tenants was shot. Opened the door to his place and bang." She made the shape of a pistol with her thumb and forefinger.

"Who?"

"A young kid. Lived one floor below me. With two older guys. Unusual name. One you don't hear every day."

"Was it Derek? Derek Janowitz?"

The woman's face smoothed out. "Yeah. That was it. Janowitz. You know him?"

The eerie, spinning feeling returned, and with it a high-pitched whine. The woman looked at her curiously. Lauren dropped her umbrella, spun around, and stumbled back to her car.

CHAPTER TWENTY-NINE

THE BELL rang. Recess was over. Everyone had to go back inside. But Georgia lagged behind. She'd been sitting on the stone ledge that ran the length of the playground watching two robins hop across the grass. One of them held a piece of straw in its mouth, but as Georgia looked more closely, the straw turned into a snake, writhing and twisting in the bird's beak. The robin dropped the snake, and it started to slither across the grass, leaving bloody entrails in its wake. The bell rang again, sharper, more piercing this time. An acrid, fishy odor permeated everything. The birds disappeared, and Georgia slowly swam to the surface.

The phone. She covered her head with a pillow. A morning dream. They were always exceptionally vivid, even more so when she'd been drinking. The phone rang a third time. *Shit.Who the hell had the nerve to call so early?* She let the machine pick up.

After the beep, a familiar voice growled, "Davis. If you're there, get the damn phone."

She cracked an eye and checked her clock. It was fuzzy, out of focus. She squinted. Ten AM. *Christ. How did it get so late?* She rolled over and pulled the phone off the base, forcing back the wave of dizziness that rolled with her.

"Davis here." She croaked. Her mouth felt like sandpaper.

"It's O'Malley." His voice was accompanied by a high-pitched rushing noise. "Dan, where the hell are you? In the middle of tornado alley?"

"You know how hard it is to find a pay phone these days? I'm at the train station."

"Why?"

"Wake up, Davis. Smell the coffee."

She swung her legs over the bed and tried to focus. O'Malley was at a pay phone because … It came to her in a heartbeat.

"Shit. I'm sorry. I'm moving slow this morning," she said.

He grunted in response.

"What's going on?"

"I got wind of something. Thought it might be of interest to you."

She sat up straight. "Yeah?"

"You didn't hear it from me, right?"

"Course not."

"Uh-huh." He didn't sound convinced.

"Dan, you know me."

"I don't know anyone anymore." He paused. "But that's not your problem." He sighed. "Here it is. There was a homicide in Deerfield last night."

"Monday night."

"If today is Tuesday …"

"Sorry. Go on."

"They activated NORTAF and some of our guys are on it. A young kid. Name of Derek Janowitz. Lived in an apartment with a couple of Serbians."

"And?"

"He used to go to Newfield but dropped out a year or so ago. But here's the kicker. The dicks went through his stuff and found a PDA with all his phone numbers on it."

Georgia held her breath.

"Sara Long's cell was one of them."

***

Georgia got out of bed carefully. Her head felt like it might explode, and her stomach felt like a battalion of tiny soldiers were running maneuvers through it. She swore she'd never take another drink. Ever. She thought about toasting a bagel but couldn't stomach the thought of eating. She did manage to down two glasses of water and three Advils.

Before hanging up, O'Malley told her the Deerfield cops had interrogated the victim's two roommates. They claimed to know nothing about their friend's murder, and so far their alibis checked out. When she asked if Robby Parker, her former partner and the detective handling Sara Long's case, knew what had happened, O'Malley said,

"If I know, Parker knows. Of course, the fact that Sara's name was in the vic's PDA might just be a coincidence." O'Malley added.

"Right."

"Hey. I figured you'd want to know."

She'd thanked him. He'd gone out of his way to call her on an untraceable line. He was still looking out for her. She owed him. After getting dressed, she booted up her computer and Googled the name "Derek Janowitz." Nothing popped up. She tried some of her other databases but came up cold. O'Malley said the kid worked at the gas station on Shermer in Northbrook. She should drive over.

Before she left, she called Kelly. He picked up right away. "Good morning, Davis," he bellowed cheerfully. "To what do I owe the honor of this call?"

She grunted. The dizziness was gone, but her head was still pounding, and his reedy voice didn't help. If they were face to face, she might have slugged him. Instead she told him what O'Malley said.

"Really? Now that is interesting. You're gonna follow up, right?"

Now she did want to slug him. "That's the plan."

"See if you can get me something by Thursday, okay?"

"Why Thursday?"

"Well, if you mosey on down to the courthouse around two, you'll find out."

"What's going on?"

"I filed a motion for a bail reduction for Cam Jordan."

"You did?"

"Three million dollars is obscene."

"That's great!" she replied. "I'm glad. That poor boy needs to get out. When do you—"

"Hold on, Davis," Kelly replied. "I wouldn't get your hopes up."

"Why not? We thought the fact that the hazing was out would make a difference."

He snorted amiably. "Not enough, I'm afraid."

"Then why—"

"I want to feel out the judge."

A wave of pain shot across her forehead. "I don't get it."

"There's no chance Cam Jordan's sister could pay ten percent of a hundred grand, much less a million, right?'

"Yeah …"

"So if the judge does lower it—even a little—then I know he's listening to what I got to say."

"And …"

"And I might go for a bench trial rather than a jury. But if he doesn't lower it, I know to take my chances on a jury. *Capiche?*"

"*Capiche?*" Last time she'd checked, Kelly was Irish.

"It's a figure of speech, Davis."

He pronounced figure "figgure." She sighed. "Good strategy."

"I think so, too," he said jovially. They made arrangements to meet outside the courtroom in Skokie on Thursday. After disconnecting, Georgia stared at the phone. She'd never heard him so happy. Had to be the Irish in him. He was gearing up for a fight.

***

Jerry Horner was stooped and had glasses that slipped down his nose. He wore a grimy uniform with "Jerry" on his shirt pocket and a faded gimme cap low on his forehead. When Georgia arrived, he was slouched in a corner of the garage in an reclining leather chair so old there were more cracks than material. He had to be in his sixties, but right now he was staring fearfully around like a kid who'd been separated from his mother.

Georgia stopped at the edge of the garage. There was no work going on, but the fumes of gas, oil, and cleaning solvents combined with her hangover made her queasy. She angled herself so she was facing out.

"Sorry to intrude, Mr. Horner, but I need to ask you some questions."

Horner looked over, and a frown spread across his face. "Don't know what else you could possibly want to know," he said wearily.

"Excuse me?"

"You done asked me everything except whether I take my coffee with cream."

"I'm not with the police, Mr. Horner," Georgia said. "But I am interested in Derek Janowitz."

"You gotta believe me." He blathered on as if he hadn't heard her. "I had no clue what he was doing."

"What are you talking about?"

"Janowitz, of course. And what he was up to."

Georgia nodded, playing along.

He rocked forward and adjusted the recliner to an upright position. "I'm just trying to make an honest living, you know? Janowitz started here about nine months ago. Kid seemed to know what he was doing. He was good with computers. Understood the digital crap. Used to say the future of the world was online. That you could get everything you wanted with a damn mouse. But I never guessed ..."

"What he was really up to."

"How could I?" The chair squeaked as he shifted. "In all my years, I've never been in trouble with the law. Thought Janowitz was a good kid. Lived around here, used to go to Newfield." He fixed her with a knowing expression. "Just goes to show you can't trust anyone."

"Tell me again what you discovered about him."

"Me? You're the ones that came to me. I—"

"Mr. Horner, I'm not with the police."

He looked bewildered. "You're not? Then who—"

"I'm an investigator. I'm working on a different case, but your employee had the name and number of my subject in his PDA. I need to know—"

"What's a PDA?"

She massaged her temples. "It's a small electronic device that has a digital address book in it, among other things."

"Oh." He wasn't sweating but he wiped a sleeve across his forehead.

"So I'd need to know if you've ever heard of her. Her name was Sara Long."

Horner snorted. "The creep had a lot of girls' names. And that's just for starters."

Georgia rubbed her temples again. Her headache was worsening. "What are you talking about?"

"Janowitz. He was a pimp, the bastard. Running whores right under my nose."

His words slammed into her like a runaway train. Her hands dropped. "What?"

"You heard me," he leaned back in the chair and folded his hands behind his head. He seemed to sense that his response had given him the upper hand in the conversation. He almost smiled. "He was a pimp. Pandering. Solicitation and prostitution, the cops said."

Georgia steadied herself against the wall of the garage.

"The cops were here before I opened this morning," Horner volunteered. "Five squad cars; I counted 'em. I swear to God, I thought they were after me. But they wanted to talk about Janowitz. They'd picked up a couple of his hookers overnight. They admitted the kid was running 'em." Horner spread his hands again. "A fucking prostitution ring. In my gas station. No wonder they brought five cruisers. They probably thought I was keeping 'em locked up in the garage."

Outside, a silver Beamer pulled up to the pump. Georgia glanced over, then back at Horner. She recalled a case she'd worked where they did keep the women locked up. The pimps in that case were hardened criminals. But Derek Janowitz was a teenager. A woman got out of the Beamer and started pumping gas.

They'd given her a heads up about teenage prostitution when she was on the force. It was on the rise, she'd learned, and while a lot of the prostitutes were illegal immigrants, drug users, or runaways, a growing number of younger teens were coming from seemingly stable middle class families. As usual, money was the draw, but not for the next fix.

These girls were hooking for triple mocha lattes, iPods, and four hundred dollar jeans.

Georgia recalled the expensive clothes in Sara's closet. The digital camera and iPod. She remembered Melinda Long saying the family was just making it; they couldn't afford luxuries. But Sara could. On her minimum wage job. Which, it turned out, she'd lied about.

The woman climbed back into her Beamer and pulled out of the station.

"Like I said, the cops were all over me," Horner was saying. "They thought I was his partner. I don't need that, you know? I got four grandchildren, for crying out loud." Georgia made herself listen. This had to be the most significant thing that ever happened to Horner; he needed someone to witness his fifteen minutes.

"The cops are sure he had a partner?"

"They sure as hell acted that way."

"And they thought it was you."

He cocked his head. "Where you been for the past five minutes, lady? That's what I been saying."

"Sorry." Georgia rubbed her temples again. "Can you describe Janowitz?"

"Skinny kid. Not tall. Maybe five six, five seven. Long hair. Wore as much jewelry as a girl. I told him to take it off at work." Horner shrugged. "Oh, yeah. He had a big nose, too. Sharp. And his eyes were always watching you. Taking it all in."

Georgia stopped massaging her temples. Where had she heard that before? Someone else had described a young kid in the same way. Recently. She wracked her brain, willing it to come. The afternoon manager at Burhops. He was describing the kid who picked up the fish guts. "Small. Skinny. Sharp nose. Jewelry."

Horner started shaking his head. "I kept telling the cops I've never done a dishonest day's work in my life. No way was I his partner."

But someone else was, Georgia thought. And that someone might know who killed Sara Long.

"Mr. Horner, I'm sorry you've had to go through all this, but I wonder if you would do me a tiny favor."

"What's that?"

"You have Derek Janowitz's address and phone number. I'd like to have them."

"Whatever for? It's not like he's gonna be answering his phone."

"The information might help me figure out who his partner is." She smiled. "And take the heat off you."

Horner squinted at her, then leaned forward and planted his feet on the floor. He took his time getting out of the chair. "I guess it don't matter to me. Just as long as you leave me out of it."

CHAPTER THIRTY

GEORGIA WASN'T surprised to see Robby Parker in court on Thursday, but she was to see O'Malley and Jeff Ramsey. Neither needed to be there—the outcome was a foregone conclusion. Knowing Robby, she would have predicted he'd show up. Anything to get out of real work. But O'Malley? Dan never liked coming down to the courthouse. He'd said—more than once—it was just for show and usually a waste of time. And surely the first assistant State's Attorney of Cook County had better things to do than appear at a bail reduction hearing. Unless he was there to make a statement. Which, if he did have political aspirations, would make his presence understandable.

Georgia nodded to O'Malley and Parker. O'Malley dipped his head, but Parker refused to make eye contact. She shrugged, making sure O'Malley caught it, and made her way over to Paul Kelly.

To his credit, Kelly didn't seem to be bothered by Ramsey's presence. Seated on a bench outside the courtroom, the older lawyer, in a spiffy suit and tie, looked unusually crisp. With his bald head gleaming in the fluorescent lights, he seemed vigorous and happy. In fact, he couldn't keep from chuckling as they waited. Ruth Jordan, wearing a gray skirt and white blouse, sat next to him on the bench.

Georgia told him what she'd found out about Derek Janowitz. Kelly rubbed his hands together gleefully when she finished. "Good work, Davis! Now we're getting somewhere. You gonna find his partner?"

"I'm on it. But so are the cops. I heard they're zeroing in on his roommates. The Eastern Europeans."

"Which could mean it's a large, organized ring."

"Exactly," Georgia said. "But I'm not real excited about tangling with the Russian mafia, or the Serbian mob, or whatever gang is running hookers on the North Shore."

"You think it's a turf war and the Long girl was caught in the middle?"

"I don't know. Depends on the connection between Janowitz and Sara."

"But you suspect."

Georgia frowned. "The girl was killed in the Forest Preserve."

"So?"

"You'd think if she was a hooker and her murder was related to prostitution, she would have been killed at a job, coming or going. But she was with her high school friends. A universe away from her other life. If she had one."

"Maybe the killers were counting on that." The door to the courtroom opened and several people came out. Kelly stood up, held the door open, and motioned for Ruth to enter.

Georgia followed them. "Well, at least things are pointing away from Cam Jordan."

"It won't make any difference today," he said. "And you know in your heart Sara did."

Georgia cocked her head.

"Have another life."

✳✳✳

When the judge entered the room, the clerk ordered everyone to rise. The judge arranged himself behind the bench. Georgia sat next to Ruth behind the defense table. She'd never had an occasion to sit with the "people" before. She'd always been at the cops' section on the dais. For the first time she noticed how much the Skokie courtroom looked like a church; pews for the congregants, the seal of Cook County above the altar, and the judge's bench the priest's lectern.

Parker and O'Malley positioned themselves on the cops' dais. Parker wore a flashy suit—it probably cost hundreds—and his shield was prominently pinned to his pocket. When detectives were promoted, at least on the North Shore, they got a shield and a clothing allowance and not much more. Promotion to detective was considered a lateral transfer. But Robby seemed to be milking it. He still pretended not to see her.

O'Malley on the other hand, was wearing the tight-fitting navy suit he'd worn to court for years. He looked older: the lines on his forehead looked deeper. His stoic expression didn't hide the fact he'd rather be fly fishing in the Northwoods of Wisconsin.

She remembered the day she was suspended six months ago. She'd been working her first substantive case, and it was a tough one. A video of a woman getting shot. It wasn't a snuff film; the video hadn't been staged. It came from a surveillance camera. It was the middle of winter, and Georgia had been trying to do it by the book. But when she came up against the Russian mafia, procedure took a back seat to survival. She'd ended up in a strip club in Des Plaines with Ellie Foreman, Rachel's mother, and an unarmed civilian. Georgia had faced down the bouncer and taken his gun. The problem was she never quite got around to turning it in. It didn't matter that she cracked the case, saved lives, got the bad guy. Olson suspended her because she hadn't followed procedure.

O'Malley tried to talk Olson out of it, but Olson was adamant. He'd been named chief after a corruption scandal that forced three officers to resign, and he needed to project a squeaky clean image. Georgia was his scapegoat. That was when she realized that, despite being a cop, her world would never be black and white. She would continue to embrace the gray.

Now, Parker nervously toyed with his shield, as if he needed physical proof he was a detective. O'Malley shot him a stern look. Parker dropped his hand and looked apologetic. Was O'Malley baby-sitting him? Is that why he was there? It was possible. This had to be Parker's his first homicide—he hadn't worked the video murder with her—and he didn't have much court experience apart from traffic tickets and DUI's. She didn't miss that part of being a cop. Or the paperwork. But she did miss the solidarity, the ability to talk across the desk with someone who knew. Who understood what people could do to each other.

She turned her gaze to Jeff Ramsey. He was at the prosecutor's table, hands folded. His dark suit wasn't flashy, and with his rep tie, blue shirt, and a shock of brown hair that kept falling over his forehead, he looked like one of those pictures of Bobby Kennedy she'd seen in books. And just as earnest. He occasionally whispered to a dark-haired female assistant sitting beside him.

The judge had to be in his sixties. Probably a lawyer who'd given up practicing law in return for a steady paycheck. Most circuit court judges commanded respect, and some had amassed a good deal of power. Looking at his sober face and black robes, Georgia wondered if this judge considered himself a successful judge or a failed lawyer. And how that would affect his decision.

Kelly introduced himself and told the judge he'd brought a character reference for Cam Jordan.

"And who might that be?" the judge asked.

"His sister, Ruth."

"What's his sister going to say?"

"Your honor, she will attest that Mr. Jordan is not a violent individual and that he poses no threat to the community."

"Is she a psychologist or a psychiatrist?"

"No, your honor, she's not."

"Then, why do I need to hear from her?" The judge rubbed a finger under his nose. "Sorry, counselor. Proceed with your argument." He looked conspicuously at his watch.

Kelly nodded, and without missing a beat, went on to argue rather eloquently, Georgia thought. The three million dollar bond was totally unreasonable given Cam Jordan's condition, he claimed. The boy was insane—when Ramsey objected, Kelly quickly retracted it and substituted "very disturbed." He could not reliably tell what was real and what wasn't. Though he was biologically an adult, Kelly continued, the boy had the mind of a child. He didn't understand what was happening to him, and the harsh treatment he'd been subjected to at Cook County jail—Kelly stopped short of calling it abuse—was compromising the boy's physical as well as mental health.

The boy did have a record as a sex offender, Kelly admitted. However, if the record was examined closely, it would reveal Cam had never touched or had any physical contact whatsoever with another individual. His activities were grounded in self-gratification. Only. If he were remanded to his sister's care, his sister being an exemplary member of the community, by the way, there was no chance he would flee. To be honest, Kelly said, the boy wouldn't know where to go. The home he had with his sister was the only one he knew.

Compassion alone dictates that his bail be reduced, he went on. The family has limited means and simply cannot pay an exorbitant bond. Compassion, Kelly repeated, and one additional factor.

"We have been collecting information that will cast serious doubt on the evidence against Cam Jordan," Kelly said solemnly. "In fact, our information points away from Cam Jordan as the killer. We will be making that information available to the court at the appropriate time, but let it be said now that the person who murdered Sara Long is very much an open question."

"Counsel," said the judge. "Wouldn't this be that 'appropriate time' to inform the Court of this information?"

"Judge …" Kelly struggled with his response. "It concerns the hazing situation. We are still looking very carefully at the events of that day, and will reveal what we've learned at the appropriate time. At this juncture, though, we don't feel comfortable sharing this information—"

"But I'm supposed to feel 'comfortable' just taking your word for it? You're asking me to reduce bond based on information you won't share, Counsel."

The courtroom was hushed. Kelly tried to fashion a response about the sensitivity of the information and protecting his client's rights. Even Jeff Ramsey paid close attention, and O'Malley was still. When Kelly finished, he headed back to the defense table. The only sound in the room was the soft clicking of the court reporter's keys.

Then it was Ramsey's turn. He rose from the table, pushing his hair back off his forehead. *Nice gesture*, Georgia thought. Then he tightened the knot on his tie. A woman in the courtroom cleared her throat.

"May it please the Court?" Ramsey said.

The judge held out his hand.

"I appreciate the obvious feeling and compassion Counselor Kelly has toward his client. In fact, I would expect nothing less from my esteemed colleague. And I concur that Cam Jordan has faced challenges in his life because of his—difficulties. Some he has mastered. Others, he still struggles with. But, if it please the court, let's go back to basics. The question of this hearing is really very simple." He paused and turned around to face the audience. "Do we let an alleged child murderer back on the street to possibly strike again? Or do we keep him where he is and make sure our children and our community are safe?"

Georgia blinked.

"The defendant is thirty-five," Ramsey went on. "And he stands almost six feet tall. His sister …" Ramsey pointed to Ruth, whose face turned crimson, "… is quite small. Let's be candid. If the defendant wanted to break free of her supervision, how difficult would it be? All he would have to do is push her, or shove her, or—God forbid—hit her, and she would likely be compromised.

"But the issue isn't even whether he might or might not harm his sister. The real issue is what he would do if he were allowed out on the street. Here we have a very disturbing pattern. This is a man whose daily walks take him past our public schools, the gathering places for our young. This man is a registered sex offender, with a history of sexual offenses. How are we to believe he won't commit another one, or two, or three offenses? Because the defense promises he won't? How can anyone control this man, given his—personality? Regardless of what the defense claims, the answer is we don't know. And when we don't know, we must err on the side of caution."

Ramsey stepped to the side and brushed his hair off his forehead again. *Damn, he looked sincere.* "Add to that the fact we have incontrovertible evidence that places him at the crime scene when the murder of Sara Long occurred. We have her blood on his shirt. His fingerprints on the bat. Your honor, no matter how you parse it, Cam Jordan is a dangerous man. The law does not allow you to lower his bail. The law does not allow him back out on the street. Indeed, your Honor, if you care about our children, if you care about their safety, you cannot in good conscience agree to this motion. I beg you. Do the right thing."

"Are you running for something, counselor?" the judge asked dryly.

"Your honor, I would run a marathon if it would keep Cam Jordan where he belongs."

Good save, Georgia thought. And he didn't mention a word about the hazing.

Ramsey looked at the judge, then down at the floor, allowing his import to filter through the room. He went back to the table and sat down. The hush in the courtroom deepened. Even the judge was quiet. Georgia looked over at Kelly. When they made eye contact, she knew from his expression they'd lost big.

***

Georgia was on her way out of the courtroom when someone called her name. She turned around. Robby Parker. O'Malley was a few feet behind him. She sighed inwardly. She'd known they'd have to talk at some point. Parker caught up to her, playing with his detective's shield again. *Was he even aware of it*, she wondered.

"How are you, Davis?"

They'd been partners for years, and he still called her Davis. "I'm good, Robby. Congratulations on your promotion."

He drew himself up. "It's a job." He didn't do modesty well. Never had. "I just learned you were working for the defendant."

She didn't say anything.

"Why are you wasting your time on a slam-dunk?"

She tried to hide her irritation. "Obviously, I don't see it the same way."

"How you do or don't see it isn't really the issue."

Was he trying to mimic Ramsey? "What are you talking about?"

"I—we've been getting reports that you've been talking to people. Asking questions."

"That is what an investigator does."

"Most investigators don't impersonate a social worker."

Her muscles locked, and she felt the heat on her cheeks. Tom Walcher, Lauren's father. He'd threatened to go to the cops. She sputtered, casting around for something to say.

O'Malley caught up to them. "Hey, Davis." He looked at her, then at Parker. He must have sensed the hostility between them. He should, Georgia thought. It was rolling off her in waves.

"What's going on?" He asked.

Parker drew himself up. "I was just telling Davis that impersonating a social worker is the kind of thing that can get you into trouble."

"Parker, lay off."

But Parker barreled on. "Not that I blame her. When a case is this clear-cut, people get desperate. They grasp at anything."

"That's enough," O'Malley snapped.

Georgia's throat got thick with anger. She folded her arms and planted herself in front of him. She debated whether to mention Derek Janowitz's homicide and what Sara might have been doing. But why give him a lead, if he didn't already have it?

"Glad you're so confident, Parker. Must be all the great investigative work *you're* doing."

"Oh yeah," he kept going. "There's something else, too. When someone starts asking questions about the daughter of the State's Attorney, they create problems for themselves. Especially if they ever want to come back onto the force."

How dare he patronize her? She hadn't intended to get into a tussle, but now the words tumbled out. "You know something, Robby? If the force is run by people like you, I don't want to come back."

O'Malley cut in. "Look, kids, play nice. You may not realize it, but you're both in the same sandbox." O'Malley loosened his tie. "Parker, you need to learn when to keep your mouth shut. And Davis," he looked over, "You—you …"

She finished for him. "I need to let things slide off my back. Isn't that what you were going to say?"

O'Malley sighed. "From your mouth ..."

But she'd had enough. "Look, Dan. I owe you. You know that. But him ..." She flicked her hand at Parker. "I got no use for him anymore. Keep him away from me."

Before either of them could answer, she wheeled around and went back into the courthouse, shaking her head. She'd become a cop ten years ago because of the loyalty and structure it imposed: the rules, clear procedures, and, despite the occasional squabble, the implicit knowledge that if you watched your partner's back, he'd watch yours. It was like being part of a family, a family she never had. Now, though, that loyalty and structure had frayed, and the family ties were in shreds.

Inside, she started down the hall to the court room. Maybe she'd find Kelly, take him to lunch; congratulate him on his argument even though they'd lost. But as she opened the door, she saw Kelly and Ramsey at the side of the now-empty room, deep in conversation. They were out of earshot, but Ramsey didn't look happy. Georgia turned around and headed back outside.

CHAPTER THIRTY-ONE

GEORGIA MULLED things over as she drove home. Tom Walcher must have gone to the police after all. Or maybe it was Ramsey he'd complained to. He'd boasted of having connections; but she had no way of knowing how strong they were. Was there a relationship between the two men? Did the men have business connections? Did their spouses work together on Newfield school activities?

Or was Walcher just the kind of guy who liked to buddy up to cops? She'd run into cop-wannabes when she was on the force, guys who scanned police radio frequencies and showed up at crime scenes, sometimes even before the cops. Others hung out at cop bars and restaurants. You had to be careful with them. From time to time they might actually have valuable information, but there might be a quid pro quo when they surrendered it.

She wouldn't have figured Walcher for a wannabe, but, ultimately, it didn't matter which type he was. Or who he'd talked to. Parker was a pompous asshole, but he was right about one thing. It had been a mistake to impersonate a social worker. It wouldn't happen again.

She drove west on Old Orchard Road. A country club took up one side of the road; a cemetery the other. It was a gray day, and the air felt wet and raw. A few dispirited leaves still clung to tree branches, but they weren't able to muster much fire.

She reviewed what she knew about Derek Janowitz. Was he the one who spread fish guts in the hallway of her apartment? The descriptions matched. But was it his idea? Or could it have been his partner's? And how could she find out who that partner was? She needed to. Whoever it was could be the only remaining link to Sara Long.

She thought about going to Derek's apartment and trying to bully her way in to question his roommates. But they'd just endured a rough police interrogation; they'd slam the door in her face. The police had his PDA in any case. A better solution would be to get his cell phone records. She knew his number.

Some people might bicker about the ethics and legality of obtaining cell phone records without subpoenas. Frankly, before she was suspended, she might have, too. But if she was going to be a PI and work big cases, she couldn't be squeamish about her sources. The police had resources—indeed, access to them was one of the things she missed about being a cop. As a PI, she was a lone ranger, relying on contacts and connections to get what she needed.

Sure, there was a trade-off: tracking bad guys versus infringing—at least a little—on people's privacy. Still, for a couple of hundred dollars, she could get Derek Janowitz's cell phone records, and she would have a slew of new leads, any number of which might lead to his partner.

Back home, she called a PI who'd referred a case to her a few months ago. He gave her the name and number of someone in Florida. Five minutes later, after surrendering her credit card number, the number of the cell she wanted to trace, and the dates she needed, she was told they had a heavy backlog. The results would be emailed to her within seven business days.

She hung up the phone and looked around. It was on nights like these that she felt the weight of time and how untethered she was. She had no ties any more, emotional or otherwise. Her mother abandoned her when she was a child, leaving her with a father who ended up loving the bottle more than her. He'd died seven years ago. She was alone now. But she was free, white, and twenty-one, an expression her father liked to repeat between shots. She'd decided that freedom was an overrated concept.

She went around her apartment and lit candles. Although she didn't collect things anymore, she couldn't bring herself to throw out her candles. Some were scented, and she breathed in mint, coconut, and berry. When they were all lit, she lay down on her couch and watched their lights flicker. The candles helped chase away the void, providing clarity and definition. They reminded her that, like them, she'd once had fire and heat.

***

Friday morning Georgia went to the gym to work out. Afterwards she stopped for a cup of coffee at a gas station. A radio inside the mini-mart was tuned to the all-news station. She had just forked over a dollar to the guy behind the counter, congratulating herself that she wasn't springing for a three-dollar latte, when the female anchor came on in the tense, breathy voice that says they have important news. "This just in. State's Attorney Jeff Ramsey has announced he will recuse himself from the murder trial of Cameron Jordan. Jordan, if you remember, was indicted for killing teenager Sara Long in the Cook County Forest Preserve last month."

Georgia looked up, startled. The man behind the counter didn't notice.

"In a statement, Ramsey said the situation has turned out to be more complicated than first thought. Ramsey admitted that his teenage daughter was present in the Forest Preserve during the hazing incident that preceded the homicide. Monica Ramsey is a senior at Newfield High School.

"Ramsey turned over the prosecution of the case to his second in command and said his daughter will cooperate fully. He hastened to say she is not a suspect in the homicide, nor is she directly connected to the crime. He made the decision to recuse himself to avoid even the appearance of conflict of interest. Stay tuned for more developments in this breaking story."

The broadcast cut to a commercial about a car dealership in Arlington Heights. The man behind the counter absently handed over her change. He hadn't heard a word. Georgia pocketed the coins and took her coffee outside. She thought back to the bail reduction hearing. Ramsey had won. No contest. Then she flashed to his conversation with Kelly in the courtroom afterwards. Ramsey hadn't looked like a winner then. He'd looked worried.

Sliding the coffee into the cup holder in her car, she pulled out her cell and punched in Paul Kelly's number. The call went to voice mail. She left a message.

Kelly had berated Georgia about going after Monica Ramsey. So what if the girl was at the Forest Preserve, he said? You don't make a case out of innuendo and hearsay. They couldn't go after the State's Attorney's daughter. Evidently, something had changed.

By evening she still hadn't reached Kelly but at least now she knew why. He'd been giving interviews to the press all day. The story was all over the news, with dueling sound bites from both Ramsey and Kelly. First, Ramsey: "The most important thing to remember is that nothing that's happened has altered the facts of Sara Long's murder. We have the offender. We believe he did it, and that he acted alone. However, our office will make every effort to get *all* the facts."

Then, a quote from Kelly: "It was clear from the beginning that the State's Attorney's Office was attempting to rush Cam Jordan through the system without the proper investigation and care. Now we know why. I think the charges against my client should be dropped." Kelly turned his head so he was looking at the camera when he spoke, which gave the impression the he was talking directly to the people. *Slick,* Georgia thought.

Sandwiched between the sound bites were reporters, most of them broadcasting live from the Skokie Courthouse. However, one enterprising woman was staked out at Sara Long's Wilmette home. The Longs wouldn't comment on camera, but issued a statement that read, in part: "We hope today's developments will not deter the course of justice. There is not a minute of any day that we do not grieve the loss of our daughter and what she suffered. We want to see justice served, no matter where it leads."

Did they really? Georgia wondered. What if the pursuit of justice revealed that their daughter was a whore?

She switched to the public television station and found pundits shouting at each other in the rude discourse that passes for debate these days. Republicans clamoring for Ramsey's head suggested he pack his bags and go back to New York.

"Don't be absurd," countered a woman with long hair and a dour expression. "He'll ride this out. And rise above it. It was a gutsy thing to do."

"It was the responsible thing to do," someone else said.

"It was the only thing to do," said someone else.

A discussion about ethics followed, and a florid-faced man with white hair pronounced the real winners the people of Cook County. The system worked, and we were all the better for it, he proclaimed.

Georgia snapped off the TV and went into the kitchen. Rummaging through the fridge for something to eat, she settled on a grilled cheese sandwich. She threw bread and cheese into the frying pan. She didn't know who was right about Ramsey, but she did know one thing. It was easy to be gutsy when your back was up against the wall.

CHAPTER THIRTY-TWO

HER CASE was heating up. Matt continued to tail her up and down the North Shore. To Burhops, the courthouse, even to Mickey's, where she had dinner with her neighbor. He checked out the guy later; a state bureaucrat. Probably nothing to do with her case. He read the reports about Ramsey, and he wondered if the State's Attorney's recusal had anything to do with her work.

Things were heating up for him, too. Especially after he reported how she'd tailed the Walcher girl to the health club. Matt wasn't part of the inner circle, but he noticed several closed-door meetings between Lenny and his employer, and when the man wasn't in conference, he was on the phone. Then, a few days ago, Lenny disappeared. Just up and left. R&R, his employer said; the guy needed a break. Just a coincidence that Lenny took off right after the kid who worked at the gas station was killed. The one she visited.

With Lenny gone his employer was pressing Matt. Calling his cell ten times a day, demanding to know where she was and who was she talking to. He knew better than to ask why, but he sensed something had shifted. Intensified. He started to watch more carefully, measured every word, alert for clues, subtle mood shifts, even double entendres.

He wasn't sleeping well. The stress was getting to him. But this was his gig—he'd wanted it. Except this time he was flying solo. There were no rules, no guidelines about what to do when. He wondered how he'd perform when they gave him a job that required more than surveillance. He needed to come through. He had a feeling he knew what that job was going to be. And he couldn't let his personal feelings get in the way.

CHAPTER THIRTY-THREE

AT FIRST Georgia didn't hear the knock at her door. She was working on the computer and the TV was on. When the tapping persisted, she thought about ignoring it. She was in the middle of searching articles on teenage prostitution. Then she realized whoever was there probably could hear the TV's babble from the hall and knew she was home. Easier just to get rid of them.

She opened the door to see her upstairs neighbor, Pete Dellinger, leaning on a pair of crutches.

Her eyes widened. "What happened to you?"

He smiled sheepishly. "Fractured my ankle playing basketball two days ago."

She opened the door wider. "Well, I guess you'd better come in and sit down." So much for getting rid of them.

He hobbled in. He'd cut off the right jeans leg, and the leg was encased in plaster from his toes to his knee. She examined the cast. "All that for an ankle?"

He shrugged, or as good a facsimile as he could while manipulating the crutches. When he reached the couch, he turned around and leaned the crutches against it. Plopping down on the cushions, he blew out a breath.

Georgia followed him over. "Does it hurt?"

"Not too much." He patted his shirt pocket. "Vicodin."

She nodded. "What can I get you?"

"You got a beer?"

"You're on Vicodin."

"One beer won't kill me."

She eyed him, then shook her head. "Sorry. I don't drink."

He frowned. "Then what were you doing at Mickey's the other night?"

"Making a mistake." She shot him a look, daring him to contradict her.

He looked back. Then his eyebrows smoothed out. "No problem. I'll take whatever you have."

She went into the kitchen, got out a couple of Snapples and poured them into glasses. Coming back into the living room, she handed one over. "Did you at least make the shot?" She pointed to his foot.

"Nope. Lost by two points."

"The final indignity." She settled on the other end of the couch. "What about your job? Can you work?"

"I'm a bureaucrat. I'm always able to push paper around."

She thought back to his comments about fish waste and how to dispose of them. "You do environmental stuff?"

He grinned. "Nope. But I used to go fly fishing with my father in the North Woods." He paused. "I work for the State of Illinois. In the Department of Agriculture's Bureau of Weights and Measures."

"Never heard of it."

"I'm the director."

"Oh." She crossed her legs uncertainly.

"Don't worry. No one else knows we exist either," he said. "And with any luck, we'll keep it that way."

"What do you do?"

"I travel around the state measuring and weighing products."

"Why?"

"To make sure you get what you pay for. For example, I make sure you're really getting a gallon of gas, a bushel of potatoes, or a pound of hamburger."

"How?"

"I weigh things. With my scales."

"You have a special set?"

"I do. See, most people take for granted they're getting what they pay for. But the cost of even tiny inaccuracies can add up. For example, an error of one tablespoon per five gallons of gas can mean $125 million a year."

"No kidding." She tried to look interested.

"Yeah." He seemed to be warming to his subject. "And when you compute the added costs of—" He cut himself off. "Hey. You don't really care about this, do you?"

"Not really," she smiled.

"That's okay. No one else does either." He sipped his drink and looked around the living room. "You live—sparingly."

Her smile disappeared. "What does that mean?"

"It's just that you don't have a lot of things, you know? Pictures, knick-knacks, vases."

She imagined the home he used to share with his wife. It was probably stuffed with "things." She looked around, trying to see her place through his eyes. It did look bare. Untended. Still. She felt a grain of irritation. "I'm not into clutter."

He backtracked. "I didn't mean to—actually I like it this way. More space."

She figured he was lying but let it go.

"So, what's been happening with your case?"

She set the glass on the coffee table. "You watch the news tonight?"

He nodded. "I had a feeling you were involved."

She filled him in, including her suspicions about Sara Long and Derek Janowitz. He listened so intently that her irritation dissolved, but when she finished, he shot her a disbelieving look. "Are you saying a bunch of suburban teenagers are running their own prostitution ring?"

"It might be tied into a larger operation." She explained about Derek's Eastern European roommates. "You wouldn't happen to know anything about that, would you?" She teased.

"Me?" A flush crept up his neck. "No. But I don't run in those—oh, never mind." He threw his arm over the back of the couch. "Tell me something. Why would girls do something like this?"

He'd asked the same question she'd been mulling over. "Money, mostly."

Pete shook his head. "Pretty extreme way to make it."

"Depends on your perspective," Georgia said. "You make a lot of money in a short period of time. And all you have to do is take off your clothes and fuck someone."

He gazed at her. She wondered what was going through his mind. Then he said, "Does that mean the Monica Ramsey angle is a dead end?"

"I'll continue to pursue it. But this—well, this could lead in a very different direction. It might turn out the only thing the Ramsey girl is guilty of is showing up at the Forest Preserve on the day Sara Long was killed."

He went quiet again and sipped his Snapple, then held it out and examined it. "This is good. I've never had it before."

"It's pricey, but I like it too."

He set down the glass and motioned to the computer. "I interrupted you."

"It's okay."

"What are you doing?"

"You really want to know?"

"It's got to be more interesting than weighing produce."

Georgia pulled one of the kitchen chairs over to her desk. Pete got himself across the room on his crutches.

An hour later, they'd printed out and skimmed half a dozen articles about suburban teenage hookers. How girls were approached at malls and recruited with promises of clothes, makeup, and accessories. How one girl started stripping in hotel rooms and "graduated" to placing ads on a personals service. How the term "Trix are for Kids" had a new meaning when girls as young as nine were recruited. They read how educated girls—particularly blondes—were considered preferable, because they worked harder and brought in more money. How the johns in the suburbs were mostly family men in SUVs with baby seats in the back. They also found an article on a new breed of pimp: "Popcorn pimps," high school students themselves.

"Maybe I'm hopelessly naive, but I still don't get it," Pete said.

"Get what?"

His brow wrinkled, and he looked almost pained. "Why?"

Georgia pointed to the pile of articles. "What it says there. Money. Independence. A sense of power."

"Still, for a girl to go to bed with someone at that age, just for what you can earn … ."

"Actually, I think there's something else at work."

"What?"

"Peer pressure."

"Huh?"

"Status—the acquisition of things—is so much more important for kids today. I saw that when I was on the force. It's not about having a pair of jeans from Gap. It's about having a four hundred dollar pair of jeans. It's not about having a Walkman or a stereo; it's about having an iPod. Or an iPhone. Or a Blackberry." She paused. "You can't get those things working at Starbucks or McDonald's."

"So they're having sex for them?"

"Tell me something. If your parents can't afford to buy them for you, and you can't earn enough money to buy them yourself, what are your options? Besides shoplifting?"

The monitor cast a bluish light over his face. He looked upset.

"Think about it," she went on. "For years girls have been getting the message that flaunting and using their bodies is okay. Some of them have just taken it to the next level. So what if you give a few blow jobs? Fuck a few men? If that's what it takes to buy a Michael Stars shirt or a pair of Jimmy Choos ..."

"I suppose I could understand if they were older. Over twenty-one and on their own. But these are teenagers. Living at home. From good families."

Georgia didn't answer.

He fidgeted on the couch. "Whatever happened to kids going steady? Dating? Proms?"

"There's still some of that." She leaned back. "But a lot of teenagers don't date like we used to. Or do romance."

"Come on."

"I didn't say they're not having sex. They are. In fact, it's all about hooking up. Friends with benefits. That's what they call it."

"Call what?"

"Sex without complications. Or consequences. Or even real connections. Like I said, maybe teenage hookers are just ..." she paused "... the natural evolution of that."

He frowned. "How do you know all this?"

"I told you. I used to be the youth officer on the force."

He didn't say anything. Then he flipped his hand sideways, knocking his crutch off the chair. It clattered to the floor. "What about their parents? Do they know what their kids are doing?"

She leaned over and picked up his crutch. An image of Sara Long's parents came into her mind. "They're working their asses off, trying to make ends meet and give their kids a better life."

He went quiet. Then, "Both of my parents worked. I'll bet yours did too. But you didn't turn into a hooker, and I didn't end up a pimp. Doesn't it bother you?"

"It bothers me more when one of those girls gets killed."

Pete laced his hands behind his head. "You've got it all figured out, don't you?"

Georgia stood up. "Do you have a sister?"

Pete nodded. "She's twenty-nine. Lives in California."

"What would you do if you found out she was hooking?"

His brows knit. "She wouldn't."

"Are you sure?"

"Why? What are you implying?"

"I'm just asking."

"I guess the real answer is I don't know. We're not that close."

Georgia glanced at the monitor, then back at Pete. "Maybe you should be."

***

After Pete left Georgia went through the articles again. One mentioned how prostitution had gone online. How if you knew the right websites, you could register by email, enter your zip code, even request a specific girl. Twenty-four hours later you'd get a response—guaranteed. The article went on to say how pimps no longer had to troll the streets any more. With a computer and a high-speed modem, they could run girls from the comfort of home.

She took the empty glasses into the kitchen and rinsed them. When she interviewed Jerry Horner at the gas station, he'd told her how Derek claimed you could get anything you wanted online these days. "The future of the world was in that damn little mouse," he'd said.

She hurried back to her computer. Starting with Google, she entered "Escort Services." A flood of websites surfaced; so many she was overwhelmed. She re-entered the words, this time adding the word, "Chicago." She was still inundated. She started clicking through them. Most had photos of nude women—all of them young and glamorous—in provocative poses. The text invited you to request either a blonde, a brunette, an Asian. Others touted European beauties or Polish princesses.

She ran an irritated hand through her hair. How were these websites allowed to operate so brazenly? Granted, the term "escort service" was a euphemism, but judging from these websites, there was no difference between "escort" and "prostitute." There ought to be some way to come down on them, shut them down. Then again, vice was always the poor stepchild of every police operation. The oldest profession still didn't merit the same attention as narcotics or rape or even identity theft. Moreover, a lot of these websites originated offshore, well beyond the reach of U.S. law. In the unlikely event they were shut down, they would simply resurface the next day on another back alley of the Internet.

She kept going, tunneling deeper into online sex. It disturbed her to see pictures of women touching themselves or each other with rapturous, come-hither expressions. Who were these girls? Did they come from families like Sara Long's? Most looked over twenty-one, but how could you really tell? Were some of the girls' smiles pasted on? Did some of those toothy grins mask an air of desperation?

She remembered a woman she'd met last year. Mika had left her home in Eastern Europe after the Soviet Union collapsed. She'd fallen into a white slavery operation run by the Russian mafia. Georgia remembered her own rage and helplessness when she'd heard about it. Rage at the exploitation, helplessness because she couldn't do anything about it.

She stared at the screen, wanting to transfer some of that rage to Derek Janowitz. He was the pimp. The recruiter. But he was dead. Whether or not his death had anything to do with his pimping, he'd paid dearly. And to be fair, she couldn't hold him solely accountable. She thought back to the expensive clothes she'd seen in Sara's closet. If Sara *was* hooking, presumably she was profiting from the arrangement.

After slogging through more websites and come-ons, Georgia spotted a link to a site that offered "hot young babes."When she clicked, another montage of naked women popped up. The text claimed they were under twenty-one, but some of the women, clearly older, had braided hair tied with gingham ribbons, and wore bobby sox on their feet. Others had no pubic hair and were positioned in gangly teenager poses.

She clicked on the photo of the youngest looking girl and was immediately taken to a website with no name, just an IP address. There were no photos or text on the site either, with the exception of a request for a zip code. She entered the zip for Newfield High School. A moment later, a registration form popped up that asked for her email, a user name, and password. Underneath that, she was to fill in what she was looking for and the dates she wanted her "escort."

She started to fill out the form. She typed in her e-mail address, entered "Everready" as a user name, and chose a numeric password. She said she was looking for a sixteen year old blonde, and that she was available any weekday after four. She was about to enter the information when she paused, her finger on the enter key.

She had no idea what she was signing up for, no idea if it would get her closer to Derek Janowitz's operation. She wasn't even sure he used the Internet to get johns. The fact that it asked for a zip code made her think the site was part of a national consortium or partnership, but for all she knew she might have stumbled onto a mob-run operation. It could be dangerous to give them her email address. She deleted her entries, wrote down the IP address, and clicked off

She started to pace around the apartment. When you were puzzling out a case, O'Malley used to say, change your environment. Get up, take a walk, go work out. He claimed it restored the right-brain left-brain balance, made it easier to receive new input.

She went to the window and opened it. Spits of water clung to the glass, and the streets had that pleasant but sandy wet asphalt smell. It must have rained earlier. The wind was whipping the leaves. Her favorite part of autumn, the sweet part, was coming to a close; the harsh winds of November would soon strip the trees, leaving nothing but bare, gnarled branches.

Directly across the street from her was a two-story bungalow. Three little kids lived there. A tricycle and wagon lay on the front lawn. A modest embankment edged the back. The kids' mother must have been too tired or too frazzled to bring the toys inside tonight. Georgia hoped no one would steal them. She liked the kids, thought they were cute. But the thought of having her own family filled her with dread. What would she do when they became teenagers? How would she keep them from turning into Sara Longs?

She closed the window. She just couldn't see herself as a mother. When she tried, the picture went all snowy and gray, like a TV station that's signed off for the night.

CHAPTER THIRTY-FOUR

GEORGIA REACHED Kelly Saturday morning. He sounded like he was still high from his adventures of the previous day.

"So, what did you think?"

"You said you weren't going to play Ramsey. That it could be dangerous."

"I rethought it. And hey, it worked."

"Temporarily. They're still moving ahead with the case."

"They're just trying to save face. Public opinion is swinging our way. They know it's not a slam dunk anymore."

"What about Cam Jordan?" Georgia asked.

"What about him?"

"Given Ramsey's recusal, and the fact that people are taking note of it, wouldn't this be a good time to try again to get him released on bond?"

"Already done."

"Really?"

I filed another motion for a bail reduction hearing. It's on Tuesday."

***

This time the hearing was perfunctory and short. The news had been full of stories about Jeff Ramsey and his political future over the weekend; public opinion was running high. Both newspapers ran editorials disparaging Ramsey's behavior, radio and TV commentary followed suit, and the political blogs kept the issue front and center. Reporters staked out in front of his house. There was a shot of Monica coming out the front door with her face averted—her father must have warned her about the cameras.

Despite earnest arguments by a senior assistant State's Attorney, the judge entered a decision to release Cam Jordan on bond. Georgia drove his sister over to Cook County jail. Cam Jordan emerged a few hours later, looking pale and thin. Georgia, who gave them a ride back to Ruth Jordan's house, felt optimistic. Although it wasn't over—the legal process would go forward—for the first time since taking Cam's case, something had gone right. She was serving the cause of justice.

Back in her apartment, she brewed a pot of coffee and sat in the kitchen. Afternoon sun glittered through the leaves, splashing shifting patterns of light and shadow across the table. She was staring at them, sipping her coffee, when an idea occurred to her.

She went to her computer and connected to Craig's List. Accessing the Chicago page, she clicked on "Erotic" services. A warning about adult content popped up, along with a plea for safe sex and an admonition that users must be over 18.

When she clicked again, she was taken to a succession of messages, all offering sexual services of one kind or another. Page after page, in groups of 100, contained come-ons, ads, and photos of women, many in lewd poses. Georgia scanned them, paying close attention to pictures of blondes. She didn't expect to see a picture of Sara, not really. Still, she had to check.

An hour later, she'd found nothing. No face even remotely familiar. She took that as a good sign. Then she pulled out a list of the prostitution websites she'd visited with Pete. She'd written down over thirty URLs. She went back to the computer and clicked over to WHOIS, a database of websites created by the largest domain registration service on the Net. WHOIS catalogued who owned each site, and provided both an administrative and technical contact.

One by one Georgia typed in the URLs from her list. Most were registered to corporations, which, when she cross-referenced them on Google, turned out to be hosting websites. The contacts led back to the web host's customer service department. She wasn't surprised—web hosts were as sensitive to privacy issues as everyone else and usually honored their customers' request for anonymity. If she was still on the force, she might have been able to get a subpoena to break through. Unfortunately, she wasn't.

After checking twenty websites, she became frustrated. Some of the sites, although they featured American girls, were registered in countries like Russia or Poland. Others were in Barbados, even the Sudan. She'd only found the names of two individuals: one was in Toronto, the other in Santa Monica. Derek might have been connected to them—geography has no meaning on the Internet—but she had no way to verify it.

Only ten websites were left on her list. She typed in nine more URL's. Nothing. She sighed. It'd seemed like a good idea an hour ago. She plugged in the last URL and watched green bars march across the bottom of the screen, followed by the jump to a new page. Nothing.

She got up. Her back ached, and she had a headache from too much time hunched over the monitor. If Janowitz did run a prostitution website, he must have known enough to cloak himself in cyberspace. She'd wasted almost an entire afternoon.

She was back in the kitchen staring out the window when she heard the chirp of an incoming email. She went back to retrieve it. The message was from her Florida contact, and it contained an attachment. The cell phone records. She'd almost forgotten.

She clicked on the attachment. At the top of the page was 847-555-4586, Derek's cell number, followed by the dates she'd requested, and a list of at least three hundred calls. She scrolled down. Derek received almost forty calls a day. Most of the calls were preceded by 847, the area code for the North Shore. That made sense. But there were a few 773's, 312s, and two she didn't recognize.

She went back to the top of the list. If Derek had a partner, she reasoned, the partner's number would show up more than once or twice. She reviewed the log carefully. Six or seven numbers popped up frequently. Of those, two numbers recurred more than the others. Both had an 847 area code. She reached for the phone and punched in the first number. The phone rang once. A tingle ran up her spine. It rang again. Then it clicked. "The number you are trying to reach is not in service at this time."

Was that Sara's cell? Had it been disconnected now that she was dead? She ended the call. Then she dialed the other number. She closed her eyes, waiting for the call to connect. It rang once. Again. A third time. Then it went to voice mail. She held her breath.

"This is Lauren. Leave a number and I'll call you back."

***

Lauren leaned over, picked her Cole Haan purse off the floor, and put it in her lap. She was in History class, and you weren't supposed to have your cell on in school. She kept hers on vibrate so the teachers wouldn't notice.

In fact, she had two phones: one for business and one for her personal use. Her parents didn't know about the business phone, and she intended to keep it that way. She looked inside the bag. The call had come in on her personal cell, but the number was blocked. That bothered her. No one she knew had any reason to block their number when they called her. Did someone have the numbers mixed up? Doubtful. Derek and Sara were the only ones who called both numbers, and they were both dead.

Maybe it was Heather, playing another of her investigative reporter games.

She and Claire both—although how could you get mad at Claire?—still called or text messaged her six times a day with stupid questions like "what do you think of Alicia's nose ring?"; "Will you pick me up on Saturday?" "Did you see what Cash was wearing?"

Lauren had been like that, but moved on when she started the business. So did Sara. They'd put immature games behind them.

Which made it awkward when the girls still peppered them with questions. They'd kept the business a secret, but it hadn't been easy. That's why Sara was always asking questions about who knew what about whom. Lauren had warned her to be careful, not to push it, but Sara was stubborn. Part of it was that she wanted to be liked—doesn't everyone?—but that wasn't what drove her. Some girls, Heather for example, equated power with beauty or information. Not Sara. For her it was simple. She craved the things money could buy. She'd been clear about that from the start. But she didn't want the slightest whiff of attention focused on the business.

The funny thing was that when you stopped to think about it, Sara was probably better suited to the profession than Lauren. Money wasn't important to Lauren; she'd grown up with it. Sara hadn't. In fact, Lauren had been meaning to talk to Sara about the amount of time she spent turning tricks. She never said no, and there were times she should have. But they'd drifted apart recently, and their friendship had become strained. Lauren wasn't sure why.

Now she stared at the blackboard, only dimly aware of the discussion about the Monroe Doctrine. The PI knew Sara came to the Forest Preserve to talk to Lauren. Sara's mother told her. Lauren figured Sara was concerned that someone might have discovered the business. But what if she was wrong? What if something else was on Sara's mind? Maybe Sara came to the Forest Preserve to tell Lauren she was sorry they'd grown apart. That she wanted to get close again. A pang of regret shot through Lauren. Maybe if she had, things would have turned out differently.

No. That was retarded. It wouldn't make any difference now. Lauren crammed the phone back in her bag and tried to pay attention in class. If the person who called wanted her badly enough, they'd try again.

***

But no one did, and by that night, she forgot about it. She was busy working the website; it was almost the middle of the week; requests were heating up. Usually she didn't mind. She liked the online side of the business. Working online made it seem more remote. Cleaner. Derek had set everything up. He'd even created a simple file sharing system for notes and records. She could match up a customer and a girl in less than five minutes.

She opened the incoming messages. Two requests for the next afternoon. She started to check the girls' schedules to see who was available, then stopped. First Sara was killed. After her, Derek. Was there a connection? Could the PI be onto something? Maybe the crazy guy in the Forest Preserve didn't do it. Lauren couldn't see how—the cops were sure he did. But maybe—somehow—it was somebody else. Someone in the business. Did Sara stiff someone? Did Derek? She didn't know, and not knowing made her anxious.

What if someone wanted them out of the way? She remembered warning Derek not to get too big. That they were inviting trouble. Bigger fish might swallow them up. As usual, he didn't listen, and now he was dead. Not even a month after Sara. Could Sara's death be a warning? A warning Derek didn't any pay attention to? Was it possible they might come after her now?

A knot of fear tightened her stomach. She hadn't counted on anything like this happening when she started the business. She'd wanted to keep it local. Small. But then Derek got involved, and suddenly they were running a dozen girls up and down the North Shore. Without Derek, though, it was too much. She couldn't do it alone. Especially if someone had it in for her.

Maybe she should scale back the business. Keep a low profile. Stay out of trouble. At least until things settled down. Sure. That's what she would do. She'd email her clients. Tell them they would be on a reduced schedule—a few girls were on vacation. Yes. That sounded good. They'd be back in a few weeks, tanned and rested and hotter than ever.

She sent the email to her client list, then plugged her iPod into her computer, and downloaded some Ashlee Simpson. She could hear her mother puttering around in the kitchen. She was on the phone, as usual. Lauren remembered a book—by Dean Koontz, maybe—where people actually melded with their computers. Sentient machines swallowed up the humans—body part by body part—in a morbid, kinky attack. The result was a monster half human, half computer. She imagined a phone growing out of her mother's ear. Knowing her mother, she'd see it as some kind of achievement, something to lord over the rest of the world.

Lauren transferred the music to her iPod. Usually she could figure out who her mother was talking to by her tone. If it was cold and hostile, her mother was talking to her father. If she was cool and patronizing, to a repairman or a store employee. But occasionally, there was a soft, honeyed tone. Lauren didn't want to know who that was.

She was lying on her bed, just starting to relax, when her business cell chirped. She considered ignoring it. She didn't want to do any business tonight. But the ring-tone, ironically cheerful and upbeat, persisted. Reluctantly, she rolled over and grabbed it.

"Yeah?" Derek always told her not to identify herself. As if she didn't know.

It was a girl's voice. Halting. Tearful. "I—I need help."

She checked the caller ID. She didn't recognize the number. "Who is this?"

"Jj- Ja- Jathmine."

One of the girls Derek recruited. Korean, she recalled. "What's the matter?"

"I'm—I'm in trouble."

A panicky feeling lodged in her throat. "What's the problem?"

"I'm hurt," she stammered.

"Where are you?"

A flood of tears kept Lauren from hearing her reply.

"I can't understand you."

In between sobs, the girl repeated herself. She was at a motel in Chicago. On the North side.

"What are you doing there?" Lauren said sharply. "You're supposed to be at—"

The girl's sobs filled her ear.

"Never mind," Lauren said. "I'm coming."

"I'm in Room 254. Hur—Hurry. Pleathe."

Lauren snapped off the phone. Her heart was pounding. She looked around her room, trying to figure out what she should bring. A first-aid kit? Tranquilizers? Vicodin? Derek usually handled the onsite things. That was their system. She was just back-up. She didn't even know the girl. Derek had found her at Golf Mill. She was smart, he said. And ambitious. Wanted to put herself through college.

She quickly grabbed some antiseptic, bandages, scissors, and gauze from the bathroom. She wasn't at all sure that's what was needed, but she had to take something. She stuffed the things into her bag. Then she crept downstairs, tiptoed past the kitchen, and out the front door.

CHAPTER THIRTY-FIVE

THE FAIRVIEW Motel sat just off Clark Street on a seedy, forgotten block near the city line. The view from its windows was mostly fast food places and shabby warehouses. Whoever named the place must have had a sense of humor. The "E" in the motel sign sputtered and the "W" was missing altogether.

Lauren had never been here before; she made sure the girls went to upscale hotels on the North Shore. In fact, she'd only been to one other rescue job, and the girl had been waiting in the bar of the Hyatt. Thankfully, nothing showed, and the girl had been able to blend in.

Lauren got out of the car. The asphalt in the parking lot was cracked and littered with cans, bottles, and food wrappers. The smell of grease from the burger place next door stuck in her throat. She was alone. And she was about to rescue someone she didn't know. A trickle of fear slid down her back. She took a breath and fastened the buttons on her Urban

Outfitters blazer. Room 254 was around the back. She walked up to it and knocked. Twice, then three times. That was the signal.

The girl who opened the door was tiny, with black, shiny hair that hung to her waist. Ordinarily, she would have appeared cute, elfin, but now her hair was tangled and matted, and her clothes, a tight black tank top showing plenty of midriff and a black miniskirt, were torn. She cradled her left arm in her right.

But it was her face that made Lauren gasp. Bruises under one eye made a swollen mockery of her features. An angry red gash streaked across her cheek. Smaller slashes swept across her arms and legs. It looked like someone had taken a razor blade to her skin.

"Jasmine?" Lauren gripped the door.

The girl nodded, swaying unsteadily.

"Who did this to you?" Lauren's voice was hoarse from fear.

The girl shook her head. Shit. Lauren should have checked the file before she came. But there was no time for self-recrimination, because the girl burst into tears and pitched forward. Lauren broke her fall. The girl screamed.

"I think my arm ith broken."

Lauren released her and sat her down on the bed. She gently touched Jasmine's arm. The girl howled. Lauren went to the bathroom and snatched a towel off the rack. Slipping it under Jasmine's arm, she fashioned a clumsy sling and tied it around her neck.

Jasmine looked up, tears streaming down her cheeks. Then she collapsed against Lauren, as if she'd been hoarding her last ounce of strength until she arrived. Lauren put her arm around the girl's good shoulder. It felt unfamiliar and awkward. She wasn't sure how long she sat there, listening to Jasmine weep. Eventually, the cries subsided.

Lauren dropped her arm. "Can you stand? We need to go into the bathroom so I can check you out."

Jasmine stood up and started to walk but stopped abruptly. A fresh round of tears materialized. "Hurths," she cried. "Down there." She tried to point to her crotch.

Lauren half pushed, half propelled her into the bathroom, and made her sit on the toilet seat.

"What happened?"

Jasmine pointed to the bed. When Lauren looked she saw drops of blood on the sheets. Bright red. Her throat tightened. She forced down air.

"He—he hurt me."

"Where?"

Jasmine shook her head. "My legth."

Lauren relaxed fractionally, then realized the girl was lisping. "What's wrong with your mouth?"

The girl opened her mouth and stuck out her tongue. Lauren recoiled. Her tongue had been pierced, but someone—or something—had torn the stud from its hole, and the tip of her tongue was a bloody pulp.

Lauren squeezed her eyes shut. "How did this happen?"

"He got mad when I took out my tongue stud. He had a razor."

"He cut your tongue?"

She nodded.

"Oh my God."

"It hurts," Jasmine wailed. "Really bad."

Lauren's mind raced. The girl needed a doctor. But she couldn't take her to the ER without answering a lot of questions. And which ER should she go to, anyway? How would she pay for it? She and Derek hadn't planned for this contingency. Sure, they knew there were perverts out there, but Derek was supposed to have screened them out. Unless Jasmine was freelancing. A strange hotel, not in the prescribed geographical area. Lauren's eyes narrowed. "Who was the john, Jasmine? How did you hook up with him?"

"Derek hooked us up."

So much for freelancing. "Was this the first time?"

Jasmine shook her head and held up three fingers.

"What about the first two times?"

"He wath fine. Then, I don't know. He'd been drinking. I didn't want to come here. The latht time we went thomeplace nicer. But when I told him I'd meet him there, he thaid no. We had to come here."

"You shouldn't have."

"He thaid he'd talked to Derek and it wath okay."

"It wasn't."

"I want to go home. I want my mother. I'm—" Fresh tears welled in her eyes.

Damn Derek. And damn Sara. Damn them both for leaving her alone. Things were out of control. Maybe she should just drop the girl at the ER and drive away. No. The police would be there in a heartbeat, and Jasmine would tell them everything. She pressed her lips together. "I'll take care of you. Just give me a minute."

"What are you gonna do? Where are we gonna go?"

Lauren looked around the room, refusing to meet her eyes. For the first time in her life, she didn't know.

***

Georgia watched as Lauren emerged from the motel twenty minutes later. Her arm was draped around a tiny Asian girl. Together they shuffled toward her SUV. The dim light cast patchy, elongated shadows over the parking lot, but Georgia could see the girl was hunched over and favoring her left arm. Both girls kept their heads down, but when Lauren looked up to flash the remote key at her car, she looked shaken.

Georgia, parked about two hundred feet away, threw open the door to her Toyota. "Lauren!" she called sharply.

Lauren froze. "Who's there?"

The girl couldn't see her in the dark. "It's Georgia Davis." The girl stiffened. Georgia got out of her car and jogged over. For a moment, Lauren looked like she wanted to bolt, but then, as if realizing it was a lost cause, she sagged against her car. The other girl looked fearfully from Georgia to Lauren.

"What are you doing here?" Lauren asked.

"I've been following you." She stepped closer and studied the other girl. "This girl needs help."

"I know."

"Where are you taking her?"

Lauren looked at the ground. "I—I was going to call one of my—a friend."

Georgia frowned. "Why?"

Lauren looked at Jasmine, then back at Georgia. She shrugged help-lessly. "I—I didn't—I don't know what to do."

Georgia nodded. She took a step toward Jasmine. "Help me get her into my car."

"Where are we going?"

"To the ER."

Lauren cried out. "No! I can't!"

"This isn't about you."

"But—we'd be—the police—it would ruin everything!"

Georgia shook her head. "Too late. She's got to be seen by a doctor."

"Can't I just—drop her off or something?"

"Nooo!" Jasmine started to wail again. "I don't want to be alone."

"Please." Lauren turned around and shot Georgia a beseeching look. "There's got to be another way. Please. I—I'm so scared." It wasn't cold out, but she was shivering.

Georgia considered it. Lauren was clearly in over her head. And she was right about one thing. If they went to the ER, it would only take a cursory examination of Jasmine before the police were called. She remembered reporting to the ER for a couple of domestics when she was on the force. She'd filled out paperwork for days.

Georgia weighed her options. Lauren Walcher was at the heart of this case. If Georgia could get Jasmine the help she needed without getting the authorities involved, Lauren would owe her. Big time. She thought about where they were. Not far from Clark Street. A Woman's Place was just around the corner.

"I know where we're going."

"Where?"

"We'll take my car." She made a sweeping motion with her hand. "Let's go."

"Why should I?"

Georgia stopped and stared at Lauren. "Because you don't have a choice."

"What are you going to do?"

"Stop talking and help me get her into the car."

Lauren looked like she wanted to argue, but Jasmine started to cry again. Lauren squeezed her eyes shut. "Okay." She was herding Jasmine toward the Toyota when Georgia intercepted them. "Here. Let me."

She braced herself, bent her knees, and scooped the girl into her arms. The girl was tiny, but a hundred pounds was a hundred pounds. Georgia felt the strain in her muscles. Still, she carried the girl to the car.

"Open the door," she ordered.

Lauren did what she was told, and Georgia settled the girl in the back seat. She seemed dazed and limp, but her eyes were open, and she yelled when her arm was touched.

"What's your name?" Georgia asked her.

"Jathmine."

"What day is it?"

"Tuethday."

"Where are you?"

"In your car."

"Okay." Then to Lauren, "You get in too."

She waited until the doors were closed and seatbelts were buckled. Then she keyed the engine, backed out of the lot, and headed down Clark.

Traffic was light, and ten minutes later Georgia turned right onto Diversey. In the heart of Lincoln Park, Diversey Parkway was a street that reinvented itself every few years, evolving from a strip of seedy bars and storefronts to an upscale shopping area. But while the stores catered to the affluent of any orientation, the bars were mostly gay. One of those bars was sandwiched between a bookstore and a florist.

Georgia parked in front of a neon sign of a silver slipper that winked at passers-by. "You two stay here. I'll be back."

But Lauren, who seemed to have recovered some of her confidence during the drive, groused self-importantly. "What are we doing here? We need to—"

Gerogia glared through the window. "Not another word, Lauren."

Lauren glared back. Then she blinked.

A wave of heat, perfume, and beer rolled over Georgia as she pushed through the door of the Silver Slipper. Couples, most of them women, idled at tables and booths. Singles drank at the bar. Georgia went to the end of the bar and looked around. It was well after ten, but she didn't see the person she was looking for.

A room in the back held more tables. She headed back. A tiny dance floor took up the center of the room. The lights were low, and a jukebox blared out a slow Patsy Cline number. One couple was dancing. Another couple kissed, oblivious to everyone else. Georgia was curious in spite of herself. What would a woman's lips feel like? As soft as Matt's? And a female body—would it feel the way Pete's did, his limbs weighing her down, making her feel wanton but protected? Pete. Where had *that* come from? *Matt*. The way Matt's did. She felt her cheeks get hot.

She should go back to the bar. As she turned around, Red Sladdick appeared in front of her. She looked just like she did at the poetry reading: dark hair, scarlet lips, thigh-high boots. Tonight, though, she was grinning from ear to ear. "What brings you down this way, sweet Georgia?"

Georgia waved off the grin. "Didn't you say you were a nurse at Illinois Masonic?"

"I am indeed." Her smile wavered.

"I need your help. Now. Please," she added.

"I don't—what are—"

"It's important."

Red's smile faded, and her eyebrows arched. Then she nodded. "I'll get my things."

CHAPTER THIRTY-SIX

AN HOUR later, Jasmine was resting comfortably in a small room at Advocate Illinois Masonic. Red had sneaked them in through the employees' entrance and found an intern who agreed to treat the girl, no questions asked. He put a cast on her arm and bandaged the worst of the wounds. Her mouth had been treated with an antibiotic, and the intern promised that of all the wounds, the tongue would heal the fastest—probably within a day or two. Until then, he advised Jasmine to eat plenty of jello and ice cream. That prompted a giggle from the girl, which made Georgia realize how young she really was.

"I'll be back," Georgia said. "I'm going to tell Lauren you're okay." Lauren was in the waiting room.

"Thank you for everything," Jasmine said.

Georgia nodded and stepped into a corridor. Red was waiting for her. "So what happened?" Red asked quietly.

While she was grateful for Red's—and the doctor's—discretion, she didn't want to tell her what was going on. Still, Red had risked her job for them. She was entitled. She made it brief. "She was hooking and she got a bad trick."

Red winced. "How old is she?"

"Maybe sixteen."

Red blew out a breath. "How'd you get involved?"

"It's one of those long stories."

Red looked over. "I'd invite you over just to hear it, but I get the feeling you have things to do."

"You're right. But thank you for everything. You had no reason to help me, but you did. You could have been fired."

"All in a day's work."

"I owe you."

"Just my luck," Red smiled wryly. "To be owed by a straight woman. And a former cop."

It was Georgia's turn to smile. "How about dinner when this is over?"

"It's a date." Red slipped a hand into her bag and fished out a card. "Tell you what." Her smile widened. "You take *my* card this time."

Georgia slid it into her jacket pocket. She started to walk away, then retraced her steps and gave Red a quick hug. As she exited the corridor, she saw Red shaking her head.

***

Georgia drove Jasmine to her home in Niles, leaving the girl to explain to her parents what had happened. She was no longer responsible for her and didn't want to be involved further. She did get a description of the john, though. She would call O'Malley tomorrow. She wanted to nail the bastard.

Lauren Walcher, however, was a different story. She was sitting in the passenger seat as they headed north. Georgia checked her watch. Almost midnight, but Lauren's parents were probably used to her staying out late. She cut back east, taking side streets to avoid the lights.

Many of the houses were decked out for Halloween. As a kid, the holiday used to be Georgia's favorite: no gifts, no church, just costumes and bags of candy. She was a fairy princess one year, a fireman the next. One year her father, a battalion chief in District Three, brought her a real fire hat. Her mother stuffed tissues into it so it wouldn't fall off.

Now though, as she passed homes festooned with ghosts, ghouls, and monsters dripping blood, she was creeped out. Some of the decorations were more elaborate than Christmas, but they all looked bizarre and sinister, as if neighbors were competing for the most gruesome display on the block. How had people become so attracted to the grisly and the morbid? Whatever happened to smiling jack o'lanterns, candy corn, and friendly ghosts? If people knew what real darkness was, they'd flock back to Casper in a heartbeat.

She stole a glance at Lauren. The girl was leaning against the window. Who knows? Maybe it all contributed to a lawlessness, a rebellion against morality that allowed kids like Lauren to operate at the margins. She doubled back to Oakton and crossed over the Edens. When she looked over again, tears were rolling down Lauren's cheeks.

Georgia pulled to the side of the road. "What's the matter?"

Lauren shook her head and started to sob.

Georgia waited, watching the play of light and shadow on Lauren's face. The girl continued to cry, long wrenching sobs that tore her heart out. Georgia leaned across her, opened her glove compartment, and pulled out some tissues.

"What's going on, Lauren?" Georgia asked softly.

"You remember what you said about secrets?"

Georgia tipped her head. "You mean how sometimes you can be a better friend if you tell someone about them?"

Lauren nodded. "I—I can't do this anymore." She sobbed. "It's all coming apart."

"I know."

"No. You don't." She turned a tear-stained face to Georgia. "You don't know anything."

"Then tell me."

The girl swallowed a sob. Her face filled with fear. "I think whoever killed Sara wants to kill me next. And I don't know why."

CHAPTER THIRTY-SEVEN

JUST OFF Willow Road between Northbrook and Glenview is a shopping center with a Steak-n-Shake that stays open until one in the morning. Relentlessly cheery and clean, the décor tries hard for an art deco look, but its black and white striped awning is too modern, its red accents too bold, and the obscure Indian sign lit up in red neon too bewildering. Still, it is one of the only places on the North Shore where young and old, monied or not, can gather for late night snacks. Georgia pulled into the parking lot and slid out of the car. The spill of artificial street lights buzzed with an electric tension, rendering the dark into faux brightness. Lauren sat in the car, not moving.

Georgia leaned back through the open door. "Is there a problem?"

Lauren folded her arms. "This place is a stoner's paradise. Half of Newfield hangs here. We're bound to run into people I know."

"And that's a problem because ..."

She looked down. "People know who you are," she mumbled.

"Which means you'll be branded a snitch?"

Lauren didn't say anything.

"Why don't you just tell them I'm your dorky cousin from Oklahoma?"

Lauren almost cracked a smile. "Georgia's more like it." But she opened the door of the Toyota and slid out.

Inside, a middle-aged waitress in a white-collared t-shirt, black slacks, and a hat that looked like something a short order cook would wear led them to a small table. She slapped two menus down. "Something to drink?"

Lauren nodded as she sat. "Coffee."

"Two coffees, please." Georgia sat down, too.

"Coming right up."

When the waitress brought their coffee, Lauren grasped hers in both hands. Georgia scanned the menu. "Order something if you want. I'm going to."

Lauren swiveled around and gazed at the back wall where three huge colored photographs hung. One photo was of a banana split, another a milk shake, the third a hot fudge sundae.

"Can I have a banana split?" Lauren asked.

"Why not?"

"With hot fudge on top?"

Georgia waved the waitress over. "A banana split with hot fudge sauce. And a burger—rare. With fries."

The waitress scribbled on her pad and went away. Lauren looked around and promptly slumped in her seat.

"Incoming?" Georgia asked.

Lauren nodded. "I know those kids."

Georgia twisted around. Four kids, three of them boys in sweat shirts and jeans, and one girl conspicuously chewing gum, shot curious glances their way. They looked away when Georgia glared at them. She swiveled back to Lauren. "Problem solved."

Lauren arched her eyebrows but did sit straighter.

Georgia pulled her coffee cup closer. "Okay. The way I see it, you've got a choice. You cooperate with me and I'll protect you as best I can. But you have to tell me everything. And you have to shut down your—business."

"You know about that?" When Georgia nodded, she asked, "How?"

"I *am* a PI."

Georgia could see possibilities being pondered, choices being made. Finally, "What about the police?" Lauren asked in a low voice.

"What about them?"

"Are you going to turn me in?"

"If you cooperate, no."

"What if I don't?"

"Then we're out of here. And I take you in tonight."

"You can't do that. I won't let—" Her expression hardened. "I'll call my father."

Georgia sighed. "Daddy can't get you out of this one, Lauren. You broke the law. Repeatedly. And the two people who broke it along with you are dead. You either talk to me, and we buy ourselves some time to figure this thing out together, or I go to the police."

Lauren's spate of overconfidence vanished. "How much time?" Her voice was meek.

Georgia thought about it. It wasn't her job to find out who killed Sara Long. All she needed to do was to raise enough reasonable doubt that Cam Jordan did. Exposing Sara as a prostitute would do that. And yet, Georgia realized, that wasn't enough. She needed to find out who was preying on these young girls. She needed to make it stop. "As much time as it takes to find Sara Long's killer."

Lauren eyed Georgia. "You don't think the crazy guy did it."

"No. And, apparently, neither do you."

Lauren leaned forward to say something but was cut off by the arrival of their food. Georgia sliced her burger in half and wolfed down the first half. Lauren scooped up a tiny piece of banana, carefully spooned ice cream and sauce on top, swallowed it, then did the same thing all over again. Georgia remembered how as a kid she'd try to make it all come out even. Is that what Lauren was doing?

As if reading her mind, Lauren flashed an embarrassed smile. Georgia recalled during the interview at her house, how she dangled her leg over the side of the chair, as overbearing and arrogant as her mother. Trying to show everyone how tough she was. This wasn't the same girl. Had Georgia finally broken through?

She bit into the other half of her burger, then wiped her hands on her napkin. "Let's start at the beginning. When did Sara start hooking?"

Lauren gazed at Georgia in the antiseptic light. The last trace of resentment disappeared off her face. She must have come to a decision. "Six months ago. I recruited her."

"Not Derek?"

"The whole thing was my idea."

Georgia hid her surprise. "You?"

"I'd had—a few encounters," Lauren said.

"You were hooking?" Georgia hoped her face was impassive.

Lauren nodded. "Strictly freelance. It was—well—I liked it. It made me feel—well—like I meant something."

Georgia stared into a face that was barely past childhood. A face that had seen every advantage, been given every benefit, and yet found it all lacking. What—or who—had made her feel that way?

Lauren must have seen something on Georgia's face. "You don't get it, do you?"

"Get what?"

"What an amazing feeling it is to see a man want you—in—that way."

Georgia didn't answer. She picked up her fork. "When was the first time?"

"The first time I fucked for money, I was fifteen. It started out as a lark," she said around a mouthful of ice cream. "I met this guy at the mall. He was from out of town. He bought me a necklace. I knew I shouldn't accept it, but I did. He called that night and asked me to have lunch with him the next day at the Hyatt."

"Did he know how young you were?"

"How could he not? I probably told him at some point."

"Go on." Georgia dipped a few fries in ketchup and stuffed them in her mouth.

"I ditched school, and we had a nice lunch. Afterwards he told me he had to get something from his room and did I mind coming with him. I knew what the score was. I wasn't a virgin. Not since I was thirteen. When we got upstairs, he locked the door and started groping me."

She stopped and eyed Georgia.

"I pushed him away but I could see it in his eyes. He'd just had lunch, but he was—hungry. Just—hungry. I knew from that moment I was in control."

Suddenly Georgia lost her appetite.

"So I stripped for him. One piece of clothing at a time. First my shoes, then my jeans. Then my jacket. My tank." She smiled. "His eyes got huge. His cock too. He started to groan and stroke himself. Then he told me to stroke him." She paused. Then she giggled. "Then we fucked. It was a real high. Talk about leading a man around by his—well, you know. Afterwards he slipped two hundred dollar bills into my purse."

She picked at the banana split with her spoon. "Shit. I would have done it for free."

"So it's all about power?"

"Men are so—predictable, you know? They think they're in control. But we're the ones who choose it. No one's making us. We're getting paid." Lauren put the spoon down. "I just can't understand why women have problems with men. Like my mother. I can't believe she can't handle Gumby."

"Gumby?" Georgia called up a dim memory of the rubbery cartoon character.

"I call my father that because he bends over and stretches in any direction just to keep the peace. Even with all that, my mother still fights with him. All the time. She ought to be fucking his brains out."

A shrink would have a field day with this kid, Georgia thought. Aloud, she said, "Let's get back to you. What happened after that first time?"

"I decided I wanted to do it again. But I was careful. I only chose guys who looked nice. Family guys who looked like they weren't getting any at home."

"Where did you find them?"

She smiled. "Everywhere. It's easy. Hotels. Restaurants. The mall. They're all over." She dug into her ice cream. "A few months later, I was so busy I couldn't keep up. Then one day last winter, I ran into a woman in a chat room who—"

"A chat room?"

"Yeah. Sometimes I'd meet guys in chat rooms, you know?"

Lauren was talking freely now. Georgia had seen it before. There was comfort in confession. Relief that everything was now in the open. And there were some people who needed to be praised for their accomplishments, no matter how criminal or grisly. People so hungry for praise even a cop's would do. Truth be told, Lauren *was* shrewd. It wasn't easy to pull off a business—any business—

whether you were a kid or an adult. Georgia wondered how much she was raking in.

"Anyway, this woman—at least I think it was a woman—said I could make a lot more if I recruited girls myself. I thought about it and decided she was right."

"You weren't worried it was wrong?"

Lauren shrugged. "It's a great way for girls to make money. Men get their rocks off. Everybody wins."

"What about the fact that it's against the law?"

Defiance lit the teen's face. "Why do adults always get down on us for wanting to make something from sex? Isn't it better than a woman being raped? Or priests doing it to little boys? That's against the law, too. This is just sex for money. A business transaction. Everybody knows what they're there for."

Georgia folded her hands. This wasn't the time to be judgmental. "How did you recruit Sara?"

"Last winter Sara was complaining about her job at the bookstore. She was making minimum wage. Hardly anything. And her parents couldn't afford to buy her things. She'd seen my stuff for years—I know it bothered her. I mean, I'd lend her my music, my makeup, even clothes sometimes, but it wasn't the same." She took another bite of banana and ice cream. "So I told her I might know a way she could make some real money."

"She wasn't bothered by the idea?"

"No." Lauren's face filled with insolence. "She knew her way around. At least that's what she said."

"Meaning she wasn't a virgin."

"There aren't many girls my age who are, you know."

Georgia didn't reply. "So, at the beginning it was just you and Sara?"

"Sara was the only one from Newfield."

"What about Claire? Or Heather?'

Lauren snorted. "Are you kidding?"

"Why not? Were you worried what they would think?"

"Of course not. They weren't—they just weren't the type."

"But there were others," Georgia persisted. When Lauren nodded, she asked, "Where did you find them?"

"Grocery stores, restaurants, 7-11's. The best place is the mall."

"Why?"

"It gives you a chance to analyze them. See where they fit in." Lauren pushed a strand of hair behind her ear. "You look for girls who're by themselves. If they're thin and tall and blonde, even better."

"Why?"

"Everybody wants a blonde. They work harder."

Her matter-of-fact tone was chilling. "Like Sara."

Lauren nodded. "So you go up to them and make friends, like. You talk about clothes or makeup or CDs. You get them to tell you they need money. Then you tell them you know where they can get it."

"What if they tell you to get lost? Or threaten to go to the police?"

"Some say they're not interested. But plenty more are."

"And after they say yes?"

"We email back and forth. Sometimes I went shopping with them for the right clothes. Told them how to act. How to get the money up front. Made sure they knew what's expected. What to do, what not to do. The best birth control stuff. You know, I'd mold them."

Georgia sipped her coffee. Was Lauren playing the role of mother/madam to compensate for the mother she never had? "How many girls are—were you running?"

"Last spring and summer about a dozen. But after Sara and everything, I'm down to four. Not including Jasmine." She waved her spoon in the air. "They look up to me. I'm their friend, their big sister, their mother, whatever it takes to keep them happy. And," she said proudly, "I always make sure they're home by curfew."

Georgia nearly spit out her coffee. "How—how did Derek get involved?"

Lauren explained how they'd first met up in a sex chat room and started emailing. "At first I thought he was just a john. But then he started to negotiate. He wanted a discount on girls, but said in return he'd help me expand the business." She scraped up the last of the banana, the last bit of ice cream and put them in her mouth.

She did it. Made it all come out even.

"Turned out he'd gone to Newfield. I didn't know him, of course. Anyway," Lauren went on, "eventually we became partners."

"When was this?" Georgia picked up the remaining half of her burger.

"Derek got involved around May. It all happened pretty fast. I figured I needed a guy anyway. For the heavy lifting. He helped me set up the website. Which brought in more customers. Then he brought in even more."

"Through his job at the gas station?" Georgia said between bites.

"I guess. I never asked. After a while, we got into this pattern. He would get the johns, I would get the girls. But then, a couple of months ago, he started recruiting girls, too. He kept saying we needed to expand faster." She played with her spoon. "I told him to cool his jets. That he was going too far too fast."

"Tell me. The fish guts? Was that Derek?"

Lauren hesitated. Then, "Yes."

"Why?"

"After you came to our house, I told him you were causing trouble. We agreed we had to do something."

"Why fish guts?"

"I figured you'd think it was related to the Forest Preserve and the hazing. I wanted to keep the focus off us."

"So it was your idea."

Lauren kept her mouth shut.

"Tried to outsmart me, huh?"

She shrugged.

"The same way you did with Monica Ramsey."

Lauren's mouth opened. "How did you—"

"It wasn't a bad move. You had me going for a while." *And forced me to waste precious time*, Georgia thought.

Lauren tilted her head, as if she wasn't sure whether to be proud or ashamed. Good. Keep her unbalanced.

"Let's get back to Sara." Georgia polished off the rest of her burger. "Was anything strange going on with her tricks, as far as you know?"

A sad look came over Lauren.

"What's the matter?"

"Sara and I were—well—we weren't close anymore. I still don't really know why. We used to be best friends. We spent all our time together. But then, I don't know. We drifted apart." She looked down. "I had this Uncle Fred, you know? My mother's brother. When we were younger he used to take us out to dinner. Sara and me."

Georgia smiled. "Sounds like fun."

Lauren nodded. "Sara liked him a lot. She used to say she'd adopted him as her own uncle. Which made us a special kind of family, she said. But then he had a stroke. And then he died." Tears rimmed her eyes. "And then Sara did, too."

Georgia swallowed. She knew what it was like to feel abandoned. To feel like you've been cast adrift, torn from the moorings of people you loved and whom you thought loved you back. She wanted to reach out to her but didn't. It wasn't the right time. She waited for Lauren to pull herself together. "You were saying—about Sara?"

Lauren cleared her throat and nodded. "Yeah. Something changed. Over the summer."

"Your relationship changed?"

She nodded. "I don't know what or why. She just started to get—distant."

"This was how long after she'd started turning tricks?"

"Months. She started in February."

"So at least four or five months." Lauren nodded. "Did Sara ever report any abusive behavior, like the guy with Jasmine tonight?"

Lauren shook her head.

"Would Derek have known if she had?"

"I don't know. I guess I should check the files."

"Files?"

"Derek had me fill out notes on each girl and enter it into a file sharing system. Along with the clients and the girls they went with."

"Why?"

"He said you never knew when it might come in handy."

Was Derek setting up a blackmail scheme—just in case? Georgia wouldn't be surprised. Who were these johns, anyway? What kind of man takes the risk of hooking up with a prostitute he knows is a minor?

"I do think you should check the files. For now, though, think. Are you sure there wasn't anything strange going on with Sara?"

The girl's brow furrowed. Then she jerked her head up. "You know? There was something. But I don't know if—it probably doesn't mean anything."

"What?"

"I got a text message from Derek."

"A text message?"

"On my cell. The day he died. He texted me about a client."

"Which client?"

"One of our regulars. Charlie."

"And?"

"He asked if I'd heard from him recently."

"Who was Charlie?"

"He hooked up with Sara all the time."

Georgia sat up. "Any idea why Derek would be asking about him?"

"No. But Derek was killed a few hours later."

CHAPTER THIRTY-EIGHT

DESPITE THE worldliness and sophistication attributed to the North Shore, its residents live in small enclaves and villages. They all walk the same streets and patronize the same shops, which, in effect, makes for a tiny, insular community. Georgia waited for Lauren the following Saturday at one of those shops, the Starbucks in Glencoe.

Lauren had called that morning to report what she'd found in the website's files.

"It isn't much," she began. "But I did—"

"I'd rather we do it in person." Georgia cut her off.

"Why? Do you think someone—" Lauren's voice was tense.

Georgia didn't answer directly. "I'm going to need a print-out of what you have, anyway. Why don't I swing by and pick it up?"

"Not the house."

"Right. How about the Starbucks in town?"

"Okay."

Now Georgia sipped a latte, watching the Saturday morning pulse of village life. Soccer was in high season, and harried parents with kids in tow hurried in and out. The kids wore brightly colored uniforms and socks. Other adults, past the young-children-at-home stage, relaxed over the *Trib* or the *New York Times*. Not too many *Sun Times* up here.

A few minutes later Lauren came through the door. She was wearing black jeans and a tight gray sweat shirt. But her jeans had rhinestone stitching and her sweatshirt looked like silk. Georgia felt underdressed in her Costco jeans and turtleneck.

"So what did you find?" Georgia asked when Lauren joined her.

"Like I said, there wasn't much." She threw her bag on the table and extracted a large manila envelope. "Just a bunch of entries for Sara with Charlie. Including her last one."

"Her last trick was Charlie?"

"I think so. It's the last entry in her file."

"What about Charlie? What's in his file?"

"Not much." Lauren gestured to the envelope. "Just when he first signed up."

"When was that?"

"The end of May. After Derek got involved."

"Go on."

"And how many times he'd used us."

"Which was?"

"Over two dozen."

Georgia whistled. "That's some 'regular.'"

"He was one of our best customers."

"Do you know who he is or where to get hold of him?"

Lauren shook her head. "He was Derek's john."

"You have his email?"

"I have the email he uses to contact us. It's probably not his real one. Most johns have anonymous or secret emails when they deal with us."

"But they check them regularly."

"Sure."

"There's nothing in the files that would indicate whether he was a crazy?"

"Sara wouldn't have been seeing him if he was," she said confidently.

"And you know that because ..."

"Because of what I said before. Most of our johns are just family guys who aren't getting any at home."

"What about the asshole last night?"

Lauren didn't reply for a minute. "There is one thing."

"What?"

"In the file, it says he only wanted to see girls who were seventeen."

"Really? Why would he do that?"

"Because seventeen is the age of sexual consent."

"Of course." Georgia shifted. In Illinois a john caught with a minor under seventeen could face statutory rape charges. But if the minor was over seventeen, the penalties were less severe. Which meant that Charlie knew the law. Although that might not be significant. Wouldn't most professional men check before engaging in this kind of sport?

Lauren handed the envelope to Georgia. "Look. I answered your questions. Now, I need you to answer mine. Do you think I'm in danger?"

Georgia stowed the envelope in her lap. "The truth is, I don't know." An anxious expression came over Lauren. "But I'm going to do my best to protect you."

Lauren threw her a look that said she wasn't sure her best was good enough.

Georgia shifted. "So that's it? From the website?"

Lauren nodded.

Georgia was about to ask another question about Charlie when Lauren's purse started to vibrate.

"That's my cell," Lauren picked up the purse, fished inside, and pulled it out. "Oh." Relief flooded her face. "It's just Claire. On the personal line. I'll call her back." She put the cell on the table and smiled, then leaned back against her chair. She seemed much more relaxed today.

Georgia pointed to it. "You have more than one cell?"

Lauren dug into her bag and pulled out a second phone. "This one's for business. The other is personal."

"Your parents don't know about the business phone."

She slipped the business cell back into her bag and shot Georgia one of those disdainful glares that told Georgia that despite her sophistication, Lauren was still a teenager.

Georgia sipped her coffee. It was cold. "Lauren, you know how I told you to close everything down on the website?"

"I—I haven't had the chance," she stammered. "But I will. Today."

"I've been rethinking it. I think we should keep it going for a while."

"But—"

"Not you. Me."

"You're going to run the business?"

"I want you to give me the passwords and talk me through whatever I need to know."

A sly look came over Lauren. "You're gonna fake Charlie out, aren't you?"

Georgia didn't answer, but Lauren's expression said her opinion of Georgia had just gone up. "Let me help. I can—"

Georgia cut her off. "No. You're out of it. But I will need you to help me delete the whole thing when it's over."

Lauren's face scrunched into a frown. "At least let me—" Suddenly she stopped and slouched deep in her seat. "Oh, shit."

"What?"

Lauren's chin jutted toward the door.

Georgia turned. Andrea Walcher had just walked in and was heading to the counter. She was perfectly dressed in a pair of corduroy slacks and a plum sweater, but her expression was grim. Did the woman ever smile?

Lauren shot Georgia a panicked look and started to squirm. "Shit on a stick. I'm not supposed to be in the same state as you. What do I do?"

Georgia sucked in a breath. There was no way to prevent what was coming. "I'll do what I can," she said quietly.

It was another few seconds before Andrea wheeled around and saw Lauren. Her eyes flicked over to Georgia, then narrowed. She was at their table in three angry strides, her body so tense she was almost quivering.

"What the hell are you doing here?" she barked in a voice that carried through the coffee shop.

Lauren seemed to shrink.

Andrea glared at her daughter. "How dare you meet with this—this—"

"Private investigator," Georgia finished. "Nice to see you too, Mrs. Walcher." She smiled coldly. "How are you?"

"Don't you dare suck up to me."

Georgia marveled at the woman's fury. It took enormous energy to be so hostile. "Mrs. Walcher, your daughter was a friend of Sara Long's. I'm investigating Sara Long's murder. Lauren could have valuable information."

"My husband's warning was clear. You are to stay away from us and our daughter. I should call the police right now. I'm quite sure I could have you arrested for stalking, or trespassing or—"

People from other tables shot curious glances their way. Georgia put on her game face. "Mrs. Walcher, I understand your animosity. And I know you want to protect your daughter. But I have a job to do."

Andrea frowned, her behavior seeming to waver for an instant. She faced her daughter. "Did she force you to talk to her? Did she threaten you in *any* way, baby? Because if she did ..." She looked angrily at Georgia.

The girl looked at Georgia, then her mother. After a pause, she said, "No. She didn't force me."

Georgia felt the knot in her gut loosen a notch.

"Are you sure?" Andrea's voice was rich with doubt.

"I'm sure."

Andrea Walcher threw up her hands. "I don't know whether to believe you or not. I come in here to get coffee and I find you cozying up to a sleazy investigator who's trying to get a murderer off the hook." She spun to Georgia. "How much are they paying you?"

Georgia stood up and folded her arms. Protection was one thing. Abuse was another. "Not nearly enough to deal with the likes of you."

Rage poured into the woman's face. "If I ever find out you and my daughter have been in contact again, whether by phone or email or even smoke signals, I'll have you put in jail. You can count on it." She turned to her daughter. "Lauren, come with me. Now."

A stubborn look came over Lauren. She shook her head.

Georgia made a quick decision. She wanted the girl to trust her, but she couldn't insinuate herself into a mother-daughter relationship. Andrea Walcher could cause serious problems. She waved her hand dismissively. "Go ahead. She had nothing to say, anyway."

Lauren shot Georgia an uncertain look and stood up. Georgia frowned and lowered her eyes. Meanwhile, Andrea Walcher grabbed her daughter's arm and steered her toward the door. Lauren looked back as they pushed through. Georgia shook her head.

Once they exited, Georgia ran a shaky hand over her face. People like Andrea Walcher enjoyed making waves. And there was nothing she could do about it. Andrea's reactions, and any repercussions from them, were beyond her control. She just hoped the woman had something more important to do with her time. She started to clean off the table, willing herself to stay focused on the case. But as she pitched napkins and cups into the trash, she still felt disturbed, and she realized it wasn't all because of Andrea Walcher.

Georgia had dealt with prostitution as a cop. Underage prostitutes, too. But Lauren's breed was different from the whores she was used to. The hookers she picked up as a cop, whatever their motive—usually money for drugs or their pimps—would avoid looking her in the eye. They might gape at the male cops, even come on to them, but woman to woman, they knew. Despite their tough exteriors, Georgia could see that kernel of guilt.

Lauren, though, showed no remorse. For her, and Sara too, apparently, prostitution was as legitimate a way to make money as any other. Better, since you raked in so much more. Nonchalant, almost arrogant, they refused to think that prostitution was self-destructive, demeaning, or even dangerous. And for what? To impress their peers—mostly other girls—with designer clothes, purses, toys. It wasn't just Lauren and Sara, either. Lauren was running other girls. Georgia wiped down the table, with rapid, vigorous strokes. Lauren claimed it was a win-win: the men got laid, the girls got money. Maybe Lauren was right. Maybe *she* was the only one with a bad taste in her mouth.

She grabbed her bag off the back of the chair, almost enjoying her anger—it was a good, clean anger, directed outward for a change—when she noticed Lauren's cell phone on the table. In the commotion, the girl had forgotten it. Georgia picked it up and dropped it into her bag.

CHAPTER THIRTY-NINE

GEORGIA DROVE the few blocks to the Walcher home, planning to leave Lauren's cell phone in the mailbox. She wasn't eager for another encounter with either Walcher. She parked on the road at the edge of the stand of evergreens that shielded the house from view. Grabbing the phone, she climbed out of the car and looked around. The houses up here were huge, and many of them had private drives, which meant the mailbox could be hundreds of yards from the house. She checked both ends of the semi-circular driveway, but didn't see it.

She started to trudge·through the trees, enjoying the crisp, snappy scent of pine and juniper. It must have rained overnight, because the ground was soft, and chunks of dirt clung to her shoes. She was about to break through the cover of trees when she stopped. A black Jaguar was parked in the driveway, its engine running. A man was in the driver's seat, and Andrea Walcher was leaning over the driver's side window.

Georgia stared at the man behind the wheel. She could only see his profile, but he had curly gray hair, and he was wearing a warm-up jacket. He looked familiar. She ducked behind a tree.

"I need to talk to you," Andrea said to the man in the car. "Is everything kosher with the land deal?"

Georgia saw the man's head bob up and down.

"Then why did Fred say it wasn't?" Andrea's voice was tense.

The man cocked his head. Georgia could just make out his reply. "I haven't the slightest idea."

Andrea straightened up and folded her arms. "Look. I know he was upset about something. But he didn't have time to get into it before he died. Tom won't talk to me about it, so I'm asking you what's going on."

His response was so low Georgia had to strain to hear him. "Everything's fine, Andrea."

"Don't patronize me. He was my brother, Harry."

Harry Perl. The real estate developer she'd seen at North Shore Fitness with Tom Walcher and Ricki Feldman.

"I would never do that." Suddenly his tone oozed empathy. "It's just that—well, Tom took care of the details. We're almost ready to start construction. Things are proceeding nicely."

Andrea cut him off. "Then why did Fred say he wanted to go to the authorities?" Her body language spoke anger, but something else was there too. Worry. Maybe a touch of fear.

The man's shoulders hunched. "I wasn't aware of that. Ask your husband."

Andrea stared into the car for a moment, then turned on her heel and went inside.

Perl rolled up his window and pulled away from the house. Georgia waited until the Jag was out of sight. The mailbox was in front of the house just to the right of the goldfish pond. She quietly placed Lauren's phone inside.

***

Fred was Andrea's brother. "Uncle Fred," Georgia recalled on the way home. He had suspicions about a land deal he and Harry Perl were involved in, but he died before he could do anything about it. Now his sister, Lauren's mother, was following up.

Georgia thought back to the conversation she'd overheard between Perl and Walcher and Ricki Feldman at the health club. She'd been distracted by seeing Ricki, but she thought she remembered something about a deal that required Tom Walcher's help. Walcher was expected to soften up the village board. Perl—or was it Ricki?—had told him to use his "leverage." Whatever that "leverage" was. Was this the same deal?

She parked on Asbury and headed back to her apartment. Andrea Walcher had been livid in Starbucks, throwing around wild accusations and threats. Was this part of what was troubling her? Maybe Georgia should look into it. It wasn't directly related to Cam Jordan or Sara Long, but she couldn't move forward with the prostitution angle without Lauren's help, and the last thing she needed was to be cut off from the girl. If she uncovered anything significant about the land deal, maybe she could use it to convince Andrea to let her keep talking to Lauren. Apply a little "leverage" of her own.

Back in her apartment, she sat at the computer and Googled Harry Perl. Perl Development came up right away. The website was a class act—he must have paid some agency a fortune to design it. Too bad. Her friend Sam would have killed for the job and probably charged a lot less. A string of pearls were used to tout the "pearls" of the company's properties. Clicking on any one of them took you to a different project, including a skyscraper off Michigan Avenue, several shopping centers, and housing developments in Will and Lake Counties.

Then there was the Glen, a commercial and residential community built on what used to be acres of Midwestern prairie. It had been a controversial development. Environmentalists fought to keep the land pristine, holding meetings, staging protests, even pulling off a tricky legal maneuver or two. Ultimately, though, the project was green-lighted, and Perl had built dozens of town houses, a nursing home, and a motel.

Now Perl was announcing a new project just east of the Glen. 2500 Chestnut would be twin condos with a small, enclosed, upscale mall. During his conversation with Andrea Walcher, Perl said they were almost ready to start construction. Georgia searched his website for other projects under development. 2500 Chestnut was the only one. The Glen was only a few minutes away. She grabbed her jacket.

***

A dirty overcast grayed the sky, and a damp, earthy scent hung in the air. Georgia turned off Waukegan Road onto Chestnut. The street resembled a war zone between residential and commercial tracts, and the commercial side was winning. An apartment house lined one side of the street, but it was overwhelmed by a strip mall, cemetery, and small office complex on the other.

The property she was looking for occupied the southeast corner of Lehigh and Chestnut. Surrounded by a chain link fence, it was about the size of a football field. Georgia walked through an open gate. Hugging the perimeter were a couple of cranes and earth moving machines. A white RV was parked at the edge of the field. Perl wasn't wasting any time.

In the center was a hole in the ground. Georgia started towards it. For the second time that day, mud caked the soles of her shoes. She picked up a stick and scraped it off. She peered into the hole, wondering what had been here before. She wasn't a tree hugger, but she found herself regretting that another piece of the past was gone, unable to serve as a guidepost to the future.

She made a 360. On one side of the field were a couple of newly built townhouses. On the other, a bank and park district facility. But across the street on the north side were five flat-roofed houses that seemed almost defiant in their shabbiness. Most of them had peeling paint, rickety porches and seedy lawns. Between houses two and three was a space that looked like a giant gap between teeth in a kid's mouth. An "Under Contract" sign staked the lawn of the house on the end.

Georgia picked her way across the street to the most ramshackle house and rang the doorbell.

A young Asian girl opened the door. "Yes?"

The girl looked to be the same age as Lauren. "Hello. Are your parents home?"

The girl looked blank for a moment, then turned and called out rapidly in another language. Chinese? A pot clanged from somewhere in back, and a woman emerged in the hall. When she saw Georgia, her eyebrows arched.

Georgia smiled. "Hello. My name is Georgia Davis."

The woman frowned and looked at the girl.

The girl translated, then said to Georgia, "She doesn't speak English."

"I wanted to ask her about the property across the street." Georgia waited while the girl translated.

The woman stiffened. Her response was curt.

"She says she doesn't want to sell and to please go away."

Georgia held up a hand. "Please tell her I'm not here for that."

The girl translated, but the woman launched into another diatribe. Embarrassment shot across the girl's face. "I'm sorry. You have to go." She closed the door in her face.

Georgia headed back to the sidewalk, wondering whether to try another house. What she was doing probably wouldn't help her find Sara Long's murderer, and she wasn't fond of having doors slammed in her face. Then again, she was here. May as well do a thorough job. She gazed at the other three houses. A rusty commode leaned against the side wall of the house two doors down. Next to the commode was a group of plastic buckets.

She walked over and rang the bell. Nothing happened. After a moment, she rang again. Still nothing. She was about to leave when the front door squeaked open. The woman on the other side was gnarled and old. Patches of pink scalp shone through wisps of straw-white hair, and her wrinkled face wore a dour expression. She was dressed in a bathrobe so threadbare it was impossible to tell what color it had been. On her feet were a pair of incongruously new-looking fuzzy blue slippers.

"Yeah?" She coughed into her hand, a rasping, phlegmy cough that made Georgia want to cover her face.

Georgia nodded. "Hello. I wonder if you could tell me about the property across the street."

The woman shifted, her manner suspicious. "What about it?"

"I have a few questions." Georgia made sure to smile.

"Who wants to know?"

"My name is Georgia Davis."

"You from that realty company?"

"No, ma'am. I'm a private investigator."

The woman shook her head. A draft of sour-smelling air wafted out of the house. Georgia backed up. "I told them I wasn't gonna sell. But they keep nosing around. You gonna do something about that?"

"Who's nosing around?"

"Them realty people." She looked down at her slippers, as if she was afraid they might dance away from her feet.

"Do you know their name?"

"Something like a jewel."

"Perl Development?"

"That's it. Some guy in a fancy suit waltzes in and tells me they wanna buy my house. Building condos and stores, they say. I told 'im I didn't think so. That they'd be taking me out of here feet first. He's been back a couple of times, but I won't talk to 'im. I been here over forty years."

"That's a long time."

"You said it. I mean, where am I supposed to go? My nephew says he'll find me a place, but Lord knows, he's got his own life to live. Three kids and a bitch for a wife. But now my taxes are going up so high, I may have to." She sighed. "I just don't know any more. They got no heart. No soul, either, you know?"

"What was there before?"

The woman slid her fingers along the sash of her robe. "There was a gas station. And body shop. Been there ever since I moved in."

"Did you know the owner?"

"Of course, I knew Fred. Fred Stewart."

Andrea Walcher's brother. Uncle Fred. "Did you like him?"

"Everyone did. He was real people. Always willing to help out, cut you a break if you needed it. My nephew used to work there over the summer. Never had a bad thing to say about the man. 'Course, after he took ill, he had to close up."

"When was that?"

The woman squinted. "Over a year ago, now. Last summer. He had a stroke, they said."

"Who said?"

"I don't know. The builders he sold it to, I guess."

"And when did they start coming around—the builders?"

"I guess it was about six months ago when Mr. Fancypants said they were gonna build them condos. And I was gonna have to sell and move." She glared at the "Under Contract" sign on her neighbor's lawn. "I'll probably be the last holdout."

"I see." Georgia nodded. "Well, thanks. I appreciate the information."

The woman spat on the ground. "So you gonna be able to stop 'em?"

Georgia hesitated. "If I was you, I would call my nephew," she said carefully. "And take him up on his offer."

CHAPTER FORTY

GEORGIA WAS cleaning her apartment. She'd been fantasizing about cooking a dinner—lamb roast, baby potatoes, a vegetable, probably broccoli, and salad—and had stopped in at the grocery store earlier that morning. She wasn't sure who she was cooking it for, but the notion was surprisingly appealing. The phone rang in the middle of sweeping the floor. She'd been thinking about salad dressing, a balsamic vinaigrette. She picked up the phone.

"Cam Jordan's BCX is back," Paul Kelly said. "It's not good."

"BCX ..." The behavior clinical exam. The fantasy dinner melted away. "It came back fast. Didn't you just ask for it?"

"Less than a month ago. At the arraignment, first week in October."

"So what does it say?"

She heard paper rustling. "I'll read it. 'Pursuant to your Honor's order, the undersigned'.. yadda, yadda.. Hold on. Here it is. 'Based on the above examination and review of pertinent records it is my opinion with a reasonable degree of medical certainty that Cameron Jordan is presently fit to stand trial. He does not manifest any active symptoms or signs of any mental disorder which would—"

"No signs of 'disorder'? Is that a joke?"

Kelly snorted. "Listen. 'He is cognizant of the charge, understands the nature and purpose of the court proceedings and shows the ability to co-operate with counsel if he chooses to.'"

"That's bullshit. The guy doesn't know what day of the week it is."

"I told you before. Mucho heat on this case."

"But Ramsey's out."

"Doesn't mean squat. It's still a heater case. Maybe even more now that everyone knows his daughter was there. Who knows who's really calling the shots, anyway?"

"Who did the testing? Who wrote the report?"

"Says here a shrink from Forensic Clinical Services."

"I don't get it. How can they come back with something so—inaccurate?"

"You can't tell me you're surprised."

"I guess not." She sighed heavily. "What happens now?"

"I'll ask for a second opinion, of course. From a private shrink. But I don't know if the judge will grant it or how long they'll have to put it together."

"What's your best guess?"

"A few weeks. Maybe a month." He cleared his throat. "But I don't think we can ignore the signals. We've got to start dealing the cards we have."

"What are you saying?"

"I start talking plea."

"But he didn't do it."

"We still can't prove it."

"You don't have to. Cam's home, and public opinion's swinging our way. Put Ruth Jordan in front of the cameras."

Kelly harrumphed.

"Actually, we're closer than we were." She told him what she'd learned about Sara Long and the teenage prostitution ring.

Before she finished, Kelly' interrupted. "So the girl really *was* a whore."

"Yes."

"You're sure?—you can't make that kind of allegation without proof."

"I've got it."

"What?"

"More like who. The girl who was running her."

"Her pimp was another girl?"

"Her best friend."

"Christ Almighty! Were they on drugs?"

"No."

"Runaways."

"No."

"Did their fathers sexually abuse them?"

"No."

"Then what the hell are teenage girls—"

"Money."

"Huh?"

"Sara Long wanted to buy things her parents couldn't afford. Clothes. Makeup. Fancy cell phones."

"And the other one? The—pimp?"

"That one I'm still trying to figure out. It's—it's nothing I've ever seen before."

He went quiet. Georgia wondered what was going through his head. Then, as if remembering he was a jaded lawyer who wasn't supposed to be shocked by anything, he switched gears. "This is wonderful! It'll throw the case wide open! How'd you find out?"

"Long story."

"Which you're going to tell me, right? In fact, you're on your way down even as we speak, right?"

"Not really, Paul. I have a few things to nail down."

"Davis——"

"I have a lead on one of the johns. Someone Sara Long was seeing regularly. Maybe even her last trick."

"No. Let the police run with that. We need to tell them—Christ! This could be our big break. What we've been waiting for!"

"Wait a minute, Paul. This isn't some pimp running whores for the Outfit. We can't just throw it out there and——"

"Davis, our job isn't to find the killer. It's to raise enough doubt about Cam Jordan so a jury won't convict him. This goes a long way toward that."

"I understand, but——"

Kelly made a throaty sound, somewhere between a grumble and a snort. "No you don't. You're still thinking like a cop. You want to find the offender and revel in the glory."

"Is it that obvious?" When Kelly didn't answer, she went on, "Paul, just a couple more days. Cam's not in jail anymore. And you can request another BCX. This thing is moving. We're going to get the asshole. I know it."

"I should be talking to the state right now. And taking the evidence with me."

"I'll get it to you. I promise. As soon as it's in my hands."

"I thought you already had it."

"I do. But I want more."

"Like what?"

"Documentation. A confession." She paused. "Maybe even the guy who did it."

"And just when is all of this going to fall into your lap?"

"A day or two. A week at the most."

"You're killing me, Davis. I'm too old for this." He sounded exasperated.

"Thanks, Paul," she said cheerfully. "You won't regret it."

He grumbled again. "So what else have you found that I need to know?"

He was in a chatty mood. "Well, as a matter of fact, there is something. I don't think it's connected to the case, but I had some time, so I kind of looked around, and—"

"Get to the point, Davis."

She told him about Andrea Walcher's conversation with Harry Perl and the property near the Glen.

"Walcher? Why do I know that name?"

"He's the lawyer who's working with Perl. And the father of the girl who's running the prostitution ring. You checked him out."

"He's back?"

"Maybe."

He blew out air. "Circles inside circles ..."

Georgia went on. "Anyway, the land in question belonged to Walcher's brother-in-law. Fred Stewart. He sold it to Harry Perl six months ago. It used to be a gas station, but now they're building a condo and an indoor mall."

"A gas station?"

"Yeah."

"And the land was sold six months ago?"

"According to the woman who lives across the street."

"You say they're already building?"

"They're about to."

"Interesting."

"Something wrong with that?"

"You happen to know if anybody got an environmental impact statement on the land?"

"Why?"

"Any time you have a gas station or dry cleaner, there's all sorts of contamination and crud that needs to be cleaned up. I had a client once with a dry cleaners. It was an EPA nightmare."

"What do you mean?"

"Those businesses spill all sorts of crap into the ground. With dry cleaners it's chemical solvents and shit. With a gas station, it's worse. You can have underground storage tanks that leak; accidental spills that drain into the ground. The dirt is laced with all sorts of toxic stuff. You have to clean it up. If it leaches into the water supply, for example, you're up the creek without a paddle ..." Kelly was clearing warming to the subject. "Even if it doesn't, you pay a frigging fortune to clean it up."

"So?"

"The point is that the clean-up can take at least a year. Usually more. First you got to test it and get the land classified. Then you got to do the clean-up itself, test it again, and submit a final report. Anyone who's building just six months after they bought a gas station is cutting it pretty close."

"Really?"

"I told you. My client who bought the dry cleaners couldn't do anything with the land for nearly three years. It just sat there, sucking money and blood out of everyone."

"Maybe I should find out more about it."

"Maybe you should."

"Thanks."

"Hey, Davis?"

"Yeah?"

"This case is finally going places. Be careful."

"Sure."

Then, "Teenage whores on the North Shore. Christ Almighty."

***

On the Illinois EPA website, Georgia learned about brownfields, abandoned lots and eyesores that were never redeveloped because of abnormally high clean-up costs, lengthy clean-up processes, or liability risks.
The dry cleaners Kelly was talking about must have been one of those. But
Fred Stewart's gas station wasn't. It was being redeveloped right away.

She combed through the website trying to find an EPA field office on
the North Shore so she could talk to someone in person, but the closest
she came was a post office box in Elgin. She did find a staff directory for
Community Relations officials in Springfield. She picked up the phone.

On the third transfer she got a live human. She explained what she was
interested in and was promptly transferred. A new voice mail said to press
"0" for assistance. She did.

A female voice with a decidedly southern Kentucky twang answered.
"Zane here."

"Hello. My name is Georgia Davis, and I'm interested in the status
of a specific site. I was transferred to you by ..." she back-clicked on the
website. "... Ginger Mitchell."

"Uh-huh," Zane said after such a long pause that Georgia wondered if
she was still there. "And what site is it?"

Georgia gave her the location of the land.

"Hold on."

Georgia took the phone into the kitchen, grateful there was no music
or annoying radio station chatter while she was on hold. She opened the

298 LIBBY FISCHER HELLMANN

refrigerator to check the leg of lamb she bought that morning. She had enough to feed a dozen people. The only problem was she didn't know a dozen people. She was starting to wonder why she'd bought it in the first place when Zane came back on.

"I see the report here, but you'll need to file a request under the Freedom of Information Act to get a copy."

"How do I do that?"

Zane told her there was a website through which she could request the file. Or she could write a letter.

"I'd like the website, please."

Zane gave it to her.

Georgia clicked to the site and started entering information while she was talking. "This is great. In the meantime, while I'm waiting for the report, could you answer a question for me?"

"What's that?"

"Can you tell me the name of the company that submitted the report on that property?"

"Well, ma'am, technically, I should wait until I get the FOI request."

"I'm just sending it now."

"Uh-huh." She paused.

Georgia waited.

"Well, I guess it's okay. Says here the company is Environmental Engineers, Inc."

"Thank you. Do you have an address for them?"

Zane reeled off an address in Skokie.

Georgia decided to press her luck. "I assume everything was in order? I mean the report met your specifications and all?"

"Well, ma'am," Zane said, stretching the two words into five syllables. "The NFR letter went out two months ago."

"The what?"

"When a piece of land is cleaned up right we send out a letter that says no further clean-up is required. It's called a no further remediation letter."

"And that went out two months ago?"

"Ma'am, I've already told you more than I should. You're going to have to look at the report yourself."

"Of course. Thank you very much." Georgia disconnected and finished sending her FOI request. They said they'd send her the report within two weeks. Too long to wait. She checked the time. Despite Andrea Walcher's threats, she and Lauren had exchanged hurried emails yesterday. Lauren promised to call after school with the passwords to the website.

That was still hours away.

CHAPTER FORTY-ONE

ENVIRONMENTAL ENGINEERS was in the industrial backwoods of Skokie, a locale that was dotted with warehouses and small plants. There was a quiet sameness to the buildings: most were one-story, flat-roofed structures made from indistinguishable yellow bricks. Georgia skirted the grass, almost the same pale yellow as the buildings, and walked up to two glass doors. White letters on the left-hand door indicated she'd arrived at the best kitchen remodeler on the North Shore. Black letters on the right spelled out the company she was looking for.

Inside was a small room with a hallway off the back. A young woman in a black t-shirt, black pants, and black fingernail polish sat behind a gray desk. She looked up from a magazine as Georgia walked in.

"May I help you?" she asked in a voice that bordered on surly.

"Possibly. I'm looking for Mr.—uh ..." Georgia pretended to search in her bag for a piece of paper.

The girl failed to help her out. "He's not here."

Georgia smiled. "I'm sorry. What is his name?"

"Jimmy Broadbent."

"Of course. How could I have forgotten?"

"Who are you?"

"My name is Georgia Davis, and I wanted to ask him about a project he worked on."

"He's onsite today."

"Where?"

The girl sighed, as if Georgia had asked for the impossible, and rummaged around the desk. Finally she picked up a slip of paper. "Des Plaines."

Georgia waited. When no further information was forthcoming, she cocked her head. "Des Plaines is a big place."

The girl's eyes narrowed. "What do you want him for?"

"We had an appointment. You know, if you would just tell me where he is, I'll get out of your hair and you can go back to work." She gestured to the magazine.

The girl glanced at her magazine, then at Georgia. She shrugged. "He's at Wolf and Dempster. The old Malden plant."

Georgia made sure to smile. "Thanks."

***

Jimmy Broadbent looked like his name: stocky, lots of brown hair and a thick neck. Georgia wondered if he'd been a boxer once upon a time. Dressed in jeans, work boots, and a windbreaker with a Sox logo, he was leaning over the ground about ten feet from an abandoned building. As she drew closer, she saw him shove a hand auger into the dirt. An open suitcase with test tubes in two neat rows and a glass jar lay nearby. After a moment, he pulled out the auger, dug deeper with a hand trowel, and poured what he'd collected into the glass jar. She waited until he closed the jar and made some notes on his clipboard.

"Mr. Broadbent?"

He looked up, startled.

"I'm sorry. I didn't mean to—Your office told me I could find you here."

He leveled a cool glance her way. "I'm pretty busy right now."

"This will only take a minute. I'm interested in a project you did for Perl Development."

He didn't move, but Georgia sensed his muscles tightening.

"You do recall it, don't you?"

Broadbent frowned. "I work a lot of sites."

"This was an old gas station. Belonged to a man named Fred Stewart."

His eyes went flat. "Sorry. Doesn't ring a bell."

"Are you sure? Illinois EPA said they sent you the NFR letter about two months ago."

He shrugged. "Like I told you, I work a lot of sites. Maybe they gave you the wrong information. Those government types screw everything up."

"Sure. I understand."

He examined her more closely. "Who'd you say you were?"

"My name is Georgia Davis. I'm working on a matter that—that involves the man that used to own the gas station."

"You got a card?"

Something in the way he was looking at her told her to back off. "Sorry. I didn't bring any."

He didn't say anything. Then he nodded.

"So you don't remember the Glenview job at all?"

He shook his head slowly. "Nope."

"Well, in that case, I'm sorry to have troubled you."

She felt his gaze on her as she went back to her car. Broadbent was lying, that much was clear. But why? She tried to piece it together as she drove back to Evanston. Fred Stewart has a piece of property. There's good reason to think it was contaminated. He sells it to Harry Perl, and Broadbent cleans it up. Paul Kelly said the clean-up could take years. But Perl gets a clean bill of health in record time.

There was no reason for Broadbent to lie unless he had something to hide. Then again, there was no reason for him to tell the truth, either. He had no idea who she was or what she wanted. Why extend himself? In fact, why was she? The land deal didn't have anything to do with Cam Jordan or Sara Long, and she didn't have much ammunition to pressure Andrea Walcher. Still, one nagging thought kept bouncing around her brain: anything was possible when you had the right lawyer to fix things. And Tom Walcher, Harry Perl's lawyer, was a fixer.

***

Georgia was back in her apartment when the phone rang a few minutes past four. It was Lauren.

"Where do the requests come in?" Georgia asked after they'd clicked onto the website.

"Clients fill out a form, and that form gets sent as an email to my Yahoo account. I get back to them with the dates and the girl and how they're going to hook up."

"How can I access those emails?"

"First you need to know how to get around the website." Lauren gave Georgia the URL, a user name, and a password. Georgia entered the information.

"How do I make changes?"

"It's a little complicated. We use Dreamweaver. Then we upload it to the server. For now, you might just want me to do it." She paused. "What changes do you want to make?"

"Nothing right now," Georgia replied. "But I might later. What about the email account?"

Lauren gave her another password and user name. Georgia clicked to the Yahoo account, then entered Lauren's user name and password. The website jumped to a page which said "Incoming Messages." There were none. "How come there aren't any messages? I thought you had clients writing in every day."

Lauren's voice got small. "Well, see, I kind of sent a message to everyone."

"What kind of message?"

"I—I told them we were going on vacation. That there wouldn't be any action for a while. But we'd be back."

"Why?"

"After Derek, well, I—I got scared so I decided to stop work until things cooled off."

"Probably not a bad idea," Georgia admitted. "Did Charlie get that message?"

"Sure."

"Good. Now, how do I send an email?"

"Once you're signed onto the account, you just send out an email like you would on your own computer."

"When I send out an email, who will it say it's from?"

"I've been using the name 'Yvonne.'"

"Did Derek set this up?"

"Yes. But it's not rocket science," she said. "People do it all the time."

Georgia heard a trace of petulance in her voice. "How are things with your mother?"

Lauren hesitated. "She doesn't like you very much."

Georgia laughed. "That's no surprise."

"Actually, she didn't dwell on it, you know? Aside from saying you were a turd. She was freaked out about something else."

"What?" Georgia played innocent.

"Something about Uncle Fred, I think."

"What about Uncle Fred?"

"I told you he died a few weeks ago, remember? Well, I have a feeling stuff isn't going the way she thought it would."

Georgia tapped a pencil against the desk. "What stuff?"

"His will or something. I don't know." Lauren said impatiently. "Georgia …"

Georgia stopped tapping. This was the first time Lauren had called her by name.

"If Sara and Derek's murder are connected to the business, what— what if I'm next? Please …" Her voice trailed off.

"What?" Georgia asked gently.

There was a pause. Then, "Please don't leave me out there by myself."

"I won't." Georgia stopped short. She was surprised; she'd almost said "sweetie."

She considered calling O'Malley. If someone was targeting Lauren, the cops had better resources than she. If she did, though, everything would go public, and Lauren's life—as well as her parents'—would never be the same. Plus, the police never did much to protect people until after the fact. She cleared her throat. "Look. You're doing the right things. You stopped the business. You're divorcing yourself from the operation. And you're talking to me. I'm on your side." She hoped she sounded convincing.

"Thank you." Lauren's voice was small.

She toyed with her pencil. "Listen. I have another question. Where did Charlie take Sara for their—" She couldn't bring herself to say tricks. "Where did they meet?"

"Charlie likes the McCormick." When Georgia didn't answer, she added, "You know, the one they call the Colonel's place? It's in Highland Park. It's more upscale than the Hyatt, but——"

"I know it." Georgia snapped the pencil in two.

* * *

The Hotel McCormick was named for a powerful Chicagoan, Robert Rutherford McCormick. Known as "The Colonel" from a stint as an artillery officer in World War I, McCormick inherited the *Chicago Tribune* from his grandfather and ran it for several decades. His politics were to the right of Attila the Hun, and he often went over the top, labeling FDR supporters "Soviets," for example, and skewering Eastern liberals with withering epithets. But Colonel McCormick was a well-bred, sophisticated man, and the elegant hotel that bore his name reflected it. Tucked away in the woodsy part of Highland Park, it catered to people with business in Lake or northern Cook County. Georgia knew this because she'd spent a weekend there with Matt. It was the weekend they broke up.

She got up and poured herself a glass of water, drank it down. When she got back to the computer, she clicked on the mailing list and found Charlie's email. She opened the email program, started a new message from "Yvonne", and proceeded to type.

"For our special customers only! A new shipment has arrived: young, blonde, sexy, and guaranteed to give you pleasure over every inch of your body. To introduce you to these new beauties, we're cutting prices by 50 per cent! This offer only good for three days, so if you're interested, act now."

She was just checking it over when the phone rang. The sound made her jump. She reached over. The caller ID said "Private." She picked up.

"Hello?"

No response.

"Hello? Who's there?"

No words, but she thought she heard someone breathing. She quickly disconnected. She didn't play phone games with creeps.

She went back to the email. It sounded okay. She clicked "send." Then she changed the password to both the website and Lauren's email account. Just to be sure.

That night Georgia lit candles. She brought one over to the couch and placed it on the end table beside her. She'd bought it in Galena two years ago during a weekend with Matt. It had a vanilla scent. She lay down, breathed in the fragrance, then gave herself up to sleep.

CHAPTER FORTY-TWO

LENNY WAS built like an eighteen wheeler with an extra-wide load. Matt didn't want to tangle with him. He wasn't talkative, either. He didn't say much about being away, and he didn't look like he wanted to be asked. So it was a surprise when Lenny told him they would be doing a job together.

"What kind of job?"

"You're the marksman, right?"

"Yeah? So?"

Lenny led him over to his SUV and opened the back door. Lying on the seat was a Remington 700 Bolt Action rifle. Lenny eyed him. "You know your way around one of these?"

He nodded.

"Good. " Lenny leaned over, picked up something from the floor, and handed it to him. It was a DNWS26 Day/Night Sniper Scope. "Saves me the trouble of teaching you."

Matt slid his hands in his pocket. "Pretty high end stuff."

"Only the best."

"So what's the target?" He asked casually.

"The P.I. She's a problem. Boss wants the broad out of the way."

"The one I was doing surveillance on?"

"Yeah. And you're gonna do the deal."

"When?"

"Tonight." Lenny tipped his head and gazed at him with a curious expression. "You got a problem with that?"

Matt didn't react. Then he slowly shook his head. "No problem. None at all."

***

They met in the back yard of the house across the street from her apartment at two in the morning. Lenny handed him the Remington. He'd attached a suppressor to the barrel.

"It's still gonna be loud," Matt motioned to the suppressor.

"No problemo." Lenny peered across the street. "Ridge is only a block east. If anyone hears it, they'll think it's a truck." Lenny turned around and pointed to an embankment in the back that rose about ten feet above the rest of the yard. "Set yourself up there."

Matt took the rifle and retreated into the shadows of the evergreens on top of the embankment. A kid's tricycle was in front of him, a red wagon to the side. He thought about using the wagon to brace the rifle but then kicked it out of the way.

Below him Lenny paced back and forth, muttering about the window and where he should aim. He could see for himself. She was on the couch. She hadn't moved. A candle was burning beside her.

Lenny stopped pacing and looked at his watch. "Okay. Do it."

He looked through the scope. He could just see the back of her head. He slid the bolt back, chambered a round, and aimed. Then he squeezed the trigger.

The shot went wide. "Shit!"

"How the fuck did you miss?" Lenny exclaimed. "You're supposed to be a crack shot!"

He shook his head. "I don't know. I had her in the crosshairs. Maybe she moved." But she never moved in her sleep. "Or maybe it was the window. Shooting through glass can deflect the bullet."

"God dammit fuck it all," Lenny said. "What am I gonna tell the boss? He was counting on you."

"I'm sorry, man. Just tell him the truth."

Lenny glared at him. "Yeah. Well, I hope you weren't getting real attached to this job."

Matt stared at the window and saw light flickering from inside. "Oh, my God."

Lenny twisted around. "What the——?"

"The candle!" he whispered. "There was a candle. The bullet must have hit it. I think it started a fire!"

Lenny squinted and peered across the street. The flickering seemed to grow brighter. "Fuckin' A! I think you're right." He twisted around. "You're one lucky sack of shit, you know that? You better hope that does the job."

Matt ran his tongue around his lips. She still wasn't moving. "I guess so."

Lenny looked around. "Hey, let's get out of here. Before the fire department comes."

"Yeah. Shit." He tore his gaze from the window and forced his eyes on Lenny's. "I'm really sorry, Lenny."

Lenny grabbed the Remington and headed around the corner to his SUV. "Meet me back at the house."

He nodded and went to his car. At least they'd driven separately. He keyed the engine and racked the wheel. Before he put the car in gear, he pulled out his cell and dialed a familiar number.

CHAPTER FORTY-THREE

A SHRILL sound woke Georgia. Dimly aware she was still on the couch she rolled over and fumbled for the cordless.

"Yeah?" She croaked, her eyes still closed.

No one, she thought groggily. Damn. When would these hang-ups stop? She tossed the phone back on the floor. A band of pain shot around her head, and she felt hot and sweaty. Had she turned up the heat last night? She should go into her bedroom. It was always cooler there. Slowly she opened her eyes.

Light flickered behind her head. For a moment, she was disoriented. Then a smoky, roasting smell assaulted her nostrils. She shot bolt upright and jumped off the couch. Flames were licking her curtains, producing waves of thick, black smoke. She sucked in a lungful of hot, acrid air. The fire was contained to the curtains, but it was moving quickly. And she didn't have a fire extinguisher. She ran to the bathroom, grabbed a towel, and drenched it in water. Tossing it over her head, she backtracked to the living room and threw open her front door.

Shit. She shouldn't have done that. The sudden draft fanned a new line of flames that crept across the floor to the sofa, the same sofa she'd been sleeping on just a moment ago. She bolted into the hall. The fire alarm box was on the opposite wall. She smashed the glass and pulled the lever. A piercing siren blasted through the building. She banged on her neighbor's door.

"Fire! Everyone out! Fire!" She shouted. "Someone call the fire department!"

Her neighbor across the hall, a graduate student at Northwestern, opened his door. A portable phone was glued to his ear. His roommate hovered behind him. Both were in t-shirts and boxers. "I just called."

"Good. I'm going up," Georgia yelled. "Get the first floor on your way out."

The men sprinted down the steps. Georgia slammed her door closed and raced up to the third floor. She banged on Pete's apartment. "Pete. Get out. There's a fire!"

A woman with a panicked expression opened the door across from Pete's. Inside a baby was crying.

"Take the baby and go," Georgia shouted. "Now!"

The woman nodded and spun around. "Okay, sweetheart. Mommy's coming."

Georgia looked downstairs to the second floor. Despite the fact that she'd closed her door, curls of smoke were seeping under the edge. Eventually, they would rise and balloon out on the ceiling. If she kept low to the floor, she'd be okay. Pushing the towel further down on her forehead, she pounded on Pete's door again.

"Pete. Wake up! Now!"

Georgia counted to five, then banged again. Pete's neighbor charged past her, the baby in her arms. "I haven't seen him all day," she shouted as she hurried down the stairs. "Maybe he's not home."

Georgia stopped. If Pete wasn't home, she was wasting precious seconds. She should get out of the building while she could. But Pete had a broken ankle. He was on crutches. She thought about breaking down his door and doing a quick search. But that would take time.

The smoke in the hallway thickened and started to billow on the ceiling. She tasted grit. It was getting hard to breathe. She threw herself against the door one last time and beat on it until her knuckles were sore. "Pete Dellinger. If you're in there, get the hell out. There's a fire!"

Another ten seconds went by. Smoke blanketed the air, and heat pressed down on her. Beads of sweat broke out on her forehead. She looked back down the steps. An uneven light under her door told her that flames had reached the wall. She couldn't wait any longer. She sprinted down the steps two at a time. She had just cleared the second floor and was on her way to the first when she heard a latch turn upstairs. A thin voice called out.

"Help!"

She stopped. "Pete?"

"Georgia?"

She spun around and raced back up to the second floor landing. She saw orange under her door. Smoke rolled over her in waves, thickening her throat and nose. She kept going. "I'm coming!"

She scrambled back up to the third floor where she found Pete leaning on his crutches. His face was covered with sweat, and he was wheezing. She slipped the towel off her head and tossed it over. "Cover your head with this." Then she squatted on the third step from the top. "Throw the crutches away and climb onto my back."

He took the towel but shook his head. "No. You won't be able to support me." His voice was raspy and tense.

"We have to try. Hurry. We don't have much time."

She doubled over, giving him her back.

"This will never work," he said shakily.

"Damn it, Pete. Get your ass on the floor and scoot yourself onto my back. Then grab on and don't let go."

He did as she said, but when she felt his weight settle on her back, whatever air she'd managed to keep in her lungs flew out. She grimaced. She couldn't carry him down two flights of steps. But she had to try.

"Ready?"

"Yeah."

She bumped her rear end down the stairs, one step at a time. She got three steps down, but the strain on her back was excruciating. She glanced downstairs. Flames were in the hall now, climbing the wall outside her apartment. The heat was unbearable. She heard sirens cut through the air. Thank God. But they were still minutes away.

"Georgia, stop." Pete said. "We can't do this."

"Shut the fuck up!"

She inched down another step. Two more and she'd be at the landing. She tried to take a breath but breathed in hot, smoky air. She kept going. She made it to the landing.

"I have to rest," she gasped.

He let go and rolled back on the floor. She took in more smoke and started coughing. She twisted around. Pete struggled to sit upright. She crawled to him and propped him up. When he was stable, he shook his head. "You keep going. I'll—I'll get myself down."

The sirens were louder now. Someone yelled from downstairs. "Georgia, where are you?"

She tried to answer, but her voice came out as a whisper. Pete's voice overrode hers. "Second floor." He croaked. "Need help!"

"We're coming. Just hold on!"

"Georgia …" Pete's voice sounded muffled, as if from a distance. "You've got to get out of here. I'll—I'll manage."

She tried to stand, but the heat and the flames and the smoke were too much. Her feet slid out in front of her. Everything started to spin. Black crept across the edges of her vision. Then there was nothing.

***

When she came to, she was lying on a shriveled patch of lawn. She heard the staticky sound of two-way radios, voices shouting, the drone of idling engines. Slowly she cracked her eyes. On her left, a whirling mass of red and blue lights. On her right she sensed, rather than saw, a crowd of people.

"Hey, she's coming to," a male voice called out. Blurry faces appeared in her field of vision. "Give her some room. Everybody back off." The faces retreated, leaving only two. As she focused, she saw that one was a cop in uniform. The other was a woman in blue surgical scrubs and a sweat shirt. A paramedic. She took Georgia's wrist and stared at her watch.

"How's … Pete?" Georgia croaked. Her voice sounded muffled. Her mouth and nose were covered with an oxygen mask.

"Don't talk," the woman ordered, keeping her eyes on her watch. A few seconds later, she released Georgia's wrist and wrapped a blood pressure cuff around her arm. Georgia waited for her to finish, then stripped off the mask.

"The guy with the broken ankle," she said again. "How is he?"

The paramedic took her stethoscope from her ears and unwrapped the cuff. "He ate some smoke, but he'll be okay. We're taking him in for the night." She reached for the mask.

"Everyone else?"

"They made it out just fine, but you need to put this back on."

Georgia shook her head and raised herself on her elbows. She sucked in cold air. It tasted so fresh.

"Did you hear me?" the paramedic scolded. "The mask." She adjusted the mask and put it back on Georgia's face. "Don't want you to hurt yourself before a doctor sees you."

She shook her head again. "I'm not going to the hospital." She muttered through the mask.

"You may not have a choice."

Georgia stared her down.

The paramedic blinked, got up, and went back to the ambulance. Georgia turned to the cop, checked to see that the paramedic was out of sight, and tore off the oxygen mask. "So? What was it?"

"One of your candles fell over and started a blaze. At least that's what we think."

"That's never happened before."

"Not to you, maybe. But it does happen. A shitty accident, but an accident just the same." He cocked his head. "I have a couple of questions. Feel up to it?"

"Do I have a choice?"

"Not really."

"Help me up."

The cop pulled her to a sitting position. A wave of dizziness passed over her. She kept her head down until it passed. Someone brought a blanket and draped it over her shoulders. She looked up gratefully; now that the fire was under control, the night air was chilly. Smoke was still wisping out of her window, and an occasional ember floated seductively to the ground.

Hoses stretched to the front door and curled up a ladder to the second floor. Firemen and cops milled around, some cracking jokes with the forced levity people assume once danger has passed. Back by the ambulance Pete was laid out on a stretcher, and the paramedic who'd taken her vitals was with him.

Suddenly, a movement out of the corner of her eye caught her attention. On the fringes of the crowd a figure slipped around the rear of a fire truck and into the shadows. She only caught a glimpse, but she was sure it had been a man with curly dark hair and a slender build that was all too familiar. Matt-familiar.

"Officer."

The cop at her side looked up from a form he'd just attached to a clipboard. "Yeah?"

"Who was that?"

"Who?"

She pointed to the fire engine. "The man who just disappeared behind the truck."

The cop squinted in that direction. "I didn't see anyone."

"Someone was watching us. Over there. Then he moved away."

An engine turned over about a hundred yards down the street. A car pulled out and drove away.

Georgia craned her neck. "There he goes." She stretched her hands out and tried to get up.

The cop blocked her. "You can't do that now. The paramedics'll kill us."

She let him move her back into a sitting position. A cloud of unease settled over her.

CHAPTER FORTY-FOUR

DESPITE THE paramedic's insistence that she go to the hospital, Georgia borrowed a cell and called her friend Sam, who drove over and took Georgia back to her place. The next morning Sam drove her back to assess the damage. The hardwood floor was badly burned with black scorch marks across it, and her living room furniture was beyond repair. Between the smoke and the flames, most of her clothes in the hall closet were ruined, too. Had she been the type of woman who liked to shop, it would have been a windfall, but for her, replacing them would be a chore.

Her neighbors had fared better. Aside from the smoky odor that permeated the building and would linger for days, no one had suffered a significant loss. In fact, everyone, including Pete, was back in their apartment.

She was making another tour of the place when she noticed a ring of spidery concentric circles on the bottom of the living room window. She stopped to examine the markings. In the center of the circle was a small but distinct conical hole. She knew what made a hole like that. It wasn't a fire.

A chill ran up her spine. She peered through the window at the house across the street. She saw the tricycle and the red wagon, the embankment in back. Plenty of space for a sniper's nest. She turned around, imagining the trajectory of a bullet across her living room. She hurried to the opposite wall. There was a black hole in the drywall, the kind of hole that could have been made by a bullet that penetrated into the wall. She looked back at the table where she'd placed the candle that started the fire. It was along the same trajectory.

***

"Who did you tick off?" the Evanston dick asked.

"I don't know," she said. She'd debated whether to call the police, then decided it was stupid not to. When they arrived, she pointed out the embankment across the street where the shooter was likely holed up. She wasn't surprised when they didn't find any shell casings or footprints or other evidence. They didn't find the bullet, either. It had probably burrowed into the wall and was buried somewhere in the building's studs, maybe even the brick on the other side.

"So you have no idea who might have taken a shot at you?"

She told him she was working on the Sara Long case but said she had no idea who might be responsible. He said they'd investigate. He also said he'd talk to Robby Parker.

"And Dan O'Malley," Georgia said.

He nodded, but she didn't expect much. Evanston PD would run with it for a while, but without hard evidence beyond a bullet hole, or a victim, they'd move on. Drive-by shootings weren't unheard of in Evanston. Still, she was glad that they'd tell Parker. Maybe it would make him think twice about the strength of his case. And if anything happened to her, at least it was on record she'd been threatened.

After the detective left, Georgia drove to Carson's and bought three pairs of jeans, a couple of sweaters, turtlenecks, and a new jacket in less than an hour. Then she stopped in at the drug store to pick up a few essentials. She spent the rest of the day filing an insurance claim, replacing her driver's license, cell phone, and calling around for estimates on new furniture.

She thought about calling Lauren to suggest she ditch school for a day or two. Whoever was coming after *her* might turn their attention to Lauren instead. It wouldn't be a bad idea for her to lay low. But she didn't; she didn't want to scare the girl more than she already was. What she *should* do was call Lauren's mother and tell her to take care of her daughter. To stop drinking her Goddamm wine and pay attention to someone else. No one, even Lauren, should have to cope with the lack of a mother's protection.

But she didn't do that either. Andrea Walcher would almost certainly hang up on her before she delivered the message.

***

That night at Sam's, Georgia borrowed her friend's computer and went online. She entered the new password for "Yvonne's" email account. Her breath caught. A message had come in. She stared at the screen for a moment, then clicked to it.

"I would like to sample the new stock. Tomorrow, 4PM. The McCormick Hotel. Charlie." Her pulse pounding, she emailed back a confirmation.

***

Georgia was back at Carson's the next morning waiting for the doors to open. She bought a pair of black pants on sale and a black bolero jacket. This was probably as formal a get-up as she would ever wear, she thought as she drove back to Sam's. Later that afternoon, she dressed and started to put on makeup.

"Big date?" Sam grinned.

"You could say that," Georgia said, applying mascara to her lashes.

"Is it the guy in your building?"

"You mean Pete?"

"Who else?"

Meeting Sam's gaze in the bathroom mirror, Georgia realized she wished it was. She shook her head.

"So? Who's the secret admirer?"

"It's work related."

Sam cocked her head. "What kind of work takes you to Carson's to buy new clothes? And put on makeup?"

"It's not what you're thinking." Sam would never go the extra mile for work. Sure, her career was important, but her personal life took precedence. Sam had never understood why Georgia wanted to be a cop. Happily, it didn't affect their friendship.

Still, Sam rolled her eyes. "Priorities, kid. Priorities."

Georgia had her priorities. She kept her mouth shut.

***

Georgia reached the hotel by three-thirty, parked in the back, and headed through a large revolving door. The lobby looked just the same as she remembered: crystal chandeliers, tufted upholstery, thick oriental carpets, and lots of dark wood. A bar took up most of the space on the left. A coffee shop was off to the right. A ten-foot marble fireplace occupied most of the back wall. Three comfortable chairs were grouped around it. She went into the bar and positioned herself on a stool where she had a view of the entrance. Her plan was to watch who came in, then tail them when they left.

She ordered a Perrier. The place was empty except for a man in a suit, talking in the too-loud had-a-few-already voice, and a woman, also in a suit, who looked bored.

She nursed her drink and tried to collect her thoughts. The fish guts were an immature prank. But the bullet through her window was serious. Someone wanted her out of the way.

The only person she'd been in direct contact with recently was Lauren Walcher, and Lauren was cooperating. There was the incident in Starbucks with Andrea Walcher, but that had been serendipitous. Which left Fred Stewart's land deal. She'd talked to Jimmy Broadbent, asked him pointed questions about the clean-up, tied him to Harry Perl. That night someone took a shot at her. She sipped her Perrier. She hadn't mentioned the real estate deal to the Evanston cop. Maybe she should have.

She checked her watch. Ten till four. The entrance to the coffee shop was directly across from the bar. She remembered that coffee shop. She and Matt had come down for breakfast the morning they broke up. The weekend was supposed to be a special getaway, a few romantic days together. They'd planned it for months, making sure they both had the weekend off.

But when it came, everything went wrong. They didn't make love, and Matt wouldn't look her in the eye. When he ended it the next morning, he was mercifully brief. They hadn't even ordered coffee when he told her he'd met Ricki Feldman and was in love with her. He should have canceled the weekend, but he didn't know how. He knew how much she'd been looking forward to it. He was so sorry. Then he left.

A numbing coldness had swept over her, her face freezing into a block of ice. She didn't dare move a muscle. If she did, she'd crack. So she stayed at the table—she never knew how long—trying to decide whether to go on living. Eventually, the hostess of the coffee shop walked over carrying a pot of coffee. "You look like you could use this," she said sympathetically. She poured coffee into a delicate china cup, smiled down at her, and walked away.

Georgia could still see the delicate china cup. And the woman's kind face. She wondered whatever happened to the woman. Was she still at the hotel, doling out free cups of coffee to jilted lovers? Georgia didn't remember how she'd gathered the strength to go home. How she drove from the hotel back to her apartment. She was surprised to find she had no memory of the ride. In fact, she was so steeped in the past that she almost missed the swing of the revolving door. She snapped back. It was ten past four. She slid off her stool and slipped back into the shadows of the bar.

A man wearing a suit and carrying a brief case pushed through. He stepped into the lobby and looked around, as if he was expecting to meet someone. But he was at least forty feet away, and Georgia didn't have a clear view of his face. She took a few steps forward, still hugging the shadows. When no one came to greet him, the man shoved a hand into his pocket. A moment later, when no one had yet approached him, he looked at his watch and tapped his foot in irritation. When another minute passed, he spun around to leave.

As he did, Georgia finally caught a clear view of his face. The man had blond hair, ruddy cheeks, small eyes, and a weak chin. Tom Walcher.

CHAPTER FORTY-FIVE

GEORGIA GRIPPED the wheel as she drove back to Sam's. Tom Walcher was Charlie. Charlie was having sex with Sara. Sara had serviced her best friend's father. Made possible by the actions of his daughter.

In one way, she wasn't surprised Tom Walcher was catting around. His wife Andrea was a cold fish, and a hostile one, at that. She could understand Walcher seeking comfort elsewhere. But screwing his daughter's best friend? An underaged teen? What would make a man so reckless? Was he that arrogant? Or just stupid? The website files said he'd hooked up over two dozen times. He'd put his entire legal career in jeopardy. How could he risk it?

She turned south onto Sheridan Road. It was one thing to discover a supposedly respectable lawyer was making it with a teenage hooker. It was another thing to accuse him of murder. She had no evidence Walcher was involved in Sara Long's death. And it was possible his showing up was a coincidence. Still, she knew she should go to Kelly with what she did have. They had enough reasonable doubt to sink a battleship.

But something inside her rebelled at doing that. Maybe Kelly was right. Maybe she still was a cop at heart. Cops didn't just create reasonable doubt. They solved crimes. Or maybe it was her ego. Maybe Georgia just wanted to prove to Robby Parker and the rest of the force that she knew what she was doing. Or maybe it was just that since the fire, the case had become personal. Self-preservation was an excellent motivator.

She stopped at a light just south of Winnetka Road. Twilight came quickly this time of year, cloaking everything in a hazy purple light. She glanced through the windows of homes she passed. Women were preparing dinner in cheerfully lit rooms. Kids lounged in front of the TV or sat at tables. As a little girl, she remembered playing outside on brisk fall afternoons, stopping only when it turned dark and she was sniffling from the cold. She loved coming inside to the warm, cozy house where her mother was waiting, where the aroma of a hearty dinner floated through the air. That stopped when her mother left. Georgia was twelve. She hadn't seen her since.

Which brought her to another reason she wanted to keep digging. She'd promised to protect Lauren Walcher. No one else was looking out for her—no parent, no one in school, not even her friends. How many times had Georgia wished for someone to watch her back? If she went to Kelly now, Lauren's life would be shattered. She wanted to delay that—at the very least cushion the repercussions—until she could find a way to shepherd the girl through them. A seed of trust had sprouted between them. She didn't want to let her down. A shiver ran through her. Was this what it felt like to love a child?

Although she knew the route by heart, she stared through the windshield, suddenly unsure where she was. Dark shadows loomed on both sides of the street, and the landmarks she normally took for granted fell away. Was she still on Sheridan Road? Had she made a wrong turn and wandered into lost territory? The landscape looked eerie and alien, like a dream that was only half-familiar. She was about to pull over when the trill of her cell phone broke the trance. She snapped back. Yes. There was the strip mall with the 7-11. And the print shop next door. She pulled into the 7-11's lot and answered her cell.

"Davis, it's O'Malley."

"Dan, I was just thinking of you."

"Evanston told us about the fire. And the shooter. You okay?"

"I'm fine."

"That's good." She heard relief in his voice. "I think it's time for you to fold your tent, Davis. Things are—forgive me—getting too hot to handle."

She ignored the lousy pun. "I'm fine, Dan. In fact, I was—"

"I didn't expect you to say anything different."

She transferred the phone to her other ear. "Look, I know you feel responsible because you handed me the case. But I'm making progress. I'll have it nailed down soon."

"Assuming someone doesn't use you for target practice again."

"I can take care of myself."

"Look, I'd feel better if you turn it over to us. We're on it."

"Does that mean Parker is rethinking the Cam Jordan angle?"

"It's clear there's something else going on besides a mental running around the Forest Preserve."

"I appreciate it, Dan, but I'm not quitting."

"I figured you'd say that, too. Can't blame me for trying." He sighed. "Listen ... do you still have your—what you need to protect yourself?"

"I'm fine, Dan." She assured him. "Don't worry. Now I have a question. I know it sounds crazy, but, have you—or did anyone say they'd seen Matt recently?

"Matt Singer?"

"Uh-huh."

"Not for a long time. Last I heard he was running around the Holy Land finding religion. Why?"

She frowned. "Nothing. Hey, take care of yourself, okay?"

CHAPTER FORTY-SIX

GEORGIA SPENT another night at Sam's going over the events of the past few days. Tom Walcher figured prominently in Sara Long's activities. As Harry Perl's lawyer, he might also have been involved in a land deal that was, at the very least, suspect. He might have some connection to Derek Janowitz's death. Maybe even to the attempt on her life. At any rate, she had enough questions about him to warrant a closer look. But to do that, she needed help.

She woke up early the next morning, dressed, and crept out of the apartment without waking Sam. Twenty minutes later she was staked out down the street from the Walcher home. About 7:45 Lauren's Land Rover rolled down the driveway and turned onto the street. A few minutes later, Tom Walcher left too. Andrea Walcher was alone.

Georgia slid out of the Toyota. She was about to walk up to the house when Andrea Walcher emerged at the end of the driveway. She was wearing a fancy warm-up suit, and a sweat band was stretched across her forehead. She looked both ways, but didn't appear to notice the Toyota. She started to power walk down the street in the opposite direction.

Georgia followed her, hugging the trees to stay inconspicuous. But after a few minutes, Andrea broke into a jog. It was a crisp, sunny November morning, and Andrea was in good shape. Georgia was too, but her thick work boots and jeans slowed her. Within a few minutes Andrea lengthened the distance between them. Georgia abandoned her pursuit and trudged back to the car.

Thirty minutes later, Andrea walked slowly back up the street, breathing deeply, her arms pumping. Georgia waited until she was walking up her driveway. She stepped in front of the Toyota.

"Mrs. Walcher."

The woman turned around and looked at Georgia. A mix of emotions: surprise, recognition, and anger roiled her face. "Get away from me, or I'll call the police."

"That might not be a bad idea."

Andrea's eyes narrowed.

"I know about your brother Fred. And the land deal he was involved in."

"So?"

"Someone tried to kill me, and it could be connected to the sale of that land. I need you to tell me what you know about it. And what role your husband played in the deal."

"You can't just show up here, make wild accusations, and demand that I talk to you. Who the hell are you? I won't do it."

"I understand completely. In that case, maybe you'd rather talk to the police. Or the State's Attorney."

A flash of panic streaked across Andrea's face. "You can't do that."

Georgia stood her ground. "Someone took a shot at me a few days ago. I haven't given them your husband's name. Yet. But I will, if you don't talk to me."

"What are you talking about?"

Georgia explained.

"You can't possibly think my husband was trying to kill …" she paused. "… *you*?" Her face was a mask of annoyance, but Georgia could see an underlying anxiety. Andrea fixed her eyes on Georgia. "What do you *really* want? How much?"

"I don't want a dime. But I do want to know who took a shot at me the other night. And who killed Sara Long. And if they're related."

"Related? How could they be? You're grasping at straws. People like you—you'll do anything to get at us. Take us down."

Georgia shrugged. "If that's the way you want to play it, fine. But you might regret that choice."

"Are you threatening me?"

Georgia tried to remember that rage was the flip side of fear. No one could sustain it indefinitely. "Of course not." She made her voice sound conciliatory. "It is in your self-interest to talk to me, Mrs. Walcher. There are things going on that aren't right. And your husband is in the middle of them. It might take me some time, but I will get to the bottom of whatever he's doing, be assured of that. This could be your last opportunity to help yourself. And your daughter."

"Opportunity? How can you call it an opportunity when you strong-arm your way onto my property?"

"You'll understand after we talk."

Andrea gazed at Georgia, seemingly trying to gauge her seriousness. She ran her tongue around her lips. Then she took a quick look around, as if checking to see whether anyone was watching them. Finally, she capitulated. "You'd better come in."

She went to the kitchen door and opened it. Georgia followed her in. Andrea motioned to one of the stools at the granite-topped island and went to the coffee pot. She poured herself a mug, then held the pot up.

Georgia nodded and sat down at the island. Andrea filled another mug and brought it to the counter. "What is it you want to know?"

334 LIBBY FISCHER HELLMANN

"Let's start with your brother's gas station. Did you know the land underneath it was contaminated?"

She took a sip of coffee. "Yes," she said quietly.

"And did you know it got a clean bill of health in record time?"

"I was the one who told Fred. After Tom told me."

"And?"

"And what?"

"How did your brother react?"

"He—Fred—was angry."

"Why?"

"Because—because he knew it couldn't happen that fast."

"He told you that?"

Andrea looked at the floor and nodded.

"Suppose you start from the beginning."

She hesitated. Then, "After the stroke Fred was very weak. It was clear he couldn't go back to work. We all thought—Fred included—that selling the place would be the best idea. He'd have some money to take care of himself; he wouldn't have to worry. So Tom helped Fred sell it."

Georgia took off her jacket and draped it over the back of the stool. "To Harry Perl."

Andrea looked up. "Perl wanted the land and was willing to pay top dollar. It seemed like the perfect solution. Tom brokered the deal."

"What about the fact that it was contaminated?"

"My understanding is that Tom promised Fred that Harry would take care of it. It was part of the negotiations."

"Didn't you wonder how the land came to be cleaned up so quickly?"

"I didn't think anything about it." She shrugged. "Not my business. But when Tom mentioned it was done, I told Fred. He knew right away something was fishy. He said you can't have toxic ground on Monday and then find it's gone by Tuesday. He said he was going to look into it. And that he might have to go to the authorities." Her lips tightened. "He always wanted to do the right thing."

"Did Tom know Fred was upset?"

She nodded. "They had a fierce argument about it."

"When?"

"It was—must have been a couple of days before he died." Andrea stopped herself. "Oh, God." She clapped a hand over her mouth.

Georgia didn't say anything.

Andrea's face crumpled. "I—I don't want to know any more."

"You don't have that luxury, Mrs. Walcher."

Andrea squeezed her eyes shut. Then she slowly opened them. Her voice was tight. "I'm sure you're wrong. There's probably a perfectly reasonable explanation for the speed of the clean-up. And the attempt on your life. It could have been a random shooting. Evanston isn't nearly as safe as people think."

"Right." Georgia shifted. "Tell me about your brother."

"Fred was the only one in my family I talk—talked to."

"Why is that?"

"The rest of them—well, they were just looking for a hand-out." Andrea looked around her kitchen. Georgia followed her gaze, taking in the granite counters, the hand-painted tiles, all the latest appliances and gadgets. She looked like it might be the last time she ever did. "We didn't come from money. It was always a struggle. We were what you call 'lace curtain Irish.'"

Georgia winced, then tried to cover it up.

But Andrea caught it. "You know what I'm talking about, don't you? An abusive father, a mother who hid the bottle under her bed, siblings always in trouble. The only one who looked out for me was Fred. I got out of there as soon as I could. Became a legal secretary. Met Tom. Put that part of my life behind me. Except for Fred. When Tom found the gas station, we arranged the down payment, and Fred moved up here." She bit her lip. "It was the least I could do."

"Until now," Georgia said.

Andrea gazed around the room one more time. Then her eyes landed on Georgia. "What do you want me to do?" She whispered.

Was she ready to trade off her husband for her brother's memory? Or was she just trying to protect her life-style? Either way, Georgia knew she had her.

"I need to know how that property came to be cleaned up so quickly," she said. "I have my suspicions. But I need proof. I want to know whether anything related to the environmental situation precipitated Fred's—well, I need to find what lengths they went to get that clean bill of health. I want you to keep your eyes and ears open, and call me with any information you find. Does your husband keep records at home?"

"He has an office upstairs."

"That's a start. I need information. Documents. Records of meetings or conversations between Perl and your husband. Or any other people. Jimmy Broadbent, for example. Anything else you come across about 2500 Chestnut. You need to report back on anything. Even if you don't know if it's important."

A calculating look came over Andrea. "I thought you were investigating Sara Long's death."

"That's right."

"How is that girl's death tied into this?"

Georgia didn't like Andrea Walcher. She considered telling her about her husband and Sara Long. Maybe the woman's shock and revulsion—and fear of reprisals—would persuade her to be even more helpful. But she couldn't tell Andrea about "Charlie" without revealing Lauren's part in it, and she wasn't prepared to do that yet. "There might be a connection."

"How? What?"

Georgia shook her head. It took an effort to muzzle herself. "Not now. Not yet."

Andrea's nostrils flared. "How am I supposed to tell what's important? I don't know the ins and outs of real estate."

"You're smart," Georgia said. "You know more than you think."

"And in return? What do I get out of this?"

"In return, I'll try to protect you. And your daughter."

Andrea wrapped both hands around her coffee cup, took a sip, and gazed at Georgia over the rim. "You're going to destroy my life, aren't you?"

"Your husband started down that road a long time ago, Mrs. Walcher." She stood and shrugged into her jacket. "Just keep me informed."

CHAPTER FORTY-SEVEN

ANDREA WALCHER might not know the ins and outs of real estate, but Georgia knew someone who did.

The area just north of the Chicago River is more upscale than the Loop, and the office Georgia drove downtown to was no exception. Harry Perl had taken over construction of a 93-story glass and steel tower on the lot of the old Sun-Times building after Trump backed out and another developer, Max Gordon, defaulted. Georgia had dealings with Gordon when she was on the force. He was in prison now, serving a life sentence.

The cheapest parking lot was several blocks away under Grant Park, but she didn't mind the walk. Downtown Chicago was as beautiful as any European capital these days, mostly because of Millenium Park. Despite a multi-million dollar cost overrun, the park had created a corridor of graceful architecture, parkland, and sculptures that stretched from the Field Museum to Randolph Street. As Georgia cut across a wide concrete plaza, she gawked at the outdoor amphitheater. The arrangement of metal on the roof looked like a giant soup can that had been opened the wrong way, but it was supposed to deliver the best acoustics in the world.

She walked from Michigan Avenue to Wabash, then north over the river to the skyscraper. The marble floors, soaring ceilings, and walls of the lobby were as elegant as they were cold. Georgia tugged on her jacket. She'd started out dressing in a pair of nice slacks, an angora sweater, and makeup. She made sure her hair looked good. Then, in a sudden about-face, she changed back into jeans and a turtleneck, washed off her makeup, and pulled her hair back in a ponytail. She'd be damned if she would compete.

The elevator whisked her to the 54th floor. To the right was a law firm with five unpronounceable names, but on the left were two huge glass doors embossed with the words "Feldman Development." She took a breath and opened the door.

The waiting room was spare and modern and looked like an art gallery: abstract pastels on the wall, area rugs, and an Asian-inspired flower arrangement. She could have sworn there was some kind of fragrance in the air, too. A sweet cinnamon, she thought.

The receptionist was blond and might have been attractive if she hadn't worn so much makeup. She was dressed in a low cut blouse and miniskirt, and she looked Georgia up and down, taking in her jeans, turtleneck, and boots.

"May I help you?" she asked with that patronizing smile that usually means the opposite.

"Yes," Georgia replied evenly. "I'd like to see Ricki Feldman. I don't have an appointment."

"I'm so sorry." The receptionist frowned, revealing lines in her forehead that put her closer to forty than the thirty she clearly wanted to appear. "Ms. Feldman is booked all day."

"Tell her it's Georgia Davis. And it's important."

Either her voice carried more authority than she thought, or the name meant something to the receptionist, because the woman's patronizing attitude vanished, leaving only the frown. She lifted the receiver of a phone with about twenty-five buttons and pressed one of them.

She spoke softly, and Georgia only caught a phrase or two. "Yes. She's here now." A pause. "Okay." She disconnected and looked up. "Please, make yourself comfortable." The smile was noticeably absent. "Ms. Feldman will see you shortly."

"Thanks." Georgia went to a grouping of low slung chairs near the windows. An assortment of magazines was fanned across a table. She remained standing and looked out the east window, which provided a spectacular view of Lake Michigan. She usually found solace in the whitecaps that sparkled in the sun, the horizon dotted with a few snowy sails. But today was November grim, and a gray curtain of fog hovered over the water, revealing glimpses of angry steel waves underneath.

"Hello, Georgia," a voice said behind her.

She spun around. Ricki Feldman was standing across the room by a glass coffee table. Her eyes held a curious, appraising expression, but something else was there, too. Georgia couldn't tell what it was. "Hello, Ricki."

Ricki sported the obligatory business casual look: a pair of sharply creased gray wool pants, a thick black sweater, and dark but soft looking leather boots. Her silky brown hair, swept back in a knot, made her eyes look enormous. For a moment Georgia regretted she hadn't worn nicer clothes. Then she rebuked herself for the thought.

"I'm working on a case," she said, "and I need to ask you some questions."

Ricki nodded as if she'd been expecting her. "Come into my office." She turned around.

Georgia followed her down a hall. The same sweet cinnamon scent she'd smelled in the reception area grew stronger. Ricki's perfume. Ricki led her into a corner office. Light poured in through two large windows, one looking south to the Loop, the other east to the lake. Ricki went to her desk, a huge slab of granite on a steel base, and waved her into one of two red upholstered chairs. Glass and metal shelving units behind the desk were filled with African masks, cloisonné bowls, cuckoo clocks, and other knick-knacks, all no doubt designed to show visitors how well- traveled she was.

Ricki sat, leaned her elbows on the desk, and steepled her fingers.

"I'll try to be brief," Georgia said.

Ricki nodded again, but the submissive angle of her head and a slight narrowing of her eyes puzzled Georgia. It was almost as if Ricki was expecting a blow. Georgia dismissed it. Probably her imagination.

"I know this is awkward," she began.

Ricki cut her off. "In a way, I'm glad. I've been wanting to talk to you."

"About what?"

"Matt and I—well, it was wrong from the start. We—we weren't compatible.' She paused. "We—it was like a fire that burned itself out."

Georgia jerked her head up.

"I'm sorry. That wasn't what I meant to say. It just—We were just— well, from such different worlds. I'm sorry I caused it."

Georgia kept quiet, marveling. Ricki couldn't stop aggrandizing herself even when she was trying to apologize. As if she was the sole party responsible and Matt had nothing to do with it.

"He broke it off, you know. Before he went to Israel."

She didn't know. She remembered Matt talking about Israel when they were together. He wanted to make Aliyah, he called it. A pilgrimage to the Holy Land. At one point, he'd asked her to come with him. She would have. She didn't believe in God, but Matt did, and if it was important to Matt, it would have been important to her. She was even willing to consider converting to Judaism. But then a few months after he and Ricki hooked up, he'd taken a leave of absence from the force. Georgia assumed they went to Israel together. She'd been wrong.

"I'm not here to talk about Matt," she said finally.

"No?" Ricki looked genuinely surprised.

"I told you. I'm working on a case, and I need information."

Now Ricki looked flustered. "For the police?"

"I'm working as a private investigator."

"Really." Her perfectly plucked eyebrows arched, and the imperiousness returned.

This was the Ricki she knew. "What can you tell me about Harry Perl?" She leaned back in her seat.

"Harry?" Ricki shot her a sidelong glance. "He and my father, and then I, were partners on several projects. He's a dynamic businessman."

"Are you still partners?"

"Why do you want to know?"

"I told you I'm working on a case, and his name has—come up."

Ricki stared at her.

Georgia's breath hitched. She'd been counting on Ricki's need to impress, to flaunt her knowledge, especially in front of a "rival."

"Yes," Ricki answered after a pause. "We have been and continue to work together occasionally."

"There's a specific piece of land I'm interested in. On Chestnut Street. Near the Glen."

Ricki shrugged. "I'd have to check. I'm more or less a silent partner. I don't know all the specifics."

Georgia didn't believe her. "Well, maybe you could answer—on a purely theoretical level. Let's say there's a property in the Glen. And the owner was trying to redevelop it quickly. In fact, let's say there was some urgency to do it fast. Why would there be such a hurry?"

Ricki steepled her hands again. Did she think that made her look thoughtful? "It could be a number of factors," she said. "There could be pressure from the investors. There could be construction warranties or deadlines. Or zoning issues."

To her knowledge Perl didn't have any other investors, and Georgia doubted there were any construction deadlines. She recalled the conversation she'd overheard in the health club. Someone had mentioned the zoning board. "What zoning issues?"

"Low income regs, for example."

"What are they?"

"New state regulations require a village to have a certain amount of low income housing available. Ten per cent, I believe. But a lot of villages on the North Shore aren't in compliance."

"Why am I not surprised?" Georgia cracked.

"The problem is that in a year the governor will establish a statewide panel. The Zoning Board of Appeals. It will have the power to overrule any decisions made by a local zoning board. Which means there's a chance local villages could lose control of their own zoning process. Particularly if they aren't in compliance with the low income housing regs."

"How would that affect our theoretical property owner?"

"Villages are running scared. They're afraid that if they have too much commercial property now, there won't be enough land to provide enough affordable housing down the road, and they could lose local control of their zoning, and, ergo, their land."

"But that's over a year away."

"It takes at least a year—usually more—from the time you get the zoning until the building goes up. Your theoretical owner would want to make sure the land is zoned now, the way he wants, before the shit hits the fan."

Georgia scratched her cheek. "There's really a chance that could happen? That land could be rezoned?"

"Probably not if it's a going concern, but if the land has been vacant or idle for a while, who knows?"

"And might he hire a lawyer to help him push things through?"

"What are you getting at?"

Her answer was cut off by a knock at door.

"Come," Ricki said.

The receptionist poked her head in. She was holding a pink message slip. "Sorry to interrupt, Ms. Feldman." She paused for such a long moment that Georgia wondered if the interruption had been planned. "Come into the office five minutes after we start talking, Sally—" Ricki could have whispered over the intercom.

"A message just came in. From Mr. Perl."

Ricki motioned with her hand. "Bring it over."

The receptionist stepped in front of Georgia, blocking her view, and handed the pink slip to Ricki.

"Thanks, Ashley." When the receptionist didn't move, she added, "You can go."

Ashley turned around and shot Georgia a look. "Yes, ma'am."

Georgia smiled up at her. Ashley walked out of the room. "Guess you're not such a silent partner after all."

Ricki waved a dismissive hand. "Oh, Harry uses the phone the way some people use email."

"What do you mean?"

"His grasp of technology stopped around 1972. He won't get near a computer."

Georgia motioned to the slip of paper. "But he manages to stay in touch."

"He tracks people down all over the world. He once called me from Greece. At home. At three in the morning. Made me wish I'd never given him my number." She laughed nervously. "Now, if that's all ..."

Georgia made a decision. She leaned forward. "One more thing. Let's say this theoretical piece of land had been a gas station in its former life."

Ricki shifted.

"A gas station which leached all sorts of toxic chemicals into the ground. How long would the clean-up take before it could be redeveloped? Theoretically."

A muscle beside Ricki's eye began to tic. "I couldn't begin to say. Years, I imagine."

"So if this property—this theoretical gas station—was cleaned up in record time, say six months, and had an NFR letter from the state, that would be unusually fast."

"It was?" She looked concerned, then tried to hide it. "What are you talking about?"

"Nothing. I figured you would be up to speed on all the appropriate waste disposal regulations. Given your—history."

Ricki blanched. "You know, I really need to end this meeting. I have another appointment."

"I thought you might." Georgia smiled. "Well, thanks for your time."

She left Ricki staring anxiously at the pattern of her granite desk.

CHAPTER FORTY-EIGHT

THAT EXPLAINED the urgency, Georgia thought as she drove north on Sheridan Road. Harry Perl wanted to cash in on the Glen property by building condos and a mall. He couldn't risk it being rezoned in light of the upcoming low-income housing regulations. So after buying the land from Fred, Perl got Walcher to use his "leverage" with village officials to make sure the zoning went his way. He probably used the same "leverage" with Broadbent to come up with an environmental report that got a clean bill of health from the state.

A weak sun broke through the overcast. Georgia rolled down the window, bracing against the rush of cold air. She was close. When you examined Walcher's business practices, factored in his relationship with Sara Long, his possible involvement with Derek Janowitz's murder, maybe even the attempt on her life, even the most aggressive prosecutor—including Jeff Ramsey—would have to take a closer look.

But it wasn't a slam dunk. She still had no proof Walcher had a hand in Sara Long's murder. Kelly would insist that wasn't necessary, that they had enough reasonable doubt to clear Cam Jordan, but Georgia wanted to find Sara Long's killer. Not just for her own safety, but for Cam Jordan and his sister Ruth. For the Long family, as well, for Lauren, and for all the teenage girls who made decisions that put themselves at risk. The problem was she wasn't sure of her next move, and she was running out of time to make it.

Her cell phone chirped. "Georgia Davis."

It was her landlord. They'd finished the repair work, installed a new floor and window, even thrown a fresh coat of paint on the walls. She could move back in.

That afternoon she packed up her clothes, thanked Sam profusely, and went home. The living room was virtually empty, but the walls and new floor gleamed, and they'd put a special chemical coating on the walls and floor to seal in the lingering odor of smoke. The new furniture she'd ordered, thanks to a speedy resolution of her claim by her insurance company, hadn't arrived, but her new computer, which the super had brought upstairs, was in a large box in the middle of the floor.

Her bedroom furniture was still intact, but her mattress reeked of mildew and smoke. She lugged it down to the curb and, anticipating the insurance reimbursement, went to buy a new one. It must have been a slow period at the mattress store, because they said they could deliver it that afternoon. She swung by Target on her way back and picked up new bedding, towels, and a pillow.

The mattress arrived on schedule, and she made up the bed. She was just pulling the computer out of the box, thinking she'd order a pizza before she assembled it, when there was a knock on the door.

Pete Dellinger grinned when she opened it. "I saw your lights were on. When did you get back?"

"Just now." Georgia returned the smile. "Good to see you up and about. Are you okay?"

"The hospital kept me overnight, but I came home the next morning." He kept one hand behind his back. "What about you? I heard someone tried to take a shot at you."

"Looks that way."

"Are you holding up?"

"Do I have a choice?"

"Everyone in the building got a call from the detective in Evanston, you know."

"I didn't."

"I asked if they had any leads. He said there hadn't been much movement, but the case was still open."

"That's cop speak for 'we don't have a clue, and we can't spend more time on it.'" When Pete frowned, she shrugged. "Happens all the time."

"How can they just give up?"

"They don't have a choice. There are always new cases that demand your attention. Cases that haven't gone cold."

"Do you think the shooting is related to your case?"

"Probably."

"Jesus! How can you be so—so calm?"

"What makes you think I am? Hey, let's talk about something else, okay?"

He looked at her unblinkingly for a moment, then cleared his throat. "Okay," he said, pointing to his leg. "Look."

She did. His cast was gone, and he was wearing a sock and sandal on his bad leg. His ankle seemed thick. "I'm down to an Ace bandage. And a cane."

She looked around. "Where is it? The cane?"

"Still upstairs." He moved his other hand from behind his back and held out a bouquet of flowers. "These are for you. To thank you."

Her cheeks grew warm, her neck too. She couldn't remember the last time anyone had brought her flowers. She felt suddenly shy. "Let me find something to put them in," but even as she said it, she realized she didn't own a vase. The empty mayonnaise jar under the sink would have to do. She started for the kitchen, then stopped and turned back to the door. "Oh— I'm sorry. Would you like to come in? I promise to scare off any snipers."

He grinned and limped inside. He was wearing his usual khakis and a button-down shirt. The light blue color set off his sandy hair. She remembered the first time she'd seen him, the day he moved in. He'd been wearing a t-shirt with the sleeves cut off. She remembered how his biceps strained against the load.

"Sorry," she heard herself say again. "I bought some new furniture, but it hasn't come yet."

"No problem." He carefully got himself down on the floor near the computer box. "New?"

She nodded.

"Need help setting it up?"

She didn't. Computers were easy to assemble. Even a kid could do it. "Sure."

An hour later, it was done. Including the cable connection, which had somehow survived the fire.

"Did you salvage data from your old machine?"

"I haven't tried. It's in the basement."

"Well, let me know if you want to try. Maybe I can help."

"Thanks."

"You want to go online now and send me a test email?" he asked.

"How about we order a pizza first? My treat."

"Deal."

After finishing the pizza, they tested out the broadband connection. Everything seemed to be working.

"Do you ever wonder whether all this email has made a difference in the amount of snail mail?" Pete asked. "I mean, the post office ought to be thankful, don't you think?"

"Why? Their business is shrinking. Then again, we still get mountains of junk mail, so I guess they're not suffering."

"And there are always some Luddites who will never use email." He laughed. "It's a major accomplishment for them to use a cell phone."

Georgia stopped short. She stared at Pete.

"What?"

"I'm sorry," she said. "I—you just said something that made me think."

"About your case?"

She nodded.

"What? What did I say?"

"Cell phones. You said—" She shook her head. "Oh, never mind."

He continued to gaze at her for a moment. Then, "You never stop, do you?"

"What do you mean?"

He shook his head. "Never mind."

Georgia didn't know what he was thinking, and that made her uneasy. Pete must have felt the same way, because he said goodnight soon afterwards and went upstairs. As Georgia closed the door, she wondered if she should feel bad the evening ended on a sour note.

Then she pushed Pete Dellinger out of her mind. Ricki Feldman said Harry Perl didn't go near computers. He used his cell all the time. He didn't care who or what he interrupted. What if Walcher was with Sara Long when Perl called him? Lauren had said Sara had a special relationship with "Uncle Fred." How Sara thought of him as the uncle she never had. What if Sara overheard something about Fred and his land and what Perl and Walcher were doing to get it? And what if Walcher realized she'd overheard? What would Sara have heard? And what would Walcher have done?

CHAPTER FORTY-NINE

GEORGIA CALLED Andrea Walcher's cell, hoping to get Tom's cell phone number, but Andrea didn't pick up. Georgia left a message to call her back. She considered calling Lauren for her father's number, but decided not to. Now that Andrea Walcher was cooperating, Georgia needed to "manage" her relationships with mother and daughter. They were both her allies—for the moment—but it was a tenuous balance. If Lauren knew her mother was involved, she might pull away. But Georgia needed Andrea—she was more informed about her brother's property and in a better position to help.

She paged through the website files Lauren had printed out for her. According to the files, Sara's last trick with Charlie was Wednesday, September 14. Three days before she was killed. And barely a week after Fred Stewart died in the fire.

She went online and downloaded a picture of Walcher from his law firm's website. His bio said he'd been with Phelps and Mahoney for twenty years, and was head of the Real Estate Practice in Chicago. He had gone to the University of Chicago Law School, and he was a member of the firm's Executive Management Committee.

Early Saturday morning, Georgia drove back to the McCormick Hotel. Most of the business clientele had departed the previous day, and the lobby was quiet. The coffee shop was virtually empty, but a fire roared in the fireplace, and a man sat before it poring over a newspaper. A hotel employee in a white jacket and black pants whisked the surfaces of tables with a brush.

Georgia went to the clerks at the front desk. At resort hotels, the weekend shift was the most important and was manned by senior staff. Not here. A young man and woman, neither of whom looked more than twenty, stood behind the marble counter. They both wore crisp white shirts, red ties, and gray blazers with the hotel insignia embroidered in gold on their pockets. Georgia debated which one to approach. The girl might be more cooperative, and she didn't want suck up to the guy just to get information. Then again, the girl could be the type who always played by the rules.

Deciding to take her chances on the girl, she had just stepped up to the counter when another woman joined them. She wore same uniform as the others, but she was older and rounder, and when Georgia looked more closely, she spotted the word "Manager" on her jacket insignia. A pair of reading glasses was perched on her nose. She started to talk to the two clerks, gesturing to a sheet of paper in her hands.

Georgia was only a few feet away, and after a moment the woman looked up. A jolt of recognition seized her. It was the same woman who'd given her coffee the morning she and Matt broke up. The woman flashed her a puzzled smile that said she thought she knew Georgia too, but couldn't quite place her.

Georgia recovered first. "Good morning. You probably don't remember me, but you did something very kind two years ago."

"I did?"

The other two clerks stopped what they were doing. The woman smiled triumphantly, as if to say "I told you service was important."

"You were working in the coffee shop. I had just broken up with my boyfriend. You poured me a cup of coffee. Said you thought I could use it."

The woman's eyes widened. "I remember." She studied Georgia. "You were looking quite poorly that morning."

"I felt poorly."

The woman's glance swept the lobby. "You're—you're not back with him ..."

"No." Georgia laughed.

"Good. So where's your new guy?"

"I don't have one. My name is Georgia Davis, by the way." She extended her hand.

"Sherry Diehl." They shook. "How can we help you?" Her gesture included the two clerks.

"Actually, it's a personal matter."

The woman gazed at Georgia, then turned to her charges. "It's still slow. Why don't you two head into the office and catch up on invoices?"

The clerks retreated into the back room. Once they were out of earshot, Georgia leaned slightly forward and placed her hands on the counter. "I'm an investigator and I'm working on a case. I have a photo of a man, and I'd like to know if you recognize him."

Suspicion registered on the manager's face. "Are you with the police?"

Georgia told her the truth. "Up until last winter, I was. I'm working privately now. But the police are working the same case. You may have heard about it." She summarized it.

Although the lobby was warm, the manager shuddered. "I did hear. I have a fifteen year old daughter." She frowned. "Wait. I thought they got the guy. A sex offender, something like that? Preying on young girls?"

"There's evidence that suggests he didn't kill the girl."

"Is that so?" When Georgia nodded, she added, "And you're trying to find the real killer?"

"We think a man who—may be connected to it—stayed here several times." She pulled out the picture of Tom Walcher. "Do you know him?"

Sherry studied it. Then she looked up. Georgia saw the recognition in her eyes.

"Thank you."

Sherry nodded. "Is that all?"

"Well, there is something else. I have reason to believe he was here on September 14th. It would help me out a lot if you could confirm that."

"You want me to check our records."

Georgia nodded again.

Sherry didn't say anything for a moment. Then, in a quiet voice she said, "I can't do that."

Georgia winced. "We can subpoena them, but you could save us a lot of time. And money."

"I don't think you heard me." Sherry's voice was firm. "Our records are highly confidential. I could get fired for going into them without authorization."

"You wouldn't have to speak or say anything," Georgia persisted. "Just nod or shake your head." When the woman didn't reply, she laid it on thick. "This is a bad guy. If we don't get him, he could go on killing. Do you really want him out there? What if he runs into your daughter?" It was a shitty thing to say, but she needed the information.

Still, Sherry shook her head. "I'm afraid you'll have to go through our corporate office. I can give you a name if you're interested."

Georgia's shoulders sagged. In a perverse sort of way, though, she wasn't sorry. Sherry Diehl was no pushover. The world needed more women like her. She let Sherry write down the name of some corporate officer and headed back to her car.

She had just exited 94 on Dempster heading toward Evanston when her cell trilled. She pulled to the side of the road and answered. It was Andrea Walcher with her husband's cell number. Georgia could have kissed the woman. As soon as she got home she called her source in Florida. He said she'd have to pay double for a 24-hour-over-the-weekend turnaround. She gave him her credit card number without complaint.

CHAPTER FIFTY

"GODDAMMIT!" MATT'S employer thumped his folded newspaper on the table. "What the hell happened?"

Lenny hung his head, as if he was a kid on his way to the woodshed. "The fucker missed."

His boss spun around. They were in his Lake Bluff study, a paneled room with a painting of a bearded rebbe and a student poring over the Torah on the wall. "I thought you were supposed to be a crack shot, Singer. The Mossad told me you could split a Goddammed hair."

Matt frowned, but inside he felt relief. His cover was holding. He and the Bureau had created it, step by painstaking step, making sure the right people would vouch for him, back him up. "I don't have an excuse, Mr. Perl. The window glass I was shooting through must have been too thick." He shrugged. "Shit happens. I take full responsibility."

Harry Perl glared at him. "You take responsibility. You … ." He shook his head. "Give me one good reason why I shouldn't fire you."

He stared back. "I can't."

"Well, boss …" Lenny shuffled his feet. "You could—"

"Was I talking to you?" Perl snapped.

Lenny closed his mouth.

Matt waited. This could be the end of his job. And his undercover work. Maybe even his life.

Perl's cell phone jangled. "Perl …" A pause. "I can't talk now, Ricki." Matt went on full alert. "What are you talking about? You can't!" Another pause. "I know what what happened to your father. He was my partner. But what you're proposing is unacceptable." Silence. "*Your* reputation? This isn't about you, Feldman. I'll call you back."

Perl broke the connection and tossed the phone down on the desk. He gazed at Lenny. "As long as the checks keep rolling in, everyone's happy. Then the first time something is off, they all want to jump ship." He picked up the phone and tapped it against the desk. "I told her father I'd look out for her, but she's turning out to be a problem."

Lenny nodded.

"Stop bobbing your head like a fucking chimpanzee. If I want your input, I'll ask for it."

Lenny looked chastened.

"If I weren't so Goddamned busy, I'd—" He cut himself off, then sighed. "One step at a time." He gazed at the painting of the rebbe. "I'll give you one more chance, Singer. Here's what I want you to do."

As Perl explained, Matt felt a buzz along every nerve in his body.

CHAPTER FIFTY-ONE

WALCHER'S PHONE records came back in less than 24 hours. Georgia pored over the calls he received on September 14. Six calls from one number, one of them around 4PM. After making sure her own number was blocked on Caller ID, she dialed it.

"Perl here …"

She hung up. Her heart was pounding hard enough to rattle her teeth.

***

Lauren lay on her bed, eyes closed, earbuds blasting Metallica. If she could only make the black penetrate everything in her mind, her problems would disappear. Nothing would be real. She concentrated on the darkness, hoping the rough, pounding beat would crush her thoughts into dust.

A gust of air rolled over her, and she opened her eyes. Her mother stood at the door. She came to the foot of her bed. Lauren couldn't remember the last time her mother had actually come into her room. Usually, she'd buzz her on the intercom or shout up the stairs. She was wearing the same grey sweater and taupe slacks she'd worn this morning. Her mother never wore the same thing all day. And her hair looked as if she'd been trying to pull it out.

Lauren propped herself up. Her mother's lips were moving, but she couldn't hear her words. Her face was bathed in anger—it never went away—but something else was there, too. It took her a minute to figure it out, but when she did, a chill crawled up her spine. Fear. Her mother was afraid.

She waved her arms. Lauren removed the earbuds. A tinny bass spilled out of them.

"That Goddammed noise ..."

Lauren pushed a button on her iPod, and the room went quiet. Her mother lowered her arms.

"What's the problem?" Lauren asked.

"Someone called a few minutes ago. You answered the phone."

"So?"

"Who was it?"

"Why do you care?"

"I need to know."

Lauren cocked her head. Her mother rarely asked that kind of thing. "It was for Dad." She had been trained from a young age to ask a caller's name before transferring them to her parents. What if it was someone they didn't want to talk to? A stranger, or, God forbid, a salesman? "A woman."

"What woman?" her mother said.

"Ricki Feldman."

"Did she say what she wanted?"

"No. But she sounded pissed."

"She did?"

Lauren reached for her headphones.

"Did you transfer the call to your father?"

"Do I look stupid? Of course I did."

"Sorry." She gazed around Lauren's room. "So, what are you up to tonight?"

Lauren frowned at her mother. "I don't know. Why?"

"I—I thought maybe we could watch a movie or something …"

"Together?"

"Something wrong with that?"

Had her mother been drinking? She didn't look high, but after a lifetime of wine and martinis before dinner, who could tell? Lauren shrugged. "I guess not."

"Good. I'll be back. I just need to check with your father."

✱✱✱

It was Sunday night, and Georgia was gazing out the window at the red wagon across the street from her apartment when Andrea Walcher called. "I can't talk, but something's going on."

"I'm listening."

"Ricki Feldman called Tom half an hour ago. Lauren answered the phone and said she sounded angry. Afterwards Tom called Perl."

Ricki hadn't wasted any time. "And?"

"I went into his office and asked him what the calls were about. He wouldn't tell me, but he said he might need to meet with Perl tonight."

"On a Sunday night?"

"That's what I said. He said it was important."

"Did he say where? Or when?"

"No. But his expression—it was something I haven't seen before."

"What was it?"

"It was—empty. Absolutely empty."

"Don't let him leave," Georgia said. "I'm on my way."

"You can't come here. He'll—"

"Make him wait. I'll be there in twenty minutes."

Georgia hung up and grabbed her coat. She'd wanted Ricki to raise hell about the fake clean-up; apparently, she had. She tugged on her boots, then stood up and scanned the shelves above her desk. She took her digital tape recorder and slipped it in her bag. She started down the steps two at a time, then paused at the second-floor landing. She turned around and went back up.

Inside her apartment she went to her closet and pulled out a shoebox. Lying underneath a soft cloth was her Sig Sauer 229. The Sig had the smallest recoil of any nine millimeter she'd used. She liked its feel, too. She'd had two Sigs when she was on the force. When she was suspended, she turned in one along with her badge. The other went into her closet.

She lifted it out along with the kydek holster it was nestled in. She'd bought the holster for times when a concealed carry was necessary. Although it wasn't leather—a fact which Parker always pointed out—the plastic hugged the contours of her body.

She slipped the Sig out of the holster and checked the magazine. She found a small box of spearhead Gold Dot hollow points and loaded them into the clip. Then she went into her bedroom and changed from the thin black turtleneck she was wearing to a bulky white fisherman's sweater. She snapped the holster over the belt of her jeans and slipped in the Sig.

As its weight settled against her hip, she realized she'd forgotten how safe a gun made her feel. She was no Robby Parker—her partner used to say that they could take down anyone they wanted, anytime. They were "the Law." And yet, the Sig *did* make her feel safe. And powerful. Maybe she wasn't that different from Parker. She rummaged through the closet again, pulled out a pair of handcuffs, and dropped them in her pocket.

Outside, a light mist spit tiny droplets on the Toyota. She climbed in and turned on the defroster. The wipers smacked against the windshield. She eased out of her parking space and headed north on Green Bay Road. An accident was slowing traffic in Wilmette, so she cut over to Sheridan. As she made the turn, the rain started in earnest. She caught the sandy scent of just-wet concrete.

Despite Illinois's reputation as a flatland, a string of bluffs hug the shoreline of Lake Michigan from Winnetka north to Lake Bluff. Between the cliffs are steep ravines, and Sheridan Road cuts through them. For a few miles, especially in Glencoe, the road turns into a sharp winding thoroughfare that's wonderfully scenic but can be treacherous, especially in bad weather.

As Georgia sped north on Sheridan, she accelerated up a hill, crested the top, and started down a straight decline. At the foot of the hill was a sharp curve. She was winding around it when a sudden flash of light seared the darkness behind her. A loud crack accompanied it, and her rear windshield exploded. Glass shattered on the back seat. The sudden rush of air made the Toyota fishtail. She struggled to keep control of the wheel.

Air and rain poured in. She shot a glance in the rear view mirror. Headlights pierced the black void. The downward angle of the beams suggested a high-riding SUV or small truck. She could make out two figures in the front seat. The figure in the passenger seat was aiming a rifle out the window.

Another muzzle flash. She jammed the accelerator, preparing to swerve from side to side. But this stretch of Sheridan was only two lanes, and as she careened around a curve, another pair of headlights swam toward her: a car, speeding into the Toyota from the opposite direction. She jerked the wheel. The Toyota skidded and swerved on wet road. She barely missed the oncoming car. The other car's horn blasted for a full ten seconds.

Georgia shot another glance into the rearview mirror. Her pursuers were still behind her. Suddenly a driveway materialized on the left, practically on top of her. She wrenched the wheel. The Toyota lurched off at an angle. Tires crackled on gravel. Trees flashed past, and she felt the car bounce wildly onto gravel and rocks. She slammed on her brakes and heard a terrifying screech. The car started to spin. The force propelled her forward, and she strained against the seat belt. She thought she might sail through the windshield. The belt threatened to slice her stomach in half. Another powerful shove threw her back against the seat. Her neck snapped back, but the seat belt held.

Then it was over.

She sucked down wet air and mentally checked herself. Except for a cramp where the seat belt squeezed her chest, and a throbbing in her neck, she seemed to be okay. The Toyota sat partly on a driveway that stretched back into such dense blackness that she couldn't see where it ended. It was probably one of those private roads that spider-webbed through the North Shore. Her eyes raked the darkness Whoever was shooting at her hadn't made the turn. She shivered in the rain-soaked cold. They could be coming back. She needed to get to her destination fast. She threw the Toyota into reverse.

CHAPTER FIFTY-TWO

WHEN GEORGIA pulled up, the floodlights above the Walchers' garage flickered on. The lights cut irregular stripes on the grass, which was covered by a carpet of wet leaves. She parked in the semicircular drive. So far no one had followed her. She got out of the car and inspected the damage to her rear window. There wasn't much glass left, except in the corners, and the back seat was a blanket of glassy pellets.

She started toward the house, then slowed. Did she really want to confront Tom Walcher? Maybe she should turn it over to the cops. They could bring him in for prostitution. Question him about Sara's death, Janowitz's, his brother in law, Fred's. The attempts on her life, too. No. She'd come too far. She crossed over the fishpond and rang the bell.

Footsteps inside clacked. Her hand casually brushed the Sig and she moved to one side, just in case, but it was Andrea who opened the door. When she recognized Georgia, she scowled, and, without as much as a greeting, led her into the kitchen. A cup of steaming tea sat on the granite counter. A fruity aroma wafted through the air.

"Where is your husband?"

"Upstairs. In his office." Her face grew worried. "What are you going to do?"

"What happened to the meeting with Ricki Feldman?"

"I don't know. Why?"

"Ricki might be in danger. I need to warn her."

"What are you talking about?"

"I told her about the 'expedited' clean-up on your brother's land. She's not happy about it. I'm sure that's why she called Tom."

"What do you think they'll do?" Andrea's expression was a portrait of fear.

Georgia glanced around the room, wondering the same thing. Then she heard a squeak from the hall.

Andrea's face went ashen. "It's Tom," she whispered. "If he finds you here ..."

Georgia cut her off. "Why don't you let me worry about that?"

Her hand slipped to her holster, but before she could draw the Sig, Walcher burst in. He was clutching a .38. "Don't move. Either of you. And keep your hands where I can see them."

"Tom!" Andrea's face twisted in shock. "What are you doing? Put that down!"

"Do what I say, Andrea." Walcher's voice was ice.

Andrea raised her hands. He waved the gun at Georgia. "Now you."

Georgia slowly lifted her hands in the air.

His chin shot up toward his wife. "How did she get in here?"

Andrea didn't reply.

"You let her in." His eyes strayed to his wife's cup of tea. "Planning a tea party?" He took an angry step toward the counter.

Andrea shot a look at Georgia that was a silent plea for help.

Georgia cut in. "Walcher, come to your senses and put the gun down. Let's talk."

"I heard plenty of talk out in the hall. I have nothing to say to you." Walcher flicked his eyes to his wife. "Or you. I should have known you'd turn traitor. What did she promise you? A pass if you turned state's evidence? She can't do that, you know. She's only a PI."

Andrea wouldn't meet his eyes.

"I want both of you in the living room where I can see you." He pointed the gun at Georgia. "You first."

Georgia moved cautiously. So far he hadn't noticed the concealed carry. She was glad she was wearing the fisherman's sweater. Andrea followed Georgia, and Walcher brought up the rear. Georgia's shoes thudded across the marble floor, then grew silent as she hit the carpeted steps in the living room. She stopped a few feet from the picture window. The glass was beaded with rain, but their reflections were sharp against the blackness. How could she get to her Sig?

Andrea spoke up. "Tom, put that thing away before Lauren sees you. This—"

"Keep your mouth shut."

Georgia spread her hands. "She's right. This won't help your situation."

"I told *you* to keep your hands above your head. And what do you know about my *situation*?"

She raised her arms again. "You helped Perl fake the environmental report on your brother-in-law's land. Then you and Perl killed him so he couldn't scuttle the deal. But too many people know about it now. Ricki Feldman. Your wife. Me. You can't keep killing just to cover it up."

A muscle in his jaw twitched.

"You had Sara Long killed, too."

Andrea looked astonished. "Sara Long? What does *she* have to do with this?"

Walcher's eyes looked dark, large, and dangerous. She had a sudden vision of what evil looked like.

"You killed Sara because she overheard you and Harry on the phone talking about Fred and the land. You and Harry were afraid she'd tell someone. Like her pimp, Derek."

"I didn't kill her." Walcher spit out.

"You know the law. Doesn't matter if you pulled the trigger. You're an accessory."

"It wasn't me!"

Georgia pretended to give him the benefit of the doubt. "Then put the gun down and tell me who did. And why you were just on the phone with Perl."

"Perl can be—he's impulsive. I was trying to talk some sense into him."

"He wants to go after Ricki, doesn't he?"

"I told you. He's under control."

"For how long?"

Walcher leveled the .38 at Georgia. "No more. You don't get twenty questions."

"Why is she bringing up Sara Long?" Andrea cut in. "And talking about pimps? What the hell is going on?"

"Stay out of this, Andrea."

"If it wasn't you," Georgia ignored Andrea. "It had to be Perl. Put the gun away and save yourself, Tom."

"Stop!" Andrea hugged her arms. "Both of you! I want to know what's going on!"

Yanking her thumb toward Andrea, Georgia faced Walcher. "Do you want to tell her or should I?"

When Walcher didn't answer, Georgia turned to Andrea.

"Your husband had Sara Long killed. And her pimp, too."

Andrea Walcher tipped her head to the side. Her voice was thick and slow. "Sara—Long—had—a—pimp?"

Walcher's eyes skimmed Georgia then settled on Andrea. "Don't believe anything she says, Andrea. She's trying to drive a wedge between us. She'll say anything."

"Sara Long was a prostitute, Andrea, and Tom was one of her best clients." Georgia said it quietly, but her words cut the air like a scream. She hadn't promised Lauren not to reveal the prostitution ring, but she had delayed the telling of it. Now it was coming out, and Lauren's role in it would follow. This family, this girl, would be destroyed. Despite being held at gunpoint, a profound sadness came over Georgia.

Andrea's body went very still. "Is this true, Tom? Were you screwing Lauren's best friend? A teenager?"

"You have no proof." Walcher's voice was laced with venom.

"You're wrong," Georgia said quietly. "There is proof. Right in this house, as a matter of fact."

"Don't believe her, Andrea."

"In your daughter's bedroom."

Walcher scowled. Andrea stared at Georgia.

"Your daughter has been running a teenage prostitution ring on her computer."

Andrea's jaw dropped.

"In fact, she's responsible for setting Sara up with you, Tom."

"NO!" A strangled shout came from Walcher. "You're lying!"

"For our special customers only," Georgia recited. "A new shipment has arrived: young, blonde, sexy. Guaranteed to give you pleasure over every inch of your body. Sound familiar, *Charlie?*"

For a moment Walcher didn't move. Then, very slowly, he took a step towards his wife. "I didn't know it was her. I swear. She looked older. Not like one of Lauren's friends. I didn't know until—"

"Until she overheard the call from Harry about Fred," Georgia interrupted.

"I swear I didn't know." He continued to move towards his wife.

Andrea threw out her arms. "Don't come any closer."

Walcher stopped.

"But once you figured out who Sara was, it gave you another reason to kill her," Georgia went on. "Aside from not wanting anyone to know you were screwing your daughter's best friend."

Andrea's mouth was working and her lips were moving, but nothing came out.

Georgia tried to muster some pity for the woman, if only because she was Lauren's mother. She felt nothing.

Walcher was another matter. She hated that he was a fixer with no conscience. She hated him for killing—or allowing others to be killed—so casually. And she hated that he abused young girls, using sex as his private currency. No wonder Lauren had no scruples about prostituting herself and finding a way to profit from it. She started to edge toward him, thinking she would throw herself at him and force him to drop the gun, when a scream split the air.

"I hate you! I hate you all!"

Tom whipped around, the .38 still in his hand. Lauren stood at the entrance to the living room, teetering on the top of the carpeted steps. Her eyes were huge, and her cheeks had spots of crimson on them.

Georgia quickly drew her Sig. "Lauren, get out! Go away! Walcher, drop it!"

But Lauren stayed where she was. She faced her father, her chest heaving. She didn't seem to notice the gun in his hand. "Is it true? Are you Charlie? Did you have sex with Sara? My best friend? And then have her killed?"

"Lauren, go upstairs. Now!" Georgia yelled again. "Walcher, drop the gun! I'm not gonna say it again!"

Walcher hesitated for what seemed like forever, then closed in on his daughter. Grabbing her arm, he pulled her towards him and thrust her in front of his body like a shield. He slid the .38 against her temple.

"Daddy, what are you doing?" Lauren shrieked. "Let me go!"

"Quiet, Lauren," Walcher spun her around so they were both facing Georgia. Walcher's eyes locked on hers. "Your turn. Throw your gun on the floor. Now."

Georgia didn't move. Her pulse roared in her ears. "You don't want to do this, Walcher," she said slowly.

"Drop it! Now!" His voice was ragged.

Lauren's eyes filled with panic. A thousand thoughts tumbled through Georgia's brain, but one took precedence. She'd promised to protect Lauren. And Andrea. Slowly, she extended her arm and lowered the Sig to the floor.

"Now, get your hands in the air," Walcher barked.

Georgia straightened and raised her hands.

Walcher motioned with his chin. "Andrea. Get the gun and give it to me."

But Andrea didn't move. Her face wore a puzzled expression, as if she was watching a movie in a foreign language with no subtitles.

"Did you hear me, Andrea?" Walcher's voice was so taut it was almost a whisper. "Get her gun."

"Daddy, please …" Lauren broke in. Her face started to crumple.

"I said be quiet, Lauren."

Andrea remained as immobile and silent as a statue. Georgia looked at Lauren. The girl's shoulders were hunched, and her muscles were coiled. She looked scared, but Georgia thought she saw something more just under the surface. Determination. When she threw Georgia a calculating glance, it registered. She was waiting for Georgia to give her a signal. Georgia looked at her Sig, still on the floor.

"Andrea!" Walcher shouted. "Are you deaf? Do what I tell you!"

Suddenly Andrea came alive and launched herself at her husband. At the same time Lauren shoved against her father, broke his armhold, and lurched toward Georgia. Georgia pulled her onto the floor, grabbed her Sig, and threw herself on top of the girl. Walcher struggled with his wife and stumbled. A shot rang out. There was a loud pop, and an abstract but colorful canvas fell off the wall. A wisp of smoke floated out from the point of impact. Andrea dropped to the floor.

For a moment, no one moved. Georgia wasn't sure if Andrea had been hit along with the painting. Then,

"The Chagall!" Andrea shouted.

Georgia rolled off Lauren, propped her elbows on the floor, and steadied the Sig. Walcher extricated himself from his wife, stood, and pointed the .38 at Georgia, but she was ready. She aimed and squeezed the trigger.

The flash from the Sig was accompanied by a deafening roar. Walcher's face got soft and rubbery, and his lips curled in a baffled smile. Then his body seemed to fold in on itself, and he collapsed almost gracefully on the floor. Georgia watched a small pool of red soak into the white carpet.

Andrea pushed herself up and covered her face with her hands.

Georgia stood, then helped Lauren to stand. The girl looked at her father, then at Georgia. Her bottom lip quivered, and an anguished sob escaped her lips. Georgia holstered her gun and opened her arms to the girl.

CHAPTER FIFTY-THREE

IT WAS a long night. The Glencoe cops took Georgia back to the station. Andrea was taken to the hospital. Lauren went too and was treated for shock.

Georgia was put in a windowless interview room with cinderblock walls where she was interrogated for several hours. The NORTAF task force was activated, and three detectives wandered in and out. They treated her cautiously: Walcher had been killed in his own home, and they had no way of knowing how or why she was there. Still, she wasn't too worried. Lauren and Andrea's stories would back her up, and the fact she'd been a cop should work in her favor.

After going over what happened several times, she told them what she'd uncovered about Harry Perl's land deal, the bribes, the fake environmental report, the murders, and the attempts on her life. But when she connected everything back to Sara Long's murder, they looked troubled.

Two of the dicks who'd been questioning her left, presumably to check out her story. One of them came back an hour later.

"We called Robby Parker. He says the whole thing is fucked. The Long case is sewn up. They've got their man, and they're ready for trial."

Anger stung her. "I could have told you he'd say that. I'm working for the defendant."

"He said you and he used to be partners, but you got suspended. He says you never got over it."

Her hands clenched into fists. She slipped them into her pockets. "If you've been anywhere near a TV recently, you know that's bullshit. The women backed me up, didn't they?"

"We're already looking," he said tiredly. "Especially into Perl. But as for the rest of it ..." He shrugged. "It's not our case, for starters."

Georgia paced the room, trying to control her frustration. She should have expected there'd be no help from Robby Parker. But she was sure O'Malley would vouch for her, once he heard about it. Paul Kelly, too.

For the moment, though, she needed to focus on a more critical problem: Harry Perl was still out there. If you believed Tom Walcher, he was a loose cannon, particularly when he was crossed. And Ricki Feldman, her unhappiness over the environmental troubles on record, had crossed him.

"You know," the dick said, "You've been through a lot tonight. You shot someone. Doesn't happen often. I'll bet the shrink who counsels cops in your area would be glad to see you."

Georgia stopped pacing. She'd grapple with that on her own time. "I don't need a shrink. I need to stop a killer."

The detective eyed her. "I have no idea what you need, but if half of what you said is true, what you need is to be careful."

They let her go home around seven the next morning. First she called Henry, a friend who had a body shop on Fullerton. He told her if she brought the car down he'd have it fixed in two days. She said she'd bring it in.

She couldn't confront Perl—the cops had confiscated her gun—but she might be able to do some reconnaissance. Tail him or his goons. Make sure they weren't closing in on Ricki Feldman. She told herself she should warn Ricki, too. She also wanted to check on Lauren.

She knocked on Pete's door, hoping to catch him before work. He was there. She convinced him to lend her his Acura.

After a quick shower, she raced up 41 to Lake Bluff, a well-heeled village adjacent to Lake Forest on the tip of the North Shore. She wound through the village to a street that ended a few feet from Lake Michigan. Overlooking the water was a huge estate that looked like an Italian villa, with carved stone work, Roman arches and gargoyles above.

The driveway in front of the house was empty. Georgia backed up to the road and parked at the curb. Clear morning sunshine threw an innocent light over everything. She'd staked out the house for about thirty minutes when a dark Chevy turned onto the street behind her. She checked the rear view. At the wheel was a lean man with curly, dark hair. Her heart started to hammer. As he passed her and turned into the driveway, he glanced over, and their eyes met. Her breath sucked out, and she felt like she'd been punched in the gut.

***

Matt was still in the Chevy, his hands on the wheel when she climbed out of her car and went over.

"It *was* you."

He rubbed the back of his neck. "Hello, Georgia."

There were the same brown eyes she'd lost herself in. The curly hair she'd run her fingers through. And glasses. She liked it when he wore his glasses. They gentled him, she said. She started to speak, but her throat closed up.

"You look good," Matt said.

Georgia gazed at him. Then she blinked it away. "You mind telling me what the fuck you're doing here?"

"I work here."

"For Perl?"

He nodded slowly. "It's a long story."

"The man's a monster."

"I know. "

"Walcher is dead."

He looked shocked. "When?"

"Last night. I shot him."

A gleam came into his eyes. "So that's it ..."

"What?"

"Perl and Lenny went out about an hour ago. They told me to stay here."

"Lenny?"

"My—my supervisor."

"We need to find them."I think he's going after ..." She pressed her lips together. "... Ricki Feldman."

"What?"

"It's my fault. I set her up." Georgia explained how she'd gone to her office and told her about the fake report. "If she didn't already know about it, I was hoping, given her father's history, she'd raise hell with Perl. And if she did know, I figured she'd warn him I knew. Either way, I figured I could use her to flush them out."

Matt interrupted, a knowing look in his eyes. "It worked."

"How do you know?"

"She called Perl. I was there." He paused, putting something together. "Now it makes sense."

"I should have warned her. I screwed up."

He shook his head. "You did what you had to."

"There's more. I think Harry Perl had Sara Long killed."

"The girl in the woods?" Matt looked worried. "That was before I signed on."

"Walcher was screwing her," Georgia said "She was a hooker. I think she heard something she shouldn't have."

Matt's mouth opened and then shut.

"Where did they go? Do you know? "

When Matt shook his head, she pulled out her cell and punched in a number. "Is Ms. Feldman there yet?" She paused. "And you haven't heard from her? Okay." She disconnected. "She's not at her office. Hasn't been in all morning." Georgia's pulse started to race. "Where does she live?"

"Hold on." Matt pulled out his cell phone and punched in a number. "Korman, Singer. I need a GPS fix on the SUV." He paused. "Yeah. Call me back." He disconnected.

"A GPS locator?" Georgia narrowed her eyes. "What's that about?"

Matt didn't answer.

"Who was that?" He still didn't answer. "You're working undercover!"

He didn't answer for a moment. Then, "Yes."

"For Olson?"

He shook his head. "When I got back from Israel, the U.S. attorney set me up with the Bureau. White collar crime unit."

"How did that happen?"

"I've known Perl was dirty since Ricki and I were together. It grated on me. I came home to deal with it."

"The avenging angel." It came out sharp.

A guarded look came into Matt's eyes. "Would you believe me if I said I wanted to make restitution?"

She wondered whether to apologize. "For what?"

His cell trilled. "Yeah? Where? Okay. I'm going there now. I need back up." He dumped the cell into his shirt pocket. "The SUV is on Barberry Lane in Lake Forest." He swallowed. "That's where Ricki lives."

"Let's take my car." She headed toward the Acura, then turned around and caught his arm. "Matt, I don't have a gun. They took my Sig."

"I can fix that."

CHAPTER FIFTY-FOUR

MATT DUG a Glock 27 out of the trunk of the Chevy. He rummaged around, pulled out a box of .40 caliber bullets, and handed them over. She loaded the clip, chambered a round, then slid into the driver's seat of Pete's Acura.

"Where did this come from?"

"Lenny makes sure we're well stocked." He got into the passenger seat.

She started the engine and pulled away from the house. "What exactly do you do for Perl?"

"I'm his bodyguard. Among other things."

"Were you the one who shot through my window and started the fire?"

He cleared his throat. "I shot wide."

"It was you on Sheridan Road, too. The rear windshield."

"You have to believe me. I would never have hurt you."

"Why should I trust you? I could have been killed."

"You wouldn't have let me get into the car if you didn't."

He was right. She turned south on Green Bay Road.

"Why Perl?" She asked after a pause. "Other men have done worse."

He hesitated. "I—I think it's because he claims to be such a devout Jew."

"Perl?"

"He has all the trappings. Keeps kosher. Goes to shul. Observes the Sabbath, at least, when it's convenient. But he's a hypocrite. He recites a *barucha* out of one side of his mouth and bribes a village official out of the other. And when he doesn't get what he wants ... well ..." His voice trailed off.

"Maybe he thinks his piety gives him special dispensation. You know, larceny, pay-offs, and murder in God's name?"

"You mean like a jihad for Jews?"

"It's been done before."

"Harry Perl isn't spiritual. There's nothing at his core but greed." Matt sighed. "And Ricki wanted me to study Talmud with him."

"You knew him before you left?"

"Ricki wanted to introduce us. She knew I was trying to be more observant, and I guess he was the most observant Jew she knew." He grunted. "She thought we'd have something in common. But we never met."

"Why not?"

"I was privy to some deals she and Perl were working on. I got suspicious so I started to do some digging. I didn't like what I found, but I didn't have the stomach to do anything about it then." He looked over. "Ricki and I were wrong from the start. We should never have been together."

Georgia tried to ignore the lump in her throat. She needed to keep on track. "Did you know about Fred Stewart and the property at the Glen?"

"Not until I got back. But there were other deals. Just as dirty. The Feds know about them."

"When did you realize I was working the case?"

"I knew you were working the Sara Long murder, but I didn't know it connected to Perl."

She tightened her grip on the wheel. "So they wired you?"

"That's how they cracked Greylord, remember?"

She nodded. They'd studied the scandal at the Academy. Twenty years ago an Assistant State's Attorney, upset with the operations in Cook County court, which included regular bribes to judges, suddenly became a defense attorney. He insinuated himself with the people who were lining the judges' pockets. No one knew he was wearing a wire. Over 92 people, including 13 judges, were eventually indicted.

Aloud, she said, "How did you land the job with Perl?"

"We let them think I was on the take and was moving 'product' in Israel. Arms, mostly. It worked."

She was quiet for another long moment. Then she turned to him. "What you're doing—it's gutsy, Matt."

"I don't look at it that way. It's just something I need to do."

"I know."

His eyes softened. His cell phone rang again. "Yeah?" A pause. "Okay." He put the cell down. "They're on the move."

"Where?"

"They're heading south on Green Bay. We have a choice. We can follow them. Or we can go to Ricki's house. Make sure she's okay."

"Back up's on the way, right?"

Matt nodded.

"Let them check the house. We should follow the SUV. She could be with them."

Georgia kept driving. "Where do you think they're going?

"Depends what they're planning to do."

"What does Lenny carry?"

"He has a frigging arsenal. A Remington Bolt action rifle, a few semi-automatics, a couple of revolvers."

Green Bay jogged east and then south again. "What about Perl?"

"I've never seen him handle anything. But that doesn't mean he couldn't. He might have one of the revolvers. Or a snub nose."

His cell phone rang again. He listened, then put it down. "They're moving east on Tower Road."

"East?" Georgia scowled. "There's nothing there. It's all residential."

"There must be something."

"Shit! I know where they're going."

"Where?"

"The Lagoons!"

***

The Skokie Lagoons, which are actually located in Winnetka, are a series of marshy ponds just east of 94. Originally built by the Civilian Conservation Corps in the 1930s, the Lagoons have been restored. Now there's fishing, boating, bird-watching, and if you happen to be looking west, you might see the sun set over the water, a rare treat for Chicagoans. Surrounded by woods and thick underbrush, the Lagoons offer something else of value: a treasure trove of hiding places.

"They've got plenty of choices," Georgia said. "If they do it right, the body might not turn up 'til spring." She gestured to Matt's cell. "Find out if they turned south on Forestway."

Matt called his handlers and asked. He listened, then nodded. "We're there in five," he said into the phone, then disconnected. "They did."

Georgia turned south onto Forestway, a street with the Forest Preserve on one side, the Lagoons on the other. The trees, now bereft of leaves, seemed bowed by the brittle air. On the Lagoon side were parking areas, behind which were stretches of grass and dirt, and finally the shoreline. She slowed down.

"We're looking for a dark Ford Explorer."

EASY INNOCENCE   385

They came around a sharp curve. A parking area appeared on their right. No car. Georgia kept going. She drove around another curve and reached another parking area. A Black SUV was parked at the far end.

"There it is," Georgia said.

"Keep driving," Matt said.

She cruised past the car until they were out of sight, then bounced the Acura up on the curb and parked. They got out and jogged back to the SUV.

Georgia felt the hood. Still warm. A pale sun hung in the cold sky, but everything was quiet. No sound of moving water. No birds. No breeze rustling the tree branches. Even the faraway noise of passing cars and trucks on the Expressway was hushed. It was the silence of impending winter. And death.

Matt pointed to the ground. The dirt hadn't dried out from the rains of the past few days, and she could make out some partial impressions. They looked like striated shoeprints, prints that could have been made by a man wearing rubber-soled shoes. Matt started to follow the tracks. Then he stopped, turned around. He held a finger to his lips and motioned straight ahead.

In front of them was a thicket of cattails, canary grass, and other prairie grasses. Through it she caught a glimpse of nickel-colored water. Georgia closed her eyes to concentrate. Gradually, she became aware of faint sounds: Rustlings. Grunts. Then a higher-pitched sigh.

She opened her eyes and tiptoed forward. Matt tapped on her shoulder, gesturing for her to go one way. He'd go the other.

She nodded and let out a breath. It left a tiny cloud in the air. She waited while he circled around the thicket. Then she started to pick her way through from the other direction, going slowly, trying not to make any noise. A moment later, a twig snapped under her foot. She froze. Nothing. After a long moment, she edged forward again. The underbrush started to thin, and she could hear voices. Low. But urgent.

She stopped and peered straight ahead. Ricki Feldman was lying face up on the ground in a clearing near the water's edge. She wasn't moving. Georgia squinted and thought she saw her breathing shallowly. What had they done to her?

The two men were a few feet away, their backs to Georgia, talking in low tones. One of them was dressed in warm-up pants and a fleece vest. Perl. The other, bigger and brawnier, wore canvas pants and a pea jacket. He'd drawn a gun—it looked like a Glock—and kept glancing back at Ricki, as if he expected she might rise, brush herself off, and run away.

Georgia waited for Matt. He had more ground to cover; it would take him longer to get in position. She quietly unsnapped the flap on her holster and drew out the Glock. She stood for what seemed like a long time, willing the goon to keep talking. Finally, she spotted a subtle movement across the clearing. Matt drew his weapon. She knew he expected her to, also. She pointed the Glock at the two men. Suddenly, Matt emerged from the thicket.

"Lenny, drop the gun!"

Lenny whipped around, surprise on his face. "What the fuck?"

Perl spun around too.

"Don't move, Perl," Georgia stepped forward from the other side. "I shot Walcher, and I'll shoot you too!"

Perl froze, mouth open, eyes huge, but Lenny swung around toward Georgia. A slight smile played on his face. He pulled back the slide on his automatic and aimed. She jumped back and sideways. She lost her balance and fell to the ground.

A shot rang out. Then the quiet rushed in again. Georgia rolled onto her stomach and raised her head. A look of surprise had unfolded across Lenny's face. His body tensed. A hole in his stomach gushed blood. He fell forward onto the ground. His hands still clutched the Glock.

Perl still hadn't moved. Georgia scrambled up and trained her gun on Perl, but Matt was already on him.

"Are you okay?" He shouted.

"I'm good, Matt."

"Okay." He sounded relieved.

Georgia looked at Ricki. She was still breathing shallowly, but her eyes were open and filled with panic. Matt stayed where he was. He kept his gun on Perl.

"Cuff him," he called to Georgia.

She pulled out the cuffs from her pocket and bent over Perl. Pulling back one arm, then the other, she snapped them in place.

"Thank God you're here!" Perl suddenly found his voice. "He ..." He gestured with his chin at the fallen security guard. "... He went berserk! He took us hostage. He was going to kill us both. He—"

"Save it," Georgia said.

"You have to believe me. I would never do anything to hurt my partner's daughter. He—"

"Shut up, Perl," she repeated.

Perl's mouth closed. The distant sound of a siren cut through the air. Georgia glanced back at Ricki. Her skin looked clammy, and Georgia could see sweat on her upper lip. She went to her and dropped down on her knees.

Ricki cringed. What was she anticipating Georgia wondered. A blow? A shot to the head? Or something worse?

"Am I going to die? Please," she said, her voice weak but desperate. "I don't want to die."

Georgia pressed two fingers against Ricki's carotid. Her pulse was racing. She turned over her hands. Her palms were sweaty, her eyes still panic-stricken.

"What's happening? Am I dead? Help me, please!"

Georgia studied her nemesis. She thought about what she would want, were she in Ricki's position. Then she slowly raised her hand—it might have been the hardest thing she'd ever done in her life—and brushed her fingers across Ricki's brow. "You're safe now," she murmured gently. "It's over. You're going be okay."

CHAPTER FIFTY-FIVE

"IT'S A race to see who gets him first: the Feds or the locals," Kelly said over breakfast next morning. He'd gone out of his way to drive up to the Lucky Platter in Evanston.

"Has anyone filed charges yet?" Georgia was famished. Between the interviews and debriefings with NORTAF and the Feds, she hadn't eaten much the past two days. She bit into a strip of bacon. It was perfect: crisp, dry, not too salty.

"Not yet. But there's a laundry list of 'em coming."

"Lenny, the security man, did all the hits, right? Including Sara Long?"

Kelly nodded. "Perl's trying to finger him, claiming it was all his idea. But no one's buying it."

She sniffed, taking in the aromas of fresh coffee, fried eggs, and biscuits on her plate. "Why the bat? He was already carrying."

Kelly shrugged. "Probably one of those opportunities that just presented itself. Someone brought the bat to the hazing. He saw it lying around and figured it might be useful."

"It got Cam Jordan indicted," she said quietly. Then, "You know what I keep thinking about?"

"What?"

"The girls hazed Sara Long because she was too nosy. Insinuating herself in other people's business. But that was her way of finding out whether anyone knew she was hooking. It was all so ... incestuous."

Kelly reached for his coffee and blew steam off the surface. "Tell me something. You ever kill someone before?"

"No."

"You holding up?"

"I'll make it." At the Academy, they'd warned she might have a reaction if she ever shot someone. They made sure she knew about the resources that could help them through the trauma. But Georgia didn't need counseling or pills or even booze. Her training had kicked in, and she'd shot Walcher on instinct. Kill or be killed. She'd do it again.

"How much would you say Fred Stewart's land was worth?" She asked.

"Hard to say," Kelly replied. "In today's market, with four or five acres, in the middle of the North Shore, probably a few mill. Maybe more."

She felt a profound weariness. A murder investigation was all-consuming. It compelled her to forsake everything except the search for the killer. She had gone over every lead, every interview, every detail, almost obsessively, making sure she hadn't missed anything. In the end, though, a young girl's life had been snuffed out because of money. It seemed so futile. Even trite. Perl was the ringleader, but it wasn't just his responsibility. Or Tom Walcher's. All of them, Andrea, Lauren, even Sara Long, had become broken, in one way or another, because of greed. They were all accountable.

Kelly folded his hands. "You did good, Davis."

"It was my job."

A young waitress in jeans and a t-shirt padded over and freshened their coffee. Her shoes hardly made a sound.

"Listen …" Kelly leaned across the table after she was gone. "You wanna take on another job? I got a few lined up. And—well—it turns out I don't mind working with you."

Georgia smiled weakly. "Well now, that's a ringing endorsement."

"Hey." He looked injured. "I mean it."

"I got a call from Eric Olson this morning. He's the Chief of Police where I used to work."

One of Kelly's eyebrows went up.

"When I was suspended, I—er, accidentally forgot to turn one of my Sigs. The Glencoe cops confiscated it Sunday night."

"So?"

"Olson said he knew I kept it when I was suspended. And that he had to make a decision whether to bring charges—"

"The shithead."

"Or invite me back on the force so I'd be legal."

Kelly's other eyebrow joined the first to form a perfect arch. "What did you tell him?"

"That I'd think about it and let him know."

Kelly didn't say anything for a long while. Then, "Make the right decision, Davis."

***

"What's going to happen to Lauren?" Pete said that night, scrubbing sweet potatoes over Georgia's kitchen sink. Georgia had surprised herself by inviting him, along with Sam, and Sam's boyfriend, for Thanksgiving dinner. He'd surprised her by accepting, though being a vegetarian, he'd skip the turkey. But he came down later waving his mother's secret sweet potato pie recipe, which he claimed he'd wangled after begging and pleading and a bribe or two.

"She's been charged with pandering. And if it turns out any of her girls were under sixteen, they'll add juvenile pimping."

"What does that mean in terms of a sentence?"

"Pandering's a Class Four felony." At his blank look, she added, "One to three years. But she has a shot at probation. Especially if I testify on her behalf."

"Which you're going to do."

Georgia turned on the flame under a large pot of water. "She's not a bad kid once you cut through the crap. If I were the judge, I'd get her into therapy right away. And make her do community service with abused women."

"What about her mother?"

"She appears to be remorseful."

Pete frowned. "But wasn't she in on the scam?"

"Not really. She didn't know anything about the deal until her brother died."

"Do you believe her?"

Georgia didn't like the woman, but that didn't make her a liar. She nodded.

Pete dropped the potato into the pot. "This life of yours. How can you do it day after day? Doesn't it get to you? Don't you ever want to be—normal?"

She rinsed her hands and dried them with a dishtowel. "Who says I'm not 'normal,' whatever that is?"

CHAPTER FIFTY-SIX

A BLEAK November chill descended the day before Thanksgiving. It was accompanied by unrelenting gray skies above and a layer of frost below. Georgia wandered around her living room, marveling at her new furniture which had been delivered yesterday. A cushiony beige couch, two brown easy chairs, and a real, honest-to-God bronze coffee table. The earth tones gave off a tranquil feeling, and with her desk and shelves, the room looked full.

She was thinking about doing some last-minute errands when the intercom buzzed from downstairs. Thinking Pete must have forgotten something, she pressed the button.

"What did you forget?"

There was no answer.

"Pete?"

"It's Matt."

She froze for a moment, then pressed the buzzer to let him in. She thought about hurrying into the bathroom to run a comb through her hair, slapping on some blusher. She stayed where she was. She cracked the door and went into the kitchen and filled a glass with water. While she was drinking it down, her front door squeaked. She went back into the living room.

Matt stood there, unwrapping a plaid muffler. "Hello."

"Hello, Matt."

He peered around. "The place looks great."

"A fire's a great excuse to get new stuff."

"May I take off my jacket?"

She folded her arms. She could smell the outdoors on him, a chilly, damp, pungent scent.

He kept his jacket on. "We did great work the other day. It was—a seamless operation."

She studied his expression. "Your superiors are happy, I'm sure."

"They are. And thank you for not pressing charges against me."

"You did what you had to." He'd said the same thing to her the other day. "I'm okay. And," she waved her hand, "I got new furniture out of the deal."

He nodded gratefully. "I have enough to work out between me and Hashem."

"Your God can't be that capricious. And if He is, why believe in Him?"

The glimmer of a smile crossed his face. "You get right to the point, don't you?"

She kept her mouth shut.

"Well, then, I guess I will, too. We make a good team, Georgia."

A wave of uneasiness washed over her.

"Will you give me a second chance?"

She blinked, trying to will away her disquiet, but it stayed in her gut, hard and heavy.

"I made a mistake," he went on. "I left a piece of me behind when I went away. It stayed with you. I want to be whole again. Let me make it up to you. You can't say you haven't thought about it. Especially the past few days."

"That's true. I have."

"And?"

She bit her lip. "The thing is ..." she paused. "I don't need you any more."

"You never did."

Easy for him to say.

"The question is do you want me?" He went still.

She weighed what to say, surprised herself with her response. "Matt, I hope you find what you're looking for."

He let out a long breath. "There's someone else, isn't there?"

"Not really. Just me." As she said it, she realized it was the truth.

He hung his head. Then she heard a tap on the steps, followed by a thump. Then another tap, another thump. A knock on her door.

When she opened it, Pete was there, leaning on his cane and grinning. His smile faded when he saw Matt. "Oh sorry ..." He looked at Georgia. "I didn't mean to interrupt."

"It's okay."

"I just came down to say I've been working on my sister's stuffing recipe and I think I've got it pretty good. I wanted you to try it."

"I'd like that. I'll be up in a minute."

He glanced uncertainly at Matt, then at her. "OK."

She watched him ascend the steps, one at a time. She closed the door. Matt looked at her. "There's no chance, is there?"

"Matt, what would you do in my place?"

He didn't answer for a long time. Then, "I'd tell me to go to hell."

She smiled then, and reached her hand up to his cheek. She traced the line of his jaw with her finger. "I would never say that. You taught me so much."

"But ..." His chest heaved.

"But ..." She shook her head. "Not now. Maybe not ever."

He swallowed and turned away quickly. He opened the door and started down the stairs. She closed the door and leaned against it. She heard his foot clomp on the steps, heard the vestibule door squeak when he went through.

She leaned against the door for a long while, then wiped her hands on her jeans. Pete, Sam, and Sam's new boyfriend would be coming tomorrow. The new furniture looked good, but something was missing.

Plants. Living things. It was time to buy a ficus. Maybe a fern. She checked the clock in the kitchen. If she went now, she could get them today. She grabbed her coat and her bag.